...ath's...d to waver before my eyes, becoming an image of smoke. My eyes watered in response. When I could see the image again, my brother Dolph no longer sat across from me. Now it was an elderly woman in a dress with many petticoats, her beautiful shawl held in place with a cameo, her cap trimmed with a wide band of lace. The gaze upon me was sharp. She seemed to be sitting on air, as if an unseen chair was present.

"Do you understand about the triad yet, Allie?" Her voice was low for a woman's, almost gravelly, as if she had spent her life speaking through smoke. My great-grandmother Emma had been a great practitioner in her time...she had read a lot of futures in the curl of a smoking fire.

So...not only could I question Death; Death could question me.

❧☯❧

Praise for Katharine Eliska Kimbriel and *Kindred Rites:*

"With a clear, distinctive voice, Katharine Kimbriel invents and re-invents magic on America's frontier, a place hardly explored by writers and long overdue for a visit. (Or should I say a visitation?) Love the book."
—Jane Yolen, award-winning author *of Briar Rose*

"It is good to see this back—the Alfreda stories are one of the reasons YA is so dynamic today. ...*Little House on the Prairie* meets Harry Potter, with a dash of Stephen King."
—Sherwood Smith, author of *Crown Duel*

"charming...unusual...delightful...definitely worth checking out"
—*Locus Magazine*

"Allie is a compelling character... Her world feels real, her studies feel real... This is one of the best historical dark fantasies I've ever read. I deeply enjoyed Allie's second tale, and plan to re-read it many, many times over the years to come."
—Barb Caffrey, *Shiny Book Review*

"**A skillfully woven tapestry** of American history, multicultural folklore, and dark fantasy for readers of young adult and above. (*Kindred Rites*) is one you will revisit from time to time when you need an old friend."
　　—Rebecca McFarland Kyle, Amazon Top 500 Reviewer

"**She has a real gift for** taking a story into interesting situations, and in directions you don't expect. I keep dipping back into the book!"
　　—Ru Emerson, author of the *Night-Threads* books

"**Katharine Eliska Kimbriel's** Allie books do *Harry Potter* one, or two, maybe even three better. ...These are the kind of good books that help a reader get through a bad night."
　　—Alexis Glynn Latner, author of *Hurricane Moon*

"**Take *Little House on the Prairie,*** mix in a large dose of magic, shake well for adults and settle in for a very fun ride. I want the next installment of Alfreda Sorensson's adventures right now."
　　—Laurell K. Hamilton, *NY Times* best selling author

ꝕ·⫰·ꝕ

Praise for *Night Calls,* the first story of Alfreda:

"**If you can imagine** *Little House on the Prairie* with werewolves, vampires, and magic, you've got an idea what this dark fantasy novel is like. ...The strong characters, the matter-of-fact tone, and the strong sense of place make this something special."
　　—*Locus Magazine*

"**I am so glad that** Katharine Eliska Kimbriel's *Night Calls* is getting out into the world again. If anything, I believe this story's time has come—it's the dark fantasy with an underlying glint of the numinous that I think so many readers are looking for and not finding."
　　—Sherwood Smith, author of *Crown Duel*

"**To protect those she loves**, a pragmatic young witch finds faith and magical lessons in the natural world—compelling, fantastic tale, beautifully, wondrously written!"
—Patricia Rice, best selling author of the *Magic* series

"***Night Calls* will keep** you up all night and leave you anticipating the sequel."
—Rebecca McFarland Kyle, Amazon Top 500 Reviewer

"**There are very few books** I reread on a regular basis. *Night Calls* is one. When I read *Night Calls* I thought, first, that Robin McKinley's *The Blue Sword* had at last found a proper shelf-mate...."
—Laura Anne Gilman, Nebula Award Nominee
for *Flesh and Fire: The Vineart War* series

"**The underlying horror** in *Night Calls* builds slowly and inexorably to an exciting climax. Nordic superstitions and spirits combined with unusual ways to combat the supernatural make this a unique read for horror fans."
—Rochelle M. Bilz, *Voya*, October 1996

"**I have not been so** enthralled with a novel since Wrede's *Thirteenth Child*. It takes talent to build a world so rich and lush that the reader cannot imagine it ever being differently, but that is exactly what Ms. Kimbriel has done."
—April M. Steenburgh, *So Many Books, So Little Time*

"**A really nicely done story**, well-written, lovely character development, and a magic system that has real costs and dangers as well as rewards. I'm looking forward to reading more. Highly recommended."
—*Lis Carey's Library*
(*NetGalley Member/Professional Reader*)

"**So there's the value of hard work.** There's the value of personal sacrifice. There's the value of human dignity. ...And there's a rousing action-adventure going on throughout that makes you forget about all of the above until the book is over and you start thinking about how wonderful it all was before you turn back to read it all over again."
—Barb Caffrey, *Shiny Book Review*

KINDRED
RITES

Also by Katharine Eliska Kimbriel

The Night Calls Series

Night Calls
Kindred Rites
Spiral Path (forthcoming)

The Chronicles of Nuala Series

Fires of Nuala
Hidden Fires
Fire Sanctuary

KINDRED RITES

KATHARINE ELISKA KIMBRIEL

ILLUSTRATION
MITCHELL DAVIDSON BENTLEY

BOOK VIEW CAFE

Kindred Rites
Copyright © 1997, 2014 by Katharine Eliska Kimbriel

Book View Cafe Publishing Cooperative
   PO Box 1624 , Cedar Crest, NM 87008-1624
Dragonrain Studio
   PO Box 202045, Austin, TX 78720-2045

Library of Congress Cataloging-in-Publication Data
LCCN 98-815545

Kimbriel, Katharine Eliska
   Kindred Rites/Katharine Eliska Kimbriel

ISBN: 978 1 61138 357 7

Subjects   Magic—Fiction
 Form/Genre Fantasy fiction
          --Horror fiction
 Notes Sequel to: Night calls.
 Alfreda Sorensson, a young girl on the American frontier of a alternate earth where magic is a part of everyday life, learns the Wise Arts

First printing, November, 1997
HarperPrism®, an imprint of HarperPaperbacks®
A division of HarperCollins*Publishers*
10 East 53rd Street, New York, NY 10022

Cover art "Don't Fear (Summoning) The Reaper"
by Mitchell Davidson Bentley ©2014
Used under contract, all other rights reserved
Cover design by Atomic Fly Studios

Interior design by Hypatia Press
For information address: alanbard@alanbard.com

A Work of Fiction

DEDICATION

To Roger Zelazny
We ran out of time, friend. I miss you

KINDRED RITES

ONE

THE DEAD ARE ALWAYS WITH US.

Most folks don't fully understand that. People wrap a corpse in ritual and custom, say their good-byes, and try to move on. But it doesn't work. We carry our dead, always. Long years later, something will bring the past to mind—a child's motion, a woman's perfume, a man's sputtering laugh. For a brief moment, the past is now, and our dead live again.

As long as we remember them, we are shadowed by our dead.

It wasn't the brightest of thoughts while riding through a crisp winter day, but we were very close to Christmas, and Christmas has long been a time for ghosts. Since I suspected I had seen one of my first ghosts only the day before, death was fully on my mind. Do we ever really die?

The fact that the ghost had been a cat hadn't diminished either my awe or my interest. There had been a tiny mackerel tabby staying close to her mistress' skirts, curling up on a flounce of petticoat. The woman had smiled sadly when I asked if she had always been fond of cats. It seemed that Mistress Johnson had just lost her sweet Bess, champion mouser and fire watcher, whose rumbling purr had carried across a room.

I was so surprised, I didn't tell Mistress Johnson that she hadn't lost Bess at all . . . not the part of Bess that was eternal. Hadn't thought before about animals having souls.

I was thinking a lot about it just then.

It was things like seeing ghosts that had gotten me where I was—learning the Wise Arts of hand and forest from my kinswoman Marta Donaltsson. I was only one of a long line of practitioners, as we called ourselves, though I was the first in three generations in Momma's family. And oh, had that caused a ruckus, 'cus Papa had expected it, and Momma had feared it. Therein lies a tale . . . but not the story I've decided to tell.

A gust of wind startled me, swirling a pile of dried oak leaves into the air, and we rode through a small blizzard of brown fragments. The sharp smell of promised snow made me sit up straight in the saddle. I'd been riding half-asleep, for we'd worked hard the past few days, readying Marta's farm for deep winter. It would never do to let the mild beginning to the season trick us into carelessness. That's how people freeze to death—or starve.

Oh, was I ready for a whiff of our chimney smoke! I hadn't been home for months, what with moving from herb lore to magic, and I hungered for the sight of my parents' farm.

My cousin Marta—Papa's cousin, really—had been quiet for most of the trip, lost in her thoughts or bemused by the good weather we'd been blessed with. Her stallion, Sweet William, moved smartly along with his liquid walk, bypassing frozen ruts and ice patches with equal ease. We traveled in his wake, Old Ned and I, and I secretly wished that I, too, had a plantation horse from back east. Not much for jumping, was William, nor a great runner, but he could do that smooth, running walk of his most of the day. Old Ned, on the other hand, didn't have any gaits—he just went along like a rocking horse.

A sharp crack of splitting wood caught my attention, and I looked swiftly around for its source. The spell carefully maintained by the region's practitioners protected us from hostile tribes, but there wasn't much you could do about panthers. A panther attacks because it's hungry, not because it's angry. Only some types of wards can protect from animals—and a practitioner needs to keep an eye on a ward.

Not a sign of a panth— A large dead branch suddenly crashed through the tree limbs above, landing on the trail between Marta and me. Sweet William hopped forward and pranced lightly, but Old Ned just stopped dead and flicked an ear my way.

That was one good thing about that ol' bay gelding—*nothing* bothered him.

"Strange," Marta said softly, her sharp blue gaze studying the bare branches above. "Snow's not heavy enough yet, and there's no sign of squirrel or flock."

Shrugging, I replied, "I suppose sometimes dead things just break loose." Eyeing the large limb, I nudged Old Ned into going around it. I was grateful the thing hadn't hit either one of us, but it's better not to imagine troubles.

There are enough *real* dangers in the world.

"It is possible," Marta agreed, and her grip tightened on William's sides. The big stallion obediently continued on down the rutted path.

I didn't waste any more thought on tree limbs, since we were coming to an open stretch of the track. But there did seem to be an awful lot of dead leaves and twigs dancing at our feet.

The wind didn't seem strong enough to move twigs. . . .

Suddenly I was very tired, and anxious for a glimpse of Papa's solid oak fence.

$\cdot$$\mathcal{D}$$\cdot$

We were already losing light when we worked our way up the frozen dirt road to the clearing before my parents' home. The wind had picked up a bit, pulling at our clothes and lifting stray hairs. There was definitely snow on the wind, and I was grateful we'd arrived before dark.

Little Ben and Joe bounded out to greet us, chattering like magpies and each insisting he could take our horses to the barn. I could have sworn they'd both grown since I left late in the month of Vintage. How could I call Joe little when he came up to my shoulder? Josh came out behind them and promptly shocked me by helping Marta off her horse. Then he gave me a big smile, and I was sure he'd been touched in the head. I mean, Josh had two years on me, but acting like a grown-up? And treating me like one?

"I'm sure Aunt Marta could use some help with her bags, Joe," Joshua pointed out, using the courtesy name for our cousin that we'd learned as children. "Maybe you'd better go see what she brought." He leaned over and whispered something to the younger boy, and Joe immediately became very helpful.

"Is your mother inside, Joshua?" Marta asked, allowing Joe to carry her carpetbag but keeping her bag of herbs and tools for herself.

"Yes, ma'am. Papa's in the barn."

Pulling the reins forward, I watched for Josh's cue. Only when he nodded casually did I hand the reins to Ben. I had no doubt Ben could handle Old Ned—a tiny child could handle Ned—but Momma was protective of her baby, seven years strong, so I waited to be sure Josh had his eye on things.

"Momma's easing up on him," Josh said softly as he pulled my saddlebags off my horse. "She's saving all her worry for the new one coming."

"Sounds like Momma," I agreed, taking my bags over one shoulder. "What did you tell Joe, anyway?"

That grin, so like Papa's, popped out. "I reminded him of those great cookies Aunt Marta makes, and how she might have brought some—or could be talked into making some!"

I grinned back, and left him to make the animals comfortable.

Heat pushed against my face as we entered my parents' home, and the rich scent of bayberry candles swept past my nose. Momma had hung a juniper branch with berries on the firewall that faced the outer door, and I buried my face in it to breathe deeply of the forest.

"Now don't be heating the outdoors, child," came my mother's voice as she moved forward to greet Marta. "Wedge that door tight!" It was such a familiar command that I leaned hard on the bound door before I even thought about it. I left the latch out, though, for Papa and the boys.

Momma seemed to have shrunk in the months I'd been with Marta. Hugging her, I could tell I was already a good hand taller than she. And did I say Momma was smaller? Not in the stomach— my mother's pregnancy was so visible, her belly tried to push me away. Holding Momma, I could feel the glimmer of my new sister turning a slow somersault in her warm, safe place.

It was only a flash, but suddenly I saw her, looking more like Papa, but with Momma's rich, dark hair, my mother's pride as Elizabeth showed off her first long skirt—

"My goodness, daughter, how you've grown!" Momma said as she pulled me toward the warmth of the main room's fire. "You'll rival Marta soon."

Momma's words brought me back from wherever I'd been. Well, Marta was nigh on six feet, so I wasn't in any hurry to top her, that's for sure. I'd leave that to Josh and the others. Height in women wasn't really admired in our circle, but it wasn't like I could stop growing, so I just kept smiling as I set my saddlebags down next to Papa's big maple rocker. Pulling off my knit gloves, I stuck my hands near the ornate metal screen that shielded the fire from the room.

"We've held back our meal for you. I've been cooking some venison in a clay pot. The boys are ready to gnaw on the chair legs, so I hope we won't be rushing you if we sit down in a quarter hour?" Momma said briskly, pausing by the huge firewall of the double-sided chimney that heated both the living room and the kitchen.

"Not at all, Garda," Marta said for us both. "We're both tired and hungry, and the sooner one is remedied, the sooner we can get some rest."

"Good. I've had Joe put your bags in the stillroom, Marta, and Allie, if you would take—"

The fire chose that moment to pop loudly, a shower of sparks bouncing off the metal screen and back into the fire well. Startled, Momma stepped away from the chimney, but she was never in any danger.

"Must have found a pocket of sap," she murmured, giving the fire one of her disapproving looks. I turned away to hide a smile. As I had aged, I had begun to see the humor of those expressions. Momma was normally a slender, almost dainty woman, with big hazel eyes and a generous mouth. But there was this nervousness in her that only Papa could calm. To make up for it, she had always acted older and sterner than her years. I supposed someday her days and her ways would even out.

"We will clean up for the meal, Garda. Will you need assistance?" Marta said smoothly.

"No, no, I have everything ready. Freshen yourselves and come enjoy supper." Momma turned to walk the corridor between the living room and the kitchen, and Marta followed in her wake.

Papa chose that moment to enter the house, tugging the door behind him and pulling off his leather gloves. He walked straight up to me, his gentle smile brightening his face, and cupped his hand against my cheek. "Straight as an ash tree," he said gently, "Just like Marta." His hand was warm and I could smell a hint of the leather clinging to his fingers. "Was it a good ride over?"

"Yes," I said, grinning back at him. I was so happy to see him, but I resisted throwing myself at him until he'd had a chance to clean up and get comfortable.

Norwegian men are quiet ones, but they have great hearts.

Momma called to Papa from the kitchen, so I touched my fingers to the back of his hand and then headed for the outhouse before I took off my coat.

Both Momma and Marta were busy when I returned, and Joe was placing some of Marta's cookies on a lovely pewter platter. I heard Papa's footsteps upstairs, and knew he was washing up for supper. I was left to haul my saddlebags up the back stairs, the pouches banging against my ankle with every step. Then I rushed back downstairs for a jug of hot water and a lit candle, because it gets dark early in the month of Snow.

The small mirror Momma had hung in my room showed a tousled visage, chapped and dry from the cold wind. I freshened my eyes and teeth and gently warmed my face, carefully rubbing in some of the berry cream Marta had taught me to make. Then I swiftly unbraided my hair, groping for the comb I'd set down on top of the big trunk I used as a dresser. Somehow I had bumped the tortoiseshell over to the far edge, but I could still reach it, and quickly combed the snarls from my long, pale hair. I'd practiced French braiding a lot the past few moons, so soon I was feeling for my hair thong. Fumbling at the counterpane, I realized the thong was missing. *Now where . . . ?* Holding the end of my braid in one hand and the candle in the other, I searched the bed, the trunk and the floor, too.

Finally I spotted the hair tie peeking out from under the ruffle of the bed. Heavens, how had it managed to get that far? I picked it up on my little finger and then hurried to finish with my clothing. Removing my heavy sheepskin coat, I pulled out the clean tucker I had packed and carefully arranged the fall of lace around my shoulders. A dab more cream—my hand closed on empty air.

What was going on? I *knew* that jar had been there a moment ago. Exasperation forced air past my lips in a rush. I turned back to the mirror for a final check, and suddenly I wasn't alone—two people were reflected back at me. Not my doppelganger, praise the Lord of Light—no fetches foretelling my death—but a dark-haired girl with a shy, worshipful smile, standing next to me. It took a moment to realize that I was older in the mirror, taller—beautiful? Standing with my little sister. . . . Then the image wavered and vanished.

Throwing up my hands in disgust, I grabbed my coat and the lit candle and hurried downstairs. It would never do to keep them all waiting my first night back.

And I'd yet to give Papa his hug. I broke down and did that before we sat down.

Momma had made much more than a supper, that was certain. The venison was so tender it pulled apart with a fork. She'd cooked it with quartered carrots, onions and potatoes for extra flavor, and simmered some mushrooms in the drippings. We had fresh bread, moist and chewy, and there were baked apples for dessert, laden with cinnamon and brown sugar. I suspected Joe and Ben would be more interested in the hermit cookies, but as usual the boys made room for everything.

Marta was praising Momma's latest solstice beer when Joe suddenly said, "Where are the cookies?"

"Right behind me on the hutch," I told him, twisting to pick up the plate.

Which wasn't there.

"There it is!" Forgetting to ask permission, Ben jumped to his feet and rushed to the sideboard by the dry sink. Sure enough, the plate sat right next to the dirty cooking pot Momma was soaking.

"I thought I saw you put those on the hutch," I said to Joe.

His face was puzzled. "I did. Why did you move them, Ben?"

"I didn't move them!" Indignantly Ben snatched up the plate and carried the cookies to the table. Since the plate was going around, I took a hermit myself—they were always better a few days after baking, and this batch had a touch of cocoa in it.

"*Someone* moved my paddle," Momma announced, standing by the oven and peering around. "There will be no baked apples if we cannot remove them from the oven."

The paddle, unlike the cookies, had well and truly disappeared, so Papa folded up towels to remove the baking bowl. There was a lot of grumbling coming from Momma's direction, but the boys were loud in their protests of innocence. The big wooden paddle didn't seem to be anywhere, but that was silly. Maybe Ben had moved it to the stillroom and forgotten. . . .

After cleaning up the dishes, we all settled by the fire in the main room, curled up on the big stuffed pillows and the rockers. I sat close to Papa, just to drink in his presence. He hadn't said much yet, but his face was bright, and I knew he was glad we'd come for the holiday.

We talked a bit about what the family had been up to the past few months, and Momma shared the gossip of the area. I heard about people I'd known all my life, and found out my dear friend Idelia was just about engaged to William Adamsson, the oldest son of a local couple.

I was very pleased for Idelia—Will was a nice boy, and had always seemed kind and hardworking—but after my own involvement with the second son, Wylie, I felt a bit melancholy about the whole business. If Wylie had been tougher, Idelia and I might have ended up married to brothers. But Wylie had not spoken to me, had sent neither word nor letter, since I dealt with that vampire before leaving home—the vampire that had beguiled him. I still didn't know if it was my power he feared, or if he resented my destroying the object of his desire . . . even if she *had* been slowly killing him.

All I knew was that Wylie hadn't said good-bye when I left. And that still hurt.

"And what about you, Alfreda?" Momma said suddenly. "How are your studies progressing?"

I'd been watching Marta for some time, because I'd known that this was coming. The original plan had been for me to remain home another year before going to Marta for training, but to say I was precocious was an understatement. Everything had changed after Papa and I killed the vampire. Momma couldn't stand wondering if I was being eaten by some demon, so she'd packed me off to Marta for safekeeping.

No one had to tell me that Momma didn't need to hear about our laying the demon child of Twisted Pines, a place once again called Cloudcatcher.

"Well, Momma, I brewed my first batch of beer before we left," I started, my eyes shifting to my mother's face. "Looks like it will be a rich barleywine, for the end of winter." I was rewarded by my mother's smile, and continued in the same vein, telling her about the quilt I'd started for Idelia, both for friendship and for the wedding I'd been expecting within the next year or so.

I let Marta mention our travels, saying merely that we'd needed to go help a community with a few problems. She spoke of the well at a crossroads tavern that had needed a good word put on it, and the crazy, friendly DeBois family, whom we'd stayed with on the road. I told about the fancy brick mansion we'd seen in Cloudcatcher (for Marta had said only that the town had changed its name back) and the beautiful dresses the youngest daughter had worn.

"She said it was called *empire,* Momma, I guess for the emperor's court," I told her, demonstrating how the high waist gathered under the bosom.

Momma sniffed her response. "If the French want an emperor, they may have him. I had hoped that freedom could come from all that bloodshed, but I see war without end for the continent."

I kept my eyes cast down so Momma wouldn't see my guilty look. She didn't have any use for emperors, kings, or even presidents—but she did insist that we call our leader the president, and not "king." Lots of the old folks still talked about King Washington, but he was never a king—he turned that down. In the end, I hope we will be the better for it, we Americans. For better or worse, we choose our leaders—and if they don't do a good job, we vote them out!

But sometimes I still think of General Washington as a king. I have read about him, and he was a noble man.

"I fear there will be war for many years to come, Garda," Marta agreed, pouring herself another cup of tea. "The Bourbons and their supporters will not surrender France easily."

Shifting carefully in her rocker, Momma pulled herself to her feet. "Time for sleep, boys. Tomorrow the trap line needs attention, and that doubles our work here at home." Joe groaned his protest, but Ben rolled up without comment, so I knew he was tired. As both boys trooped to the outhouse, Josh looked over at Papa.

"You can stay up a bit, son, if you're minded," Papa said easily, pulling out his flint and steel to light his pipe.

Momma didn't look happy, but amazingly said nothing about Josh. "I will retire," was her comment. "This little one demands rest."

"Yes, Garda," Marta said encouragingly. "Listen to what your body wants. The child will take what *it* needs—do not neglect yourself."

I leaned dreamily against papa's rocker, listening to my aunt's formal speech pattern and watching the glow of a many-branched candelabrum. That was a gift I hoped I had inherited from the Sorensson family—the ability to shift speech patterns, depending on to whom I spoke. It seemed a useful talent.

I wished Momma wasn't going to bed so early, but I had to get used to it. The new baby would fully occupy her for some time to come. It was a wistful thought. I knew my mother loved me— of *course* she loved me—but she didn't show it much. And soon she'd have a dutiful daughter who wouldn't go off chasing after vampires. . . .

I didn't remember that candleholder. Papa must have made it for Momma after I left home—or asked Bear Kristinsson to make it, since it looked to be metal. As I looked harder at the candelabrum, one of the candles abruptly went out. It didn't gutter or get caught in a flaring breeze—it just went out, smoke curling from the wick.

Then another branch went out . . . and another. Momma had only lit six of the nine tapers, so our table light had been halved. As I sat watching, the two candles on the second level went out, leaving only the top candle burning.

It seemed I was the only one paying attention. Momma turned around and said, "Do you want just the fire, Eldon? Did Ben blow these out?"

I decided not to comment as she picked up the snuffer and extinguished the last candle. The two boys pounded back in, and as

Momma turned to follow them into the kitchen to the back stairs, I watched the final taper reignite.

This time I turned to look at Marta, who had moved into my mother's rocker. She had one eyebrow cocked. So—she'd seen at least the last candle relight itself.

"I thought I saw the smoke from that going out," Josh muttered, looking hard at the candle. "I've never seen one start burning again."

"It can happen if you don't hold down the snuffer long enough," Marta said mildly. "Will you have more tea, Josh?"

"Thank you, yes," he said politely, and I was impressed at how he'd worked on his manners. Then I gave him a hard look. Something sparkly about him. . . .

"Are you courting somebody?" I said abruptly.

Even by firelight, I could see him flush. So Josh had his eye on a girl. Well, well, well . . . I decided not to push. If someone didn't slip with it the next day, I'd ask Idelia. I supposed if Idelia could get engaged already, and she but a year older than I was, then Josh could start thinking serious thoughts about someone.

Still, I didn't think Idelia's parents would let her get married until she was fifteen, *at least,* so she must feel pretty strongly about William to be talking about an announcement. Hadn't Momma said something once about Idelia's family believing in long engagements?

I let my gaze slip back to the lone candle and watched it quietly go out.

There was a shout from the boys' room, and then the sounds of protest and Momma scolding. We all looked at each other, but no one said anything. A few minutes later, Momma walked back through the main room on her way to the front stairs. "Those boys," she said harshly. "Trying to get me blistered or worse. They had my oven paddle upstairs laying right on their bed!"

"Didn't hide it very well," was Josh's comment, but he quickly ducked his head at a look from Momma.

"They swear they didn't take it. You need to have a word with them, Eldon—I won't have those boys starting to lie their way out of their mischief."

Papa took another puff on his pipe and then carefully set it on the fired clay tray on the table next to the rocker. "I'll speak with them, Garda. Don't worry about it—just get some rest." He kissed my mother's cheek in passing, as he always had each night, not caring who might be in the room. I'd always thought that was nice—some couples never seem to so much as really look at each other.

When we could faintly hear Momma's footsteps in the big front room upstairs, Josh said: "What really happened in Cloudcatcher?"

"When your father returns," Marta said tranquilly, absently picking up another hermit cookie. As you may have guessed, practitioners eat a lot, yet you rarely see a heavy practitioner. We burn off the fuel too fast. That's why Marta was so angular, and I suspected it was why I didn't have any curves yet.

Papa returned a few minutes later, a slight frown on his face. Sitting down, he glanced once at our cousin, his keen sky blue gaze piercing. "They swear they didn't touch the paddle, and Joe may spice up his stories, but he's never lied to me that I know about."

"Perhaps he is not lying," was Marta's comment. "Let it go for now, Eldon." She frowned slightly, eyeing the candelabrum. "There is another possibility, but I would like to observe the household for another day." Turning toward me, she smiled and said: "Do you want to tell Joshua and your father about your *utburd?*"

I shivered as she named the dreaded ghost, but Papa looked interested, and Josh excited, so I went ahead and started. "In a way, it's a story about the sins of the father carrying on through the next generations. . . ."

To Joshua it might as well have been a tale of long ago and far away. I had his full attention, his shining eyes never leaving my face. None of it could be real to him—not the dark wind that had come on the foot taps of a child, rattling the eaves of the houses. Not the stench of *wrongness* that had woven itself through the fabric of the village. Not the tiny bones we'd found in the forest, nor the tattered pieces of flesh or the blinded woman. . . .

Not the young woman who'd drunk mistletoe tea to kill her unborn son.

It's not just a story when you've lived it. Maybe I was still too close to it.

"Sounds like you had a hard fortnight," Papa said finally, knocking his pipe against the firewall to dump his tobacco ash in the coals.

"I've had a lot better," I admitted with a sigh, straightening my spine in an attempt to stay awake.

"Time for some sleep," Papa suggested. "You've got several trap lines to check tomorrow, Josh. And you, Alfreda," he said as he stood up, "you need some time in the woods, I think. Why don't you take your brothers out and let them figure out how to keep warm in the winter?" Smiling faintly at me, he added: "I'm sure you can find a squirrel to advise you."

Well, despite my exhaustion, that made me smile. Suddenly I remembered Papa's teaching Josh and me how to make a shelter in the woods . . . with the help of a squirrel or two.

"Maybe I will," I agreed, stretching and rising to my feet.

The candelabrum suddenly burst into flame, all nine tapers. Surprised, Papa turned and stared hard at it. "Is that going to be a problem?" he asked Marta quietly.

"I'll charm all wicks," she said calmly. "I don't think we'll have trouble."

Huh. Now what did candles and things disappearing remind me of?

A ghost? But we'd never had trouble before, and there were no signs of any Indian tribes ever having lived here. . . .

Or . . . a poltergeist. Had we attracted a tricky spirit, plumb ready to scare us out of our home?

"Good night, Allie," Marta said gently, turning toward the kitchen.

Papa reached to touch my face. "Get some sleep, daughter. Riding herd on Ben and Joe takes strength."

I returned his smile and followed Marta into the kitchen. "Do you need help?" I asked her simply.

"I have it," she murmured from the stillroom, and I heard the clinking of my mother's herb pots. "We'll speak of it tomorrow, Alfreda."

When it's "Alfreda," it's time to leave. So I did.

But I was thinking about a spirit strong enough to move that heavy oak paddle.

TWO

IT STARTED SNOWING HARD THAT NIGHT, almost a whiteout, which trapped us inside except for the rope paths Papa had strung among the buildings. At least we wouldn't lose Josh in a blizzard when he went to do the milking. I was crazy to go outside, but I knew Momma's nerves wouldn't stand for that. She had other ways of coping with the boredom and temper of "trapper fever."

Momma hauled out the breaking cards and her needles, for there was wool to card and baby clothes to sew. The garments from Momma's first confinement had lasted through six births, but now new things were needed.

However, nothing drove me crazier than being trapped inside making clothing, even for babies. This time they were both boring *and* hard to work with, because needles and pins kept disappearing, and measuring ribbons were tied in knots, and fabric was inching around the room like a snake—it was *very* aggravating.

I did have to admit the tiny balls of fluffy wool chasing themselves around the planed wood floor were funny.

A poltergeist was not dull, but it was a nuisance.

Marta seemed resigned and told us to ignore it. If it didn't go away by the end of our visit, she planned to take care of the problem.

The snow slowed down two mornings later, and my choices were more sitting and sewing, or taking the boys into the forest to teach them how to survive. Well, you can guess what *I* decided to do.

❧ 📅 ❧

That's how I ended up walking through the glittering fairyland that used to be our forest. It was a perfect morning, the air crisp but not biting, a steady veil of snow dusting the landscape and filling our tracks. The boys had wanted to kick through the powder, but Papa got out the snowshoes and made us use them. So we clomped along, Ben giggling over his huge sliding footprints, following Papa and Josh into the woods.

Papa was carrying a loop of sinew cordage, his Kentucky flintlock and powder bag, and his traveling pack of old canvas stained with blotches of China tea. Of course Josh and I didn't have guns, so we had our knives at our hips. Hostile Indians were unlikely, what with the spell that protected the area. A curious, hungry panther—now *that* was possible.

Josh and I also had our small leather survival bags, filled with things like corded sinew, dry tinder, and a flint and steel. I'd also stuffed extra socks inside my coat pockets for me and the younger boys. Momma was an avenging angel on the subject of dry socks. Truth to tell, she was right—you never knew when you'd break through ice to water. Far from home, that was dangerous.

At least Momma wasn't still squawking about my wearing boiled wool pants when it was cold. A hard-fought victory, that was—and she still expected me to toss a skirt over them when I was in the village. My big sheepskin coat she put up with; I suspected she was weaving me a cloak for Sunday best.

We were headed in the same direction as the trapline, but I wasn't going to let the boys look over papa's shoulder that day— they were just too giggly and full of spirit. Hunting was pretty serious work. Papa trapped mostly for weasels like mink, skunk, marten, and wolverine. He tried not to get otter; he said sometimes they looked too human, though we kept his feelings on the subject dead secret. I'd rather watch otters play than wear them. The line was also set for muskrat and beaver, the most valuable skins. It was a water line, with snares set to grab and drown the animal quickly so it wouldn't suffer.

Marta was Papa's only real competition—she ran several lines. There were others in the region who trapped, but they didn't make much money at it because they damaged the pelts. Papa had had no luck convincing them that leg hold traps were not only cruel, but bad for the fur. I've got a feeling Papa sometimes arranged for those leg hold traps to "disappear," but I never asked him about it. You see, some stands are best made alone and privately.

"You've moved the line again, Papa," I said as we trudged along.

"I never stay in one place too long," was his quiet reply. "Animals are smart. If other critters keep disappearing around them, the sharp ones move on. And you can trap out woods quick if you're not careful." I nodded, grateful that most of the folks in the area of Sun-Return were cautious.

The steady snow made me lose any hunger for conversation. It was enough just to be with Papa and the boys. For the first time, I wasn't missing Dolph like a lost tooth, always testing the hole with my tongue. . . . I was just sorry our big brother would never see this morning.

At least he wasn't still a werewolf.

The silence of the woods was absolute, and gave me the eerie feeling that someone was watching us. Most of the trees had been blown bare, polished and shapely in their nakedness, and the swift flight of a passing cardinal was like fresh blood on the snow. Red juniper, cedar, pine and hemlock trees were flourishing, the brown cone seeds and blue juniper berries a sharp contrast to the green needles and mounds of fresh snow. I couldn't help but wonder what might be under the skirts of those evergreens. . . .

I kept an eye on one juniper as we walked by—there was a pair of cardinals in it, caroling their hearts out, and a flock of chickadees hanging every which way, chirping and calling like a holler-off. The beauty and innocence did not dispel my unease.

In the distance was the sound of a beautiful bird song, one I knew well. Not truly a bird—a forest spirit, that had come to me at

Cloudcatcher in the form of a great stag. I still wasn't totally sure what it would mean to my future—Marta was only telling me bits and pieces about "Good Friends," as those spirits were called. All I knew for certain was that the White Wanderer, as I thought of him, wasn't a demon any more than I was a devil worshipper.

It was nice to know he'd followed me from Cat Track Hollow, where Marta's home was hidden beside Wild Rose Run. I always felt better when he was nearby . . . even though he usually popped up to warn me about something.

Josh and Papa disappeared into the brush, heading down toward the creek and the trap line. We all looked after them as they headed downhill, silent figures already obscured by a soft haze of snow. There was a thick fallen tree just off the deer trail, and I waved Ben and Joe toward it.

What with that funny feeling itching in the back of my skull, I didn't want to stray too far from the trail—or from Papa and Josh.

"Aren't Josh and Papa going to teach us things?" Joe asked, craning his neck to catch sight of our older brother's retreating form.

"Of course they will, sometime," I assured him. "But today I'm going to teach you a few things Papa taught me.

"Now," I went on after we were sitting on the log, one boy on either side of me. "When you think of the wilderness—and that's what you find a day farther than any settlement, wilderness," I added quickly, thinking they looked too excited about the whole idea, "the first thing to concern you is survival. What do you need to survive in the wild?"

"A gun and a good knife," Joe said quickly.

"Why?" I asked.

"To hunt food, to cut and skin things, and to protect yourself from cougars and nasty thieves and unfriendly Indians," was his swift answer. It sounded like something he'd overheard. Ben kept quiet, his sky blue eyes, softer than mine, very thoughtful in his ivory face.

"But you know that you can catch food without a gun," I pointed out. "Papa and Josh are going right now to get some critters they caught in their snares."

"How do you cut it up, or skin it, without a knife?" Joe countered.

"A sharp rock, like a chip?" Ben suggested.

"Sharp rocks aren't jist laying around," Joe responded, leaning around me so he could see Ben.

"Something else, then. Antlers can be sharp," Ben pointed out. I waited for them to argue, letting my gaze slide over the showy scene beyond, but Joe was quiet, like he was thinking.

Suddenly I felt Joe jerk up straight. "And bone! Like that awl Papa uses!"

"All good choices," I said, rearranging my tailbone on the log. "God makes wonderful rocks, but men and women can make good tools from those rocks. That's what people used before they learned to mold metal."

"What about fighting off mountain lions and bobcats?" Ben asked, his expression worried.

I could feel a smile creep across my face. Was a cat what was worrying me? But it didn't feel like the gaze of a big cat—I'd been stalked by one before. "They can be a threat, there's no doubt. Bears, too, on occasion. But unless you're being chased by one, you've got bigger worries than a 'maybe' bear or lion. Once you finish your lessons in the forest, you'll know how to look for dens or tracks, and be able to avoid areas those animals prowl. When critters finally show up, you'll have the sharpened stake or bone spearhead to help you defend yourself." Turning my head to gave Joe a sly glance out of the corner of my eye, I looked behind us for movement. "A thief would be more likely to want your gun than anything else you carried, 'cept maybe gold."

"How about water, then?" Ben asked. "You've *gotta* have water."

"Well, yes, you do. But how soon do you need it?"

They both looked at me, and then each other. "A day?" Joe tried.

I kept silent, and tried to keep my face impassive, like Papa did when he was teaching. As I let my eyes wander over the landscape, I saw several small, sharp-edged rocks floating about waist-height above the snow!

Mother of us all, the poltergeist had followed us.

"Less?" Ben squeaked.

His question snapped me back to the moment. Oh, I hoped that tricky spirit was not going to throw rocks at us—I'd heard of them doing that. "I'll give you this one," I said quickly, trying to keep the boys' attention on me. "You can last several days without water. But water is easier to come by than you think. So even water isn't first."

"It can't be food," Joe muttered.

I didn't say anything—I was watching the motionless rocks hanging in thin air.

"Why not?" Ben piped up. "Oh—you mean 'cause you won't starve for a long time. But you need to get the snare up, 'cause it might take *days* to catch something."

"True," I said quietly, as if the rocks were listening. "But you can last a fortnight without food. Papa says some folks have survived a month without it."

"Fire?" Joe blurted out.

Lord and lady of light, don't let the poltergeist think about fire!

"Valuable, but not most important unless you're freezing or chilled from rain."

No more hints—but we could turn into snow statues while they struggled with the answer. Or get pelted with rocks.... I had wanted them to wonder whether I'd build a fire to thaw us out. They were both wearing more than one sweater, they'd be fine for a while. We'd walk a bit if necessary; in fact, walking might be a good ide—

"Shelter!" Joe shouted. "First you need some kind of shelter to keep warm and dry and safe!"

I didn't have a cane to pound in tribute, so I clapped my hands instead. "A first for Joseph," I said. "Shelter is most important. Not only does it keep you warm and dry and safe, it's also calming when you're lost and makes it easier for folks to find you. It doesn't have to be much, but a shelter to come back to makes everything else seem easier. Now, what's the most important thing to remember when choosing a shelter?"

Joe blinked. Ben drew himself up like he was going to recite in school and said, "Where you put it." It was a tone that brooked no nonsense.

I was so surprised I forgot about the rocks. Joe peered around me and said: "Why?"

"How did you know that, Ben?" I asked, curious as to how he'd figured it out.

Now, if someone had asked me that question, I probably could have worked my way around it—by pointing out that you needed to choose someplace dry, and free of things like poison ivy and ant nests and bear dens, or something like that. Not a lie, but simply a good explanation.

Ben wasn't good at stories, like Joe and me. His color got a bit high, and he shrugged just like Josh. Then he mumbled something about last summer and a lean-to.

"Lean-to?" I said, trying to get him to speak up.

"David and Sven and I built a lean-to down by the left fork of the stream," he finally said in a normal tone of voice. "Pretty good one, too. But it rained, and by midday we were flooded out. So we moved a bit higher, but even there, the bugs et us up." He gave us both a fierce scowl. "So—where you put a shelter is even more important than how you do it."

I couldn't stop grinning. Josh, Wylie Adamsson and Shaw Kristinsson had done the same thing a few years before, with the same results—only they'd gotten rained out in the middle of the night.

"A good shelter in a bad location is a bad shelter," I agreed, rising to my feet and dusting off some snow. "A first for Benjamin." I glanced quickly at the rocks—they were now dancing, moving in a stately country dance pattern. I did *not* want to have to explain—

"Allie? Why are those rocks floating?" Ben's tone was perfectly calm, as if he was asking why grass was green.

"I'm not sure, Ben," I answered, putting a hand on each boy's back and steering them down the trail. "We'll have to ask Aunt Marta, or maybe Cousin Cory next time he comes by." I'd been listening for Papa's voice, or Josh's, and I could hear them—they were just moving up the creek. "Why don't you two build a shelter?"

A wonderful thing about kids was that they'd accept any answer with a kernel of truth. Unless they were just a hair too old for whimsy.

"Rocks don't float." Joe said this with a frown. Then he looked up at me. "Can we stay out all night?"

Not yet too old, it seemed.

Joe was plainly hopeful—Momma disapproved of the boys staying out in the snow, since Papa hadn't yet taught them all he'd taught Dolph, Josh and me. I suspected Ben and Joe would be cold enough they'd want to go home, but I was willing to dangle the idea like a carrot for an ox, if that was what it took to get a hut built.

As long as the poltergeist didn't get nasty.

"We'll see," I said, moving them off the trail. "This clearing over here"—I gestured ahead of me—"has everything we need." *Including floating rocks.* I took another glance over my shoulder.

Of course the rocks were following.

Now, when Josh and I had done this, Papa had just wandered off down the trail to tend to his trapline. We'd fought up a storm before agreeing on what to build and how large. But we'd been eleven and thirteen; Ben was too young to be left out there. The silence of the woods could get to you, suddenly, and having Joe there might not be reassurance enough. And there *were* panthers out there—I'd seen tracks as we came down the trail.

I couldn't leave them, so a little nudging was in order.

They wasted half a candle mark trying to build a snow fort. When I asked them how they were going to do the top, they realized that it was going to be way too big to cover with any dead branches they could find. Papa would teach them how to build a snow hut later in the season—this powder was too fresh for cutting snow blocks. I wanted to steer them toward the easiest kind of shelter.

When they realized the snow hut wouldn't work, Joe sighed and Ben looked despondent. They went back to walking around the clearing, trying to pick the best place to build. I listened from my perch on the log, all the while keeping an eye peeled for any trouble.

So far, trouble did not include the rocks. They had multiplied while the boys were arguing—there were a full six of them now—but they were marching back and forth along the south side of the clearing. And they were still a good three feet above the ground. I kept my eyes on them while the boys worked their way through their problem.

"How about over there?" I heard Ben pipe up.

"Nah, too close to the creek," was Joe's response.

A pause. "It'll freeze up hard pretty soon."

"Might scare animals away from the trapline." Joe's tone was very definite.

"Oh." Longer pause. "But the creek won't flood now, will it?"

"Ben! You *never* build that close to water! There are winter floods, too, if an ice dam breaks! Remember what happened to you?"

"It can't rain in winter, can it? No rain, no flood."

I stuffed my glove into my mouth to keep from laughing out loud. I hadn't anticipated this kind of reasoning. The rocks paused before continuing their pacing, as if such reasoning surprised them, too.

A squirrel got tired of the rising voices and scolded from the safety of her perch. The explosion of sound startled the boys, and their argument suddenly ceased. For awhile there was only the sound of snowshoes hissing over snow. Then I heard some muttering between the two of them.

Finally—

"Allie? Can we build here?" I looked over to where they stood, on the west side of the clearing.

"Why that side?" I called.

"If we put the opening facing southeast, we'll be up with the sun and get some warmth from it," Joe suggested, already stomping down the snow in his chosen spot.

"There's no sun," Ben announced, helping to stomp and landing on Joe's right snowshoe.

"Just 'cause we can't see it doesn't mean we don't get warm from it," Joe retorted. "Remember Grandsir's stories about the great ice that will cover the world at the end of time, when the old gods fight that last battle? No sun, so the ice covers everything and never melts."

"Facing that way will also shelter your entrance from storms," I pointed out, steering them away from the old sagas. Momma would be horrified to hear that Joe spoke as if he believed the story of Ragnarok.

Joe's face was first thoughtful and then wide-eyed. "You're right, Allie. Storms come from the nor'east and nor'west, mostly." He thought of something, then, and looked up quickly into the softly falling snow. "No big tree branches to fall down."

"Good thinking—and watch for dead trees that could fall and hit your shelter," I added. "What else would you do if it was summer?"

Both boys looked lost, standing there with snow piling up on their shoulders and hats. Then peculiar looks crept across their faces. Finally Ben giggled. "You should know, Ben, you've had that problem before," I went on.

He didn't respond—he just pointed behind me.

I whirled around and discovered that the rocks had formed a half circle at my back, and were still floating several feet from the ground. There was this temptation to touch them, but I resisted. Any encouragement might make the poltergeist feisty.

Ben and Joe could learn about ant and wasp nests in the summer.

I stood up, dusted myself off, and took a quick look around the clearing. "So, what are you going to use for shelter?"

We worked at ignoring the rocks.

⚜️

There were two trees maybe six feet apart with lower branches we could place a dead limb on, so I demonstrated a crosspole. Joe and Ben scrounged up more big branches and laid them against the crosspiece, driving the bases into an oak copse, and then piled sticks, dead leaves and pine boughs on top of the wood. After the crosspole, I didn't offer any suggestions—I just let them do what they thought best.

That squirrel was darting back and forth up on her tree limb, giving us a piece of her mind. I wasn't sure if she was upset about us or the floating rocks, but she was definitely unhappy. It was a red squirrel, and there's nothing for energy or sheer spunkiness like a red squirrel, 'cept weasel. I remembered another squirrel, maybe the mother or grandmother of this one, scolding Josh and me in the same way.

I'd gone into the woods for another armful of old pine boughs, and finally I'd stopped and told the squirrel to shush.

"You've already got a nice warm house," I'd said, pointing out the leafy ball wedged into a nest of branches. "We need to do this, so hush."

I hoped that this squirrel was as talented as her kin—maybe Joe and Ben could learn something from her.

In the meantime, I scraped a place about ten feet from the lean-to, down to the frozen earth and a bit deeper besides, to make a wide spot for our fire. First I lined the hole with rocks (the nonfloating variety) and then I looked for firewood. I found several dead oak and cedar limbs that looked useful, so I snapped them off the trees and brought them back.

All my firebed rocks now were floating a few inches above the scraped earth. I froze, clutching my bundle of wood. Well, this was a pretty kettle of fish, and no mistake. I thought about it a few moments, and then squatted by the firepit, reached out, and set my hand on the rocks. No response. I pressed gently. Slowly the rocks returned to the frozen ground. Quickly I framed the area with larger limbs of wood and built a protected area for my tinder.

Joe had stopped piling brush on his lean-to and was collecting squaw wood and kindling, which he dumped next to the fire pit. When he turned back toward the hut, I pulled out my knife and started shaving some tinder from inside a dry limb of cedar.

"Why don't you two go wait inside the shelter?" I suggested as I enclosed the tinder with some of the dry twigs I'd snapped from a branch. Every piece of firewood was now under my sight, but nothing was happening.

"Why?" Ben asked, but I was so addled I couldn't remember what I'd told them, so I didn't say another word. The boys stooped and duck-walked into their lean-to.

They lasted about fifteen minutes. By then I had a nice blaze going, which was a good thing, since the inside of the lean-to was surely a lot colder than it was outside. The boys probably thought their toes were frozen solid and were gonna fall off once thawed. Sure enough, I heard the rustling that promised cold children.

My six floating rocks were worse than silent—they had vanished!

The boys didn't say anything—they didn't even look for the floating rocks. They just stood *very* close to the blaze.

I shook my head. "Should have listened to that squirrel," I murmured, feeding the fire another stick of dry hardwood. "She told you the thing wasn't finished. Squirrels build fine shelters."

There was a lot of quiet for several minutes, and then the two of them charged off into the woods and stationed themselves where they could watch that squirrel's nest. I let a giggle escape, and then I went to drag over a decent little log I'd seen. It was a fairly recent fall, still stout enough for sitting on. Might as well be comfortable—no telling if they would need more or less time than we had to figure things out.

While the boys watched the squirrel, I looked for floating rocks, but they had completely disappeared. We couldn't be that lucky. I considered what the poltergeist might do next.

My brothers were fairly quick on the uptake, so they eventually noticed that although the squirrel brought her babies food from a horde, she also brought back moist leaves she'd pulled from a snow bank somewhere. I heard the crackling of branches, and looked up to make sure it was Joe and not Ben climbing the tree for a closer look at the nest.

"Remember, don't touch the nest or the babies!" I called. I heard soft conversation, the beginning of an argument, and then the sound of snowshoes thumping on snow.

"More leaves," Joe announced when they'd returned to the clearing. "Lots more—those squirrels are packed in there like baby mice in a wool bale."

About an hour later, I could push my arm in to the shoulder before I touched the wooden frame of the lean-to. Talk about leaves and needles! The boys had found a snowdrift that used to be a ditch of leaves. It was packed solid, and the fallen gold and brown foliage in the center was soft and dry. We had a mess of them; Ben even filled the area under the lean-to with dry leaves. This time when the boys crawled into their hut, they yelled that it was a lot warmer under there—warm enough to take off a sweater.

"But the needles keep sticking us and falling on us," I heard Ben grumble, "and I'm getting poked."

"Better to be poked than frozen," was Joe's response, but Ben didn't sound happy.

"Allie, I keep pushing this falling stuff off—it itches," he called. "Without our coats, we'd be *real* cold by morning, 'cause this stuff would keep falling through the top."

"Something must be missing," I agreed, setting more wood on the fire. "Squirrels wouldn't like to be poked, either. Plus, what if the wind picked up fierce?"

Silence. They hadn't thought of that, I could tell.

"Didn't you look *inside* that squirrel house?" I asked them. "I thought you asked the squirrel how to build, but this looks more like a rabbit scrape."

ᔥ᙭ᔥ

Joe couldn't figure out what he'd missed, and was getting sulky. This time I let Ben climb and look into the nest, but I stood right underneath him and made Joe anchor him to the tree. Ben looked a little nervous, since the branches were still slick from the ice. Or maybe he was worried about an irate squirrel. . . .

Well, boys might not be as good at noticing the next trick, but I had figured out the secret first thing. Squirrels actually weave their leaf piles together with a lattice of branches. Would Ben see it?

"Allie, the leaves around the outside look different from the ones inside," he announced.

"How so?" I prompted him.

"Pressed together." He peered close, and I gestured for Joe to get a tighter grip on his feet.

"Watch your nose some squirrel doesn't bite it," I murmured, and he yanked back fast.

"They use branches, too. How did they get the branches to stay in place?" He reached toward the nest.

"Ben!" He looked down at me. "You touch it, and the babies will starve. Their momma won't come back. Come on down, and I'll show you how she did it." The babies would be good-sized this time of year, but I didn't want to take any chances. I didn't know how long a red squirrel fed her young.

"Come on, boys," I said once their feet hit snow again. "I'm gonna teach you how to weave."

"Weave? What's that got to do with a shelter?"

Gesturing, I led them back toward the lean-to. "The squirrels hold their leaves together by weaving branches and fibers and stuff, so nothing shakes loose. We need to find some branches that bend. This is easier when you have a knife, but you can do it without one."

A bit of luck meant we didn't need the knife this time. The back of the lean-to had that oak copse next to it, which meant a bunch of tall, soft, mostly leafless root suckers pretending to be baby trees. The boys could have used the copse for a minor windbreak in case any gusts swirled around from the west. Instead, we bent the branches over and pinned them under another long, arm-thick piece of wood wedged in the branches of the evergreens.

After a quick look around for floating rocks, I left them stuffing extra leaves in their firm mat and opened my coat. I dug out the canvas bag I'd looped inside over my shoulder, the one we used to feed the horses and mules when we were on the road all day. Then I slipped down to the creek and filled the sack.

Joe and Ben were testing out the lean-to again. They hadn't made quite as thick a mat as Josh and I had managed. So . . . I looked around the corner, to see where they were, and went to the opposite end.

"Ready or not, here it comes!" The surging water hit the top of the lean-to and poured down like a waterfall.

"Argghh!" In just a few moments, the two boys piled out the other side. "Allie! You ruined our lean-to!"

"I ruined it?" I asked, ready for a fight.

That stopped Joe in his tracks. "Well . . . there's water dripping all over our leaf beds."

"And?"

They were both quiet, now. "Rain and snow would get in," Ben said finally.

"Should I get some more water to check?"

"No, no," Joe said quickly as Ben scrambled to his knees, "it's getting wet in there."

"What did you forget?"

"Does it matter?" Joe asked. "Even wet, we'd still be warm, wouldn't we?"

"Squirrels sleep warm and dry," I said, buttoning my coat and turning back to tend my fire. "Stay wet too long, you get chills." The entire fire looked a bit higher than I remembered...*Please, Lord and Lady, not that....*

The boys sighed, not quite a chorus but close. Warm and wet simply wouldn't do. Back to the nest.

"Any water left, Allie?" Joe called from the base of the squirrel tree.

"A bit. You thirsty?" I kept my eyes on the fire.

"No." He clumped back over to me. "I was gonna drip some water on the squirrel nest to see what happened. They'll be fine, won't they?"

I handed him the canvas sack. "If that squirrel is good at building houses, they will be."

Well, Joe went back up and Ben stood below, watching as Joe dribbled some water on the top of the nest. Momma squirrel was on a higher branch, scolding us with all her might. I kept my gaze on the fire and waited for some encouraging sounds from the boys.

Thwap! A tiny snowball hit my back.

"Who's horsing around?" I asked without turning.

Thwap, thwap! I reached over and grabbed some loose snow, pushing the new stuff together as best I could. Whirling, I cranked back and looked for a target.

No one was close by—Joe was up the tree, and Ben was glued to the trunk. "The leaves on the outside are frozen, Joe," Ben hollered. "Aren't they? They look all shiny."

I straightened and looked around the clearing. Had Josh cut back to see how we were doing? Or even Papa—he liked a good snowball fight as much as anyone. I shot the boys another look out of the corner of my eye. There was no fresh snow clinging to their mittens, but then there wouldn't be—it was too young a snowfall.

Joe was gently touching the outside of the leafy ball. I was pleased to see that he was keeping still another leaf between his mitten and the shelter. "Seems frozen to me—wait a minute. . . ." *Thwap!* A snow spot suddenly appeared on his big sweater. He looked down at Ben from his perch in the swaying oak tree. "Don't do that, you'll scare the squirrels."

"Do what?" Ben asked.

Uh-oh.

"Allie? You throwing snow?"

"Not me," I told them, slowly moving over their way. "But I'm ready to toss some back. Can you see anybody sneaking around in the trees?" I had a feeling the poltergeist had gotten tired of dancing rocks, but how would you know for sure? Snowballs out of thin air?

"Nobody, Allie," Joe announced after taking a hard look around the clearing. "Is Josh doing it?"

"Don't know. You ready to go back to your hut?"

Thwap! Thwap! Thwap! Thwap! Thwap! It was a flurry of small snowballs, like when a gust of wind takes snow from a tree, only these were traveling with force.

"Hey! Cut it out! This is work!" Joe yelled even as Ben hollered, "Stop!"

Silence. We waited several long minutes. No more snowballs. Finally Joe said, "The only other thing that looks different is the shaggy top of the nest."

"Guess maybe you need a shaggy top to your hut?" I asked.

"Guess maybe," Joe agreed, and started climbing down the tree. "Let's get the leaves from inside, Ben."

By the time Joe was on the ground and had replaced his snowshoes, Ben was already carrying an armful of wet leaves from the inside of the lean-to back outside. The two of them heaped those damp, cold leaves on top of the shelter and added more brush, to boot. When they were done, the lean-to was almost a half-round. The boys finished by refilling the inside with the last of the dry leaves from the sealed snowdrift they had discovered.

I walked the edge of the clearing, watching for flying rocks and snowballs, but nothing was stirring. When I came back around to the front of the lean-to, I found the boys wiggling their way back out of their leaf drift. Giving them a nod of approval, I said, "Come have some dried fruit and sit." Squatting by the fire, I pulled small packets of dried apples, apricots, and peaches out of my coat pockets. "Check to see that your socks are dry," I added as I handed out pieces of fruit. We chewed with satisfaction and pinched at our socks, but they seemed dry inside.

As I let my eyes roam for signs of the poltergeist, I spotted Papa's and Josh's ghostly forms working their way through the falling snow toward us. The boys had their backs to the creek, so I kept silent. Sure enough, Papa changed direction so that he was no longer coming from the creek, entering the clearing from the south.

"Does it pass the rain test?" Papa asked as he came up.

Ben and Joe popped up with shrieks. "Papa! Josh! Come see our hut!" Ben grabbed Josh's hand and pulled him toward the structure. "Come see!"

Papa chuckled as he was led to the finished lean-to. Josh had come prepared; his wooden mug was full of water to toss on the roof. But, sure enough, not a single drop trickled through the thick mat of leaves. We celebrated with a few more slivers of dried fruit while Josh and Papa warmed their hands.

"I'd like you two to learn a few more things before we spend the night in snowy woods, so I guess we'll head back," Papa said finally, looking up at the heavy gray clouds as if reading the time from them. "Just as soon as you tell me which way is home."

For a long moment the little boys sat very still. Some folks can feel north, they say, but I've never had the gift. It was sun direction, stars, or simply paying attention to the forest that got me where I wanted to go. Josh had the knack, but Papa had had to teach him what north felt like. Would either of the little ones be any good at feeling the poles?

Joe jumped up and started examining the trees closely—and I mean closely.

"Joe?" Ben said with a question in his voice.

"Look for moss," he said crossly, without glancing around.

I clapped a hand over my mouth to keep from giggling. All it took was a tree in heavy shade during the heat of summer to totally mess up the moss theory. But surely there was something else. . . .

I walked back over toward the trees, looking for the river trail. The footprints had long since filled in, of course, and Papa had come to the glade from another path. A flash of scarlet caught my eye; I followed the flight of a male cardinal. Memory flooded back, and I started peering around for my red juniper. Even without the birds, I thought I'd remember it—

There. Almost in response to my knowledge, a fantastic trill of notes echoed through the woods. Silently I turned to see how the boys were doing.

"What makes you so sure?" came Joe's voice.

"I recognize that tree," Ben said simply.

Joe snorted in an amazing imitation of Josh when he's annoyed. "One tree in a forest? Come on, Ben, why that way and not this?" He pointed in the other direction of the trail.

Over near the lean-to, Papa was carefully extinguishing the fire. "You're not just guessing, are you, Ben?" he asked as he tossed snow on the coals.

"No, Papa. I thought that juniper was so pretty, with the birds and all, I just kept looking at it."

A big grin crept across my face. So I wasn't the only bird-watcher.

"The secret to knowing where you are is simple," Papa said as he rose to his feet. "Look over your shoulder occasionally, my children. It is as easy as that. Things change from different angles, so you must see more than one side. Otherwise, how will you recognize your return path?"

There was a trill of counterpoint, closer, and I laughed out loud. Josh started off down the trail, sparing a glance over his shoulder for us.

"Stop horsing around. It's starting to get dark, and I'm hungry!"

Glancing to see that Papa was coming, I nudged Ben and Joe toward the trail and hurried to catch up to Josh. Then I looked back again. A small row of rocks was calmly floating after Papa, following like children lined up at school.

Momma and Marta would *not* like this. . . .

A few more quick steps and I caught up to Josh, matching his steps as I scuffed beside him on the narrow path.

Once more Joshua looked back at me, this time twisting his body slightly. "Any problems?"

Josh wouldn't play games about the rocks, not after the candles the other night. So that meant—

"No, no problems," I answered, lowering my gaze to the rumpled snow of the trail. "No problems at all."

THREE

LIFE IS HARDER THAN IT HAS TO BE with a poltergeist in residence. What can be worse than a family plagued by a restless spirit? Trust me—it's worse when the poltergeist decides that it likes *you* best.

Sure enough, Papa and Josh had had a bit of trouble with the poltergeist—snares disappearing, strings of animals suddenly moved several yards away, even a pelt dancing out of the cold storage. Momma's sewing and carding tools kept popping up in odd places, too. An occasional shower of rocks on the roof was no big thing. We even got used to the footsteps upstairs when we were all at dinner. But the poltergeist loved to torment me personally.

Every time I walked into the main room, the pile of baby garments rose up and attacked me. *Every* single time! Fragments of unfinished clothes would follow me into the kitchen—sometimes they'd just pop into existence, and other times they'd dance along the split oak floor after me. I felt like I was being followed by ducklings.

The knife, though . . . that frightened me. It happened early on the morning of Christmas Eve, when I thought I was snug and warm in back, bayberry candles scenting the air. Josh had gone to pick up our order from the village. Weeks before, Momma had taken in many of her bayberry, hollyberry, and pine-scented candles, which Old Knut had no trouble selling at his store. Now our payment had arrived—fine cambric and linen from back east, and a few surprises as well. Maybe even some East Indian prints. . . .

I was alone doing the early Christmas baking, busy rolling out dough for pies and cookies, when suddenly I saw motion out the corner of my eye. Turning my head, I saw Momma's boning knife hovering in the air like a tiny jeweled humming bird.

My hands stilled. So far, all the poltergeist seemed to want was attention. But it *had* thrown the baby clothes at me. . . . Slowly I set down the rolling pin and moved off toward the fireplace. Momma's big paddle was back next to the fireplace where it belonged, and I wanted a wide, thick piece of wood between me and that knife.

My left hand closed around the handle, and then suddenly I felt my skirt pulled sharply to one side. Well, just like a toddler with her first frog, I let out a shriek, and looked behind me to find that my skirt was pinned to the log wall, the knife still vibrating.

Momma and Marta both rushed to see why I was yelling. I reached for the knife, but I wasn't fast enough. The ladies arrived to see the knife pull itself out on its own.

"Good heavens, Allie, I thought you'd burnt yourself," Marta said mildly, keeping her eyes on the floating knife.

"Alfreda!" Momma whipped herself around. "Marta, you do something about this immediately!"

"Yes," my cousin murmured, her hands on her hips. "I think it's time to limit our little friend."

At her words, the knife dropped to the floor. I swooped upon it, the paddle still clutched tightly in my left hand.

"My goodness, daughter, you've grown strong! Are you all right? Did it cut you?" Momma rushed over, fussing like a hen missing a chick. I finally realized I was holding the heavy paddle with one hand. Near the neck, maybe, but still one hand.

"I do seem to have grown stronger," I admitted, "but I'm taller, so maybe that follows. No, Momma, I'm fine, I was just frightened for a moment."

"And no wonder. My best boning knife!" She looked down at the long, slender blade, gleaming wickedly in the firelight. "I don't think I'll ever feel the same way about it again," Momma added, clenching her hands together. "I wonder if Eldon could trade it for another. . . ."

"Don't be foolish, Garda," Marta said quickly, her voice kind. "It was no fault of the knife. Alfreda was not hurt, only startled. I'll spell the knives as well as the wicks. It will take the poltergeist a great deal more energy to play dangerous tricks." This said, Marta immediately moved into the stillroom in three strides of her long legs.

"Do you need help, Marta?" I asked.

"Not right now, Allie. You tend to your baking," came her voice. This was followed by the sharp smell of fresh mint and the clink of my mother's fired clay herb crocks. At least Momma kept fresh herbs indoors during the winter, the pots dozing in the pale light that filtered through one of the few windows we had. This problem would take dried herbs as well as fresh. I slid the knife back under the counter and put the paddle by the fireplace.

With luck Marta alone could solve this problem, because I had at least three pies to make, and *then* I'd have to start the bread.

By dinner I was fair whipped, but Momma was cooking our main meal, so I had time to freshen up and catch a catnap. The snow had stopped, and it was possible that we'd have folks stop by that afternoon, on their way to visit family in the village and farther south. I wanted to present a good appearance. It was easy for people to misunderstand about practitioners and find fault.

No one was going to talk about my family behind my back, not if I could help it.

I shook out my golden dress and put it on, and then called down to ask if Marta could fasten the buttons for me. Women's clothes were so foolish—you needed another woman to get dressed! At least I didn't need help putting on a lace tucker to veil the neckline, which was a bit low but would be fine when I finally filled out.

For several long minutes I fingered my practitioner's talisman, a thin gold chain carrying several tiny charms. There was an amber bead, a chunk of polished tiger eye, and a real, shiny piece of rough diamond, bound in a tiny basket of gold threads. Shaw Kristinsson, a local boy, had made the necklace for me. Goldsmithing was a skill I hadn't known he had, but his father was a blacksmith, so it was not surprising he understood metal.

Marta had said it was good to be given your talisman by someone who cared about you. Shaw also had talent at the Gift, as we sometimes call our strange craft, and he was studying with my cousin Cory, who lived ten days away, close to the big lake. Strange to find so many unrelated folks with the talent living so close together, but there you have it. Maybe Shaw's hidden strengths made the necklace all the more powerful. . . .

Gold for his gift, amber for immortality defeated, tiger eye for creatures of air and darkness, the diamond for grace—or so I saw it. A goddess had helped me find the bones of a tiny skeleton, and so had helped me lay the malignant ghost of Cloudcatcher; Marta had formed the diamond that day by compressing a huge lump of coal during a spell. The forces involved. . . . I shivered. Much scarier than the werewolves or vampire I had helped defeat.

But perhaps not the right jewelry for a family gathering. I still thought of it as a thing of beauty, and so it was—but its purpose was power. Marta's huge, heavy necklace included animal teeth and bones—there was no mistaking its purpose.

Someday there would be no way to mistake the purpose of my talisman.

Sighing, I left the necklace in its tiny pouch and tucked it back into my saddlebag. My bracelets and choker of woven silver would have to do. They were also things of power—of protection—but looked more ordinary. My sour cream tea cake and the *verterkake* had been placed in Momma's single oven set in over the fireplace—I could smell them baking—and I needed to make sure the pies got into the pie cabinet. Time to help set the table for dinner. Time to punch back the dough for the Christmas bread.

Time to prepare for the eve of the first day of Christmas.

Momma had warmed up sliced ham and made biscuits and grits with dried apricots. We slathered honey over just about everything, and it was wonderful. My parents and Marta drank solstice ale, while the rest of us had fresh milk. I had to learn how Momma seasoned her hams before she smoked them. Never too salty or too tough—I think she could offer her extra hams for sale, and people would fight for the privilege of buying.

Josh and I scarcely finished washing the dishes before we heard a knock at the door. It was one of the blessings—or curses—of living on the road to the village of Sun-Return. Momma always had company if she wanted to invite people to stay a bit. Today, it would likely be folks we knew dropping by, and I was sure she was eager for company. After a certain point a pregnant woman avoids riding in a wagon, and Momma had been housebound for some time.

The copper teapot came to a boil, so I mixed hot and cold water to warm the china pots, and then prepared a pot of tea and a pot of hot water. Cookies were heaped in the center of a big plate, with slices of sour cream cake and dark, hoppy *verterkake* forming a rim. Then I set everything on the tea tray and carried it into the main room.

It was a large, heavy platter, and I was worried about the poltergeist, so I kept my eyes fixed to the floor just beyond the moving tray and made it to the tea table with everything intact. Setting my burden down in a cleared spot, I turned and took a few steps forward to greet the new arrivals. I'd recognized Mrs. MacDonnell's voice, so—

I took one look at handsome Mr. MacDonnell, his dark hair gleaming in the firelight, and I gasped. Exploding bursts of blackness crept across my sight, narrowing my vision into pinpoints. My legs lost strength, and I swear my heart skipped a beat.

How could the man's legs be wrapped in cloth? How could he walk that way? The material looked as substantial as my cat ghost had been, almost but not quite there, but why did his face seem blurred? With effort, I took another step, to get away from the tea service, but then the vigor drained from my body and I pitched forward into darkness.

❧ ⅅ ❧

Waking was painful . . . I had a frightful ache in my head, and I couldn't see. The overwhelming odor of herbs and wort, and the softness beneath me, announced that I was on Marta's bed in the stillroom. "How far did I fall?" I murmured, but immediately hoped that no one had heard me, for I remembered what I'd been doing—and seeing—before I fell.

"That remains to be seen," came Marta's voice. "Some fall very far." I heard the sound of dripping water, and then the blackness was lifted from my forehead and a fresh cold cloth substituted. There was no candle; through the doorway I could see the kitchen firelight reflecting off the rounded logs of the ceiling. I shivered a bit, but had to admit that the cold compress helped the ache.

"Your mother made excuses for you," my cousin went on. "Your baking since before dawn and such. Now, was that the truth, or did something else trigger your faint?"

"I don't faint," I protested. Only vaporish women fainted. Maybe I was weak, but I wasn't vaporish. Lord and Lady, had I tossed my dinner?

"New experiences teach new lessons," Marta replied. "How do you feel? Is it just your head, or elsewhere?"

"In truth, I feel as if I had an ague," I admitted, shivering once again. "I remember Momma switching me once—this is like a switching all over."

"What did you witness?"

I paused, not certain how to describe exactly what had appeared before me. Finally, I lifted up the corner of my damp cloth in a vain attempt to see and whispered, "Does Mr. MacDonnell have a long white robe of some sort on? Was he still wrapped in a blanket against the cold when he walked inside?"

Marta was silent a moment. She was naught but a stark shadow rimmed in gold against the firelight, motionless as a stone. "Exactly what did you observe?" Marta repeated.

Her distant, calm manner made me feel a bit better. "Mr. MacDonnell . . . had something wrapped around his legs and trailing off, like—" Then I realized what it was like, and pressed the cloth back across my eyes.

Like a shroud.

"It was a fetch, wasn't it?" I asked, suddenly very weary.

"Yes, I think so," Marta said somberly.

"Does it mean he's going to die?"

Again Marta paused before she answered. "Likely," she said at last. "The only time you *know* there will be a death, it is said, is when you see your own double. You'll have to learn to interpret what you have seen—and whether or not to tell others about it."

She lifted the cold compress off my head. "How is your stomach? Are you queer inside?"

I thought about it, listening to my insides. "No. I think I would like something to drink."

"That can be done." I heard liquid pouring into a cup but didn't turn my head. "When you see a double of someone half wrapped, often it means the person will die within the year. Full wrapping means dead very soon. And if you just see a fetch, without a shroud, it doesn't always mean death. Sometimes you can have a waking dream, where you see activities going on miles and even days away."

"Do you see fetches?" I asked her.

In response she smoothed my damp hair back from my forehead, and I recognized the anxious note in my voice. "No, I do not have that gift. It is not a comfortable talent, to see so much and to be helpless to change things."

"Then I shouldn't tell Mr. MacDonnell what I saw?"

"What would you tell him?"

"That—" I broke off abruptly. Tell him he'd die within the year? And that I couldn't tell him how or where? Even if he believed me, should he fear every twitching tree limb or hard-eyed stranger?

Could I take away his joy in what time he had left?

"What can we do for him?" I said instead.

"Encourage him to have his home shored up against weather and troubles," she replied. "I wish we could convince his wife to use wild carrot seed, to stop any more babies. She won't need an infant when it finally happens."

"Could the vision be false?" I said suddenly, struggling to sit up.

"It is possible, but not likely," was Marta's response as she handed me the pottery cup. "We can also get a tall, dark man to first-foot them on New Year's Eve. Is Shaw Kristinsson home for Christmas?"

I felt heat in my face again, and sipped some water. "I have not seen him," I said formally. "His brothers are all tall as well. Any of the Kristinssons could do it."

"Well, the MacDonnells are Scots, so any bit of luck we can push their way may help in the year to come. I've never understood this business with a tall, dark man with coal in his pocket, but the Scots place a lot of faith in it. Even have a special name for the new year's eve, Hogmanay or some such." Marta rose from her seat on the edge of the bed. "Are you up to visitors?"

I sat there a bit, as she waited for my answer, and then said, "Do you think I'll still see the shroud?"

"Some do, some don't," was her comment.

Draining the cup, I pulled my legs over and carefully stood up. No dizziness now. . . . Slowly I started out the doorway into the kitchen.

We paused to set aside my cup and make sure my hair and tucker were straight, and then I went back into the front room and smiled until my jaws ached. Momma and Papa knew something was amiss—I could tell by Momma's posture and Papa's stillness—but neither so much as raised an eyebrow. I don't think Mr. MacDonnell caught on, although his wife kept glancing in my direction. I didn't say a word, except to ask after the older MacDonnell brother, who lived just the other side of Sun-Return.

The shroud was no longer visible, praise the saints.

Around us the children played, Ben acting like a big brother to them. The youngest MacDonnell, barely toddling, sat quietly on his mother's lap and looked past her shoulder at some flickering candles set in a holly wreath.

It took a second glance for me to notice that sprigs of holly were twirling about the wreath, performing their own graceful dance. I quickly looked back at Mrs. MacDonnell, although I occasionally sneaked a glance out the corner of my eye. The little one watched the holly dance until another family came to the doorstep. Only then did the twigs stop moving. The MacDonnells continued into the village, while I got clean cups for the Anderssons.

I am grateful to say that I went the rest of the afternoon without seeing anything unexpected.

The evening was another matter.

ॐ ⚅ ॐ

Unlike folks across the sea, we did not exchange gifts on St. Nicholas Day—we received too few gifts to do that. Christmas in our community was family and church. Christmas Eve we had supper and leftover cake with our evening tea, and Papa read to us from the Book of Luke. What presents there were would come after church and dinner the next day, in honor of Christ's birth.

Days were short in the winter, and the solstice was just past. This meant the boys were going to bed early. Even Josh did not stay up long—he had handled all the livestock himself that day, plus run Momma's errands in Sun-Return, and he was tired.

I was tired, after standing in the kitchen most of the day. It felt good to sit on a cushion before a roaring fire and sip tea without an audience. The poltergeist had been very quiet since the dancing sprigs of holly. We'd heard footsteps upstairs while eating supper, but that was it.

It was *very* nice to sit in the living room without the scraps of fabric attacking me.

Marta was working on a square of her latest quilt, called Fish Tails for its sharp edges. She really liked working triangles, and this pattern was a challenge—it took eight colors. Since the scrap bag was full, she'd decided to deplete it a bit. I was still addled by her design, which was much more complicated than the Irish Chain I was doing. Marta was piecing the overall coverlet in her head from the center out, so that in case she ran out of a few remnants, the blocks would gradually change color.

"Ready for a lesson?" Marta said suddenly.

I blinked, surprised by the question. "Tonight?"

Marta lifted her head to meet my gaze; a half smile flitted across her lips. "No time like the present," she offered, tugging her thread back through. "Between fetches and poltergeists, I think it is time for you to learn the first of the major arcana."

Suddenly I was wide awake, and there was an ache in my chest, like I couldn't catch my breath. Between fetches and poltergeists, I'd been feeling a bit ragged, truth to tell. I wasn't sure I was ready just then for any more surprises.

"Christmas Eve?" I clarified. Marta had conducted a ritual on the solstice a few days past, but as a neophyte, I had not actively participated. Christmas was also a good time for ceremonies?

Marta looked amused. "'Tis said that ghosts walk on Christmas Eve. Can you think of a more appropriate—or safer—time to look beyond the borders of our world?"

"Ghosts?" Well, now . . . spirits were interesting. I straightened up.

"Actually," Marta began, pinning her needle in place and setting aside her square, "the first major arcana you must learn is how to call upon Death." Turning to smile at me, she added, "Nothing else is truly frightening after you have faced Death."

I just stared at her, a sinking feeling in the hollow of my stomach. "Death isn't really a person, is it? I thought that was just poetry, in the Bible. . . ."

"Death is a spirit," Marta said softly, her hands folding in her lap. "Some claim it is Azrael, the angel of death. Most people never see Death—or never know it is Death they see at the last. Death can wear many faces—Death can be anyone you have ever loved or known who has gone beyond. The face chosen is usually whomever the failing person wants most to see. And so the dying are comforted as they step over into the next life."

The angel of death. Lord and Lady, these were deep waters, now. "Do we find those people over there?" I finally whispered.

"We may. Death is ambiguous when answering questions about the other side of life." Marta looked a little evasive herself.

"Death will answer questions?"

Marta nodded as she stood up. "That is why a practitioner calls upon Death, to ask questions. But it is not done lightly. You do not ask Death anything that can be answered by anyone or anything else. You have to work at the answers—Death does not make things simple."

As she started for the kitchen, Marta added, "And you never, ever ask about your own death. That is the one question Death will not answer."

Rising to my feet, I threw the big pillow over on the pile and started after her. "What are you going to ask Death?"

"This is the only time that you call upon Death when you have no questions. When you begin learning the major arcana, you must introduce yourself to Death." Looking back at me as she lit a single taper from the kitchen fire, Marta went on: "All apprentices learn this spell first. Once you have cast it, Death will know your call, and may choose to answer it."

I thought about it, and shivered. "May choose?"

Marta smiled and went into the stillroom. "When Death is invited, Death may choose whether to come." Her voice grew lower as she continued. "The only way to guarantee Death's arrival is to kill something. Soldiers do it all the time, and rarely see Death passing by. But if a practitioner kills to demand Death's presence, it changes the relationship."

"Changes?" I hesitated at the doorway of the stillroom. *Relationship?*

Marta returned to the kitchen holding the candle and her carpetbag of wands, wards and beeswax candles. "Death is a friend to a practitioner, Allie," she said solemnly. "Death is the last, great healer, who takes away the pain we cannot ease. It's not Death people really fear—it is suffering. Death will answer specific questions concerning healing." She stopped before me, her expression grave. "Once you shed innocent blood to summon Death, you are no longer perceived as a healer. You become . . . something else. You become an enigma to watch, and perhaps a danger, a black sorcerer."

"Death no longer trusts you?" I asked slowly, watching her eyes.

Her brows lifted slightly, and she said, "Perhaps. I try not to attach emotions or attributes to Death. Death is not human, and helps us for obscure motives. Death never volunteers information— but Death always answers." Setting down the bag on the table, she began to take out things. "Sometimes the answer is no," she added.

"Is Death male or female?" I asked quickly, more to hear someone speak than to know the answer . . . which was a good thing, because Marta was done answering questions.

"Both, and neither. Get your coat." As I looked at her in surprise, she said, "We do not need ritual robes for this ceremony. Just fire and water, tobacco, blood, and honesty."

I was halfway into my coat before I realized Marta had said *blood.*

Might as well have not bothered with the coat. No mere sheepskin was going to warm my body, much less my soul.

Not this Christmas Eve.

ॐ ☽ ॐ

Marta had disappeared earlier in the afternoon, and had been gone much longer than a visit to the outhouse would require. I'd wondered where she was, but had not asked—practitioners sometimes need solitude, and prying is the worst form of rudeness.

Now the evidence of her sojourn outside lay before me. In the clearing behind the barn the snow had been scraped down to the ground in a circle about nine feet across. A small cone of wood was carefully placed in the center, ready to be lit. Marta had not changed into her shapeless purple silk gown or let her hair down. Tossed over her shoulder was a small leather bag. In oiled leather boots, woolen gloves, and a sheepskin coat covering her wool dress down to her boot tops, she seemed a strange figure to be staging a major ritual. Her only visible tool was a warming pan carrying a couple of live coals.

As we arrived at the scraped circle, Marta reached into the bag and pulled out her athame, the black-handled knife all practitioners use. She made a slashing motion on the east side of the area, and gestured for me to enter the shoveled ring. Following me inside, she gestured once again with the athame, and I felt a snapping sensation thrum against my left side. Apparently Marta had set wards earlier, when she created the circle. It looked shoveled, but who knew? Maybe she cleared it with magic.

"The ward is not necessary once the circle is drawn, but a ward is a good precaution when you have the time and strength to create it," Marta told me, sliding her knife into its sheath.

"Why isn't it necessary?" Might as well ask now, before things got busy.

"A good question, but I can't tell you why. All I know is, when the circle has been drawn and closed and Death called into it, negative influences shun the area."

So . . . even demons feared death?

Pulling her metal goblet from her bag, my cousin set it at her feet and then heaped snow into it. When the cup was overflowing, Marta touched the warming pan to the metal bowl. As the snow melted she continued heaping the goblet, until it was nearly full.

"You're not going to pull water out of the air?" I finally asked. I'd seen her do that very thing more than once—three nights earlier, in fact, for the solstice.

Marta shook her head, a gesture barely visible in the eternal twilight of a winter night. "That is a major form of magic, one you cannot yet do yourself. This is *your* ritual. Also, the air is too dry." Standing, she gestured for me to approach the center, and then poured the coals over the cone of dry wood.

A little encouragement from breath and tinder, and the wood caught fire easily. It was a fragrant blaze—oak, apple, and a sliver of resinous pine or cedar. Once the fire was burning brightly, Marta turned toward me and offered her knife to my left hand.

I hadn't even seen her pull the athame back out. . . .

"This is almost the only ritual a practitioner performs that requires blood. It demands the blood of the person casting the circle—you. Take the knife and just prick the index finger on your right hand. You need a drop of blood in the goblet. That also provides your salt for purification."

Oh, my . . . I could not *believe* what I was doing on Christmas Eve. Would Momma send Papa to look for us, or would they be mumchance about our absence? Would they even notice we were missing from our beds?

Standing there shivering, I knew full well that there was no getting out of this ritual. Marta was an adept, a fully-trained practitioner. She could stay out in the cold for *days* without ill effect. My toes would freeze off long before she agreed to go back inside.

Lord and Lady, my mind was spinning like a windmill. Sighing, I held up the silver knife to my right hand, thought about something else, and let the sharp tip slide across the surface of my first finger. The pain registered immediately, and by firelight I could see a dark drop welling up.

"Shake it into the goblet," Marta instructed. I did as she asked.

"Now—take the knife, dip it in the water and stir, preferably clockwise, three times." Solemnly I did so. "You are ready to draw your circle. Start east, as always, and end there, drawing an unbroken line with the water. You keep dipping the blade into the water to refresh the line. When in doubt, you can *pour* the circle, gently, so it doesn't roll away."

Stifling a sigh, I moved to the edge of the cleared snow and began drawing my circle. "What if I run out of water?" I said haltingly.

"You may stop, melt more snow, and put more blood into it," Marta said simply.

Ask a foolish question. . . .

I did not run out of water, I'm glad to say. I had a complete line circling the cleared area, although I could not tell by firelight if my ritual was complete. Marta solved that for me—she muttered a few words, and a faint red glow, like foxfire, was visible, as if I'd made the circle with live coals.

"Now the inner circle?" I said, looking over at Marta. At her nod, I backed up a step and made another complete circle within the first.

Then I ran out of water and had to heap the goblet once more. It's always more painful to get blood out of a cut when the slice has started to close, but I managed. Marta told me what to write between the rings—the names of the angels who are said to guard all who petition for their help. Raphael protected from the east, Michael from the south, Gabriel the west, and Uriel from the north. Between the names I drew crosses. Then I turned back to my teacher.

"And . . . ?" I prompted.

"Only those names and the cross," Marta replied.

I looked down at the circle I'd drawn, and then back at Marta. Suddenly I felt hot inside, flame searing down my veins. "This is all?" Marta nodded. "And we're protected?" Marta nodded again.

Didn't seem like enough to protect from Death. But maybe that was the point—there *was* no protection.

"Black magicians and black witches do not draw circles of this type," Marta said quietly. "They certainly do not call upon angels for protection from demons—they call upon the dark god, Satan, who has ruled the amoral and vile since the dawn of time, to protect them from his servants."

Anything I might had said seemed wasted breath, so I simply nodded.

"Remember, this is not a summoning."

I thought about it a moment. "So the forms used to call upon spirits don't really hold?"

Marta smiled and her fingers brushed my cheek. "You can't threaten Death with the wrath of angels, my dear—remember that some say Death *is* an angel. You are appealing to a force. It's not a prayer—Death cannot create life, it is not one of the powers that be. You are offering up an *invitation* to a spirit."

Her last words gave me a clue. Marta must have seen the change in my face, because she held up a finger to stop me from speaking.

"There is one last thing you need." Reaching back into her pouch, Marta pulled out a tiny leather bag. "Open your hand." When I did so, she took out a hefty pinch of a dried and crumbled plant and placed it on my palm. "Death can always be found in the coiling smoke of burning tobacco. I suspect that's part of why the Indians respect it and call it sacred. Toss this into the fire before you begin. You will end by flicking the rest of the goblet water into the blaze."

I closed my fingers over the flakes of tobacco to keep any errant breeze from stealing them. Glancing quickly at the flames in the center of the ritual circle, I thought of one last question: "What name do I use to speak with Death?"

Again, Marta smiled that sudden, twisted smile that only echoed her usual expression. "You may use your earthly name your parents gave you, or your Craft name we selected on the equinox— although you have had good luck using no name. Your calling must ring like a solitary bell, its voice known to all."

She was reminding me that I'd actually had the nerve to call on the mother goddess without identifying myself, back when we were trying to lay that ghost. It was almost enough to make me grumble. I knew I was to use my Craft name in invocations—I didn't know I was to use it when *praying*.

I'd had my first magic name three months, since the equinox, and had yet to use it. Time to break it in. . . .

Suddenly I was warm all over, almost too warm for my heavy coat. I undid the big horn toggles and let the garment hang loose. Then I turned to face the bright fire. Inhaling deeply, I took about a third of the crushed tobacco and tossed it into the flames.

The familiar smell of burning tobacco filled my nostrils. It seemed stronger than what Papa used, more biting. As the smoke rose into the cloudy sky I managed to swallow once, and then said, "I call upon you, Azrael, great healer of the ages, most compassionate of spirits, who knows all that we are and might ever be. I, Alfreda Alethia, come before you to announce my intention and offer you my service. I was born a healer, and now learn all the mysteries you have yet revealed, to better practice *my* calling."

I gulped some air and tossed more of the tobacco into the flames. "In a circle drawn with the wine of life, I ask you to look upon me and listen to my petition, so that you will know me as a healer when I call upon your name." I inhaled once more, to finish my request, but nothing else came out as I realized that someone—something—was seated on the other side of the fire.

In form it was a young man wearing buckskin, his skin the color of fresh ivory, his hair so pale a blond it looked white by firelight. I could not see his eyes, but I knew they would be a pale blue . . . and that there was a smattering of freckles, like sand, etched across his nose.

It was a face much like my own, except that my eyes were like Papa's, as blue as the sky.

Fury seized me, and I threw the last of the tobacco at Death—useless, as it floated into the fire. "How *dare* you!" I shrieked. "How *dare* you choose that face! How could you choose it?"

Death's expression did not change. "I was not uncalled."

"I most certainly did not choose my brother! Don't you have a face of your own?"

"Yes."

I stood there, suddenly uncertain. Marta had told me the exact truth—Death answered questions, and no more.

"Why do you think I chose that face for you?" I asked, my voice quieter.

"Perhaps because you felt you never properly said good-bye," Death suggested evenly. His—its—face did not change expression.

There was truth in that. My last words with Dolph had been ordinary words, brisk words dismissing a troublesome little sister.

"I miss you," I said simply. "Someday I'll forgive you for acting stupid and touching that wolf's mouth. I know you couldn't guess it was a werewolf, but still . . . to toss all your learning out with the wash water just to impress some fool young men—" I stopped, then, knowing I was addressing Death as if it was Dolph. "I loved him."

Death seemed to waver before my eyes, becoming an image of smoke. My eyes watered in response. When I could see again, Dolph no longer sat across from me. Now it was an elderly woman in a dress with many petticoats, her beautiful shawl held in place with a cameo, her cap trimmed with a wide band of lace. The gaze upon me was sharp. She seemed to be sitting on air, as if an unseen chair was present.

"Do you understand about the triad yet, Allie?" Her voice was low for a woman's, almost gravelly, as if she had spent her life speaking through smoke. My great-grandmother had been a great practitioner in her time . . . she had read a lot of futures in the curl of a smoking fire.

So . . . not only could I question Death; Death could question me.

"I know that I am rooted in life, Gran, and you in death, and that there's love between us," I told her, reaching up to finger the woven silver necklace at my throat. It, like the bracelets that matched, had once belonged to Great-grandmother Emma. "The Triad is always those three things, but what they mean changes like a breath of wind."

"The meaning never changes, my dear," she said gently, smoothing her full skirt with one hand like she always did, "but which meaning we recognize flickers like sunlight on the face of a pond. It never repeats itself."

"I'll do right by you, Gran," I said impulsively. "I'll learn these things."

Emma Schell's sweet smile slipped out. "I know you will, Alfreda Golden-tongue, Veritas. You were born to walk in the Dark on the Other Side. You will bring light wherever you tread."

I blinked and frowned. Those were not names I remembered from anywhere. "Why do you call me that? It's not my name."

"It will be."

What else was there to say? "When?"

"Sooner than you think."

So much for questioning Death. I guessed future names fell into knowing your own destiny, and such information was hard to find and uncertain.

It dawned on me that I'd gotten mad at Death and thrown something at it. Death had not responded—whether from courtesy or because response was not its nature, I did not know.

Maybe it was time to fold my cards and leave the game. . . .

"I thank you, Azrael, for your courtesy in coming to face me in this circle, and for your answers to questions I did not know I had." Lifting up the goblet, I dipped my hand into it and flicked the blood-tinged water into the flames. "Farewell to you, until we meet again."

"It will be soon," Death said implacably as it wavered and disappeared like a windblown candle flame.

I flung the water in an arc of droplets, causing the fire to hiss. Then I turned toward Marta.

She was not looking at me; she was looking at the spot where Death had been seated. "Well done, Allie," she said softly.

I would have felt better about the whole thing if she hadn't been frowning when she spoke. That ended Christmas Eve for me, as at the age of thirteen years I first met Death face-to-face.

God rest you merry, gentles all, and peace on earth to folk of good will.

FOUR

PEOPLE THINK OF THE SOLSTICE as the most dangerous part of winter, as if anything could happen on the longest night of the year. But the wise know that the most perilous time is Twelfth Night—the Epiphany, or Feast of the Wise Men. It has an older name and an ancient history, but what matters is that the sixth day of Ice is when Herne the Hunter rides the night skies with the Gabriel Ratchets, his baying pack of hounds.

Often he doesn't ride alone.

Wild geese don't travel across our skies in winter, so when you hear a strange, high whickering on a crisp winter eve, you need shelter fast—because the Wild Hunt is not choosy about what it hunts.

Normal animals can't face the Wild Hunt—it would drive them mad. The wise shut their barns tight, and the forest beasts hide, so Herne hunts only evil creatures on Twelfth Night.

He drives them to the ends of the earth.

Practitioners can call the Hunt to cleanse a place, but it is a call fraught with danger. The Wild Hunt is wild magic, and answers to no master. It is easy for the predator to become the prey. Only the desperate or the greatly skilled touch wild magic.

Christmas was the sole lull in the winter rising of the Dark, which was why we had used that evening to conduct our ceremony. Something changed for Marta after the ritual—she grew quiet and contemplative, her thoughts clearly elsewhere. Without asking I knew that our visit was coming to an end.

Sure enough, the day after Christmas we were up long before first light, packing our clothing and the food for our dinner. There was plenty of roasted wild turkey and tight-grain bread left, as well as the honey-glazed ham. We could take with us wedges from the remnants of the mincemeat and pumpkin pies (both excellent, if I may say so myself) but the spicy squash soup, baked potatoes, and chestnut stuffing remained only a pleasant memory.

On Christmas the poltergeist had settled for footsteps upstairs and snowballs hitting the side of the house. I think we were all relieved.

And yes, Momma had made me a hooded woolen cloak that brushed the ground, all dyed a beautiful golden brown from red onion skins and powdered copper. I folded it carefully when I slid it into my saddlebag; it was a lovely, soft thing to hold between my hands.

"I wish you could stay longer, Marta," my mother was saying as I walked down the stairs, my bags balanced over my shoulder.

"I do, too, Garda, but you know this is an odd time of year. I'll feel better this evening, when I have Allie back inside my permanent wards," was Marta's response.

I watched as Momma slipped some of her thick-skinned basil goat cheese in the food bag, and grinned to myself. Momma had always pushed food on people when she didn't have the sentimental words she wanted. Some things didn't change.

"Are you ready, Allie?" Marta asked me, and I realized that both women had turned my way.

"Yes, ma'am," I told her, which brought a smile to mother's face.

"Then let us say our good-byes and be off." Turning back to Momma, my cousin embraced her and said, "I'll be back for your confinement, Garda, come spring."

Momma reached for me and hugged me as hard as she could with a baby and saddlebags between us. "If you'll finish your growing up, girl, you can help deliver the baby."

"I'll work on growing, Momma, I promise," I assured her, bracing myself for Ben and Joe throwing themselves upon me.

"And Momma doesn't mean how tall you are, either," Josh whispered in my ear as he squeezed my shoulder.

I knew that.

All Papa and I did was hug each other a long time, but it was enough. He's always with me, in a funny way, and his lessons have saved my life more than once.

But that's how fathers are supposed to be.

The road was trampled flat for an entire wagon width, so we were swift passing through the eerie light of dawn. An occasional flurry of small snowballs told us that the poltergeist was keeping us company. I tapped down a sigh—I'd hoped the thing would stay in Sun-Return. Did poltergeists demand feeding, like brownies and other house spirits?

"With any luck, we will only have to deal with the poltergeist for a month or so. It will look for more interesting prey when spring rolls around," came Marta's voice from ahead of me.

"There's nothing we can do to get rid of it?" I asked.

"Deprive it of what it wants, which we can't do. All other eviction attempts are chancy."

Huh. "It wants something?" I murmured, grabbing tighter with my knees when Old Ned slid a bit.

"Always. Sometimes you can use a spell to shut down the lure, but not this time." Marta looked back over her shoulder, and she was grinning. "I've been waiting for you to guess. Poltergeists like to visit homes where there's a young person maturing. There's lots of extra energy sizzling about before a child becomes an adult."

"So Josh and I attracted the thing?" I said, wishing I didn't sound so surprised.

"Something like. And it prefers you, unless there was more than one. It will stick around until you're finished maturing—or until you manifest so much power the thing is frightened off," Marta added. "I suspect you'll finish blossoming by autumn. It's very unusual for a poltergeist to stay beyond that—and by that point, you'll be able to control all your energy, and starve it out."

Lovely. My own, personal poltergeist. What would Idelia think? We'd agreed at Aunt Dagmar's solstice party that Idelia would come visit in a few weeks, weather permitting. But if I still had a poltergeist around. . . .

Almost as if she was reading my mind, Marta said, "Idelia doesn't need to know what's pestering us. If you take it in stride, she probably will, too."

Well, that was true enough. Idelia had once fallen into a sleeping animal's mind with me, and she'd handled herself pretty well, all things considered. Maybe she *could* handle a poltergeist, too. I mulled this over as we trotted through the fresh snow, a thin veil of flakes covering older stuff packed down by horses and wagons traveling to Sun-Return. We'd have our path blazed for us almost halfway to Cat Track Hollow, and Marta clearly meant to make the most of it. There was time enough to push through drifts.

Marta had not been joking about her intentions. We practically flew that morning, and had to walk the horses cool before we ate our lunch. A league or two beyond the half-way point, we passed Gilman's homestead, and our dwindling wagon path abruptly disappeared into sculpted, drifting snow.

"Now we work," Marta said grimly, weaving to the far side of the track, where the snow was shallow.

Funny how you never think of time as something that changes, but I would have sworn that afternoon lasted an entire day. The wind had churned bizarre shapes from the snow, leaving frozen ground at one point and deep ice pellets at another. Old Ned was getting very tired—I would have had to get off and walk him if we hadn't soon reached the narrow path cleared near Cat Track Hollow.

No wagons had passed since the last big snow, so we had a track simply one horse wide. It was enough of a trail to lead us to Marta's own path before true night fell.

Marta's home was one of the oldest in the region, and built in three sections. The great room and kitchen were in the center, with the big chimney across from the outside doorway. The stillroom was to the left, and three small sleeping rooms to the right.

The barn was attached to her cabin through the big stillroom by a covered walkway, which was very handy that night. Sure, it meant she had to keep her lean-to cleaner than most, but I suspected magic helped hide any odor. Marta rode right up to the lean-to and leaned over to unlatch the doors. I stayed where I was—Ned wouldn't sit still for tricks like that.

"Inside," she ordered, backing up and waving me on in.

"Do you want a lantern first?" I said, worried about stomping a chicken, but I touched my heels to Ned's sides as she continued to gesture. The snow had been trampled down by whomever Marta had asked to tend her livestock, so we had no trouble pulling open the doors. Marta must have spelled the animals, because nothing tried to run back outside.

I dismounted and fumbled around but didn't find the lantern. Marta knew where she kept things; in moments she had pulled a lantern from a peg and lit the wick. The sudden flare of light left spots flashing before my eyes, but I'd heard her whisper a few words, so I'd known what was coming.

"Pull the door tight, Allie," Marta ordered, moving Sweet William a few steps closer to the stalls. I did as she asked.

Only then did Marta seem to relax, hanging the lantern from another peg and slowly dismounting. "It's not a good time of year to linger outside after dark," she said without preamble. "It is especially dangerous for you. You know just enough magic to get yourself into trouble, and you'll look tasty to certain creatures that eat magic."

I thought about this as I led Ned into one stall and tied him up. A nanny goat butted my leg for attention, but I ignored her. "The wards you set while traveling wouldn't be enough?" I asked.

Marta unbuckled her saddlebags from behind the cantle and set them outside William's stall. "Traveling wards aren't as strong as fixed wards," she said simply. "I laid down my circle of power when this cabin was first built, and I strengthen it each time I cast a spell." As she yanked on her cinch and pulled off the saddle, she added, "You'll stay close to home until after Twelfth Night. This time next year, your own protections will guard you from magic scavengers."

"Home" meant Marta's home, I knew. So I'd be stuck there eleven days. Well, maybe Idelia would come visit in that time, and we could quilt and talk. My current project was that quilt for her wedding, if I liked how the thing turned out, but she didn't have to know that as we sat and worked.

Eleven days is a long time when you can't even walk down a trapline. I wasn't looking forward to it.

঩·ⅅ·঩

The next few days were spent getting Marta's farm working smoothly again, returning Ned to his owner, and catching up on the baking. I also started learning how to grind certain minerals for spells. Some of them were expensive, rough gemstones, even— but when you needed only a few grains, price was not a problem. Marta told me I would be given some of Granny's stones when I was ready.

Between grindings I went back to piecing that Irish Chain quilt. It's amazing how fast you can quilt when you're not doing much else. I'd wanted to do something like Robbing Peter to Pay Paul, but that required big pieces of two colors of material. Latticed Irish Chain meant seven different colors, which were easier to collect. I had to beg the seventh color from Marta, but that was all right— she said that folks traded scraps all their lives, and sometime I'd have something she wanted.

I think I liked quilting because I was imposing order on chaos. And there was a lot of chaos in our life on the frontier. Maybe women out there quilted because if they could bring order and beauty to a blanket, then they could bring order to a log cabin, or a farm—or a village. Some women gave up and went back East . . . and some became quilters.

Pale ivory, greens and yellows, like a fresh spring morning, danced before my eyes. I cut tiny squares from cloth scraps dyed with comfrey, chamomile, horsetail, and bearberry. There was bracken, lady's mantle, and larkspur used, too, and Scotch broom flowers had made the palest green for my outside lattice rows. I wanted to finish piecing before Idelia arrived, so we could quilt on the frame Josh and Papa had made me.

Life was good that fortnight. I even had something else to look forward to.

"There's to be a barn dance on Epiphany, Allie," Marta announced one afternoon after she had been out dispensing medicines and picking up supplies. Well, my head popped up at that, because I loved dancing. "You know the country dances and the minuet, don't you?"

"Yes, Ma'am, Momma taught me and Dolph." It just flowed out naturally, and I was surprised that saying his name aloud didn't hurt. "I taught Josh some, but he doesn't have much patience with dancing."

Marta smiled as she removed her hat. "If you asked, you might find he's acquired patience. Most girls love to dance, and it's a way to hold a girl's hand without her parents getting upset."

I grinned at that. Trust Josh to think up that angle. I only hoped he didn't tell Momma *why* he was finally interested in dancing. Momma didn't approve of "forward" boys and girls. "How are your mothers feeling?" I asked as I stood up to help her put away flour and beans.

Marta had no less than three women within a half day's ride who were expecting, as well as one two days north of us. One of the local women was new to her "delicate condition," and the one far away only six months gone. But the other two around Cat Track Hollow were much closer to their times—within a fortnight for one lady, and a month for the other.

Marta was a firm believer in the benefits of powdered squawroot to promote a swift and easy lying-in, as long as the tea was given only in the last fortnight of pregnancy. Any earlier than the last two weeks, and it could bring on an early delivery.

Mrs. Johnson was drinking her squawroot obediently, but her husband had been slow to clean up the cabin for the birthing. He'd been willing, though, to pay Marta in fresh ground red wheat to do the work for him. That had made Marta mad, but she'd gone in to prepare the Johnson household.

That was one of the things I admired about Marta. She would have gone to clean that lady's house even if there was no way for them to pay, to make sure the birth was a safe one. Marta charged the man for one reason only—his laziness in caring for his wife. I'd been told that there used to be another midwife in the area, who thought Marta's "obsession" with cleanliness foolish. But that midwife lost many women to childbed fever and other sickness—babies as well—while Marta had lost only two mothers and a handful of children in twenty years of midwifing.

Who would you want at your bedside when your time came, or your lady was about to present you with a child? Marta's ideas seemed outlandish, but something she did helped protect mothers and babies. Since we didn't know *which* thing, we did all of them.

Needless to say, the midwife's family had moved on a few years back. I hoped the woman had decided to try some of Marta's suggestions, since I was sure she was still delivering babies somewhere.

"Mrs. Johnson is coming along nicely, and Mrs. Moore is still as nervous as a cat under a rocking chair," Marta announced, setting another log on the fire to build it up for our main meal of the day.

"I suppose if I'd lost two in a row, I'd be nervous, too," I offered as I pulled the current loaf from the bread box.

"Almost every woman will lose at least one if she bears long enough," Marta said calmly, sitting down on her low cooking stool and swinging the pot of venison stew over the heat. "Mrs. Moore lost one because of bad midwifing, which won't happen this time, and the other because she was traveling. Some women don't travel well when they're increasing. Did you start the wild rice?" She held her hand close to a covered pot as she spoke.

"Nearly an hour ago," I told her, glancing at the candle I'd been using for sewing.

"Good, it should be about ready. Mrs. Moore is fretting needlessly, but all I can do is give her chamomile and hops to soothe her spirits. It's too early for squawroot." Marta took a quilted pad and tilted up the cast iron lid of the rice pot. Scooping up a tiny bit, she set the lid back on. "She has two healthy children, which is more than some women ever have." As the rice cooled, she tasted it. "A few more minutes." Turning to look over at me, she asked, "Did you finish the laying-in packs?"

"All four of them are ready. Let the babies come!" This was still another reason why it was never boring at Marta's house. She made everything new and different, because she always seemed to go against the current. Only Marta would boil her own linens and fold them up to take when a woman was delivering. She even had a couple of aprons she used, only her aprons were boiled after each delivery, not blood-stained and pus-covered like the frock coat worn by the bone surgeon in Cat Track Hollow.

Just toss me in the ground and let Death come for me, before a surgeon lays a hand on me.

⁂

Idelia Pederson arrived on New Year's Day, and her dark-haired father was first across our doorstep, so we were even first-footed properly. Her arriving for the dance was a big help to me. Sometimes boys were shy about asking me to dance, because I was an apprentice practitioner . . . or because I was so tall. But Idelia was dainty and dark and growing beautiful, and I would be proud to introduce her around. Even if she was practically engaged, she could still dance with anyone she chose.

I was surprised at how interested Idelia was in Marta's home. All those chimneys got her attention, and Marta made food spicier than my friend normally ate. Mrs. Pederson was a sound cook, but she never did anything fancier than sweet bread. Marta let us cook what we wanted, so I taught Idelia how to make all sorts of things.

Maybe Will Adamsson's attentions made her nervous about all the household things she *didn't* know. . . .

"And then you just put a sprig of rosemary in the bottle?" Idelia said, frowning at the warm cider vinegar she'd poured into a pale green bottle.

"That's all," I answered, dropping five inches of rosemary in the vinegar and corking the tall flask. "Put it in the sun if you can, and shake it every day for a fortnight. Then taste in two weeks, and if you want it stronger, strain the vinegar and put new rosemary in. I—" read *Marta* there "—put a fresh sprig in the bottle when it's ready, so I know what kind of vinegar is inside."

"And you can do this with any herb?"

I frowned. "Well, maybe not any herb. Ones we like to eat, like basil, dill, fennel, garlic, marjoram, thyme—those kinds of herbs."

"I can't wait to try one," Idelia said, and sounded like she meant it. Then she gave me a glance out of the corners of her dark brown eyes. "Are you still running a trapline?"

"Of course," I replied, moving into Marta's stillroom to place the vinegar bottle on one of her few windowsills.

"Then why won't your aunt let you go farther than the privy? Is there something dangerous out there?"

Uh-oh . . . heat flushed through me at her words. Idelia was more observant than Marta had hoped. So far the poltergeist hadn't done anything around my friend, but I'd forgotten how well Idelia knew me. Thinking rapidly, I composed my face.

Then I realized what she was *really* asking, because I remembered the cougar that had attacked travelers on the road, back when we were little. I could have laughed with relief. "You're safe, Idelia," I assured her. "You can go gather eggs or help milk goats or whatever you want. I can't go out because . . . well, it has to do with the mysteries."

Would she believe me? I'd never used that phrase before, but practitioners fall back on it to spare people things they don't want to know about.

"What about the dance?" she asked, hanging a full kettle on the pothook to heat for washing up.

"I can go out on Epiphany, but not before," I replied, reaching for one of the last squares I was piecing. "It would be dangerous for me. So unless the cabin catches on fire or something, I'll be here!"

Now, I should have known not to say things like that.

۞

The days flew by with Idelia there to ease my mind. We got the entire coverlet pieced together, even the border strips with the chain blocks balanced on end, and then Marta helped us lay it over the cotton batting and beautiful calico backing I had bought.

That flowered backing was beyond my limited store of coins, but Marta had loaned me the money in exchange for my doing "extras" for her. She'd counted how well I'd done at Cloudcatcher as part of my payment. *There are journeymen practitioners who would have panicked during all that, and you never did.* Her words echoed in my head.

Surely part of that calm was being too scared to say anything, but I didn't want to destroy her faith in me, so I kept mum. I suspected she knew how I'd felt. Wasn't bravery being scared but doing something, anyway? At any rate, I was grateful for the fine cloth.

We wound that big double quilt around one side of the frame, and celebrated the first quilt on my own frame by having a quick tea party. Then we got back to work!

It was well into the afternoon on the day of Twelfth Night when a knock came at the door. Whoever it was knocked again before I reached the entrance—well, pounded, really. I pulled open the door to find Mr. Johnson on the step, slapping his hat against his thigh, his dark brows drawn together and his beard hiding what he was thinking.

"It's time," he said abruptly. "She's been having pains all morning, but she wouldn't let me come until now."

With a first baby, that was as it should be. Most likely this baby would take a while. I turned to go fetch Marta, but she had quietly come up behind me.

"Come in for some spiced cider, Mr. Johnson, while I get my things." She vanished into the stillroom, which meant I was expected to get that cider.

"Come along, Mr. Johnson, heat's escaping," I told him, trying to sound as though everything was under control. He looked at me in surprise and then stepped inside, brushing the snow from his shoulders as he did so.

Idelia had already pulled the crock from the coals, and made a pretty picture as she poured Mr. Johnson a mug of cider.

"This is Miss Idelia Pederson, Mr. Johnson. She lives in Sun-Return, and came to visit for a spell." I winced at my word choice—I try not to use "spell" in that fashion—but Mr. Johnson did not seem to notice.

"A pleasure, Miss Pederson," he said gruffly, accepting the mug of hot cider. Idelia did that to people—women were charmed by her and men admiring. It helped that the man had no idea how old either of us was; Marta didn't tell people that sort of thing. *None of their business,* she'd say.

She probably didn't tell because she didn't want folks refusing a medicine they watched me make. People are like that about young'uns.

Marta came back with one of the laying-in bundles, her herb bag in hand. In a few quick movements she pulled on her big sheepskin coat and her winter hat. "I could use your help, but we won't risk it tonight," she said simply. "I've set the wards. Good night, ladies. Keep busy, and eat some of that soup for dinner!" Touching my cheek in farewell, Marta headed for the door.

Mr. Johnson handed me the empty mug, nodded to us, and rushed to help Marta into his wagon. Idelia hurried to shut the door the man had forgotten to pull closed.

"I'm surprised he didn't drop the cup and run," she said with a smile. "It's their first child, isn't it?"

"Distracted," I agreed. "Do you want some tea before we go on?"

"You're giving me a taste for quilting," was her answer. "My mother makes three patterns over and over. I could piece them asleep."

"Then let's work," I agreed. Talking and quilting—it doesn't get much better, when you're trapped inside.

'Course, that was before I found out about marriage.

❧ ⚘ ❧

We did stop for a rich chicken soup, made with the rest of the wild rice. Marta's dilly bread was as good as Momma's, so we had a nice meal. After cleaning up, we lit several more candles—Marta was never stingy with candles, since she made her own—and got back to work.

It must have been compline, as church folks have it, when there came a pounding at the door. I was so startled I dropped my thimble.

"Ouch!" Idelia cried, quickly pressing on her finger. "Sweet lord, Allie, who could that be?"

"Probably someone with a sick child," I murmured, moving to the door with a feeling of unease. Would it be something I could make up and trust the parents to use right? "Who is it?" I yelled. Idelia flinched, but remained silent.

"Jimmy M-Moore," came a small voice. Amazed, I opened the door. There was a small, bundled creature powdered with snow standing on our doorstep. A lantern sat at his feet, hissing as it melted into the slush.

"Lord save you, boy, what are you doing here this late?" I seized his shoulder and hauled him inside, grabbing the lantern with my other hand and shoving the door closed with my hip. "Idelia, get him something hot, will you?" Quickly I stripped the child of his soaking wet coat, hat and mittens. At least his oversized shirt was still dry. "Pants, too."

"Pants?" he squeaked, his seven-year-old dignity offended.

"I've got brothers, and you've got a shirttail. Peel off those shoes and pants! There are quilts in the cedar chest, Idelia," I called as I grabbed my coat and went out to tend to the boy's horse.

Good Lord and Lady, the temperature was dropping. I hustled the restless horse into the big lean-to and quickly rubbed him down with straw. A bit of water, access to the haybin, and I hurried back inside through the stillroom.

Modesty was preserved by the shirt, but Jimmy was happier in the quilt. Idelia had pushed cider and molasses cookies at him.

"Miz Donaltsson has to come," he finally got out. "M-Momma sent word." He pointed at his coat.

I dug in the pockets and pulled out a corner of an old letter. The snow had smudged it a bit, but printed in careful letters were the words *My water broke*. It was signed in beautiful copperplate with the name *Martha Moore*.

"Dammit!" I said aloud, heedless of the child. Idelia gasped in horror. Looking up at her, I repeated the message aloud.

"Oh, dear. That's not good, is it? She's too soon," was Idelia's response.

I shook my head. A month or so early, so this was *not* good, but there was a chance for the baby—if Martha Moore did not panic. Marta hadn't actually said so, but Mrs. Moore was a flighty woman, easily upset. It might be part of the reason she lost one of those earlier babies.

"Jimmy, where's your daddy?" I said quickly. Since Jim was the messenger, I already had a pretty good idea of the answer.

"Gone to Sun-Return to buy a horse," the boy replied, shoving a cookie into his mouth.

"Is your momma having pains yet?" I asked.

Swallowing a bite of cookie, he said, "Only a couple before she sent me here. She wasn't happy, but she didn't seem to hurt much."

Early labor, then, which could last until midnight, easy, before things got difficult. Then a midwife or another woman needed, more to keep the woman from bearing down too soon and exhausting herself. Until the womb was opened enough, only trouble came from trying to force the babe along.

Someone needed to be there by midnight.

It was the night of Herne's Ride, the biggest thing Marta feared for me. I could feel my dinner trying to rise into my throat, and took deep breaths to calm myself.

"Allie?" Idelia sounded unsure of herself. I sat back on my heels and looked at her. "Come sit by the fire and catch your breath." As I did so she whispered, "Have you ever delivered a baby?"

"Helped," I told her, hearing the tension in my voice. Helping wasn't the same. There were things I could do, but there were medicines I absolutely could not make—I didn't know how to decide on the amount, which was the most important thing with strong herbs.

For the first time I bitterly resented the order of my teaching. If I'd been a boy, I'd already know a few of the lessons of Air and Fire, including throwing my mind distances to speak to those who could hear. I'd done it accidentally, to someone in the same room, and with effort to someone maybe a quarter mile away. But even if I could reach Marta at the Johnsons', I would not be able to reach her from the Moore cabin.

There wasn't actually time for a lesson . . . still, if I'd been a boy, I'd have no idea where to begin delivering the baby, because I'd have had no Water and Earth experience. At least I knew what *not* to do.

I *had* to talk to Marta. Half of me was scared witless, and half knew I had to go out into that soft, snowy night and deliver a baby. Wards, I had to have wards—

I was moving before I realized I'd stood. "Keep him here, Ida," I said, using my oldest nickname for her. "I need to do something." I rushed into the cold stillroom and shut the door, plunging myself into darkness. It was the most privacy I could hope for, short of the lean-to.

Feeling for Marta's mixing stool, I sat down, took a few deep breaths, and composed my mind. There was a rustling over in the corner, but I ignored it—we had no rats, so it was probably the poltergeist. Then I concentrated on Marta's face, her turn of words, the way her chuckle could catch your attention. The wards around the cabin might protect me, but I wanted to be sure nothing interfered with any bridge built between us.

I was as ready as I could be. Bracing myself, I tossed my thought into the night. *Marta? Marta Helgisdottir Donaltsson?* I couldn't risk using her one ceremonial name that I knew—not on Twelfth Night.

Allie? The thought was startled, but the mind *felt* like Marta's. I knew that was a silly idea, but it was the only way to describe something no one could touch.

Marta, Jimmy Moore is here, I thought quickly. *Mrs. Moore's water has broken.*

Marta didn't actually speak, but her thoughts were both irritated and distressed. *It doesn't rain but it pours,* she told me wearily. *Allie, this delivery will take every step of twelve hours, and Abigail Johnson has a good six hours to go.*

Well, I hadn't really expected better news. *Should I go to her?* This was such a soft thought I wasn't sure she heard me. *Marta?*

No! Not without wards! This was loud and fast.

But Idelia and Jimmy are in the big room. Should they see this? The permanent circle was in the main room, spelled to remain hidden, but always present. If I was going to do wards, I needed a circle—I was too new in the Craft to concentrate on linking the stones without protection.

No, Jimmy can't see this . . . and I don't think Idelia is ready for it. There was silence a while. *Do you know where the outside circle is?*

Somewhere behind the stillroom window? This thought was a little desperate—there was three feet of snow out there, and I'd used that circle only once so far.

I could feel Marta's sigh across the miles. *Not good enough, woman. You'll know where it is before the end of the week, I guarantee you.*

Marta wasn't going to make the same mistake twice.

Are the traveling wards from Cloudcatcher still set? I suggested.

Yes, but fading. There may not be much left. Another moment of silence, and then a brisk thought arrowed my way. *There is no choice, Allie. Yes, there is danger, but Mrs. Moore may lose both her baby and her life if she panics and starts pushing too soon. You don't have time to set wards, not and keep it hidden from Idelia and Jimmy. Nerves make for long rituals.*

I had a sinking feeling in my stomach. *So I take the travel wards?*

Yes. Also your necklace—and take mine, I left it in the usual place. I felt something grip my mind tight. *Go get the necklace.*

I pulled open the door and hurried back across the big room, basking in the heat as it rippled across my body. Until that moment, I hadn't realized I was cold. Idelia might have started to speak, but I understood none of it. Entering Marta's second small bedroom, I pulled the curtain closed and then rushed to the chimney shared by both sleeping areas. When Marta had guests in winter, she always moved into the other small bedroom—that meant two instead of three fires to tend.

The fire was banked, but I was able to get enough heat to light a slip and then a bedside candle. Setting the candle on the hearthstone, I reached to the brickwork on the right and counted up three and over six. The bricks were in that alternating pattern where every other one stuck out an inch, and I gripped the protruding corners and hauled back.

Desperation gave me strength—it came easily into my hands. Inside was Marta's jewel box, holding her few pieces of her mother's jewelry and her practitioner's necklace.

The coiled long chain of gold held charms of every imaginable kind, from coins and gems to cougar teeth and amber. There was a faint luminescence about it to my eye, as if power radiated from it—which it did. My own chain sat alongside it, since there was no other hidey-hole in the house.

Pulling both necklaces out, I thought: *I have them.*

Put them on. Marta had that ordering tone in her voice, so I quickly did as she asked and then shoved the box back into the crevice. Replacing the brick, I gathered my skirt and the candle and stood.

The other apron is folded between the top two laying-in packs, she told me. *Take all the usual herbs, and remember the red raspberry leaves—you'll need quite a bit. I can't explain wormwood to you this way, you must see the mixing to understand it.*

That I knew—I never thought she'd trust me to use wormwood, not yet. Red raspberry was good for pain and to both relax the patient and stimulate the womb—it would have to do.

I would have to do.

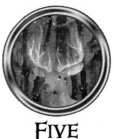

FIVE

IT WAS THE FIRST TIME I HAD ever feared the forest.

I'd had my moments of unease out in the vast world beyond our tiny homestead, but this frigid, murky night was the first time I was constantly aware of danger lurking behind every tree and rise.

Now I knew how folks who had no practitioners felt about the different Indian tribes.

Maybe it wasn't the forest that was so bad—maybe it was the dazzling light from the lantern I was carrying on a pole across my lap. I was able to walk this trail without a torch, but Sweet William needed more guidance than my hands on the reins. Instead of eternal twilight we had the strange, round gleam of a lantern surrounded by softly falling snow. It was as if tiny chips of fire were falling through the glow, sparks flaring momentarily before vanishing beneath the horse's feet. The shadows cast were muted, as if the light were at a distance.

The darkness was held at bay—just barely. It followed me, as alive as a stalking wildcat. I found myself erect, listening, as we flowed through the powder covering the trail. There is nothing like fear to improve your posture; I felt like a poker. Was that eerie whickering sound a distant flock of birds disturbed by the snow, or was it the Wild Hunt? I listened so hard my ears almost turned inside out, but the sound was fading in the west.

Take Sweet William, Marta had said. *Leave Jimmy and his horse to Idelia's care. William may startle, but he won't run unless there's reason to panic.* She'd also told me to take some squawroot along. There wasn't a lot it could do now for Mrs. Moore, but just tasting it might relax her, knowing what the herb was supposed to do.

A liquid trill of notes sounded off in the forest, somewhere to my right. I recognized the voice of my spirit friend, the White Wanderer, and clung to the sound like a child to her mother's hand. Although the Wanderer usually came to warn me of danger, I was still glad for his presence. I no longer felt so alone.

The forest was most dangerous before midnight. Still, Herne rode until dawn, and Mrs. Moore needed me soon. I could not wait until midnight had passed. I'd managed to find all the proper tools, from the laying-in pack and apron to my sharp stork scissors Momma had given me two years ago. But I'd fumbled the buckle on the back on the cantle, pulling it loose from the saddle, and I'd been too rattled to reassemble it. So my saddlebags were held on only by a rawhide thong. If we had to run, I might lose them.

Idelia had been very upset at my going, after what I'd told her about "the mysteries." She'd even nerved herself to remind me of it. I had told her simply to stay inside the house or lean-to until dawn—no matter what she thought she heard.

"I'll open the barn for you when you return," she promised.

A nice thought, but I wasn't looking further ahead than delivering that baby. And first I had to reach the Moore homestead. I pressed my elbows against my knife sheath and buckskin pouch full of sinew, herbs, and flint and steel. I'd left Marta's gun back in the cabin . . . what was out there couldn't be killed with lead.

There wasn't much else I could do but pray.

It was colder than I'd dreamed, our breath coming in great plumes of freezing drops of moisture. I was wearing my sheepskin mittens, so my fingers could still move a piece, but my toes felt like they were fading away. Praise the Lord and Lady we'd put a hood on my sheepskin coat. That and my wool scarf were keeping my neck and head warm. And when your head is covered, why, you're half-way home.

I sure hoped the Moores' young daughter was keeping the fire built up. Frostbite was not in my plans that evening.

People always lost track of time in the woods, and at night, in falling snow, it was worse. I knew I was still on the northern track—a few moments earlier I had recognized a blaze carved in a tree trunk. But I had no sense of how far I'd come or the distance yet to be covered.

I didn't remember it being so quiet, the nights I'd spent out in the forest. All I could hear was my heart hammering in my chest and the slow, muted thud of William's hooves.

And then something changed. I think it was the way the snow curled at William's knees. Before it had merely humped up as he kicked through the narrow path foraged by the Moores' horse. This time, flakes clumped into a wave that surged around his legs. I felt an icy breeze on one cheek, trying to wend its way down the front of my coat. The damp was cloying, moist like an animal's panting tongue.

Branches began to stir, their twiggy fingers scraping unpleasantly against each other. Limbs swayed and trunks creaked as the wind increased, swirling snowflakes like goose down.

Borrowing trouble like sugar, I thought, shaking my head in disgust. Still, I gripped tighter with my knees, and William's strides lengthened in response. The lantern bounced with every step, crazy shadows dancing down the trail before us. Was the snow getting thicker, or was that just the wind picking up?

Abruptly, I realized what was wrong. The breeze was pushing at my back and left side, but it was bitterly cold. True, it was winter, but wind from the south should be warm—at least warmer than what had been in my face. The temperature hadn't changed, though—just the wind direction.

Unless it was not a natural gale. Amongst the rushing waves of wind, I could hear that high-pitched whickering once again. It was coming from the west; it was heading this way. . . .

Suddenly a great gust of wind blew, setting my scarf flapping and causing the lantern to flicker wildly. Swallowing a curse, I kept a tight grip on the pole and a firm grip on Sweet William.

A hideous wailing exploded near my ear, the ghastly cry of a banshee, and William reared and screamed in response. All at once the trail was full of strange, repulsive creatures pushing and shoving as they ran blindly through the forest.

As I wrestled with Sweet William, I recognized dark, tempting goblins and twisted, trollish trows, followed by a malevolent duergar and ancient, long-taloned hags. Fanged leanan-sidhes, the beautiful vampires from the Isles, glided across the snowdrifts, trailed by redcaps drenched in wealing blood and clutching twisted branches. I saw beautiful, treacherous glaistig, the water fairies that fed on the blood of men. A kelpie ran past, fleet as the wind in its horse form, but I could see the man-shape beneath its dark coat. There were even creatures for which I had no name . . . that might not have names.

It was as if the entire Unseelie Court was around me, vomited from their fairy hills and fleeing into the dubious safety of darkness. I grabbed William's mane as he reared back again, ducking as another banshee soared over my head. There, at least, was the source of all the wailing. Myriad spirits flowed in its wake: staggering ghouls, human in their form, demons I tried hard not to look at for fear they could seize my mind, and ghosts of all types—young *navky*, some in child form, some as ravens; infant *utburds*, which sent a shiver of memory down my spine—corpses in their winding sheets, and skeletons who walked without rest.

William began backing up, shaking his head in dismay, and I realized that the decaying ghouls had decided there was time for a small meal . . . my horse and me. Powers of air and darkness! My Saint-John's-wort could repel goblins, but what could turn away a ghoul?

Spirits. Sweet Lord, I needed a spirit. Spirits had the power to repulse a ghoul—but I didn't know yet how to summon spirits. I thought of the necklaces, and simply thinking of them ignited the glow hidden within them. Suddenly light was tumbling from the pneumonia hole at the throat of my coat, which had been exposed when my scarf was pulled askew.

The silvery light reflected from the snowflakes like sunlight on a mirror, blinding in its intensity. A roar came from the ghouls, and they stepped back, shielding what was left of their eyes with their arms. The glittering motes bewildered the creatures, even as other denizens of the night swerved around them to avoid trampling us all. I took advantage of the ghouls' confusion and swung the lantern at them. You couldn't hack up a ghoul, but you *could* burn one. If a blow could dislodge a spark—

An errant curl of wind brought me a whiff of foul meat, and Sweet William screamed his protest. I glanced quickly over my shoulder and saw something huge, dark, and oozing. A massive clawed paw swept down and slashed away part of the skirt I was wearing. It missed William's flank, but the stallion had had enough. He had not been made to face such creatures.

William twisted away from the monstrous ghoul, kicking out as he did so, and caught me leaning the other way. I tumbled over the side, taking the saddlebags with me. There was churning snow, whistling wind, and the screaming of both horse and haunts.

Then the lantern went out.

I heard William scramble—then all I could hear was the unholy chorus of haunts. Rolling in the powdery snow, I got off the trail proper and covered my soft necklace light with my scarf. I used the pole to heave myself up as I struggled for footing. Several bogles knocked me against a tree, but I held on and managed not to slip.

There was no time to be afraid. I could be trampled before the ghouls could get me. Hefting the thick pole, I got ready to poke and whack.

Without warning, another creature jumped into the fray. The shambling ghoul moaned its protest as a hulking animal charged from the forest, hooking the walking corpse and tossing it into the trees.

Then I realized the stag was white.

I'd prayed for a spirit, and my own spirit had come, the White Wanderer, choosing freely to fight for me against the denizens of darkness. Flames erupted from the huge rack of antlers, igniting the tattered clothing worn by the other two ghouls.

The ghouls began to make a ghastly sound—screams from creatures who could no longer speak. They ran off into the stream of unseelie fay charging through the forest.

I'd been this close to the Wanderer only once before, and I kept my head back, well away from those tines. The buck turned, bracing his legs. Firm as a rock, the creature stared down at me, tiny flames flickering in his dark eyes, undying fire rising from his branched horns.

Beyond the terror of the fleeing fay, I heard that high-pitched, yelping cry, as if the sky was covered with shrieking birds. Suddenly

I realized there was no spit to ease my dry throat. I had to find shelter fast—but could I dig into a snowbank with ghouls sniffing out fresh meat? They preferred corpses, but they'd settle for the living.

The stag pivoted, moving a step past me, and dropped down on his knees. I stared at him.

"Do . . . do you want me to get on?" Oh, Lord and Lady, what if this was a pooka trick, and not the White Wanderer at all? As my thoughts whirled, a sound grew louder, beginning to overpower the chaos flowing around us.

Not birds. The sound of hounds, thousands of hounds, belling on the scent. . . .

I groped for my saddlebags as the stag nudged me hard. Probably he had no desire to meet the Gabriel Rachets, either. I tossed the bags over the creature's back and grabbed hold of the ruff at his neck and shoulders. Scrambling for purchase in the snow, I found a packed chunk and kicked up, settling against the curve of his spine.

My mittens clenched in the shaggy hair covering his neck. The stag rose to his full height, turning his head imperiously. Then he bolted down the trail, heading north toward the Moores' fields and homestead.

Icy wind ripped at my face, pushing back my hood, but I didn't dare reach to pull it forward. I could smell musk and fresh-turned earth, scents of life that the Wanderer had brought me before. The voice of the pack filled the sky, like thunder without end. My White Wanderer literally ran down bogles and demons who fell underfoot; others trampled each other to get out of his way.

The trail turned due north where the trees thinned, and the unseelie fey continued east, a flood of them, blackening the fresh snow with their presence. I knew the pack would chase them through the forest, in all directions, until the dogs drove the confused and exhausted fay folk to the uttermost west. Wanderer paused under a great, gnarled oak, as if waiting for something.

There wasn't long to wait.

Lightning split the heavy clouds like a knife through plucked down, and the Wild Hunt roared from heaven to earth. It was as if the Milky Way was pouring from the sky. The dogs flowed like a raging stream, their eyes glittering like stars.

Some of them actually touched the ground, snapping at the heels of terrified goblins. They were unbelievable—the size of ponies, snow white except for dark ears. As one ran close by, I could see that the ears were red.

There was no resemblance between these ugly creatures and the sleek hounds owned by farmer Adamsson. His hounds were famous trackers, with noses like bloodhounds, but they were friendly dogs. These animals burned with a dreadful eagerness. They had only one reason for living.

If they really lived.

The hounds kept coming, a foaming wave rushing like a waterfall down onto the forest below. I turned my head, looking for Herne and an end to his Gabriel Rachets . . . and realized one of the hounds was watching us.

It had red eyes, eyes that flickered with flame, just like the Wanderer's. I tried hard to swallow, and settled for gasping for air. That horrible warmth that steals your strength was creeping into my bones.

Turning calmly, the stag met the dog's eyes. They stared at each other a long moment, and then the stag took a step toward the Gabriel Rachet.

The hound turned away, blending into the darkness beyond the flaming tines. Either it saw that we weren't of the dark, or it saw something it could not challenge alone.

Intruding into the bell-like voices of the hounds came a deep-throated horn, calling out a pattern of notes. I didn't know all the commands, but I knew there was one to gather, one to send a pack after blood, and one to rally the hounds at full chase.

There was little doubt what we'd just heard . . . the Wild Hunt had found prey.

As the last of the dogs approached, the Wanderer started moving. I had just enough time to tighten my grip before the stag bounded into the fray, running not from the hounds but with them.

The Hunt surged around us. Dogs rose like the froth on fresh milk, straining as they ran after the fleeing unseelie. Other figures rode in the darkness, some of them with a faint green glow, like dead trees at night. There were those who say that ancient heroes ride with Herne, and those who say that warriors trapped in purgatory come at his call. The riders might even be demons in disguise.

I didn't care what they were—I just tried to stay out of their way.

We rode through a veil of falling snow, across frozen streams and up icy hills. We may have ridden across the tops of trees— there was a time I had wind gusting against my feet. I clutched the Wanderer as if he was my hope of heaven, and clung so tightly my legs started cramping.

I will confess it: Even paralyzed with fear that Herne might name us prey, I never in my life have felt the way I did as I tore through that dark forest on the back of a white stag. I have ridden the back of a storm and walked on raging water, but nothing has ever rivaled that first time when magic carried me away.

There was no knowing how long we rode with the belling pack. I was so tired it took me a moment to notice when we finally stopped moving. Lifting my head, I looked around. The Wanderer had stepped back against the side of a cabin, watching quietly as the Wild Hunt roared on without us, driving its prey to the western sea.

I sure hoped this was the Moores' cabin. If not, Lord and Lady forgive me, Martha Moore was on her own.

Slowly I pried my fingers loose from the ruff of the great stag. Then I dropped my saddlebags on the ground and slid after them. I didn't stop at my feet, and sat down in the snowdrift against the house, leaning against a convenient white leg.

The Wanderer turned his head, the fire from his antlers slowly dimming. Silently he bent and whuffled my windblown hair. His warm breath seemed to thaw me a bit; I felt some strength creep through my limbs.

Could you thank a Good Friend? You were not supposed to thank fay folk who did you favors. "I'm glad you were there," I said simply, patting the leg as I sat up straight.

A long, rough, wet tongue curled along my cheek, and then the creature bounded off across the clearing, following the path of the Wild Hunt.

Sighing, I pulled myself to my feet and hooked the saddlebags over my arms. I just couldn't lift them to my shoulder. Then I waded around the corner to the front of the cabin and pounded on the door frame.

Someone fumbled at the pegged wood door, and it fell open before me. A girl of eight or nine stood shivering in the wind, her delicate form outlined by the fire roaring in the fireplace beyond.

"Let's move, sweetheart, it's cold out here," I said briskly. If I was going to have the strength to deliver this baby, I had to keep moving.

Mutely the child stepped aside, allowing me to enter. The cabin was smaller than Marta's, but well chinked. The pine floor was either boards or half-rounds, and a few knots were just beginning to rise above the rest of the smoothly worn surface. Stepping carefully, I headed for the fireplace.

Mrs. Moore was standing behind a straight-backed chair over by the long table near the wall, tightly gripping the knobs on either end of the back. I was pleased to see she was taking deep, slow breaths. Either one of her midwives had had some sense, or she'd been listening to Marta after all. Sweet Lord, she was big as a rising moon. Could she be farther along than Marta thought?

"Mrs. Moore, I'm Miss Sorensson," I said quickly. That was stretching things a bit—not tossing my first name in there hinted that I had more years than I could claim. But I hoped it would make her happier to think me sixteen or seventeen. "Mrs. Donaltsson was called out this afternoon to Mrs. Johnson, so I left Jimmy with a friend. And you are . . . ?" I added, turning to the girl who had come up next to me.

"Emily, ma'am," the child said softly, actually giving me a quick curtsy.

"Well, Emily, have you been tending that fire?" At her nod, I continued, "Good. You keep doing that, and boil some water for me, will you please?"

Emily gave me a small smile. "I put the kettle on when Jimmy left. I've filled it four times."

"Good, good." I struggled to get out of my coat and mittens, and then turned swiftly as Mrs. Moore gasped.

It wasn't the baby. She was looking at my tattered skirt. Fortunately for modesty's sake, I had my boiled flannel pants on underneath.

There was no way to explain, except to say, "My lantern blew out and my horse spooked, so I had a bit of trouble getting here.

I'm fine." Tossing my coat on an empty wall peg, I fumbled with my bags. "Are your pains steady yet?"

"They just started getting hard," the woman whispered. "I've tried to keep walking, to see if I could slow things down. Did you bring the squawroot?"

Huh. Good try. I'd wait until afterward to tell her that walking might have hurried things along. At least she hadn't started pushing.

"I need light, Emily," I announced without looking around. "We're going to put these sheets on your momma's bed, and I need to see what I'm doing over there."

After the apron was tied, I rummaged for bowls and a cup and saucer. All the while I nattered on, complimenting the child and saying soothing things to Mrs. Moore. I tossed purple coneflower and goldenseal into a big bowl and steeped them in hot water, and put powdered squawroot and red raspberry leaves to steep in the smaller bowl.

Martha Moore had had her husband make her up a lying-in mattress of burlap and sweet hay, one that could be burned after the delivery. I wrestled it onto the rope frame and quickly made up the boiled sheets, laying the Moore quilts aside for later, in case she was cold. I needed to get my hands dipped in that big bowl as soon as possible. You could say it was part of the magic—if I did the steps right, chances were good the baby would be fine.

"I should check to see how you're coming along," I rushed right on as I piled up her pillows at the headboard. I couldn't *believe* I was saying that to a woman old enough to be my mother, but I guess my bustling about had reassured her, because Mrs. Moore went to sit on her bed.

She'd wisely stripped down to her nightgown, so I shooed her daughter to the cooking area and quickly checked. I was relieved to see she was just getting serious about delivering—she hadn't stretched but an inch or so, and there was no budge that promised a baby's head.

"Everything's coming along just fine, ma'am," I told her, pushing pillows behind her back. I'd dug out another basin and placed it next to the bed, in case her dinner started arguing with her. "Did you eat tonight?"

"Just a little chicken broth," she murmured, gasping as her womb tightened.

"That's fine." Less chance of tossing back the meal, thank heavens. Now that we were down to it, I was getting nervous. It's best to have two people helping a woman deliver—one to keep her calm, and grip her hand, and clean her up if necessary so she didn't choke, and one to handle the baby. Unless Emily could face her mother's pain, I was on my own.

I turned back to see if the herbs were done steeping—and saw one of the candles Emily had lighted floating to the other side of the mantle.

No! Not here! It took everything I had not to shriek aloud or burst into tears. My hands tightened into claws. *Please, please Lady of Light, don't let that thing hurt the baby.*

Trembling, I left my hands in the cooling basin until they were warm and red. Then I dried them on the towel I had brought along, and went to strain the tea. I simply fixed my eyes on the kettle and ignored the candle. Maybe if I treated it the way I had the rocks. . . .

Mrs. Moore was pathetically grateful for the tea. I decided not to tell her it was a mix unless she asked—Marta might not have discussed the delivery with her yet, and I didn't want her to think I was making this up as I went along.

Not much, anyway.

"Did you put wormwood in it?" she asked, after she'd drunk half the cup.

"We use other things than that, ma'am," I told her, trying to make it sound mysterious. I could tell she wanted to ask, but she'd finally noticed the necklaces held flat against my breast by the apron. Whatever she was thinking went unsaid.

I wondered if she recognized Marta's necklace—or thought I was old enough to have earned those honors.

Wormwood was *very* powerful; I didn't care what she wanted, I'd give her water with a sliver of wormwood for flavor just to take her mind off it, if necessary. With luck, the red raspberry would work.

"Shall I start pushing?" she asked after she finished her first cup of tea.

"No!" I took a deep breath to keep any alarm from my voice. "You've got plenty of time, there's no point rushing. You don't want to tear, so let your body decide when it's time to push. You don't feel like you need to push, do you?"

Mrs. Moore shook her head and handed me the cup. I set it aside for a moment and placed towels to catch the baby, and for the modesty of Mrs. Moore.

"Just breathe deeply through your mouth, Ma'am. As deep as you can without it hurting." I went to fill the cup again.

The teakettle was missing.

Damn, damn, damn. I was grateful these people couldn't read my mind. I looked around out of the corner of my eye, like I was thinking about something. It had to be somewhere . . . or I'd start boiling water in her cauldron.

A hiss of steam caught my attention. There on the hob was the kettle, merrily boiling away. I stalked over to the fireplace and grabbed a quilted pad to pick it up. Leaning over, I hissed, "If you mess up this delivery, I'll search for you the rest of my life and blast you into the next world when I find you." Then I whipped around and returned to the bowls.

That had to be one of the silliest things I'd ever done. But I felt better.

I carefully didn't look at either Emily or Mrs. Moore as I poured another cup of red raspberry tea.

❧·𝒟·❧

The hardest thing was keeping her from pushing too soon. More than one woman has killed herself with exhaustion and hysteria by starting to strain too soon—a simple delivery gets complicated when the mother suddenly *can't* push.

It was a good hour before I let her work at pushing. The tea had taken effect, and the opening was big enough. Now there was just popping that pea. In the meantime I got ready for washing the new baby with a basin of hot water close by. It would cool a bit come the time I'd need it. I must have looked a sight, fluttering back and forth from watching for the baby and trying to get everything ready.

I think the poltergeist must have believed my threat—it confined itself to making the candleholders swap places around the room. I did my best to keep the Moores too busy to notice.

"You keep that warming pan moving inside that blanket, Emily," I told her as she sat down next to her mother's bed.

"I *need* to push, child," she finally gasped out.

"Give your mother some sheet to grip, Emily," I said as I waited for Mrs. Moore to show signs of the baby approaching. The girl was too delicate to hold her mother's hands—Emily would have to encourage by words alone.

"Why must I always need the privy when I'm lying in?" Martha Moore groaned, falling back on her pillows.

"Breathe deeply," I reminded her. "That's a good sign, Mrs. Moore. If you feel that urge, it means the baby is pressing on your insides as it moves toward the outside." I'd carefully put the stork scissors and ribbon in the pocket of the apron, to make sure they didn't "wander off."

"You are wonderful, Ma," Emily told the woman, patting her arm gently. "I'm sure it will come soon."

Suddenly the baby was crowning, Mrs. Moore's body seeming to try to turn inside out. "Do you want to push?" I said, my words tumbling over each other.

"*Yes!*"

"Then push!" I positioned myself at the foot of the bed after one more dip and dry of my hands. Finally, for the first time I touched her, placing one hand on her stomach to make sure the baby hadn't suddenly turned funny.

A conflicting welter of impressions rushed at me, both male and female, and I inhaled sharply. For the first time since my Gift had risen, I wasn't sure what sex the baby would be.

Please, Lady, not both sexes. What a horrible fate. . . .

As the top of the head peeked out, I gently set my right hand on the top, pushing lightly to keep the head from coming too fast and tearing up Mrs. Moore. "Keep breathing deep, ma'am. It's okay to rest yourself between pushes. I'll keep watch." I moved my hand away from the head until the next spasm, and then continued the light pressure. God, I hoped it was light enough pressure. *Thank you that it's headfirst, thank you, thank you. . . .*

I suddenly remembered an important secret Marta had told me about. I'd never done it myself, but. . . . I gently felt beneath the opening with my fingertips, feeling for the brow or chin. Just a tiny bit of pressure there, to help the head along and keep anything from tearing.

It took only three pushes for the head to come out. Immediately I wiped the baby's face, trying to clear the nose and mouth as much as possible, and supported the head. I felt for the birth cord, but it wasn't around the neck, hallelujah. *Now the shoulders should turn a bit, and.* . . . My hands were sweating up a storm. *Just tiny pressure on the head, so the top shoulder can come under the bone, and lift.* . . .

A tiny, perfect baby boy dropped into my arms. I'd cleared enough gunk from his face that the cold of the room got his attention—he let out a good-sized yell.

I had been certain he'd be bigger, but he sure was beautiful, bloody and grayed out as he was!

"You've got another son, Mrs. Moore," I told her, hanging on tight to my slippery prize. I laid him on the birthing blanket and made sure his throat was clear. Then I sponged him down while I waited for him to pink up some. He kept yelling about the cold, but the water was quite warm, so I rubbed him down and wrapped him in the small quilt Emily had warmed. Only then did I use the ribbon to tie off the cord in two places, so I could cut the spot between them.

It was my first baby knot, and my hands shook while I tied the delicate cord. Good thing I knew how to embroider.

"Settle in that rocker, Emily. You're going to hold this little fellow while your mother and I finish up." Emily was nothing if not obedient, and sat deep in the rocker by the fireplace. I put a pillow on her stronger arm, and then settled the baby with her. "You keep an eye on him for your ma until she's ready to nurse him." First the afterbirth, then we'd talk nursing.

"Dear lord, these pains are still bad," the woman muttered, trying to sit up to finish pushing.

I took her hands to pull her upright, and that wave swept through me again. This time I understood what was happening.

I stuffed the pillows tighter at the base of her spine. "We've got more work to come, Mrs. Moore! Keep breathing deeply, and we'll try to take the afterbirth in one piece." I pulled out the rest of the boiled towels and plopped the warming pan into the Moores' quilt.

"More?" she whispered, trying to settle her tired gaze on me.

"There's another baby," I finally said, pulling the wash basin close.

"*Another* one? Oh, God, don't let it smother!" she shrieked, falling back on her elbows.

"Keep breathing!" I yelled at her, demonstrating with huge breaths as I pressed on her stomach. "We can get her out okay, she's in the right position. If you can push, push!"

We had some luck—the first afterbirth popped right out in mere moments. Mrs. Moore started yelling about the baby coming now, but I was warming up the bowl water for washing my hands, so I merely kept an eye on her and waited for the crowning.

Little Mary Moore began life as she lived it, always in a hurry to do things. She was out of that womb within minutes, and all I had to do was poke the birthing cord back over her shoulder as she swam out.

"It's a girl!" It was so fast I was still trying to clean her face and throat, so I smacked the soles of her feet to wake her up. I hauled out the throat blockage in one long strand, and Mary let me know exactly what she thought of the entire process, screaming her head off.

"I know, little one, it's a cold, cruel world," I whispered, sponging her off and wrapping her in the big, warmed quilt. I gave her an extra minute or two before I cut the cord, tossing prayers in the air for everything I could think of—good health, wits, kindness, a loving and prayerful heart, curiosity. . . .

It took forever to get both Martha Moore and the babies cleaned up, diaper the pair of twins, and attach them for their first meal. Then I washed my hands and collapsed on the dining chair for a while. Sweet Jesus, I looked and felt like I'd been butchering hogs . . . but I was surely pleased with my work.

Her face was pale, but Mrs. Moore was smiling broadly. "Mrs. Donaltsson told me it would be all right. Thank you so much, my dear."

I managed a faint smile and told her, "You did all the work, ma'am. My hardest job was getting here." My gaze settled on the fireplace mantel, as I watched the poltergeist do a celebratory candle dance among the mugs and china figurines.

Ah, well—a little celebration was proper. I'd just keep this part of it to myself.

Six

LORD AND LADY, I DIDN'T THINK IT was possible for me to respect my cousin any more than I already did.

I was wrong.

Around the time I was hauling in snow to fill the washtub in front of the fire, so I could soak the linens and apron in cold water overnight, I realized that Marta *always* did this alone when she had no apprentice. That thought made me even more tired.

I got the Moores' real mattress made up and pulled the birthing mattress off the frame, but Mrs. Moore drew the line there.

"You've done enough, my dear Miss Sorensson," she said firmly. "I will be comfortable with the mattress on the floor for one night. It is a better bed than we had on our trip west!"

Well, that I believed, so I put one baby snug in the cradle and the other in the bottom drawer from the Moores' big wardrobe. Then I took a quilt and the last pillow and curled up right by the firescreen—not the safest place to be, but somehow I thought the poltergeist was having too much fun to let me get burned up. I *did* remember to bar the entrance—I didn't want the smell of blood to attract anything unfriendly.

Anyway, that's all I remembered until I heard someone banging on the heavy wood door. Daylight was peeping in the room's only window, though it was trickling through a sky full of snow. I stumbled out of the quilt and made it to the door, but I won't promise I wasn't sleepwalking.

Swinging the door wide, I saw Marta, carpetbag at her feet and stick tucked under her arm, already untying her bonnet strings. Bundled up behind her was the round, red-faced man I recognized as Mr. Moore.

"I knew I needed to get home, I knew it," he was saying. "They tried to get me to spend the night, but I was so worried, I didn't know what to do." Somehow he managed not to trample Marta, but he was trembling like a racehorse waiting at the start line.

"She's fine, Mr. Moore," I managed to get out. "And your family has increased by two. Why don't you take care of all those horses while I make you some coffee?"

Marta smiled slightly and walked past me into the house. "Jimmy's with them. He might need some help, though, with three animals."

Moore just stared at me for a moment, and then said, "Two?"

I could barely smile—I'd slept maybe three hours—but I nodded. "A boy and a girl. Take care of those horses!" I promptly shut the door in his face, leaving him there on the stoop smiling at nothing I could see. A new parent needs a few moments to adjust to the idea before sharing the joy, so I left him to his own thoughts.

Marta had already greeted Mrs. Moore, checking her eyes and skin for fever and asking her about the delivery. Before her coat was even off, my cousin found the bucket where I'd hidden the afterbirths, and after poking around with the stick she'd picked up on the road, she nodded in satisfaction. I felt something relax in me that I hadn't known was tight. Mrs. Moore wasn't going to die from not finishing her birthing—at least I'd gotten that right.

I'd also ended up explaining to Emily what was *in* that bucket. Children are funny—some would be upset about the entire business, but Emily was merely curious. I just told her that a baby needed the afterbirth when it was growing, but not after it was born and could get milk from its mother. So neither baby nor womb needed the thing anymore.

I wasn't certain that was true, but one thing I then knew for sure—each baby had its own afterbirth. Twins had just proved it to me. And it had to follow the baby out, or the woman would die.

"Momma wants to bury them and plant a tree on top of them, for the babies," Emily had announced.

"That's a nice idea, Emily," I'd agreed. And it was a nice thought. Maybe I'd remember that come my own time.

Marta placed the teakettle back on the fire and then gave me a sharp look. "We'll have to scrub you down before the dance." Her sky blue eyes were twinkling. "Well done, woman. I think you've earned that calico quilt backing."

It's a fine glow when an adult hands you a compliment.

"Is Mrs. Johnson all right?" I thought to ask through my haze.

"She has a son, and her husband is bursting with pride," Marta said drily. "I decided not to remind him that she did all the work."

We shared a grin, and then the kettle whistled, and Marta made up one of her tonics for new mothers—red raspberry leaves, goldenseal and coneflower root, willow bark, and some flavoring. It was mixed back home, of course—a practitioner needs some trade secrets, or why go to the practitioner?

I was awake enough to start some porridge and warm up cider for the adults. There didn't seem to be any coffee in the cabin. It took me a few moments to remember an important question.

"Did Sweet William get home all right?" I was almost afraid to ask—I was gonna feel sick if anything had happened to that horse.

"That he did," Marta replied, and a great load was lifted from my shoulders. "You did not take his advice, did you?" She gave me one of her shrewd looks.

"There wasn't really any time to discuss it," I said carefully, suddenly very conscious of Mrs. Moore and of the sound of her older son and husband entering the cabin. I pulled the quilt tighter around myself in response to the gust of cold wind.

"I look forward to your story," was all Marta said as she poured off the shredded herbs and took the tea to Mrs. Moore.

I looked forward to sleeping. Maybe I wasn't going to make that dance after all. I reached over to wring out the sheets and hang them by the fire to dry.

❧⚶❧

As always, I was borrowing trouble. After inhaling the porridge and cider, we folded the still-damp sheets and stuffed them in an empty saddlebag. Marta left some tea and strict instructions for Mrs. Moore, and before I knew it we were bundled up and back on the road to Cat Track Hollow, Marta on Sweet William and I on one of the two mules. He'd pick it up next time he headed for town—or Marta would lead it back on her next visit.

Blessings upon us all, that animal had the smoothest gait of any mule I'd ever imagined. On that mule I learned I could doze in the saddle. And I did just that.

The snow had slowed to light flurries, but it still took more than an hour to get home. Toward the end, I told Marta about my evening. She managed to keep any questions to herself until I'd about finished.

"You did well with the delivery, Allie," she said finally. "Many people wouldn't have done as well. You pay attention when I tell you things. That's a great gift. It pleases me that you're my apprentice."

That like to made me want to cry, but I hid it best I could under cold-weather sniffles. I followed in her wake and let my gaze wander over the barren countryside; all landmarks were covered by a blanket of snow. I was pretty sure when we passed the spot where I'd lost William, but there was no sign on the trail—except for the wire handle of the lantern. I stopped and retrieved the lamp but didn't even fumble for the pole.

"Quite a thing, for the Wanderer to fight for you," Marta said softly, waiting a few paces beyond. William seemed calm, so either there was no odor left from the night before or Marta was using extra control on him. "And to let you get on his back. . . ."

"I'll never forget it," I whispered as we moved on.

"No, I don't think you will," Marta agreed.

⁂

I'm sure I don't need to tell you that Idelia was overjoyed to see me. She tossed her arms around me like she hadn't in years and was practically in tears.

"It's fine," I kept assuring her, "everything is fine."

"I stuffed Jimmy full of food and bedded him down in here," Idelia went on, trying to control her sniffing. "Before they left,

Mrs. Donaltsson asked me to boil a bunch of water for you." As I took off my coat, she looked at what was left of my hem with dismay. "Alfreda Sorensson, what did you do to your skirt? And your pants?"

I looked down. Despite the apron, my pants were splashed with dried blood. Or maybe I'd done it myself—I had the habit of wiping my hands on my clothes when taking pelts. "Having a baby is *not* tidy," I decided to say. Let her think I had needed the skirt for bandages. The truth would have kept her out of the woods at night.

The truth would have kept her out of the woods forever.

Idelia immediately went into her mothering ways, taking my coat and hanging it on a wall peg. "Well, we'll soon get you cleaned up. Do you want to wash your hair?"

"Oh, yes," I said fervently, and went to help her with the big copper washbasin. Sometimes the thought of a bath had been all that kept me moving the past night. Marta had some recipes for bath herbs she made up as gifts for friends, and I was looking forward to the one called Black Rose, with rosebuds, comfrey root, mints, and more. It was both relaxing and invigorating, if you can imagine such a thing. And oh, the sweet scent!

Still, there was one thing I needed to do. And I couldn't think of how to explain it to Idelia. You see, I didn't want an audience while I bathed. Normally, I'd use a screen to the north side of the copper tub.

But Idelia would wonder why I wanted the screen. And was there any way to explain?

If you've been paying close attention, you've probably noticed something missing in my tale. I've spoken often of the White Wanderer, my Good Friend, as practitioners name their helpful spirits—name on the sly, that is. Regular folks simply wouldn't understand. Every follower of the Wise Arts attracts a sympathetic spirit, who helps guard against malicious creatures and increases power for spells.

A Good Friend is not necessary, but it is very useful. Sometimes— like with what had happened the night before—it can be lifesaving.

I've never mentioned Marta's Good Friend. And of course she had one. I had no idea what it looked like or what she called it.

But I knew where it lived.

To the right of the central fireplace, between the stone chimney and the window, hung a huge, many-tiered elk head. The person who had mounted it had been skilled—the chips of glass that formed the eyes were marbled dark, and the nose was so shiny it had to be silk. After years on the wall, it was still sleek, a stag's summer coat.

Just a beautiful symbol of the bountiful forest. And yet there were times when the cloudy glass eyes grew dark and knowing . . . when I was certain the head was watching me.

I was *not* being fanciful. More than once I'd seen Marta touch the stag's nose in passing, like an elder might do for balance or to judge distance. But the head was high enough that even Marta wouldn't bump it, and she wasn't the type of person to pat the thing because of who made it.

Keep it for the making, maybe, but not stroke it.

So why did she touch the long nose every time she walked by? And why did she never hang so much as a hat in the antlers? Lots of folks store things on their trophies.

It was another of those things you didn't talk about, but I was certain Marta's Good Friend liked to hide inside that elk head.

I had wondered why it put up with the poltergeist in its domain . . . maybe because it never bothered Marta.

"You know, there's quite a draft from the chimney today," I suddenly said out loud. "Maybe we should use the screen."

"Of course," Idelia agreed, starting for the three-winged embroidered panels.

Turning my back for modesty's sake, I stripped out of my clothes and climbed into the high tub. Once I was in the thing, I turned and positioned myself so I could keep an eye on the trophy. This tub was special for washing, and had hinged panels that covered the top, to trap the heat. I closed myself up and hunkered down, positioning myself for some soaking. Then I glanced up at the elk head.

The right eyelid moved, dropping into a wink.

My throat tightened up and I sank into the warm water, submerging myself as much as I could. *Bother!* I wanted to stay under until Idelia had the screen set up, but that would have been silly. So I came up for air and started scrubbing my hair.

Once the screen was in place, I was able to finish washing, but I'd swear I heard a ghost of a laugh as I rinsed off.

Idelia didn't say a word, and neither did I.

❧ 𝒟 ❧

I managed to braid my hair before collapsing on my bed, but I was sleeping the sleep of the virtuous before Idelia and Marta had started emptying the washtub. I felt a little guilty about going straight to bed, but not much—Marta had pointed out in her driest voice that both she and Idelia had slept half the night, and how could I argue with that?

So I didn't argue.

Light was fading in the west by the time I stirred. The smell of pumpkin pie and cheese grits had lured me from my dreams. I woke to find Idelia working her way into her newest dress, the one I'd helped her dye with alkanet roots, that delicate plant with violet flowers and roots that tint things red. In spun wool, the color turned out a pale, rosy brown, like the belly of some fish. With Idelia's dark hair and eyes, and her creamy skin, she would break hearts.

"Get out of that quilt and help me hook this dress," Idelia told me, so I stumbled out of the double bed we shared and lined up the top hooks.

"You're going to look good enough to eat tonight," I told her. "What would William think?"

"He would think he had better get around to posting the banns. That is what he *should* think." This was said with a toss of her head, so I knew Idelia had been brooding on home. I'd noticed that about her lately. Whenever she was nervous about something, her thoughts returned to William Adamsson.

I hoped that nothing ever happened in their lives that he couldn't handle.

That was hard for me to understand, her longing for marriage. Yes, I could see wanting your own home, but I had so much still to learn, I couldn't imagine getting married yet. Marriage was followed by babies, unless you used a decoction of Queen Anne's lace to keep from getting pregnant. And a baby would slow my lessons.

A mistake about a man could be a nightmare for a practitioner. I was in no hurry—I didn't want to make any mistakes.

Once we had Idelia in her dress, I splashed warm water on my face and pulled on the bright yellow gown Momma had made from all that dyer's chamomile. I had to admit the style was flattering, now that I had some distance on those empire-waist things. It was hard to admit something fashionable didn't flatter you, but I could tell without trying—the new waistlines were not for me. I might have been small on top right then, but if I ran true to the breed, pretty soon I'd be busting out all over, with more curves than the Wabash River.

"Are you going to wear your stole?" Idelia asked, holding up the wrap Momma had dyed with red onion skins.

"I hope I'll be dancing enough not to need it," I admitted, checking to make sure my hair would pass muster. I had enough color, after my vigorous jaunt through the snow, but I could have wished for a spot of jewelry. Wearing my practitioner's chain wasn't done for pleasure, and the silver necklace and bracelets I'd inherited from my great-grandmother were for work, not for show. I hadn't felt right about wearing them Christmas Eve, though I *had* ended up working. Silver doesn't favor ivory-skinned blondes, anyway.

"We should see if your aunt needs help with the food," Idelia said, taking one last glance at her hem.

"She asks when she needs help, but we could carry the pots while she drives." That reminded me—I went over to the chest, opened it, and fished out the woolen cloak my mother had made for me. The color was close to that of my stole, so it would look good with the dress.

"Your momma would be so pleased to see you wear that," Idelia said softly. "When I go back to Sun-Return I'll tell her how nice it looked."

Holding the cloak at my shoulders, I whirled around, letting the wool swirl at my ankles. "Shall we make our parents proud?"

"Not too proud," Idelia pointed out.

"Not that kind of pride," I agreed. "But parents are allowed to be pleased if children are a credit to their families." I wasn't sure I could ever be a credit to my family—not with Momma's feelings

about magic. But at least I would do my best not to embarrass
Marta.

And with my habit of speaking and then thinking, every public
event was a trial. So I asked the powers that be for strength and
silence, and went to my first real dance.

❧ ☙

We piled into Marta's wagon, clutching the pie and grits, and
let Sweet William haul us all into town over a trail that was blown
thin of powdered snow. The rest of the white blanket was packed, I
was pleased to see, so we didn't fear ice—not that trip. The sun had
leaked through the low gray clouds, setting fire to the sky. I kept
my gaze above it, on the deep blue beyond, and said thank you for
surviving the previous night.

Cat Track Hollow was less than half the size of Sun-Return,
with its store and small church the center of the community. Six
families had built homes in the area as well, including the only
cooper for a week's riding. Many people had come in from farther
along the trail and would spend the night with the village families.
It was the only way we could have a big gathering. As many as fifty
people might be present in Cat Track Hollow that night.

As I'd suspected, there were a handful of young men hanging
around outside, waiting to escort any girl across the trampled snow
and into Hudson's store. They were eager to help Idelia from the
wagon—and once they saw the pie, they didn't ignore me, either.

Marta gave me a wry glance as she allowed Daniel Hudson to
take her wagon over by the family barn. *I would give much to
see all their faces when you finally bloom into a swan*, came her
thought.

I wrinkled my nose at her amusement. *You are thinking of my
Aunt Sunhild*, I told her, for that was what my beautiful aunt's name
meant—"swan girl." I was gonna be more like Aunt Dagmar—a
long-legged heron.

Wait and see. Marta took the grits from Idelia's hands and led
the way into the store. With a troop of red-cheeked young men
surrounding us, Idelia and I followed her inside.

Sound rose up like a wall before us as we crossed the threshold.
The regular store area had been shoved back a piece, the open
goods covered with old burlap sacks. Mr. Hudson's big wooden

counter was buried with food, groaning with hot dishes, and it was good to see that the harvest had gone so well. Marta had brought a sack of plates and forks, as well as mugs for our cider, so we could eat when we pleased. Folks must have thought about candles, because there were dozens of them, stuck everywhere around the scene, shedding their golden glow over the packed room.

It was the sound of the violin that called to me, beckoning us beyond the wavering heat of the fireplace and into the storeroom beyond. The grain and crates had been cunningly stacked, leaving room in the center for four couples to spin in a country dance. If they had started with a minuet, we had missed it.

Four couples may not seem like much—Momma had told me of a good two dozen couples lined up for a reel—but we made do with what floor we had. In summer, maybe, we would all dance under the beams of a new barn. For now, we could share the merrymaking.

We had barely shed our cloaks into the mound in the corner when we were descended upon by our hostess. Mrs. Hudson was looking very fine in blue muslin with a strand of real pearls around her neck. Her golden hair was piled high on her head, secured with a blue band and several soft feathers. She had in tow her eldest son, Charles; he was taller and his blond mane darker than I remembered. Standing beside Charles was another young man, of similar height but so fair he looked white-haired.

"Miss Sorensson and Miss Pederson, you know my son Mr. Charles Hudson?" she began, her son wincing as her casual address reduced him from trousers to breeches. "And this is a cousin of the family, also a Mr. Hudson."

The grave young stranger bowed to us both, and looked as if he would have liked to find the nerve to take our hands. His eyes were large and pale, glinting in the candlelight. I could see his resemblance to Charles's father. We favored him with a brief curtsy, and then Charles slipped past his mother and asked me to dance.

There was no surprise in this—Charles had heard me talking in the store one day, and knew I both liked to dance and did it passably well. Most of the girls here barely reached his shoulder. I suspected it was nice to dance occasionally with someone and not get a stiff neck in the bargain.

The violin was changing its tune, signaling that another set of figures was about to begin. Idelia and the new Mr. Hudson were moving into the open area as the panting dancers quit the floor and went past us toward the refreshments. Charles and I hurried, and managed to be the fourth couple.

I couldn't tell you how much I loved to dance. It did something to my blood, I think. The only thing I knew that rivaled it was a full glass of applejack on an empty stomach. Charles Hudson was not the finest dancer, not by a long shot, but he was more than enough for that night. I had survived the Wild Hunt, an attack by ghouls, and delivering my first set of twins—I was in a mood to be pleased.

Mr. Chapman, the cooper, was a dab hand at his instrument. His playing did not wring the soul, as my friend Shaw Kristinsson's did, but for a village dance he was perfect—steady on, and with an eye to the strength of his crowd. We did not pause, but did courtesy to our partners and the lead couple, in this case Idelia and Mr. Hudson. In short order we were weaving our way through several figures.

Back and forth, in and out, under and gone, till our breath was tattered. We did the fox and the hounds, a chain of dancers spiraling past Idelia hiding in the center. Then there was four corners, and windmills, and garden path. There were not many figures to be done by such a small group, but we did most of them!

At one point I looked up to see that the candles set on the crates were performing their own country dance, bobbing and wheeling in time with the music. A huge smile crept across my face, but I wasn't the only one beaming . . . just the only one watching dancing candles.

Or maybe not the only one. The new Mr. Hudson had also noticed the candles. I watched him out of the corner of my eye to see if he'd convince himself it was drink and smoke, but he seemed merely bemused. I could see laughter in his eye as he passed shoulder to shoulder and back to back with Idelia.

Suddenly the music was at an end, and we were out of breath and moving quickly to the sides. As another square formed, Charles was quick to make his bow to me and survey the gathering. I waited, amusement and despair warring within, for I knew he was looking for a bolt hole.

I was the better dancer, since I always knew where I placed my feet, but Charles had been maneuvering toward Idelia ever since she came to visit. There wasn't much chance he'd change her mind about William Adamsson, but he was welcome to try.

Idelia and her escort appeared, and Mr. Hudson said, "Are you ready for cider?"

"Oh, yes!" Charles said quickly, and then realized he had spoken too swiftly.

I kept myself from smiling and said, "Yes, I would like that very much."

"I'll fetch it," Charles announced, and disappeared into the throng. The crowd had grown—it seemed impossible that there was anyone left in the neighboring houses. There was no need of a fire—the press of bodies was enough that we could no longer see our breath. I was backed up against a pile of grain bags, and realized that one stack had been reduced to but three by some enterprising gentlemen who had carried off possible seats for their card game.

The gathering was so packed that I boosted myself up on the shortened heap, offering a hand to Idelia. My friend hesitated momentarily, but I could tell she did not care for the jostling of the throng. In short order she took my hand and accepted Mr. Hudson's assistance in joining me.

"Have you been in Cat Track Hollow long?" he asked after we were both settled.

"Since the new year," Idelia told him, her shy smile attracting many admiring stares.

"I have been here a few months," I said carefully, not in any hurry to volunteer information about myself. I had to live here a few years—I didn't want this fellow mentioning to our host that I was strange.

"It had been a long time since our families had been in contact—almost ten years," Mr. Hudson announced, making known his own tale. "I was named for Charles's father, Erik, whom my father played with as a child. Therefore, when the north and south branches of the Hudson family reestablished contact, I, as the namesake, was chosen to go north." The young man had a relaxed manner and seemed to radiate comfort. It was as if he belonged there—and since his uncle owned the place, maybe he felt like he did.

"Are you enjoying your stay?" Idelia said politely.

"I am enjoying tonight," he answered, smiling knowingly, and then Charles came up clutching four mugs of cider. It occurred to me that he'd had to find Marta and get hold of our sack. That would have taken some doing in that crowd—I hoped Idelia would be nice to him the rest of the night.

Idelia gave Charles a sunny smile as she accepted her mug; it seemed to more than compensate him for his trouble. Charles leaned into our group, planting himself closest to Idelia, but Mr. Erik Hudson didn't seem to mind. I guessed that as far as he was concerned, one girl was like another. At least at a Twelfth Night party.

The Hudson men were full of the local gossip—who had arrived in town since New Year's, and who had left for home. A few folks were wintering over before heading on to other places. I figured it wouldn't hurt to speak of safe deliveries, and mentioned the births of the three new babies.

Charles really had his eye on Idelia, but Erik (as I called him to myself) seemed to have a wandering eye. Some folks just like to watch other folks, and Erik was one of them. Since he was having fun, I saw no reason to call back his attention, and let my own gaze drift.

I could swear that sometimes things happened because I was there. Marta said that was not quite true—that the things might always be happening, and I was just one of the few who could see them. Like the older man over by the cooper, tapping his foot to the music and propping himself upright with his cane. He looked vigorous, his eyes twinkling—but I could see the winding cloth around his legs and chest. Something was going to happen there, and all that vigor would drain away.

I glanced back at Charles and Idelia, Mr. Hudson still with us, and noticed that he was actually staring at something. That surprised me—he'd been so careful and polite about meeting people's gazes. And he'd attract attention, as tall and fair as he was, and related to the town's wealthiest family to boot.

My eyes peered in the same direction as his, and I realized that he was staring at Marta! It was an intense look, as if he was sure he knew her from somewhere. He was concentrating so hard, I felt almost uncomfortable. Like Shaw Kristinsson sometimes studied at me, when he was in Sun-Return and we crossed paths.

Just then our gazes locked, and Mr. Hudson looked momentarily startled. Then he lifted his eyebrows and nodded over Marta's way. I looked back and saw several candles doing their own version of a reel square. So that's what he was looking at! I grinned, my eyes flicking momentarily to the young man, and we both broke into smiles.

"I don't know about everyone else, but I could eat some food," Idelia said suddenly near my ear. I nodded my agreement, and we let the boys help us down so we could go fill our plates.

ooo

I managed to get through the meal with only one embarrassing moment. Practitioners eat like there's no tomorrow, because magic wears at the body like water against stone. You may not notice at first, but suddenly there's a weariness as the fat of your body dwindles and the muscles sink, stripped of flesh. Magic must be fueled—and if you do not give, it will *take.*

So, I had what was known as a healthy appetite. And there wasn't a scrap of extra padding on my body. Mr. Hudson was clearly used to the delicate appetites of older women (who eat beforehand, I'm convinced.) His eyes widened at what I put on my plate, and the brows went up when the seconds mirrored the firsts.

What could I say? I didn't announce my calling casually. Smiling, I lifted my mug in a toast to him and said, "I am still growing."

I heard a bubble of froth at my side and knew Idelia had nearly choked. The heat flushed right through my body, but I didn't think anyone could see the blush in that light. *Did it again, Alfreda.*

"It is good to see you enjoying the meal," Mr. Hudson said politely. "So often the ladies seem indifferent to the efforts of the hostess."

I thought about it and decided that even if he was surprised, he wasn't shocked. That was nice. There weren't too many people who could be around me and survive their embarrassment. Would I never learn to say the right thing?

Lifting the mug to my lips, I swore to keep quiet and finish my meal. Nothing but *yes* and *no* from me the rest of this evening. Idelia could handle the flowery thanks. Turning my head, I looked toward the open front door and tried to gauge how late it was—the clouds had finally moved off, exposing the stars in the sky.

That was where I saw the Indian. I knew it was an Indian, no matter how wavy the white light—he was wrapped in a skin or a blanket, and there was a suggestion of a couple of feathers somehow entwined near the top of the form, falling down the back of his head. He was walking slowly, his steps careful and measured, as he made his way past the doorway. Nothing in his shadowy form told me which tribe he called his own.

It took me a moment to realize he was a ghost. He wasn't alone—behind him walked a smaller form, also wrapped in something bulky and carrying a good-sized bundle against its back. Probably his wife—Indian men carried nothing but their weapons, unless they were healers or holy men. The women carried everything—and owned everything, for all I knew, except their own selves.

Curious. Why was this trek so important, so memorable, that the very stones remembered? I'd probably never know.

Suddenly I could *feel* someone watching me. My skin actually crept, and not from cold. I turned my head away from the door and back to the crowd heaped around us, but I didn't see anyone looking my way.

Then my gaze met Erik Hudson's. He was startled to meet my eyes, and actually flushed. A slight smile, almost in apology, and then he asked the group if he could take any used plates to their sacks.

Almost like Shaw, the reticence in the man. But not unfriendly—also like Shaw.

Curious. Maybe someday I'd find out why. . . .

SEVEN

IT IS RUMORED THAT WITCHES MAKE their own tools for ritual spells. That may be true—but I discovered with relief that practitioners aren't expected to tread the bellows. It is allowed, but few do, because blacksmithing has its own magic.

I'd always suspected there was more to being a blacksmith than folks talked about, but I had no proof until the Feast of the Wise Men.

The morning after Twelfth Night I was up talking with Marta about the mysteries. "Silver's not very strong," I pointed out, lowering my voice and giving my cousin a long look. Idelia was still asleep and didn't need to hear any of this conversation.

"Strong enough for your purposes," was Marta's reply as she tipped out bread dough on her big board and gestured for me to take over kneading.

That suited me just fine—when I'm grumpy, there's nothing better than pounding dough. "Won't it snap?" I went on, punching a big hole in the billowy shape.

"We do not need physical strength from our blades, we need psychic strength," Marta said, turning back to the fireplace. "Your hunting knife is your physical strength. Your athame is for fighting off demons and rebellious, hostile spirits. And for entering and closing a circle."

"Can you enter a circle without an athame, in an emergency?" I asked, curious.

There was a long pause. I flipped the dough and glanced over my shoulder. Finally Marta said: "Yes, you can use any knife, as long as some of your blood is on it. Or your own hand, with blood along the little finger." Marta did look back then. "We are asked for the blood of entry only until we consecrate our athame. Then we use that blade alone, with the memory of our blood upon it. I hope you must never draw a circle without your tools. That would have to be a great need." Her voice was very serious as she spoke.

"Do I have to make my tools from scratch?" I said, turning back to the dough I had rolled and pulling in the end flaps. Another push and fold . . . I shot her a look under my arm.

"Everything but your metal tools. Those I am having made by a blacksmith with the Gift. You will prepare them and charge them magnetically, and etch any ritual signs upon them you wish to take into your journeyman training." Marta dumped some dried beans into her kettle and added water from a bucket sitting nearby. "You will also carve the symbols needed upon the handle. I will loan you my penknife, and you may practice carving on branches and scraps of wood." Giving me a short, penetrating look, she added, "You will keep bleeding to a minimum while teaching yourself to carve. Ten fingers are preferred in this profession."

Swallowing a sudden tight lump, I said, "Yes, ma'am." I *was* in favor of keeping bleeding to a minimum. "Do I start with the athame?"

Marta stood and brought the bread pans over to the table. "No, you will start practicing your carving. The knives will arrive sometime in the next fortnight. You'll also need to carve your own wand." She studied me for a moment, eyes slightly narrowed. "Oak, I suspect. None of the other woods would be strong enough for you. But we'll test to be sure, when the bread's shaped." With a nudge, Marta moved in next to me and started working half the dough.

Not nearly enough information to suit me, but maybe I'd find out more in the "testing" Marta spoke of. . . . I went back to kneading bread.

§·⚁·§

Well, the testing was a disappointment from my end of the stick, because it made little sense to me. Marta dug out tiny pots of ashes and smudged my forehead with the contents. Then she told me to go quilt until Idelia finally woke up.

"That's all?" I said, staring at her.

Marta looked amused. "That's all for right now. Come back to me in an hour, and we'll see what has happened."

I remained rooted to my spot. "What's supposed to happen? You're not going to get mysterious on me, are you?"

My cousin raised her fingers to her lips to cover her smile. "No, Allie, I'm not going to become mysterious. The ashes come from many trees—willow, hazel, ash, oak, even mistletoe. We'll select your wand wood from the smudges that remain after an hour or so. The ones that are absorbed would not be strong enough to channel your magic." She nodded once at me, the movement finishing her statement, and then closed the last of her pots.

So I went to the quilting frame and started working. I couldn't shake the feeling that I'd just taken a great leap in the dark, and who knew where I'd land? No one had ever mentioned how important choosing my wood could be.

Maybe that's why she told me to quilt and not start carving . . . I stuck my fingers several times in that hour.

What if they all absorbed? I wondered if my forehead would be shadowed forever, and if Idelia would say anything when she woke.

If Idelia noticed the ashes, she did not speak of it. Of course, there were Catholics in Sun-Return, where we grew up. Maybe she thought it was something like Ash Wednesday.

Looking fresh as a spring morning, no trace of all our dancing upon her face, Idelia was sunny and ready for whatever the day held. While Ida fumbled with the teapot and some toasted bread, Marta gestured for me to come into her bedroom. Once inside, she offered me a hand mirror.

I had felt eight streaks paint my forehead, when Marta had brought out her pots. Only one remained. Turning to her, I cocked my head in inquiry.

"Oak," Marta said simply.

I'd always liked oak trees . . . which was a good thing. From that point on, I'd be staking my life on oak in every ritual I ever performed.

※ 🐚 ※

Three other things happened that Epiphany to stick in my mind, even now. A vision, a visit, and a dream. The first was a small thing, but full of import. I'd gone out to the lean-to intending to feed the animals, when I looked out the barn door and thought I saw Shaw Kristinsson walking up the footpath and hailing the house! Lord, that boy was growing tall, and was there dark hair on his upper lip?

Well, I plumb dropped the bucket of grain I was carrying and charged through the stillroom back into the house. I came in so fast I almost ran over Marta, who was carrying something toward her stillroom.

"Saints preserve us!" Marta turned to one side to protect the bowl she carried. "What is it, a cougar?"

I careened to a stop and looked around the room. Idelia was by the fire adding ham to the beans, her eyes huge at my swift entrance. Otherwise, they were alone.

"I . . . I thought I saw. . . ." I looked to Marta, and I'm sure my face was a study. "I *did* see Shaw Kristinsson walk up to this house!"

"Did you?" Marta said with interest. "Have you finished with William and the mule?"

I could feel the blush growing. "No, ma'am."

Marta moved gracefully past me into the stillroom. "Finish with the animals and we'll talk about it."

Well . . . at least she hadn't said "Nonsense" and changed the subject. So I went out and fed and watered the livestock, from Sweet William to the Jersey cow Marta called Saffron. Goats, chickens, and geese—everybody got their turn. Then I hurried back inside for a warm fire and my promised tale.

Idelia, bless her, had warmed some sweet cider for me, so I peeled off my sheepskin coat and settled down in one of the rockers. I wasn't sure how we were going to handle this . . . the fireplace between the tiny bedrooms had been banked for the day, so we couldn't in good conscience ask Idelia to leave.

"It's all right, Allie," Marta said in her soothing voice. "Idelia can hear about this—in fact, she may already have heard about it. Generally it doesn't happen until a person's grown, but you're running true to blood. What you saw was probably what your grandparents called a *vardoger*."

I tilted my head, staring hard at her. Why was that familiar? "A forerunner?" I repeated in English as Idelia gave an excited gasp of recognition.

"Exactly." Marta paused to reach for the quilt square she was piecing. "No one is quite sure how a forerunner is created, but I can tell you from my own mother's tales of Norway that forerunners are common in some parts of the world."

"Can anyone be a forerunner, or only someone involved with the Wise Arts?" Idelia asked.

"Apparently anyone," Marta replied, a wry expression crossing her face. "Some people arrive home from the fields every night an hour or so before they really appear."

"Could it be an astral projection?" I said carefully, getting my tongue around a word from a recent lesson.

"That is one possibility," Marta agreed. To Idelia she said: "If the person is thinking intensely of where he is going, and what he will do when he gets there, he unconsciously wills his spirit body to separate from his physical one and hurry to his destination. The person briefly appears, much like a ghost sometimes is seen, and then disappears again."

"What else could cause it?" I whispered aloud, clutching tightly at my mug as I thought.

"I have always wondered if time simply falls out of order . . . that we see the same event repeated, once at its true time, and once earlier, a brief glimpse of the future." Marta bent her head over her quilt square and placed a new triangle against one side. "I've seen a few *vardogers* in my time, but not for years now. Your uncle Jon used to arrive home early every afternoon."

I thought about that for a moment . . . and wondered if Marta would be at all surprised by Uncle Jon's ghost wandering through the house. Not much surprised my cousin Marta.

Shaw was coming . . . because his father had made the knives? That fit together with what I suspected about the Kristinsson family. Although nothing had ever actually been said to me, I was pretty sure Shaw's mother and father were shape-shifters—Mrs. Kris a wolf, Mr. Kris a bear. That counted as being touched by the Gift, and "Bear" Kristinsson was the best blacksmith in a fortnight or more. I thought that Shaw also might have inherited the changling blood, because there had been a wolf that helped us kill that vampire. And he was studying with Momma's cousin Cory—to be a practitioner? Or something else?

It gave me a nice glow to think that Shaw was looking forward to visiting. I couldn't admit right then how much I'd missed home—and him. It'd been awkward, the last few times we'd seen each other, because Shaw was always staring and not saying anything. But he did make my practitioner's necklace for me, so I guessed we were still friends.

I hoped someday we could talk again.

※ 🎴 ※

It was the next afternoon that Erik Hudson and Charles Hudson first came to visit, and it was like pebbles rolling downhill on a mountain, though I didn't know it at the time. I'd spent the morning just getting used to the penknife and wood, and learning how to cut without the blade slipping. The sun was fighting its way out of a cloud bank when I heard the sound of horses coming up Marta's path.

Idelia rushed into our cold bedroom and peeked through the opening between the curtains. "It is Charles Hudson and his cousin!"

"Is it?" Marta murmured, and I saw humor cross her face. "Come to pay a call after the dance."

Immediately I got up and went to stuff my carving into the oak chest in the stillroom. Better that no one see this in the making . . . it was that sort of thing. I could hear the Hudsons open the doors to the lean-to, so that their horses could stand in a warm place with their feet off the snow.

"Some of the black tea cake, Marta?" I asked as I drew off a jug of fresh cider and brought it into the main room.

"That would do nicely, ladies," Marta answered. I poured the cider into a pot to warm near the fire, but when I turned to the cooking area, Idelia had already gotten out the plates and cake. So I collected spices for the cider, and put on the teakettle in case anyone preferred tea.

I had the cider pot spiced and beginning to simmer when the knock came at the door. Idelia flitted back from the bedroom, smoothed my hair and straightened my sash, and then moved to the door.

Lord and lady, all we need is a servant, I thought, and tried to keep my face straight. It was apparent that Marta approved, whatever her reasons. Maybe as practice for future days, when the settlement had grown—maybe because who knew where we might end up in our short lives. Surprising as it seems, knowing how to serve tea was a useful talent in our world.

Our callers had dressed in clean clothing and even polished their boots. I was impressed, and hoped our everyday dresses weren't too plain. Idelia had insisted I put on my nicest work dress, after I scrubbed the barn smell off. . . . She'd known they might come. Or had hoped.

I had no chance of learning this game. Could it ever matter to me more than my lessons?

࿐

Only a while longer. I might have been the only girl in a week's riding who was trying to get rid of two good-looking young men, but there you have it. The struggle not to say anything odd always tired me, and they'd stayed almost an hour.

I'll confess that Mr. Hudson, formerly of New York, was an entertaining guest. His tales of the great cities of the East, and the ocean beyond, kept me on the edge of my seat. In turn, he seemed genuinely interested in our stories of life on the frontier.

"And you have to check your trapline every few days?" he asked.

"I check every other day," I admitted. "Sometimes every day. If you don't, you run the risk of something robbing your traps. It can still happen, but it won't be as likely."

"Do you have a trapline, Miss Peterson?" Charles Hudson said to Idelia.

Flushing slightly, she replied, "No, I'm afraid I never learned to set traps. I can prepare skins, though."

"You never know what talent might be useful out here in the wilderness," Mr. Hudson tossed in. "Do you also run a trapline, Mrs. Donaltsson?"

"For many years," Marta said simply, pouring herself another cup of tea. "My husband and I ran the largest fur center in the territory at one time."

"Is it difficult to learn?"

I couldn't help smiling at his words. Good heavens, most things were harder than a trapline!

"Alfreda?" Marta prompted me, and I jerked back into the conversation. "Did you find it hard to learn?"

"No," I said, adding, "it's one of the simplest things I've learned in my life."

"Miss Sorensson is learning the arts of the practitioner," Charles Hudson told his cousin. "She will study with Mrs. Donaltsson for several years, I believe. Is that correct, Mrs. Donaltsson?"

My, weren't we being nice to the chaperone. . . .

Marta smiled slightly, and I was sure she was thinking almost the same thing. "The time needed varies. Some learn quickly; others need many years of study. Allie has only been with me a few months."

Of course, I had studied with a junior practitioner, my momma, before that, and I hadn't done too shabbily since . . . perhaps Marta wanted to hint that I was younger than I looked, not ready for courting?

"Miss Sorensson is learning to read the character of people in their palms," Idelia said with a smile. "I think that would be very interesting."

I blinked in surprise. Well, that was a balanced way of phrasing it. I'd have to caution her about mentioning that talent . . . and to never mention my handling the tarot. Some people went up in smoke at the mere mention of fortune-telling cards. You could be run out of some communities for the talent.

Charles Hudson fastened an astonished gaze upon me. "You can read a person's character in his palm?"

I managed a small smile; I *didn't* like being the center of attention. "Well, can't you get a feel for people's character by studying their faces? Their eyes? Their movements?"

"True," he agreed. Then: "Could you tell something about me?"

"We're still pretty young for our hands to tell our secrets," I said evasively. *Yes, I could read you down to your toenails, but I might find out something I didn't like, and then how would I face you in town the next couple of years?*

"But you could see promise in them? Perhaps in my cousin's hand, since he is older than I am?" Charles went on.

"No, thank you, Charles," his cousin said quickly. "I do not want to know my future—I might try to change it."

"That is how I feel," I added, smiling at him.

I didn't volunteer that I got enough warnings about the future in other ways, thank you very much. And, right on the hour, our gentlemen thanked us for our hospitality and rose to leave.

༄་ཌ་༄

That night I had an odd dream, one of those ones that felt like a snip of the future. I was in the forest, and it seemed to be twilight, but since there was snow on the ground and in the trees, I wasn't sure. The snow had been cleared from the top of a huge boulder, and I was melting snow in the wooden cup that I carried in my little hip pack.

I'd built a small fire on top of the big rock, and when it was burning brightly, I pulled out my hunting knife Papa had given me. After heating the tip for a time, I waved it about to cool it down and then just broke the skin on one of my fingers. I let the blood fall into the cup, and swirled it to mix.

A horsehair brush from my pack was suddenly in my hand, and I was painting a circle around the top of the boulder.

I was watching myself from several paces away, as though my sight were linked to a squirrel's or a bird's eyes. But even at a distance, I could feel the haste, the fear of the young woman I was watching. How old was I there? A year older, two years? Less? There was no athame, for some reason. . . .

Tobacco flared into warmth and light, and sticks were fed to the flames. I heard the echo of her—my—mind, whispering an invitation, and I realized I was summoning something.

Anxiety so intense it twisted my stomach brought me fully awake.

"Allie?" said a sleepy voice. "Did you have a bad dream?" Idelia rolled over to face my side of the bed.

"I guess," I muttered, burrowing deeper into the covers as we huddled for warmth. It was tempting to think of stirring up the fire, warming some milk, and chewing on this awhile. But I knew Idelia might be concerned and follow me. I didn't think anyone could help me with what I felt from that dream.

Danger.

Could the future be averted? Or were prophetic dreams our only possible fate?

Maybe it was time I found out.

※ � ※

There was a low sky packed tight with clouds the day Shaw Kristinsson actually walked up to our door. The Hudson cousins had already returned and were trying to convince Idelia and me to join them on a trip to town. It was possible they'd succeed, but not on their charm. Marta had something she wanted delivered to a client, and I was perfectly happy to let someone else drive me out and back. Driving in snow, even with the stud wheels on, was not fun.

I must admit I lost track of Erik Hudson's words when I saw the Kristinssons' Arab horse strolling up our dirt path. That white stallion was something people would ransom their homes for, he was so gorgeous, but Bear Kristinsson wouldn't part with him. More than one mare passing through had left these parts in foal to that animal. But I never got tired of watching Frostfire move.

I was partly watching to see if another *vardoger* had come to call, or if this was really Shaw. He was leading another horse, a bay with a white foot that I recognized from the Pederson's farm. My *vardoger* had come alone. There was a jingle of the bridle as he dismounted, so I was pretty sure this was the real thing.

"Someone you know?" Erik Hudson asked politely, his manner formal.

"Yes. It is. . . . Mr. Kristinsson, from Sun-Return." I glanced down at the stick sketch he had been drawing in the snow. It was supposed to be an outline of the edge of my face—the high cheekbone and oval tapering into the chin seemed like someone else. He'd been trying to convince me that my bones would age more gracefully than Idelia's sweet dimpled face.

Our guest noticed my gaze. "Someday you will be a beautiful woman."

Maybe. I just smiled at him. My Momma and her delicate sisters were beautiful—I was nothing like them. The only woman of my father's family I'd ever seen was Marta, and though she was handsome, she was not "in the established mode"—too tall, her face too strong. It was too much to hope for that both sides of the family had made something beautiful in me.

"We should go greet him," I said aloud, my head turning back toward the house. "Idelia, Shaw's here."

"Already? How nice," she said warmly. "We should go inside and see if he would like to join us on the trip into Cat Track Hollow."

I nipped the inside of my lip firmly to keep from laughing. Just what the Hudsons wanted—another man on the journey! Somehow I managed not to say a word. This was definitely shaping up to be an interesting day.

⁂

Idelia's words might as well have been prophecy. Shaw had arrived with knives in hand, their handles solid and untouched by design. It turned out I was going to have to select one from the stack, as it were. But not while we had company. And I couldn't simply nudge the Hudsons home—or send Idelia off alone with them. That just wasn't done.

Shaw looked as the *vardoger* had, taller than I'd last seen him, slim as a reed, and starting to grow a mustache! There was also a hint of beard along the line of his jaw. Lord and Lady, I was not ready for Shaw to look like a grown-up. That meant my brother Josh wasn't far behind him.

'Course, Shaw had sixteen years under his belt, and Josh would be rising sixteen soon. I realized with a shiver that it might not be too many years before Josh brought home a bride.

"And how are your parents, Shaw?" Marta was asking as we all trooped inside the house.

"Both well, ma'am," Shaw answered her, one eye on the four of us. I suspected that Marta allowed Shaw to call her by name, but that would not do before strangers. Shaw stood when we came into the main room proper, and I wondered if he had been taking lessons in manners from my momma, or from his own.

"Gentlemen, this is Mr. Kristinsson, from the community of Sun-Return," Marta said formally to the Hudsons. She then gave their identical last names to Shaw, who nodded greeting with his entire upper body.

"Mrs. Donaltsson, Mr. Hudson has offered to take us in to town on your errand," Idelia announced. "Shall we do it for you this afternoon?"

Marta turned and removed from her mantelpiece a small package wrapped tightly in butcher paper. "This really must reach Mrs. Lyons today. If you don't mind making the circuit, Mr. Hudson, I would be obliged to you." Setting the package in my hand, Marta gave me a hard look. "Be sure and ride past the barn the Smiths are building. Mr. Smith wanted to talk to us about lightning."

Ah—I knew what she meant. When we'd seen him at Sunday church, Mr. Smith had mentioned a problem with working, as if something was trying to stop him from finishing his barn. "I'm sure we can visit the Smiths," I said firmly.

"Of course," Charles said quickly, his gaze flicking swiftly to Idelia. It was plain that Charles wasn't going to miss any chance to spend extra time with Idelia. I kept my grin to myself.

While I was watching this attempt at subtlety, Marta glanced over at Shaw. "Would you care to see Cat Track Hollow, Mr. Kristinsson? I don't believe you have ever seen our little village."

Shaw was giving Mr. Erik Hudson a very peculiar look . . . it reminded me of something, but I couldn't quite grasp what. "No, I have never seen Cat Track Hollow. I'd be delighted to accompany you." His gracious nod took in all four of us, but his eyes had shifted to me. Today they were very light, almost silvery.

Idelia didn't seem to notice the odd sensations floating between the two young men. "Shall we be off, then?" Turning to Shaw, she added, "Your horse isn't too tired, is he?"

Shaw shook his head as he stepped back to let Charles Hudson open the door. "He could run all day if necessary. He needs the exercise. It's hard to keep a horse trail-ready during the winter."

Idelia nodded as if she knew just what he was talking about, which I don't think she did, but she made it look convincing. She led the way back outside, where Charles had tied his buggy while he tried to convince us to join them in town. It was the only real buggy for many days' ride, I think, the sprung seat wide enough to hold three adults.

Charles boosted Idelia up onto the seat. I knew I'd end up there, too. I was wearing a dress, despite the warm breeches I had on underneath, so I had to act like a lady. Sure enough, Erik Hudson offered me a boost up, which I tried to accept as if it was my due.

Shaw had already mounted Frostfire, and this showed a certain cunning on his part, because they were perfectly placed to walk along next to me as the buggy rolled down the packed snow of the drive. Erik Hudson was on one of his uncle's horses; his help to me left him bringing up the rear.

As always, Shaw didn't say anything at first; he just kept a steady hand on the prancing, spirited stallion. Then he abruptly said, "How are your studies?"

Keenly aware of Idelia and Charles's idle chatter, I replied, "They go well. How are things with you?" I left it oblique, still not certain what Shaw was up to, many days west of Sun-Return.

"Things are fine. I learn quickly, so Cory says I may start working with Dr. Fraser soon." This was very matter-of-fact, but I turned toward him as he spoke. Shaw going to study with a physician? But I would have bet real money that he was studying the Wise Arts. . . . Glancing sideways at me, he added, "Mrs. Donaltsson won't be ready to have me as a student for several years."

Ah. Light dawned. He was going to study with Marta for the creative female elements, Earth and Water, when he finished with Air and Fire, the male elements of transformation. I suddenly wondered just how Shaw was related to the same people I was. . . .

"How are you and Cory related?" I asked aloud.

"My great-uncle married Cory's aunt," was the prompt reply. "Cory's your Mother's third cousin, isn't he?"

"Yes," I agreed. I was still looking oddly at Shaw, and he seemed to divine what I was thinking.

"I'm not related to Mrs. Donaltsson," he told me. "I have no female relatives who actually practice. But she liked me, so she said she'd teach me, if I could wait until she finished with you."

So . . . we weren't actually related, except by marriage. That was reassuring—I couldn't *believe* that we could be related to the Kristinssons and no one had ever said anything. That just doesn't happen, unless a feud's going on. And surely we hadn't been in this part of the country long enough for fighting to break out.

That was more conversation than I'd had out of Shaw in ages. I found I wanted to make him speak again. All the time he was spending out in the orchard country was changing his speech—he was starting to sound like an Englishman. 'Course, his father was only half-Swede; the other half was Irish or Scottish or such, like me. No one knew where Mrs. Kris came from. . . . I don't think Shaw's family spoke the old tongue at home. Most folks in Sun-Return spoke English to each other—it was the one language we all shared.

"Will you stay for supper?" I said suddenly, as I realized how long the shadows were growing. If we didn't step lively on these errands, we'd need a lantern to get home.

"Yes," was the simple reply. "I'm to take Idelia home tomorrow, if she's ready to leave."

Well, I'd be sad to see her go, but I knew she missed her family and William Adamsson. I wondered if Charles Hudson would be bold enough to drive the distance—almost a full day—to Sun-Return.

Even as I thought about whether Charles had a chance with Idelia, we approached the Lyons' farmstead. Time to be gracious and make people think well of Marta's latest apprentice. I even kept myself from jumping down from the seat, and let Charles help me to the ground.

Because the cloudy sky suddenly seemed a shade darker, I turned down Mrs. Lyons's offer of tea—regretfully, because Mrs. Lyons made lovely molasses cake, and I knew she'd like the company. But it was cold enough in what little daylight was left to us—we didn't want to be out long after dark.

Mr. Eric Hudson boosted me back into the buggy, though I'd protested I could pull myself up. Once the blanket was settled back over my legs, Charles urged his horse on into the village.

This late in the day Cat Track Hollow was almost deserted. The women were spinning or carding wool, the men doing the small chores of winter and tending to tack, loose boards, sprung traps. It was a deceptively tranquil scene. Hard to credit that Mr. Smith believed someone was trying to witch his new barn.

I could hear the sound of a hammer pounding somewhere in the distance. *Someone* was getting something done. "Is that from Smith's?" I asked Charles.

"It sounds like it," he agreed, taking the right fork past the commons.

We continued past the last house and went straight to the Smith homestead, scarcely a quarter-mile beyond Cat Track Hollow. There were two other men working with Mr. Smith. Jed Hall was the only one I knew. They had set up sawbucks to support the long beams of wood and were building one of the barn doors. No one was actually working on the naked skeleton of the building.

Charles stopped the buggy a good hundred feet from the work site—the packed snow went no farther. I tossed the blanket to Idelia and, gathering up my skirts, was on the ground before any of the men could get down to help me. Shaking my skirt around me properly, I lifted the hem to keep it from collecting too much powder and walked the narrow track to the sawbucks.

I was grateful for my sheepskin coat, but I would have given a lot for my snowshoes.

Mr. Smith came toward me, his thick dark beard and mustache creased with his smile. A burly, wind-chapped hand appeared from his heavy coat to gently take hold of my fingers. "Miss Sorensson, we are so pleased that you could come."

"How goes your work, Mr. Smith?" I asked politely, trying not to shiver in the rising breeze.

"Slowly, I'm afraid." He leaned closer and said softly, "Your cousin told you what was happening?"

I nodded once, my gaze shifting to the skeleton of the barn. "But you can work on things around it?"

"Yes," he said fiercely. "It is only when we try to raise the sides of the barn that our nails will not drive straight. We've been hitting our thumbs and dropping tools, and Jedediah nearly fell off the ridgepole. That was why I spoke to your cousin."

I noticed that Mr. Smith was one of the old believers—he carefully avoided referring to either the possible cause of the problem or Marta's calling. I wondered if this was human interference, or something else. . . .

I glanced up to make sure there were no boards hanging loose, and then slowly walked into the area where the barn would stand. Looking around, I realized that this was where the hollow started rolling back up—it was the highest point just beyond Cat Track Hollow.

Could that have anything to do with it? What if this was an elf mound? It didn't really feel like one. Still, there was something here. I could feel a lingering trace of power. I paced carefully along the perimeter of the rectangle, looking at tracks in the snow, looking at landmarks nearby.

Finally I noticed something odd and stopped walking. It took a few moments to make sense of the footprints. "Mr. Smith?" I called to him. "Has your wife been to the site since the last snowfall?"

"No, she has not," he replied, starting toward me.

I held up a hand to stop him. "Wait right there. You're certain? All of you? Not your wife, your sweetheart, a daughter, somebody's granny—"

"Not since the Twelfth Night snow," Smith said gravely. He had paused when I asked him to, and was watching me for his next move.

"I need a hammer and a long nail," I told him. "Walk toward me from that way." I gestured to my right, and then looked down at the footprint before me. It was a woman's foot that made this—a small foot, in kid boots, not big fur-lined muckers like mine. The weather had been too cold for seeing the sights—especially when these men had been here working on the ridgepole. They wouldn't let anybody walk beneath them while they were in the air.

This meant a woman had come when they weren't here. And there was only one reason to come by at night. Mr. Smith was correct: Someone had a grudge against his family—or his barn. I looked around again as he walked up with the hammer and nail. This might have been the hill site of a local witch, where she did her sky ceremonies. And she clearly didn't take kindly to losing her ritual place to a barn. Or maybe she had just liked the little wooded hill.

Mr. Smith came up beside me and carefully handed me the long iron nail and big hammer. Squatting down, I whispered a prayer of protection, asking help from the Lord and Lady of Light—and then I set the nail over the small half-round of the heel print and drove the slender spike through the snow into the dirt below.

The ground was very hard, so it took some effort, but I'm no faded flower. When I had it deep enough, I stood and handed the hammer back to the man. "Try now," I said, and started back toward the buggy.

Jed was already holding a planed board to the studs to one side of the center doorway. The other man drove a nail in on one side, and another, and then moved to secure the other side.

Mr. Smith beamed and walked with me. "Was it witchery?"

"Of a kind," I told him. "I don't think anyone means you real trouble, since no one's been badly hurt. Someone didn't want you to build a barn here, and tried to make it hard for you."

"But we asked all in town before I chose this place!" He sounded bewildered. "Why not stop us before we started?"

I gave him a wintry half smile. In a way, I had some sympathy for the witch. "Did you ask the wives when their husbands weren't there?" Well, of course he hadn't, and he just looked at me. I stopped walking. "Now, I hope you know better than to loan anything to anybody or accept any gifts, now that you know someone is angry. Not even a cup of hot tea while you're working. If you do, we'll have to do something else—and you know my cousin always charges more when she thinks someone's been foolish."

The man chuckled, but his expression was a bit sheepish, which made me think he'd had a run-in with Marta's tongue. "Not even a cup of tea?"

"Not even food," I said firmly. "And don't lend so much as an egg unless the person says the words 'for God's sake.' The evil-minded have trouble speaking those words. If you lend without

those words, you'll put yourself right back into the witch's power."
I decided not to tell him that his witch was probably nursing a
bruised foot at this very moment. It would hurt for quite a while—
as long as the nail was whole—and the witch couldn't remove the
cold iron herself.

I'd probably come pull the nail after the barn was finished.
She'd know better than to mess with the Smiths once the clearing
was gone.

"I will bring Mrs. Donaltsson her fee later on this week," Mr.
Smith was telling me. I smiled and told him that would be fine, and
then let him help me back up into the buggy.

Charles and Idelia had clearly been talking up a storm in my
absence, while Shaw had kept his horse moving so the stallion's
muscles wouldn't chill. Erik Hudson had stayed close by the
wagon, watching me walk into the framed barn, and his face was
approving.

"You're very clever," he said with a smile.

"Just common sense," I told him, smiling back, and nodded to
Charles that we could move along.

Everyone was pretty quiet on the way home.

Watching ritual magic will do that to you.

EIGHT

WE HAD SIX TO SUPPER THAT EVENING, and until that day I hadn't known that there was a leaf for Marta's table. She'd been very busy while we were gone, slow-cooking a haunch of venison till it was so tender it would melt in your mouth. There was a meat sauce made from dried cherries, and some potatoes 'n gravy, too, so no one would go away hungry.

Idelia dragged me into the guest bedroom, where Marta had already lit a fire in the fireloft, and fussed with my hair, re-braiding it. "You must look your best," she whispered to me. "It's not often you have two fellows glaring at each other like that. Might as well enjoy it—I always did."

I must have looked poleaxed or something, because Idelia glanced at me and started giggling. Then she pulled loose those tiny hairs at the top of my forehead, the ones that always shift in a breeze.

"You didn't guess? Allie, you're so funny sometimes. You've had boys looking at you like that for years, and you never notice a thing." Idelia's eyes sparkled in amusement.

Me? They were mad at each other over me? "What did I do to make them mad?" I whispered.

"Not what you did, silly one—what you are." She finished with my long, thick braid and wound a piece of hair around the thong she'd used as a tie. "They both want your attention, and they don't want to share it with any other fellow."

Oh.

I considered this a moment, and tried to wrap myself around the idea. It seemed impossible that anyone would work to get into my good graces, but that was what Idelia was suggesting. "You really think so?" I started slowly, trying to fit other visits into the puzzle she'd handed me.

"I do," was her firm reply.

I shook out my dress, which had mostly dried from my standing near the fireloft, and tried to find something to say. It wasn't often that I couldn't contribute to a conversation (although I usually said the wrong thing), but that time I was speechless. Lord and Lady, worse and worse! Whatever was I going to say to those boys?

"You'll be fine," Idelia told me, slipping an arm around my waist and pulling me toward the door.

Fine? I always had trouble finding things to say! How did she expect me to talk with them *now*?

"Let them talk," she hissed as she opened the door.

Being shoved through a doorway by somebody a head smaller than me was not my idea of looking like an adult, so I threw back my shoulders and tried to walk with some grace. Perhaps that's why Momma always encouraged me to dance—she knew her chicks were gonna be tall. At least I wasn't as tall as Marta . . . not yet.

We found the three fellows standing near the fireplace and talking softly—or rather, Charles was talking and the other two occasionally answering. The rich odor of spiced apple cider floated to my nose, and I decided then and there I wanted some with my dinner. Cider is the next best thing in the world to hot chocolate when you're melancholy. And I saw a very long evening ahead, unless the Hudsons left after dinner.

Charles lost no time in the praise-the-chaperone competition. "I wish you made supper at our house every night, Mrs. Donaltsson," he said with enthusiasm as we sat down to our meal. "This is fine enough for dinner."

My nose told me that Marta had an apple cobbler in the oven, and I had to agree. I doubt we'd have eaten like that if it had just been the womenfolk. Still, you never knew with Marta—she loved to cook. Sometimes I thought she missed having her children close by . . . she needed grandchildren to spoil. Or another man to keep company with, maybe? She couldn't have been more than forty-five, and we were a long-lived bunch, we Sorenssons.

"Would you say grace, Mr. Hudson?" Marta asked Charles's cousin. Erik Hudson promptly flushed, looked down at his plate, and muttered something about "Let us give thanks for the food we are about to receive, in His name, Amen."

Typical male—either too much praying or not enough.

After all that chatter, supper was a pretty quiet affair. We all paid Marta the compliment of concentrating on our food. It wasn't until we'd cleared the plates and brought over bowls of cobbler and cream that anyone spoke again.

"Miss Pederson said that you had left home to study, Mr. Kristinsson?" Charles Hudson suddenly said.

"That is correct," Shaw replied, adding some cream to his cobbler.

When it became obvious that Shaw wasn't going to volunteer anything more, Charles asked: "Are you pursuing the law?"

"Medicine," was Shaw's clipped answer.

That *was* true . . . and the rest was no one's concern but Shaw's. I don't know why I was suddenly so skittish about our work, but I was glad that Idelia was not announcing any of her theories about Shaw's training. Flicking my gaze to the other end of the table, I gave her a hard look, just to keep her silent. She must have gotten the message, because she tilted her head down over her bowl.

I'd never actually told Idelia that Shaw was also studying the mysteries. It just didn't feel like something she needed to know. Most of the time she kept quiet about my training, but occasionally the need to boast got the better of her . . . like the other day.

Better it was only my business she was shouting from the rooftops.

Shaw had hesitated between bites, as if contemplating the apples in his spoon. He glanced over at me, his eyes dark in the subdued light, and asked, "Do you know how to make this?"

I just stared for a moment—as if I didn't know how to make a simple cobbler!—and then decided he meant the extra touch of spice that made Marta's different from, say, Momma's recipe. Not better, mind you—just different.

"Not yet," I told him, glancing up at Marta, who was across the table from me. She actually winked! "But I will."

You know, sometimes Shaw flashed a truly charming smile. I promised myself to try and make him smile more often. As I basked in the warmth of that look, I glanced out the corner of my eye at Erik Hudson. He didn't look amused—in fact, he looked glassy-eyed over the entire exchange.

I swear, I had butterflies dancing in my stomach like you wouldn't believe. And Idelia thought this business between two boys was fun? Somehow I finished my cobbler, but I was glad for that soothing cider.

Maybe someday I would understand all this courting business . . . but I doubted it.

❧·𝒟·❧

The Hudsons left after supper, and Idelia and I spent a pleasant hour packing up her things for the trip. She'd only brought two carpetbags and a bandbox, which could be easily tied to the two horses. There was extra yarn to pack—Marta had taught us a new crochet stitch, and we'd each started wool shawls. Then we returned to the main room, where Marta was quilting and talking with Shaw.

I'd listened to the rise and fall of their voices as we packed, and I'd discovered that Shaw was more talkative when I wasn't around. A lot of their conversation was about the mysteries, and I'd longed to listen, but Idelia didn't need to hear those things. And I was losing her the next day . . . in fact, the next time she could get away to visit, she might be a married woman.

Lord and Lady, to think of that. Good thing her quilt was nearly finished.

We stirred ourselves to make tea and bring in some of the scones we'd made for breakfast. While we arranged the tray, I could see Shaw studying my quilt on its frame. I wondered if Mrs. Kristinsson quilted—I'd never been in the family's private quarters, so I had no idea if she even owned a frame.

"My mother likes this pattern," Shaw said suddenly as I set the tray down before the fireplace. "She has made several versions of it."

"It's a good pattern for using up scraps," Marta replied, glancing over at the long frame. "You two have done a good job of matching your stitches. I can't tell where one left off and the other began."

"It took some work," I admitted, pouring everyone cups of tea. "I don't remember your mother ever attending a quilting bee. Does she prefer to quilt alone?"

"What with serving meals, it's hard for mother to get away," Shaw said softly. After a pause he admitted, "Sometimes Morgan and I help her. She thinks every man should be able to thread a needle. You never know when you'll be on your own."

There was no answer to that. Too many women died young in this land—it was merciless sometimes. "Dean doesn't care for quilting?" I asked instead, referring to his oldest brother.

"Not really. He has to be truly bored before he'll pick up a needle. He'll thread a handful for us, and then go reread one of our books. Sometimes we can get him to read aloud, but not always." Shaw's gaze returned to his cup of tea as if he realized he'd been speaking for a while.

Marta set aside her quilt square and broke open one of the scones. "Did you take care of Mr. Smith's problem?"

"I did," I said slowly, sipping carefully at the hot fluid. "It was very strong, and night was falling, so I didn't try to dissipate it . . . I just turned it back on its maker."

Marta studied me over the scone she was buttering. "I thought it might be too tough to dispel. Someone in the area has a real talent for witchcraft."

Idelia's gasp was audible.

"Not to worry, my dear," Marta said gently to my friend. "It is not anything that would affect you. The woman who cast that spell has a gift for small, malicious things. Her strength could not reach as far as Sun-Return."

"But she is certainly drawing the attention of Cat Track Hollow," I tossed in.

"Yes," Marta agreed. "We will need to do something about her. Mr. Forrest stopped by while you were gone and said his wife's butter will no longer come. One of us will need to go to their homestead tomorrow and help set the butter."

That trick I knew—it was an easy spell. You simply heated a clean silver coin and dropped it into the cream. Some folks used a heated horseshoe, but that was only needed when a powerful spell caster was working against a community. In this case, a coin should do fine. If witchcraft was involved, the coin would break the spell. If the problem was simply that it was too cold to churn, the heat would set the butter.

Dissipating a spell was safest, since it kept all the forces in the region balanced. Throwing it back on the sender was faster but a little more dangerous, since it was both a warning and a challenge. Then there was the third choice, the most dangerous one . . . laying a trap for the witch.

Of course, there was always the chance that you were trying to catch someone with more power than you possessed. Then there could be big trouble.

I knew better than to attempt the third. I might be *strong* enough to trap another spell caster, but I didn't yet have the control. Another power could gobble me up.

Coins in churns I could handle.

We didn't stay up much past our evening tea. Marta had prepared the master bedroom for Shaw, so any who chose could have stayed up. But Shaw and Idelia had a long ride on the morrow through snow and cold, and I needed to select my athame. The solstice season had been pleasant, but it was time to return to work.

I would miss her, though. It was almost like having a sister.

❧ ⅅ ❧

We were up well before dawn, tending to the animals and making oatmeal to warm our bellies. The cold went right to the marrow that morning; I pulled on my warmest trousers and flannel shirt before going into the lean-to. Shaw was already there, giving the horses a hot mash, so I tended to the cow and the goats. It was pleasant just to work in the soft darkness—no need to speak.

Once or twice, I thought Shaw started to say something. But he never got the words out.

Idelia had oatmeal with brown sugar and cream waiting for us, as well as coffee to make sure we were awake. We inhaled with good appetite and then went to saddle the horses. That left Marta and Idelia saying their farewells, Marta probably thanking Idelia for the sack of scraps she'd brought as a visiting gift.

The horses were on their way out of the lean-to when Shaw finally spoke. Taking hold of both sets of reins, Shaw stopped our progress and looked over at me. "Allie. . . ." He swallowed, as if not sure how his words would be received. I just held still and waited for him to speak.

"Those Hudson fellows . . . be careful of them, will you?" My face must have looked odd, because he added, "Their eyes reflect like mirrors." Then he stopped pulling back on the Arab's rein and hauled the gelding toward the front door.

I stood there a moment or two, looking after him. *What kind of thing . . . ?* Folks' eyes *did* shine, healthy folks. *Like a mirror. . . .* Finally I shrugged myself into my skin and shut the door to the lean-to. If this was jealousy, it was a strange sort of thing.

As always, we were rushed through our good-byes. I gave Idelia a big hug and told her she had to get serious about one of those fellows before they were all driven to distraction. She laughed delicately, like she always did, and let Shaw boost her up into the saddle. When it came to riding, Idelia was no fussy female—she rode astride, like most of the young women of the region.

Shaw gave me a long look after he'd swung up on the Arab. "Take care, Alfreda," he said finally.

"And you," I replied, thinking blessings upon them both. The woods should have been clear of all evil things since the ride of the Wild Hunt. But there were cougars and bears, and an Indian might creep through the barrier if he wasn't angry when he passed it. . . .

"A safe journey to you both," Marta said firmly, and with those words, Shaw turned the head of the stallion and led the way down the path. The sun would rise before too long, and with any luck, they would be in Sun-Return before sunset.

"Best wait until sunup before walking to Forrest's," Marta said as she surveyed the still woods around us. "Easier to move in snow during the day. In the meantime, let's make sure of the fire and then check the traplines. Don't forget your hip pouch."

No argument from me—I'd check a trapline any time. First, though, I stood there and watched Shaw and Idelia until they turned onto the main road and were lost to sight.

I had expected the poltergeist to mess up the breakfast dishes for me, but silence reigned in the house. Maybe I'd left it at Hudson's store?

No such luck. Marta's quilt squares had been carefully arranged on the floor of the main room. But they were unhurt—my poltergeist hadn't risked the wrath of Marta's Good Friend!

$\mathcal{x} \cdot \mathcal{D} \cdot \mathcal{x}$

I hadn't been on the trapline since we'd returned to Cat Track Hollow, and I enjoyed that romp through the firm snow. We got out snowshoes to make sure we didn't sink into a drift, and found a good catch of mink and two beavers waiting for us. It was the dark of the moon, but the eerie glow that clung to the snow let us keep to the right path.

I had wondered if I would be uncomfortable once I returned to the woods, after my jaunt on Twelfth Night. But no; they were still my trees, my animals . . . it was still my place. I knew the difference between bad things passing through and a bad region.

Still, Marta's company was nice.

We finished up before dawn, and stopped for some tea and the last of the scones. Then Marta went to her hiding place and returned with several silver coins. "English shillings," she said in response to my amazed look. "It may take more than one coin to turn the trick. Mrs. Forrest is an honest woman, she'll dig them out of the butter for you."

"Can I go like this?" I asked, gesturing to my boiled wool pants and flannel shirt.

Marta pursed her lips. "Mrs. Forrest wears her husband's smocks when she does fieldwork; she wouldn't mind. But Mr. Forrest might . . . it's one thing to see your wife that way, and another to see a young girl like that. Use the skirt."

Well, "the skirt" meant only one thing—my old dark brown merino wool that had been both turned and lengthened, a yellow ribbon masking where the flounce was attached. It was too old for anything but a winter coverall, and that's how I used it, with one too-short flannel petticoat.

But I was leaving on my pants!

I stuffed extra socks in the pockets of my sheepskin coat, and put the shillings in my hip pouch under the skirts. I made sure the

knife sheath was tied to my thigh—didn't want any funny bulges—
and then dug out my wool cap and scarf and heavy mittens.

What with my wool-lined boots, this was as warm as I could get.
But already I found myself hoping for a cup of tea at the end of my
walk.

"Don't stay too long, Allie," Marta told me as she nodded her
farewell. "You need to practice your carving."

"I won't," I shouted as I pulled the front door shut. I looked up
at the rolling clouds above, the light to the east promising that the
sun was up *somewhere.* "You could send some of that sunshine this
way," I suggested to the sky, but I didn't rail against the weather.
Sun was lovely in winter, but it could also melt snow into a blanket
of ice, which would make hard going on my return.

We'd found the snow hard enough to walk on, so I'd left my
snowshoes at home. I used the path that the horses and buggy had
trampled down, and worked my way toward the main road.

Just as I was about to leave Marta's path, there was an explosion
of dead leaves and snow, and a snowshoe hare bounded across my
path. It was a big one, pure white except for its big dark eyes. I
knew this because the animal stopped and rose on its hind legs,
turning to watch me. I had the strangest feeling the hare wanted
my attention.

For a moment I wondered if this could be my witch. It was
difficult to take on another form, and rarely done during the day—
at least not by Satanic witches. If this hare was my witch, she would
be limping after my little trick with the nail—unless Mr. Smith had
foolishly loaned something out.

Then I felt the lightest trickle of unease. A hare across your path
was not lucky for a traveler. I wasn't really a traveler, but still . . .
and white hares were sometimes ghosts. In the daytime? Or was it
an oracular hare, trying to tell me something?

Whatever its meaning, the hare was finished with me. With
a bound longer than I'm tall, the creature tore off into the forest
beyond, its huge feet scooping balls of snow and tossing them in
my direction.

Here was a dilemma. Should I go on or return to the house,
if only for the morning? Marta would not laugh at me—she took
hares seriously—but Mrs. Forrest was expecting one of us. I hated
to disappoint her.

I would be walking on the road, not through the woods. Surely the path was safe? That's why everyone paid all the practitioners— to keep hostile Indian tribes at bay. Just to be sure, I picked up a long oak branch and snapped off a few stray limbs, leaving something that was half staff and half thin club. If a cougar wanted an argument, I'd give him an argument.

The trail was partly trampled, which helped a bit. My passage was slow but steady. Not that many people went on past Marta's home. I put my feet where Mr. Forrest's mule had churned along, and was grateful for small favors. I could have been snowshoeing down the road! Sometimes it was easier to walk on top of snow, but it tired my leg muscles in different ways.

I'd been walking only a few minutes when I heard the sound of horses coming up behind me. After I'd floundered off to one side, I looked back to see Mr. Erik Hudson driving a team pulling a sleigh. There were supplies in the back, but Charles had not accompanied his cousin.

"Hello!" Erik Hudson said brightly, reining in the long-walking horses. "What are you doing on foot? Did you lose your horse?"

Remembering Sweet William dumping me on Twelfth Night, I decided to let that one pass. "Heading to Forrest's," I said instead. "It's not that long a trip."

"So am I," he replied. "Mr. Forrest's order came in, and I volunteered to take it out. Can you climb up? No sense in getting wet when I'm going the same direction. And"—he held up a pottery jug—"I've got hot cider!"

Now, Shaw didn't like the Hudson boys—he'd made that pretty clear—but I had to live in that village for at least another year or so. How could I turn down a ride when I was going the same place?

For the first time, I wished that dipping into people's heads was allowed. I'd never known Shaw's judgment to be wrong, but accusing someone of being shallow didn't mean they were dangerous . . . not on the main road.

No help for it. If I turned him down, he'd be offended and say something to his family. So. . . . "Sure," I said aloud. "Half a minute." I kicked my way through the drifts to the box seat of the sleigh and pulled myself up without much trouble. We paused while I banged the snow on hem and boots back over the side and tossed away my branch.

"There's a mug right down there," Erik said as he coaxed the horses into their long walk. "And a blanket for your knees, if you're cold."

"Not hardly," I told him. "Not a long enough trip to get cold." I pulled up the mug and took the jug from him. "Do you want some of this? You've been out a while."

"I poured myself some back a ways, when the trail was smoother," he replied, giving the horses their head over a patch of ice and gravel. "You go ahead."

What with the rocking of the sleigh, I only filled the mug half full. But I wanted the steam on my face more than anything else. The spices smelled wonderful, just like the crock at the Twelfth Night party. I waited until we were back on smooth snow before sipping at the cider.

"How is Mrs. Hudson today?" I said politely, since conversation would probably be expected of me.

"She is quite well, thank you," Erik responded, glancing my way. "Today is the day her girls have been waiting for—it's time to start new dresses for spring."

Oh, to have a father who runs a dry goods store, I thought, but something about saying that out loud didn't sound quite right, so I merely nodded appreciatively. "New material brightens the spirit," I finally said.

"Do you think it will snow today?" Erik went on, and then we talked about the weather. The various signs of a hard winter as opposed to a gentle one were discussed, as was how to gauge when spring was just around the corner. As Erik finished speaking, a ray of sunshine broke free of the cloud cover. After the eternal twilight we had moved through, the effect was blinding. The light flickered across the snow-covered trees, causing them to glitter like stars. I found myself light-headed from the reflections.

Then the dizziness didn't go away. *Uh-oh.* . . . I had been so sure we were going to be lucky this season. Neither Marta nor I had been sick since early autumn.

"How much farther is it to Forrest's homestead?" I asked, gripping the seat with one hand.

"No more than five minutes," Erik replied, steering the team around a hole where the road had washed out.

"Good," I said, closing my eyes against the glistening expanse of snow. The churn wouldn't take long—then Erik could drop me off on his way home. . . .

That thought was the last thing I remembered.

❧ 🎴 ❧

When my eyes opened, I was fully awake, like being startled out of a dream. It had been years since I'd slept like that—not since I had an ague as a child and slept an entire day and night after the fever finally broke. The dark room where I lay smelled strongly of hay and molasses.

There was no odor of herbs. Wherever I was, I had never been there before. As this thought came to me, I realized I was wearing my coat, hat and gloves. While sleeping? But the room was cold—I could hear the wind howling outside—and Mrs. Forrest would have removed my coat, and brought quilts. . . .

It was a storage area. Somewhere in an adjoining room I heard voices—at least two men, talking softly. I could see the flicker of firelight through a warped board beside the door frame. The building wasn't built well—there was a mighty draft across the floor.

I did not recognize the voices, and a knot slowly formed in my stomach. Where was I? Where was Erik Hudson? Had we been attacked by thieves? It had been years since any French had tried to take settlers back to Quebec for ransom. . . .

Carefully I felt myself over while I tried to figure out where I had been. I remembered saying good-bye to Idelia and Shaw . . . I remembered the trapline . . . I remembered walking to Forrest's, and Erik giving me a ride. That was the end of memory.

A hole in your thoughts was a terrible thing to consider.

I didn't think anyone had been taking liberties; my hip pouch and knife were still strapped on underneath my coat and skirt. Thieves would not have left me that knife, for it was a good one. I could tell my boots were still on, too. . . . That might be a good thing.

The room actually had an oilcloth window, which let in that paler darkness that tells you it's night outside. I kept my gaze away from it, trying to get a feel for the room without moving around.

There were hogsheads stacked under the window, and hay bales all along one wall . . . maybe the north wall, I didn't carry a compass in my head.

As I strained for any sense of sound, I realized I could make out some of the conversation in the next room. What with the stamping of feet and moving of furniture, I suspected that one fellow had just arrived.

"When's young Hudson coming back for her?" said a low, gravelly voice.

"Not until morning," was the response. That one sounded younger, maybe a light tenor—or maybe a little scared.

"Did he figure out what went wrong?"

"If he did, do you think he'd bother to tell me? I think he went to talk with the Keeper of Souls about it." That was definitely a scared man . . . or boy.

"God save us all then," the older man whispered. "And God save that poor boy, too, if this child dies from whatever poison he gave her. The Keeper don't care for failure."

"He said to let her sleep, so I'm letting her sleep." Very definite. "And may God have mercy on her soul . . . while she still has one."

"He's surely abandoned us," was the gruff response.

More movement. Darkness momentarily blocked the crack of firelight, but no one came toward the door. "Man's gotta live as best he can. You live here, you deal with the Hudson clan." This was defensive, and I smelled an argument brewing.

I'd heard enough. What was going on, I had no idea, but I planned to figure it out at a distance. Time to move before fear kept me from moving. I sat up slowly, but for a wonder, the planed boards beneath me didn't creak. Probably frozen. . . .

I unbuttoned my skirt and pulled it off, followed by my petticoat. Then I tied them under my coat, flat around my ribs and waist for extra padding. From the sound of that wind, it was gonna be cold out there. Who knew when I'd find more things to warm me? If I could get out that window stuffed with hay, I'd do it, but it was only big enough for me in my coat . . . maybe.

The discussion was getting loud. I untied my knife hilt and drew the fine blade, all six inches of steel and then some. It was my most precious possession, next to my practitioner's necklaces. And right then it was more useful. The only question that remained was, what was outside under that window?

I carefully nudged at the nearest hogshead and found it was full of something, maybe the molasses I smelled. Without hesitation I climbed to the top of the pile. Praise the Lord and Lady of Light that I had my wits and health about me. That "poison" he'd spoken of . . . had Erik Hudson dosed me? And if so, how long had I slept? A day? Longer? How late was it?

My hand was shaking, but the sharp tip of my knife went right through the edge of the oilcloth. I cut a slit down one side of the window, and then across the bottom. Carefully I lifted a corner, praying a gale wouldn't blow into the room and make those fellows suspicious.

The argument had died, and I paused, listening. Something about did he want coffee, there was whiskey for it . . . They weren't concerned about me. Maybe they didn't know how people with the Gift were trained, or maybe—

Praise the powers that be for small blessings—the wind was from another direction, and the cloth didn't flap. It felt dry out there, a piercing cold—a north or northwest wind, then. I could see trees, and ground sloping up behind the building. Not as far down as inside, but still a far piece.

I cut all the way across the bottom and the other side, leaving a flap. Then I sheathed the knife and prayed I wouldn't need it. I had never had to hurt anyone with it, and I didn't want to start now. But what I'd heard hadn't been good.

It was time to put a spoke in the wheel of someone's plans. Since I'm broadest in the shoulders, I stuck my upper body out the window, just to be sure I'd fit. If anyone saw me, I had no hope of escape, anyway. Then I pulled back to grip the outside top of the window opening. First one leg, and then the other . . . not much worse than a hay chute. One I was scrunched in the window, I gripped the bottom and turned to drop myself down the side.

Waiting . . . waiting . . . the next big gust of wind roared by, and I lowered myself to the length of my arms. With any luck, the wind covered any scraping noises, but still . . . my heart quailed at the thought of a hand reaching out to grab my wrist. More wind coming. . . . I let go.

There'd been snow recently; I landed in a drift of powder. Quickly I rolled to my feet and crept along the back of the building. I wanted to get out of sight quickly, but that icy hill was just too steep.

Peeking around the corner, I found that the sky was as clear as the tone of a bell. Stars blanketed the night, bright enough to give a glimmer to the land below. A new moon was fading above . . . and it was a good-sized sliver of an eye.

Two days. At least two days!

This was a place I did not know—not Cat Track Hollow, not Sun-Return. *Lord and Lady, where am I?* Frantically I scanned the skies, moving down behind a dark and silent structure. Finally I recognized Orion, already overhead. Three hours or more since sunset, but on what day?

I turned around, to sight myself on the pole star and the constellations that circled it. The Little Dipper, the Big Dipper dancing on its handle, and—

The knot in my stomach clenched tight as a fist as I traced Draco the dragon through the sky. *Too low, his head's too low on the horizon.* The two bottom stars brushed the treetops beyond. I should've been able to see a crack of night between head and trees, a strip of night dusted with distant stars.

I was breathing faster, and shoved the back of my hand against my mouth. No one could travel that far in only a few days. Not without powerful magic.

When I could think again, I did the only sensible thing I could do. I took a deep breath, and slowly I started slinking northward. *Keep filling these footprints, wind. Carry my scent far, far away.* First I needed a frozen stream to follow; then some shelter. And then there was gonna be some hard thinking.

If I finally got to tears, God willing they were gonna fall a long ways from there.

Wherever "there" was. . . .

NINE

THERE'S ALWAYS AT LEAST A STREAM near a town; people don't build where there's no fresh water. It's harder to feel the difference between the living and non-living in winter, because everything is sleeping, but I'd had my first lessons in grounding in the month of Snow. With a little work, I could distinguish a river bed from a draw.

Having something to look for kept me from panicking.

The howling wind wasn't helping how I felt. I rearranged my scarf to cover my face and plowed on. Since the wind was more friend than foe, it seemed wrong to complain about it. In such a swift, bitter wind, I was less likely to run into a predator . . . either four-legged or two-legged.

North of town I found a stream, a lumpy cap of sticks and frozen water covering its surface. Most of the snow had blown away, leaving glittering black ice reflecting candles of starlight. From the swirling shape of the ice, I guessed that downstream was to the west, and headed that way, walking carefully on the hard, ragged surface.

Downstream would take me to bigger water and a better chance of figuring out this place. There could even be someone to hitch up with—but I'd be careful. I might break down and slip into their thoughts. With as little training as I had, I was in a heap of trouble. I needed all the advantages I could find.

Wherever I was, chances were the spell to suppress aggression in Indians did not stretch this far. Go far enough south, and there were no settlements, only isolated trapping camps and a few forts. Go farther south, and you reached the lands of the Miami or, farther east, the Shawnee.

Miami and Shawnee didn't care for white folks, most times, and with good reason. Farms scared off most of the game, and white trappers were greedy. Truth to tell, most Indians hated whites, and I really couldn't blame them. We were changing their world beyond recognition.

If I got caught by Miami, I'd be lucky to end up a slave or a squaw. If I got caught by Shawnee, I'd probably end up dead.

Even farther south was a great river they called the Ohio, which the curvy Wabash met. Somewhere down that way was Fort Vincennes and a few settlements on the Ohio proper. But they might as well have been on the moon for all I knew how to find them. I couldn't imagine being that far south.

I pushed those thoughts away—thoughts in a dark wood can freeze you in your tracks—and concentrated on placing my feet carefully on the frozen stream. This path felt rock solid, but there was no sense in getting cocky. A mistake in weather like this could cost me my life.

Or my soul? I could build a fire to dry out, but if I couldn't find dry wood, the flames would smoke. Green wood was the quickest way to say "Here I am!" that I could think of, except maybe shouting.

All told, I might have walked as long as an hour. The stream had widened and the bank was getting steeper; boulders loomed far over my head. This was a harsher land than my home . . . the teeth of the earth still poked through now and then. I started watching for some kind of break in the walls.

Finally I found a small opening on the leeward side of some boulders. It would have been damp and useless without the winter ice, but right then it had potential. After sniffing for cat or bear, I squirmed through the crevice into the darkness.

The brutal wind was reduced to a steady draft, though the roar beyond the rocks was almost constant. It was a relief to be out of the gale, but I couldn't relax—this little hollow was filled with icy cold air, and my legs and socks were wet. I needed to somehow get dry.

First I felt carefully for leaves and driftwood—a pocket by a stream should have mounds of it pressed against the stone. Sure enough, I could feel both sticks and leaves. A few of the leaves crunched; I leaned to one side and snapped a small stick in half. So. Maybe I didn't have to go out again that night.

Which meant socks first. *Dry socks can save your life.* I opened my coat to untie my petticoat, and whipped it out. Then I took off my boots and socks, and rubbed my feet until they were dry. The spare socks came out of the coat pockets. Not for the first time was I thankful for the sheepskin flaps Papa had insisted I put over the pocket slits. Next time I'd stuff my extra socks in the inner pocket—close to my body, they would have been warm compared to the air.

The sock problem solved, I checked out the draft and picked a spot for a small fire. If I chose badly, I could build a larger one somewhere else and let my first attempt die. After I'd cleared a place down to sand and stone, I made myself a nice pile of leaves under a teepee of twigs. Then I put myself between the tinder and the crevice, and dug my flint and steel from my hip pouch.

Thank you that I don't have to do this without flint, I thought to any powers that might be listening. Without my hip pouch, I would be burrowing into leaves or a snowdrift, waiting for the storm to pass so I could find the tools I needed. Starting fires with bow and sinew was possible, but I was slow at it. I paused to set my hand on my pouch. *I may start sleeping with you on*, I told it as I bent over my handiwork.

It took one strike of flint to steel to see what I was doing, and three more to get a good-sized spark that took hold. Gently I encouraged the flame, first with leaves and then with dry twigs. I had tried to size wood as I sorted, and now I reached for finger-sized sticks. In a few moments I moved up to bigger sticks, and then I looked for limbs and even logs.

The limbs were pretty dry. I did find a small fallen tree, its dried roots a snarl of vegetable fiber, and I carefully set the stump close to my fire. The draft carried away any smoke, and I couldn't see it, which was a good sign. This spot would do—and I could slowly push that tree into the fireplace. It was soaking wet on one end, which would slow things down. And it wasn't pine—I wouldn't risk burning an old evergreen like that, the sap might explode.

Once I'd cleared a spot on the other side, I set my legs closer to the fire, to dry my pants. The wool steamed gently in the fierce blaze, but it felt warmer than before, which was what counted. I considered stuffing leaves in my coat, but decided to wait. Then I set my boots mouth-open toward the fire and draped the wet socks and petticoat over a pile of branches.

Shelter and a fire . . . I could drink snow if I had to, if slowly. Food would be harder this time of year—I'd have to make some snares and hope for a rabbit or a bobwhite. Pine needles for a nourishing tea. . . .

They were things I understood, and they calmed my frantic heart. Now that I'd put some distance between me and that tiny village, I had some thinking to do.

I was south . . . how far south? Far enough for the circling stars to drop lower to the horizon—not much, but some. At least a hundred miles. I had not yet been taught how to judge distance, but I would have bet I was farther from home than I could imagine. The thought made me shudder, because I knew of only one way to get the power needed for jumping a hundred miles in one fell swoop.

Something had to die to provide that energy . . . a lot of somethings, or one large thing.

I found myself praying that he'd used one of the horses. What if he'd used Mrs. Forrest? Tears slipped down my cheeks, and I didn't know how to stop them. I could not think of a single thing to make myself feel better—except that I wasn't in that storeroom anymore. God willing, they'd not look in until morning.

Could Marta find me?

Yes. I was her apprentice—somehow she had put her mark on me, and I would show up against the background of ordinary life, whether she used her own two eyes or her nighttime sight. But it's not that easy to let your spirit float to another plane, and direction counted. First she'd look close by, in case somebody'd been looking for a white woman for a wife. I was tall enough to be mistaken for a woman.

She'd have to check for my body, probably by asking Death if I'd entered the next realm.

Erik would be missing, too . . . I hoped. If he had the power to jump back and forth between Cat Track Hollow and where I was, then I could lie down and die right then and there. I had to believe that Erik had fled with me and did not intend to return.

With Erik gone, Marta might make a connection, no matter what the Hudsons said about his vanishing. Marta would not think I'd run off with him willingly.

Of course, the Hudsons might not know this cousin as well as we'd all thought. . . .

Then the hunt would begin. She might ask other practitioners to help, ones she knew. Surely she'd tell Cory and Shaw I was gone. But the expanding circle of their search would take a long time . . . could take months.

There was one thing I could try, but the idea scared me. Although I had had no lessons of Air, I did have some talent with mind speech, talent Cory had identified and Marta had nurtured. I could try throwing my thoughts to Marta. Right then she was the one I was most tied to; I needed no ritual for my mind to seek hers.

But others might hear me call into the mists. And if they could hear me, they could follow my thoughts back to my body. . . . I straightened as something occurred to me. If Marta could hear me, then I could hear *her*. By now she would be looking for me. If it had been two days, she knew I was alive and not within a day of her home. So she'd be sending out a call, trying to reach me.

I could sit still as a field mouse under the owl's wing and listen hard. If I was lucky, I might hear her call me. If I was lucky.

After gauging the fire and making sure the clothes weren't getting too hot, I settled down to open my thoughts to anyone seeking Alfreda Alethia. My only prayer was that Erik Hudson and his friends weren't already looking for me.

Being receptive to someone else's distant thoughts meant keeping your mind from focusing. It was hard to relax—I was pulled tight as a snag in the warp of a weaving. But I stared into the flames and let them fill my head. After a while I could sense the slow, sleepy dreams of tiny, furred creatures, and the dark, hungry thoughts of a wolf pack. There were big cats out there, too—more than one. But they had no interest in hunting, not in this biting wind. Even the owls were roosting.

I could feel a jumble of sleepers south of me—many of them folks with power. That was interesting, so many with the Gift together. There was a native healer performing a winter ritual, somewhere to the north. . . .

There were no thoughts that I recognized.

ও𝒟ও

I don't know how long I sat there, trapped in a daze of my own fear and loneliness. Perhaps you have known solitude, but until that moment I had never been totally alone before. Not even when I spent the night in the forest, when Papa tested our woodcraft. That time, Shaw's momma had ghosted by, hidden in her shape-shifting form of a wolf.

But this night I would stay awake and tend my fire. There wasn't enough debris in the cave to make a nest like a squirrel's. The next day I'd keep moving and look for a good place to hide a leaf hut. I'd also keep an ear to the trace that was blazed to the east . . . it was probably the closest thing around to a real trail. I might get lucky and see folks on it—or better, hear folks talking.

And just to be cautious . . . I let my thoughts slip out, floating on the warm air currents circling around me, seeking the mind of an animal. Finally I stumbled into an owl who was actually sitting out on a branch, hidden behind a trunk from most of the wind. Hiding in the mind of an owl would do nicely. . . .

Eventually my stone cave got so warm that I took off my coat. I spent the night poking at my fire, my consciousness linked with a rare snowy owl, hooting softly into the gusts and listening for the scamper of a field mouse. To my surprise, on the morning side of midnight the owl actually caught a few foolish souls who surfaced into the dying wind.

I decided to heed the lesson of the owl. Sometimes you were safe, but the owl convinced you that you weren't safe. Then you moved . . . and you died.

There was the problem. I had no real idea where I was or whether anyone in the region would be helpful to me. There are some people to whom you simply can't say, "I was magicked away from my home." I could go days, weeks farther from Marta, without even realizing it. I could end up lost in the wilderness that Mr. Jefferson sent Lewis and Clark into . . . or I could end up in Ohio somewhere.

I could get caught by Erik Hudson and his friends.

So. Unless I heard the name of a fort I recognized, or could figure out how far east or west I was, I was stuck. My plan was as good as anything else I could do. Staying warm and dry was the best idea—then I'd think about food. I wouldn't starve, not for a month or more, but I didn't think this place would be trapped out, either.

And if necessary, I could live on mice. Wolves did, when bigger game was scarce.

Really.

And you'd be surprised how good mouse stew can be when you're *really* hungry.

⋅ 🐾 ⋅

The wind had indeed died down by morning, though the intense cold remained. I let my owl slip off into sleep, while I shook myself awake for a long day. I could reach out of the crevice with my tiny wooden cup to scoop snow out of a pocket in the rocks. The flakes took a while to melt, but water would help dull the hunger until my stomach learned to do without.

Time had no meaning in a forest . . . and that was just as well. The most dangerous thing about survival was worrying about the future. If you looked too far ahead (or behind), you'd be buried under the fear. One step at a time, I could walk to the China Sea— Papa sometimes said that.

One step at a time, I would survive.

My fire was out, the ashes growing cold. It was time to move on. Crawling toward the growing light, I pulled myself out of the crevice onto the boulder by the stream. Sitting up, I sniffed the brisk air, checking for other fires, for animals . . . for unwashed human bodies.

No—no humans on the slight wind, no other burning wood. Time to get some height on the situation. I started crawling up the rocks, heading for the top.

The rocky bank of the stream wasn't high enough to top the trees, but leafless branches let me see for miles in every direction. I made sure I was sitting on my coat, and settled against the southern face of the boulders. Tucking my hands inside my sheepskin, I let my eyes grow unfocused, looking for movement.

It must have been several hours later that I slowly stretched and moved to leave my perch. I'd seen a great deal from my stone hill—I knew the major game trails and runs for several miles now. The forest was pretty old, full of beech, oak, and chestnut, but there were clearings to be seen. That's where I would look for rabbits and mice. Deer might visit those meadows to scrape down to withered grass. Animals were like humans—they lived between things. Where field and forest met, where water and land met, there you would find animals—and the humans who preyed on them.

There was neither movement nor tracks on that wide trace to the east. If it was a human trail, it was not traveled daily . . . unless that bluster the night before had been the tail end of a blizzard. In that case, people might still be digging out. I carefully chose a deer run, and then slid down the shiny rocks to where it reached the stream. This run was hard-packed snow with some gravel mixed in . . . my tracks would be scarce there.

As I started down the meandering track, I realized that deep inside I already understood what was different about this time spent in the wilderness.

For the first time, I understood how the rabbits felt.

⁂

Turned out I didn't need to start a leaf hut this early in my stay—something I was glad of, since hiding the hut might be hard. Better to wait until I could smell snow coming, and let a blizzard cover my presence.

Several hours north of where I'd spent the night, I crossed another stream and found myself a big old oak hunched at the base of a mountain's teeth. It was so wide I couldn't begin to put my arms around it.

The oak had an opening about shoulder high, filled with snow, and there were evergreens and other oaks crowded around it, the thick pines and cedar trees blocking most of the wind. I leaned into the crevice and carefully started to dig. If this hollow went down far enough—and I didn't hit a hibernating animal. . . .

Winter must have caught the region on the hop, for at the very bottom there were remnants of old nests and beds, but nothing was currently inside the tree.

First I surveyed the entire oak where it leaned into its baby mountain. It didn't look like it was going to blow over any time soon—the sides were still thick and sound, the roots gripping the frozen earth. With the help of a couple of good stepping stones, I could climb in and down with scarcely any trouble.

Evergreen boughs. I needed a thick mat of evergreen boughs for the floor of the chamber. Then dry oak leaves, if I could find any under a cap of snow.

Lining the chamber took some time, because I went a distance from the copse of trees to break off my branches. I avoided cutting—a knife slash doesn't look like much of anything except blade work. Eventually someone might come looking for me; I would leave as little evidence of my passing as I could.

My petticoat sure came in handy. Once I found a bunch of leaves and dug down to the dry ones, I could load up the flannel and make only a few trips. It still took more than a dozen bundles to get the thickness that I wanted.

Now, obviously I couldn't have a fire in there. But I'd have a warm, dry sleeping place, and that was the most important thing. There would be time later to think about a permanent camp—or camps.

Unfortunately.

There was a knot sticking into the oak hollow within arm's reach, and that was where I set my cup of snow to melt. It took a while, but, as I'd hoped, when free of the wind, the air warmed enough to give me a full cup of water. Then I tossed broken and crushed pine needles and oak buds into the water to steep. If I could find sassafras roots, even better. It doesn't sound like much, and the taste was horrible, but "winter tea" can keep you going a long time. It's best to dice up the ingredients and steep them a few minutes in boiling water, but I'd get something out of this, and the next day I'd set up a campsite.

In the meantime, I'd spotted a white oak, and white-oak acorns could be mighty good eating. Since it was already getting dark, I'd have to wait on those cattails I'd passed down by the stream—the horn-shaped sprouts growing from the tangled rootstock could be eaten raw, if nothing else had found them first.

While I was up in the oak harvesting acorns, I let my mind drift, looking for another animal to hide my sleeping mind. I was getting tired, and I didn't think I could stay up two nights straight.

An owl brushed past my thought—not the snowy from the night before, but a great horned owl. He was alone, and long-eared owls liked company in winter, so I was pretty sure he was a great horned. He was a good mile away, already hunting, in pursuit of a rabbit he'd flushed. I tried to take note of his direction—I could set a snare on a run near the rabbit burrow.

The owl landed with a terrific thump, probably breaking the animal's back. He carried it up to a big branch to eat . . . and suddenly I heard human voices.

Wildly I looked around, trying to keep a grip on both the tree and the mind of the bird. No one in sight. . . .

The owl. Owls have excellent hearing—they can find mice hidden under leaves in total darkness. Human words were so much noise to the owl, but I understood what was being said.

A spot of warmth grew under my breastbone. I had a way to gather information. Marta hadn't told me about this . . . yet. Could I even see through the eyes of an animal?

Hanging on to the tree limbs, I quietly cracked two acorns and listened to two people leading a horse, greeting a third person walking on snowshoes. I was lucky. The acorns were sweet, I could eat them without soaking them. The owl was busy with his meal, so I didn't try to borrow his eyes—I was just glad he was loaning me his ears.

"You'll reach a cleared trail in another hour or so," one man was saying. "We drag logs to scrape and pack the snow, once you get close to Heaven's Road. Down by the river bend there's a trading post where you can stock up if you're minded."

Did I know that fellow? I'd heard them speak so few words. . . .

"Thank'ee," a grizzled old voice said, and I heard the horse stop walking.

"Have you met anyone else today? We're missing a young woman, separated from friends of her family." The familiar-sounding man's words were careful, as if he'd practiced saying them a while.

"No," a younger man replied, his voice not as gravelly as his companion's. "Not so much as a deer."

There was a pause, a bit longer than you'd expect, but then people were careful meeting strangers . . . you never knew. It could be an ambush, and these men had a horse and surely had rifles—valuable possessions in our world. Finally the lone man said, "If you should hear word of her, the Hudson family would be very pleased at the news. Erik Hudson would reward anyone who helped rescue the child."

Now, that was interesting . . . I was worth a reward?

"We'll remember," the unknown young voice said, his manner even and quiet.

I could hear the passage of the snowshoes as the man from the village moved on. The other two paused, and it was several minutes before they spoke.

"Damnation. I was afraid we were too close to the Hudson camp," the younger voice muttered. He sounded real worried all of a sudden.

"Lord protect that poor child if the witches of Hudson-on-the-Bend get hold of her," was the rough response. "Haven't heard of Erik Hudson . . . must be a young one. If the Keeper of Souls was expecting the child, Erik-boy may need those prayers himself."

"I say we circle this place and head for the trading post. We may run into Hudsons, but that way we won't pass their fort." This was urgent—the young man was growing anxious.

"If we can still get out of the region with our horse and furs," came a rumbled reply.

There may have been more, but I didn't hear it. I was suddenly so scared my hands could barely grip the branches.

Witches. True witches were either harmless practitioners or Christian heretics. When power and a name were mentioned fearfully, then black sorcery, not witchcraft, was at work.

Sorcerers. I had sorcerers looking for me. *Lord and Lady of Light*.

I didn't remember climbing out of that white oak, but I found my way back to my hollow, picking up a couple more rocks on the way to make my steppingstones look more like a natural pile of rubble.

Somehow I took care of personal things, at a distance from my hidey-hole, and managed to dig my way down into my thick pile of leaves. Once I was sitting deep in my hollow, I sipped my cold winter tea and tried to calm my beating heart.

Too new . . . I was too new to the breathing exercises. It took much longer than it should have for me to stop shaking.

I hadn't realized until then that I *was* shaking.

My throat had gone dry; I took another sip of tea and tried to keep a leaf from falling on my face. *Why? What can they want with me? Did I somehow interfere with a spell they were casting?* Questions spun around in my head like children linked in a circle. Answers . . . I needed answers.

There was no one to ask. Even if I could find someone who would tell me the things I needed to know, anyone with power and training could squeeze that person dry. News of me would be everywhere before I could blink . . . and the sorcerer might hurt or kill the person who told me about the Hudsons.

No, this was my burden. I couldn't drag any strangers into it.

I don't know how long I sat there, my thoughts scampering like spring lambs, but when I came out of my daze, it was full darkness. The great horned owl still echoed in the back of my head, hooting his inquiry to any who would listen. Running like a chant through my head was the phrase *What am I going to do*? I had so little magic, almost nothing in the face of sorcerers. Who could answer my questions without fear of death?

Then I knew the answer, and I shivered at my own daring. There was only one place to turn.

I would have to summon Death to ask my questions.

Now I understood the dream I'd had the night before Shaw came to Cat Track Hollow. No wonder I'd felt haste and fear in my dream self. I had been summoning Death. It was a dangerous idea, and might prove useless—Marta taught me that Death could not volunteer information, and my questions were jumbled.

Perhaps that was all to the good. Erik Hudson might think to ask Death if I had joined the dark realm, but I doubted anyone would think of trying to use Death to track a fledgling practitioner.

Clinging to my cup, I crawled out of my warm nest and headed for the wide stream I had crossed earlier in the day. I didn't have to look for that boulder—it would almost come to me. I'd stuffed a bunch of leaves down inside my coat and petticoat, and I snapped off deadwood on my way to the water. Right now I had a powerful need for a fire.

Sure enough, there was a rough boulder in the center of the stream, a huge one, that would take me several paces to cross. Wind had scoured the top clean of snow and ice, so climbing it was easy. I'd cleaned and filled my cup before I started up—now I sat in a puff of wind, letting my warm breath melt the heaped snow. Then I wedged the cup between my knees and started building my fire.

The boulder was not in a direct line of sight from that distant road, or I would have looked for a sheltered area to build. A fire was essential; I needed blood, and I wasn't going to risk using my hunting knife without heating it. I didn't need to use any of the precious tinder in my hip pouch—those oak leaves were dry enough to burn from a spark. The limbs I'd broken off caught well . . . soon I'd have a fine blaze.

My cup was full of icy water. I pulled out the hunting knife Papa gave me, and placed the tip in the flame for a little while. Then I waved it to cool the metal. It wasn't the heat that was necessary, it was having been in fire. One of Marta's teachers had discovered that heating metal was like washing your hands in boiling herb-tinged water—people didn't get sick as often when you cut out arrowheads or bullets. Hot metal was only to stop bleeding.

Once I thought it'd cooled enough, I used the wicked, well-polished blade to break the skin on the little finger of my right hand. *Ouch.* The knife was warm and sharp, but it did its job. I let the blood fall into the cup, and swirled it to mix.

I'd changed one thing about my hip pack after my last weird dream—I'd added a horsehair brush. The brush from my pouch was now in my hand, but I asked nothing yet. I merely went to the edges of the stone and painted a thin circle around the top of the boulder. Then the second circle, so delicately I didn't run out of water. It took more snow from a crevice to finish the names of the angels, but I had enough blood to do the job right.

Marta said wards weren't necessary when you summoned Death. I hoped she was right. With water, wind and fire as protection, it was as close to warding as I could get.

Carefully I took my pouch of tobacco from my pack and opened the strings. Only the smallest bit of tobacco, no more—it was the odor, not the amount that counted. The rest of the water I set aside. Opening and closing the invitation . . . I was as ready as I could be. One last look at the blanket of stars flung across the night—

A pine branch popped at me, drawing me back to the moment. I sprinkled the tobacco over the top of the small fire, and let the smell of burning oak and tobacco fill my head. My clothes would be smoky for sure, after this . . . but animals didn't notice smoke. Not with wildfire always running through a forest.

This was as calm as I was going to get. . . . "I call upon you, Azrael," I whispered aloud, "most compassionate of spirits, who knows all that I am and might ever be. I, Alfreda,"—I certainly wasn't going to use my Wise Arts name aloud in a strange place!— "come before you for answers and for service." Now how could I phrase this, when I wasn't exactly asking for help with healing?

I let the rest of my tobacco pinch flutter into my small fire. "In a circle drawn with the wine of life, I ask you to look upon me and listen to my petition. I am in need of great healing, for I am lost amid dangers, and my heart withers in fear. Come to me, great spirit, and impart your wisdom to me, or I will not survive the test before me."

The wind whipped at my fire, sending a few sparks skyward, but I'd used very little pine, to keep distractions to a minimum. After a bit, I lifted my eyes from the flames and looked across the burning wood.

There was someone seated on the other side.

My eyes filled with tears, because it was Grandsir, gone several summers now. He was twinkling at me the way he always used to when he was pleased with me. Grandfather was wearing the

ancient wool breeches he'd loved so much, held up by a strip of
deerskin, and the shirt I'd embroidered for him. I could make out
the crooked daisy on his collar, peeping out from under his long
white beard. His hair was still red, if flicked with silver, as it'd been
at his death.

"Am I in danger?" I asked him—it.

"Yes," came its rumbling bass voice, still strong, like before
Grandsir's last illness.

"Are the Hudsons black sorcerers?" I said boldly, taking the
next fence at a canter.

"Yes."

I tell you, the sinking feeling in my stomach was eating a hole in
my chest, if you get my drift.

"Why did Erik Hudson steal me from Cat Track Hollow?" I
wished I had some idea of where I was going with my questions,
but right now I was a flock of birds startled into flight. I couldn't
light on anything.

"You were the first person of real power he had found," Death
replied evenly.

"Why does he want people of power?" *Does he intend to kill me
for a spell?* That question I was afraid to ask.

Death looked thoughtful for a moment. "Power calls to power,"
was the low reply. "If the powers are closely related, the children
born may be sickly or feeble. If there is no power, the talent lessens
in each generation."

I thought about that for a while. Then it made a horrid sort of
sense. "You mean he wants a *wife*? I'm only thirteen years old, I'm
not even bleeding yet!"

"Yes, for him or another. And yes."

I wasn't too addled to notice that Death had confirmed a
statement. Huh. That might be useful, later. . . . "Have the Hudsons
done this before?"

"Yes."

"They want wives—spouses—with power," I added.

"Yes."

Well . . . Death wasn't supposed to be a great conversationalist.
"Am I younger than they usually take?"

"No."

I let my gaze drop to the fire, and shoved another limb into it. That made no sense. Why take children to be wives and husbands—assuming they also took boys on occasion?

"Why do they want children, and not adults?" I tried.

Once again there was a long pause. Was this finally a question that Death wouldn't answer? Was it too important to my future?

Could I change my future?

"Power without training means little resistance," Death said finally.

I mulled on this a while. Ah—they took apprentices with little training. In fact, hadn't Marta said something in Erik Hudson's presence that made it sound like I'd started my lessons way late? Perfect for them—almost old enough for children, but not yet trained. So they could train me in their blood magic?

I tried to make a slightly different question out of it. "Is the fact that we can't put up much of a fight the only reason they want young, untrained Gifted?"

"No."

Clenching my teeth, I went right on. "Why else?"

"There are spells that can compel loyalty and service. And great powers can draw on the strength of weaker powers."

Uh-oh. I wrapped my arms around myself and squeezed hard. Maybe they weren't interested in teaching me anything . . . maybe they just wanted to use my strength like my papa would use a mule. The cold ran right up my spine and grabbed the back of my neck.

The only reason I was still free was that whatever Erik had used on me was so strong, he must have thought he'd nigh killed me. And then he'd gone for a healer? It was only luck that I knew how to make winter serve me.

"Will Erik give up looking for me after awhile?" I said hopefully.

"No."

"Why not?" You'd think if I could hide from them for several days, they'd think I was long gone.

"The Keeper of Souls has tasted your power. He wants you."

That name again. I swear, it gave me the shivers just to hear Death say those words. "Who is the Keeper? Erik?" I finally said.

"The first Hudson."

Frowning, I asked, "You mean the grandfather of the group?"

"Harold Hudson is the eldest, the first sorcerer."

"And the Hudsons do whatever the Keeper wants?"

"Yes." Death sounded implacable.

"Does he rule them because they respect his training?" I decided to ask.

"The Keeper rules through fear. His talent is great and spans many lives of men. They fear to be next."

"That's not possible," I said automatically. "Unless he's a vampire or something." Death did not speak. "He's not a vampire, is he?" I heard the fear in my voice. Dear Lord and Lady, a vampire strong enough to control a small village of descendants? I was in big trouble.

"No."

I took deep breaths to slow my breathing. Not a vampire . . . how could he have the talent of many lives? I was pretty sure Death meant more than a gathering of knowledge, or it wouldn't have used the phrase it did. But even sorcerers were mortal—flesh could only be pushed so far. Unless. . . .

"Has the Keeper of Souls discovered how to become immortal?" I whispered.

Would it answer?

"There are several ways. He has found one of them."

Black crept into my vision, and I dug my fingernails into my palms to keep from fainting. Now was *not* the time to have vapors, for heaven's sake! *Stop it! Marta would expect you to stay calm. There's a time and place to fret, and this isn't it.*

"How?" I decided to ask. I didn't think Death would tell me—it didn't seem like something it wanted spread around—but I'd never know if I didn't try.

Silence. I listened to the wind as it picked up, and felt my great owl swoop silently through the night, a mouse in his talons. So, Death wouldn't tell me, except that it was possible, and that I had a cunning enemy old in magic.

"The Keeper has learned to transfer his soul into a body born of his line. When the time is right, he keeps the new body." The statement was abrupt, and sounded odd, coming in Grandsir's rumble, for he never spoke to me that way—not in my memory.

Sweet Lord . . . that meant the Keeper of Souls could go on as long as a child of his line was around. Was his original body long gone?

Suddenly I couldn't breathe.

Was Erik a young man . . . or an ancient man hiding in a young man's body?

No. I forced air from my lungs. Death had said the Keeper was not Erik. But that didn't mean the Keeper couldn't take Erik's body.

"Is that why Erik is so desperate to find me?" The words came out harsh, like the rasp of a raven. "Because the Keeper might get mad and take his body?"

Death gave me a long look. "The Keeper would seek you himself if his family failed. And he would need a younger body for the search."

I tossed more wood onto my fire and stared into the flames. My head was numb—I just couldn't think. Sorcerers were looking for me, and were not likely to give up. . . .

"Which way is Cat Track Hollow from here?" It had nothing to do with healing, unless you counted keeping me in good health, but so far Death had been pretty talkative.

"Northeast."

All right, then. "How far?"

"Over two hundred fifty English miles," came Grandsir's soft rumble.

I stared at the apparition, a strange, high-pitched buzz ringing in my ears. Over two hundred . . . that was farther than New York to Philadelphia! That was over *twice* as far as New York to Philadelphia! My eyes grew unfocused as I considered, made plans, then stopped and thought again.

A forest was a good friend to me. I could find or build shelter, scrounge food and even trap animals. But could I do it with someone looking for my tracks?

Could I move without leaving psychic traces?

I shoved fear into the back of my mind. No time for that—no time at all. This far away, it made no difference if I waited for Marta's call or headed home myself. We were talking months before I'd be found.

If I started heading north, they might jump over me as they widened their search, but they'd hear the echo of where I'd been, and follow it to its source.

Home. Just knowing I'd be going in the right direction made my heart ache. Home was where you found people who wanted you near, and I was too far from those I loved.

I'd heard enough. It was time to thank Azrael and make my plans. I had a warm nest waiting for me, and I didn't want to fight some roaming animal for it.

☙ ❦ ☙

That night, buried in my column of leaves, I dreamt of a place I had not yet seen, the snug pegged log house my cousin Cory shared with his mother. But it was not Cory I was seeing—it was Shaw, restless in the night, sitting by the kitchen firepit and heating a kettle of water. He'd pulled on his pants and loose shirt without the vest, and was warming his bare feet on the hearthstone. Shaw looked very tired, as if a nightmare had roused him.

There was movement in the shadows, and Cory lumbered into the firelight, moving like a sleepy grizzly. "A bad dream?" he asked simply, scratching through his beard.

"Yes," Shaw murmured, pulling the word out almost like a soft hiss. "I can't find Allie."

"Hum?" Cory still sounded half asleep, but the dark eyes looking at Shaw were quite alert.

"Usually I can feel where she is—if she is behind me or ahead of me. But suddenly she just . . . vanished."

Cory's face grew impassive. "Is she dead?"

"I don't think so," Shaw replied. He looked over at the big man. "But what else?"

"A couple ceremonies you haven't learned yet . . . and blood magic." Shaw straightened at the last words. "If someone used blood magic in her presence, the taint would sicken her aura for a bit. Maybe that's why you can't find her. She doesn't feel the same right now."

"Blood magic? How?" I could tell Shaw was angry—his jaw was set and his eyes glinted silver despite the shadows.

"You said a witch was up to mischief in the Hollow," Cory said reasonably.

Shaw shook his head in furious denial. "She was nothing. Marta could deal with it without leaving her own land."

Cory sighed and seemed to stare into the fire for a while. "Something caused a power shift in the region. I think that's what woke me." He leaned forward and lit a spill, setting it to a candle on the mantle. "Come on, then. We'd best write Marta and find out what's up. Too much curiosity is not a restful thing."

They moved away from the firepit toward an opening in the wall, and then my dream darkened, and I saw no more.

⁂

When I woke in the false winter dawn, I knew I carried summer in my heart. I had people I loved, who loved me.

Might it be so forever.

TEN

MY GREAT-GRANDMOTHER WAS AN OLD, old woman when my momma's family made the move West. When Momma was a little girl, before I was ever thought of, Gran was the wise woman for the region. Those who believed in her Gift were constant visitors to the Schell farm. What they wanted most from her were glimpses into the future.

Gran warned them to be careful what they asked for, but they didn't listen.

You can't refuse to prophesy in the face of a question. It's said you risk losing the Gift if you do. When they asked a second time, she would tell them what she could see. It wasn't always useful knowledge—where you were viewing things *from* was mighty important—but folks kept asking.

One time I tried to talk to her about why people came to listen. She merely told me that folks wanted to know when storms were coming, so they could prepare.

"What's it like, seeing the future?" I'd asked her.

Gran had given me one of her long looks. Had she already seen snips of my life? Finally she told me, "Mostly dark. Shadows can be so long, they arrive before the sun."

The days following my summoning of Death made her words come back to me. I was trapped in shadows . . . and I'd had no vision of life beyond the moment.

My head start dwindled quickly—I knew people were looking for me. Voices floated on the breeze, and I found evidence of snowshoes. I was careful to walk frozen streams and rocky outcrops when I could, so I wouldn't leave tracks, but that made for slow going. Half the time I was looking for secure hiding places; the other half I was looking for food to scavenge.

They knew they were close to me . . . and they were destroying my snares. One trap yanked from its tether might be an animal pulling loose, but all three? They wanted me hungry—which I was—but they were in for a surprise if they thought I'd give up.

I'd worked my way down to a good-sized river and was following it north. When pushed, Death had given me some pretty specific instructions. The first was simple—follow the river against the current until it branched. I knew to take the left fork, but it became a stream at that point—it eventually would go east, and I wanted north. Then I would question Death again. For whatever its reasons, Death had decided to help me.

I must admit that made me uneasy. But Death never lied . . . although Death might not volunteer everything it knew about something.

Trouble was brewing. A ward of some kind would hide me from Indians, but other magic-users could sense a ritual ward. So if any of the Hudsons were helping in the search, they'd be able to focus on my spell.

I could survive in a winter forest, or I could hide from magic-users. I wasn't sure I could do both.

The intense cold had eased some—the great dark river was flowing steadily on its course south to the mighty Ohio. Broken ice was pushed toward shore, where it froze each night into fantastic mounds and peaks. With the river for company, I never felt alone. The water seemed to sing to me in a young girl's voice, and I felt that was a good sign.

I was six days out when my heart rose in my throat and showed me that I was in strange waters. With my thoughts tucked behind first the mind of an owl and then that of a hawk, I had left the

Hudsons and their friends stumbling the night before. The boulders lining the riverbank at this point were dry enough for easy walking, and I was busy thinking about a quail dinner. I'd managed to sneak up on a covey while they were scratching at the edge of a meadow, and I'd used a heavy stick to brain several of them before the flock took off.

Properly gutted, they were hanging off a sinew line while I walked. Birds just taste better after they've hung a bit. That night I planned to have a fire and a real supper. Acorns are fine, but they get old after a while. In that cold, cooked quail would last for days.

I was debating how to move around a huge stone outcropping— it might have been time to walk the ground next to the rocks— when I heard voices in the wood to the east. Sound carried easily in the crisp winter air.

"We got no sign she's this far west," came one loud exclamation.

I was belly down on the rocks and crawling into a crevice before anyone could answer him.

"Keeper said her shadow was west," was the steady reply.

"Huh. And how can that old man see her shadow when the sun hasn't shown a face in weeks?" said the first. "I ain't seen her shadow."

I peered over the lip of the stone, looking for the two men. Up the curve of the bank and beyond I saw the boughs of a cedar shudder, the snow slipping from higher up to fall on branches below.

"Damn wet," muttered the first voice, his words followed by the sound of a heap of snow falling. "We been at this all morning and then some. I say we bide a spell."

I wasn't ready to swear, even to myself, but I sure wished I could. A perch between two cold boulders was not my hiding place of choice. At least my mind was still hawk-masked. Would they come down to the river for water, or look for a stream? Would they stop and build a fire?

"The widow Cole has a good fire going—I saw smoke from the chimney," came the slow-talking second voice. "She can add to this bread and meat we're packing."

"Maybe," grumbled the sour one. "And maybe a blind woman don't bother to cook a meal at midday. She sure don't have no love of Hudson's crew."

"We can ask her if she's seen the girl." After this statement there was a coarse laugh and a crash of snow and ice, and I figured that meant the complainer had picked up his pace.

I fumbled around for my birds and grabbed the sinew. It was finally my turn to track someone. These fellows and their friends had kept me moving hard for almost a week. I was tired and past hunger, but I now had a new hope.

There was someone out there in this part of the woods, someone who didn't care for the Hudsons. Someone who had been blinded by the Hudsons? Perhaps I could use these birds to trade for a water bag—something that I could put in my shirt and warm with my own heat. Melting snow took a long time, and I was tired of scrubbing frost off rocks with my petticoat—it tasted of the material.

And if she was blind, she could honestly say she hadn't seen me. I wouldn't have to barter her safety for my own.

❧·⫱·❧

When I speak of a log cabin, you may think of a big structure, because both my parents' and Marta's homes were large. But they hadn't started out that way—they were added on to as the families grew. Most houses were very small, and stayed that way while the children were young. Only after the kids were big enough to help farm was there time to build an addition.

There was no way one old woman could have built this home by herself. But someone had built it, small but snug, well chinked with dried mud. I could have lain down in it twice head to toe in either direction—no more. A small lean-to was attached to the side of the cabin, filled with things like a washboard, trays for separating milk, tack for a horse . . . one pregnant she-goat.

No sense in taking any chances—I crept past the shed and to the solid side of the cabin, walking carefully on a fallen log and the woodpile. The breeze was just brisk enough to cover any scraping noises I made.

A half hogshead was turned over on a frame, to keep it from filling with snow and ice. I slid under the rack and up into the wood barrel, letting the shadows swallow me. As I'd hoped, I could hear the voices of the men inside as they questioned the owner of the cabin. Her replies were soft—I could make out only a word or two.

"She don't know anything, Rafe," said the whiny one. "There's nothing in her mind about any visiting girls."

So. The steady one kept the irritating one around because he was Gifted. Was Whiny a Hudson?

"Then pour us some tea, Mz. Cole, and we'll be on our way," the other said in his even voice. It reminded me a bit of that young trapper back on the road . . . I hoped the Hudsons hadn't caught up with him.

The men didn't leave at once, of course—not with that nice fire burning. I could smell oak and applewood smoke, of all things, masking other odors around me. It took me a bit longer to realize that there was very little snow against that side of the building. The stone and mud wall just beyond my reach was the chimney.

Oh, glory! I'd been comfortable enough, doing my best to keep dry, but real warmth was a treat. I hadn't had a fire in three days. I settled on the frozen earth under the hogshead and extended my legs so my boots were pressed against the dark stone. Now, if those fellows would leave in a different direction. . . . I had snow heaped just beyond, a pretty good barricade against anyone noticing me under the barrel, but I couldn't take chances. I'd have to pull my feet back under once I heard those men leave.

The voices inside had grown louder again when I noticed the hazy, foglike patch floating near the chimney. Having nothing else to do but listen, I watched the mist swirl in place, stretching and then squeezing itself tightly. It was almost relaxing—I felt as if I were watching fluffy clouds tumbling like balls of cotton. . . .

It took the form of a man. I felt my throat shut tight. A third Hudson on the loose, tracking me? *What kind of spell—?*

Then I realized I was looking at a ghost.

As I tilted my head and peeked up at the softly glowing apparition, details began to form. Stiff leather boots, a suggestion of fringe on the deerskin jacket, a battered tricorner hat in hand. . . . By the time a long, thick beard formed, if I'd known the man before his death, I'd probably have recognized him.

The spirit hovered there, as if waiting for an invitation to enter the building. In the sharp, clear air, I could hear the cabin door opening and the two men walking back into the early afternoon light. Not quite sunny, but almost—you could tell the sun was up there, behind the heavy sky.

What would the ghost do next? I sat still, fascinated, wondering if it was aware of me. Even as the thought crossed my mind, the spirit turned my way. If he chose, a wooden half keg was no barrier to spectral sight. The old man did not stoop to look under at me—I felt him staring right through the oak planks. I couldn't pull the same trick without considerable effort, and I wasn't going to reach the astral plane during the day.

The sound of crunching snow told me that my trackers were moving on, toward the river. I let the footsteps fade into the distance before moving to stand. As if in response, the ghost nodded my way and passed through the wall, vanishing to my sight.

Well, here goes nothing, I thought grimly. It was unlikely the ghost would attack me, as long as I didn't threaten the current owner of the cabin. Most ghosts didn't have the power to do anything but frighten people. Fear and belief made them more tangible—and the more solid they were, the more they could harm you.

A few kinds of ghosts, like *utburds*, were very dangerous. If you met a demon ghost, you needed cold iron and running water at hand . . . and prayer. If it was an old spirit, you hadn't a chance without prayer and magic.

Slinging my birds over my shoulder, I moved carefully around the cabin, keeping my grip on that hawk's mind. He was currently sitting in the top of a beech tree, watching and listening for any signs of movement. I hadn't tried yet to look through a bird's eyes, but if I had been able to do it, I'm sure I would have seen those two men pushing their way through the undergrowth.

Don't come back, I thought at them. I would offer my birds to this woman, in exchange for something to carry water. I'd even pluck the silly things for her . . . if I could figure out how to speak to her without endangering her. Could she not think about me? If Whiny could look into her mind to see remnants of visits. . . .

Maybe I should wait until dark and swap her the birds for a watertight pouch.

The decision was made for me. As I hesitated a few steps from the door, it was pulled open, dragging on its leather hinges. A tiny, elderly woman stood in the doorway, dressed in the full skirts of a generation ago, the faded red muslin now a rich burnt orange. She wore a lace shawl, a fine one, perhaps even from over sea, and a cap trimmed in a lace pattern I did not recognize. Her thick white hair was braided down her back, but it was under her shawl, perhaps to keep it from falling into the fireplace.

Her eyes looked as if they were filmed by fresh cream. I wondered if she could even distinguish light from shadow. How had she been blinded? A spell? Had they forced her to stare into the sun? What should I say to her, if anything?

"Joseph tells me everything," she said in a soft, pleasant voice touched with the shires of the old islands. "He suggested that I might enjoy inviting a few other ghosts in for the day. So I, Hannah Cole, open my home to all without ill intent in their soul, that I may feel once more the presence of friends." With that, the woman turned her back and walked away from the open door.

Well . . . either she was getting a bit odd, living in the forest, or she was crafty as can be. If she thought of me as a ghost (after all, no young girl would be out in the wilds alone), then she would remember my visit as merely that of another ghost.

There was a third possibility. Some folks could see ghosts . . . perhaps their presence could be felt as well. Maybe Hannah Cole did know when a spirit was around her; maybe Joseph even made audible sounds. If so, then if she did not touch me, I was merely another rustling spirit come to call.

I paused for a moment, letting my inner senses get a feel for Hannah and her tiny home. No, Hannah was not an active user of magic. There was no echo of power in that place. But still, she was not in the common way. I walked into the cabin and closed the door behind me.

ও𝒟ও

The shadowy one-room building was stuffed to the eaves with hooks for hanging and chests for tucking things away. A big bed was shoved in one corner, and a work table stood opposite. I could faintly smell herbs and smoked pork. There was no odor of tallow or beeswax . . . no one there had needed extra light for a long time. The floor under my boots was polished smooth—there was no sound of grit between leather and wood.

There was a pot of beans soaking near the fireloft, and I found Hannah moving them to a pot hook. A second, larger pot hung to one side of the fire, its lid tight against escaping steam. I could smell brown bread cooking.

The ghost was sitting on a chair set next to the fireplace, across from the only rocker.

"Joseph told me that the forest was buzzing about a powerful child taken by the Hudson clan," Hannah said to the leaping flames. Settling in her rocker, she leaned forward to stir her dinner. Adding a handful of lean salt pork, she continued: "Seems young Erik thought he'd poisoned the girl, and went off for a healer. He chose lazy watchdogs for her, poor boy. Now she's put a spoke in his wheel and vanished like morning dew. Seems she has a talent for woodcraft. At any rate, there's been little sign of her."

I kept quiet and paused between the chairs. The dark room, lit fitfully by firelight, was already warming back up, but I waited a few minutes before removing my outer clothing. Looking for a spare hook for my coat and petticoats, I discovered where Hannah Cole hung her cooking knives. I took the smallest one and sat down between the chair and the rocker, pulling the quail close.

"Been a long time since I roasted a skewered bird of any kind," Hannah murmured softly. "Several irons are hanging to one side of the fireloft. I keep the barding and yarn in the box sunk in the corner, where I store my root vegetables."

So—she had a very good nose. Even though the quail were half frozen, she could smell the blood and fresh meat. I'd heard that losing one sense sometimes strengthens the others. Grabbing the first bird, I set the small knife aside for pinfeathers and started plucking the carcass.

We sat in silence for a while, with me forcing my cold fingers to close on the feathers and pull. After a few moments Hannah reached down to her left and pulled a bird off my game line. A bag appeared between us, and I realized it held some duck feathers. Good, they wouldn't go to waste.

I moved quickly to the pinfeathers, using my forefinger and the tip of the knife to pull each offending barb. Out of the corner of my eye, I noticed that Hannah Cole had wisely looped the sinew of her plucked bird over the back of her rocker, saving the pinfeathers for me. I left the tugging to her and took care of my part.

"Joseph tells me that you were a dab hand in life at tanning," Hannah said suddenly. "Your coat looks warm and well cured, and also your boots and gloves."

In life? She was sticking to my being a ghost, then. Well, God's power to her deception, might it fool that whiny tracker. I wondered if her ghosts talked to her.

"You must have had a great potential for magic, for Erik to search for you so desperately," Hannah continued. "And the Hudsons could use more woodcraft. I don't think any of the women know how to survive in the forest."

Huh. That explained why he'd been so confident about leaving me . . . even if I woke, he thought, I wouldn't have gone far. I looked for something to set the plucked birds on, and took a pewter platter sitting over the mantel. While I was up, I got the skewers from the hooks by the fireloft. The barding I'd get in a few moments— quail were so lean, they cooked better with a layer of salt pork tied around them. And I had feet to remove . . . the tendons would be soft, the birds had been young.

During Hannah's conversation with herself, I kept one eye on the ghost. He seemed to be doing something with his hands . . . whittling, maybe? Or stitching leather? It was strange to see the fellow sitting there as if he belonged. So like he must have looked before he died. Had this been Hannah's husband? Brother? A son worn by hard years of homesteading?

"Forty years we were married," Hannah said softly, leaning forward to stir her beans. "Joseph died a fortnight before our forty-first anniversary. Elijah and Daniel had gone south by then, to the river and beyond. They're in O-hio, now, and married, both of them. They don't know that their father's dead . . . I don't want them worrying about me."

So she did have someone. Made me tempted to ship a letter east and say "Send your oldest son to get his grandmother!" But I decided long ago it was no use giving people advice—they probably wouldn't take it, anyway, and I'd just be frantic watching them mess up their lives. Telling folks stories so they knew how others had handled something, maybe, but Lord protect me from becoming a busybody.

"This bread should be done steaming." Scarcely a murmur. I thought about taking it out for her, but decided not to risk startling her so close to fire and scalding water. I watched as she moved aside the hook for her largest kettle and carefully removed the lid. With quilted pads, she used big tongs to pull two copper molds out of the pot. Then she replaced the kettle's lid and laid the tongs down next to the pudding molds. I'd heard that the blind always put things back after use, and it seemed Hannah was true to rumor—she either replaced a tool or kept it right where she herself sat.

"We'll give them a few minutes to cool before pushing them out of the molds," she announced. I nodded my agreement—the ghost wasn't ready to say anything—and kept yanking pinfeathers. What if Whiny could pull the memory of voices from people?

I was gonna singe, bard and roast those birds, and maybe heat some water for a sponge bath. Might be the last one I had for a long, long time.

Then I'd decide whether or not the new ghost was a mute.

❧⊘❧

Supper was roasted quail, beans with a bit of ham, and thin-sliced raisin brown bread with a mild goat cheese spread. There was honey in the cheese. I'd never done that to cheese before—it was as good as honey butter, only sharper.

Joseph didn't have any dinner. I think he enjoyed smelling the warmed cider, though.

I went ahead and cooked all the birds, and placed the third one in Hannah's cold box, where she stored things that spoiled fast. The wood lining would keep any animals from digging to it. The fourth bird I would take with me.

It was time to wash up and think about leaving. I cleaned the dishes for Hannah, so she could put her feet up and rest. Then I put the teakettle on the hob for wash water. How far away did I need to get from the cottage? There was a temptation to pull that hogshead over next to the chimney and stuff it with leaves, but if I was going to stay that close, it would be easier to sleep before the fireplace.

Hannah wouldn't toss me out, but I wondered if Whiny might come back during darkness. . . .

"They won't stop looking for you, little ghost." Hannah faced the flames as she spoke. "They know you exist, and that you're not strong enough to magic yourself back to wherever you belong. The Keeper wants your power. Perhaps even your body would be useful to them."

I sat close to the straight-backed parlor chair, clutching my arms and wondering if she could be right. I'd always believed that what gave me power was linked to my soul. What if I was wrong . . . what if something else could occupy my body and pass my power on to others?

Could the Keeper take a woman's body? But I wasn't of his blood. Death had told me the Keeper used his descendants. Hannah couldn't know that, though she might suspect.

"You're a good little ghost, or you wouldn't be hiding away. You didn't leave with young Hudson willingly. So it may be hard for you to think of this . . . but you must." Hannah paused, and took a deep breath. "You can't outrun them, child, not Hudsons and the Miami, too. The Hudsons ward each homestead, not the area." She looked down at her hands, which were clutched in her lap. "You must fight them, ghost child. Whatever magic you have, you must hide yourself and fight back. Otherwise, they will destroy your traps and dog your tracks. They will wear you to a shadow. No one can elude them for long . . . not if the Keeper joins the search."

At her words, two thoughts came together in my mind. One was that the Hudsons were warding in the area . . . the people here might fear Hudsons, but they were willing to use Hudsons when needed. Potential allies would be few. The other thought was that Hannah sincerely believed the Keeper would personally come after me. My flesh crept at the name.

I could not stay here long . . . maybe not even that night. I'd stack some logs near her front door before I left.

Now I knew I needed help. Breath left me in a long sigh. My choices had narrowed, but all paths led the same way. I knew how to call Death. And Death was perhaps the greatest magic of all. Could Death teach me something I could use to ward myself?

It was worth asking.

❧ ☼ ❧

Once again I found myself painting a bloody circle on solid stone. Twilight was deepening around me, spreading out from copses of oaks like fog off water. I gently nursed my tiny fire, adding dried tinder I'd taken from Hannah's small box. I'd decided to use some of Hannah's dried logs—I would split some of the bigger stuff for her before I left. I needed answers, and I didn't have hours to search for dry limbs to break off trees.

This boulder was surrounded by other big rocks, all of them hunched over in a circle like gnarled old men seeking warmth from my fire. It was the best I could do for protection right now. If things went wrong and the Hudsons found me, well . . . I'd already be halfway to Death's kingdom.

There were much worse ways to die.

When the small logs were burning well, I took a pinch of tobacco into my palm. "I, Alfreda, call upon thee, Azrael, greatest of healers, greatest of mages, greatest of teachers," I whispered formally, tossing half the tobacco into the flames. Then, dropping all ritual, I rolled into my plea. "Come to me, angel of mercy, for I am in need of instruction that only you can provide. My path is laid before me, but I cannot reach my goal. I have enemies behind and before, and they are drawing near. Teach me, angel of all that has been and ever will be—give me the knowledge to dismay my enemies. Let me live to return to those I love."

A swirl of sparks rose into the blanket of clouds above, and then I saw a figure standing on the other side of the fire. She was small, as she'd always been, but in life her presence had loomed, overshadowing generations of descendants. Emma Schell was wearing a full-skirted dress of lilac blue, her beautiful ivory shawl of lace held on her shoulders by an antique cameo. A thick lock of pale dove gray hair peeped out from beneath her cap, but she paid it no heed.

Her face was solemn but not stern, as Gran had always looked when someone was consulting her about the future. "What do you ask, Alfreda Golden-tongue? What is your need?" The low, rough voice was so familiar I could have wept to hear it.

"Can you teach me magic?"

Silence. *Lord and Lady.* What if that was something too tied to my future? *I am doomed.*

"Why do you want me to teach you magic?" Gran's voice asked me.

"I need to hide from sorcerers and the Miami, from folks tracking me and folks seeking my mind," I said promptly. "I don't know how to hide from one threat without betraying myself to the other. Can you teach me a way to ward that the Hudsons won't detect? I can hide in this forest, if only I don't have to worry about magic."

Death's eyes were unreadable. I was studied for a long moment, and I wondered what she—it—saw, and whether I'd be found wanting. Finally, Death smoothed one hand down a panel of its skirt, its eyes following the movement.

"There is a way to block that even the greatest sorcerer cannot detect," Death said calmly. "But it is not a ritual such as your teacher has shown you. It is magic free of ritual and free of blood."

I stared at the spirit. Either ritual or blood—or both—*had* to bind a spell, or else anything could happen. Anything at all. Why, without a binding, you would have pure elemental magic. You'd have only your own strength to—

Then I realized what Death was telling me.

Wild magic. Controlled only by the will of the one who summoned it, it was something few sorcerers, much less practitioners, dared to use.

"You . . . you think I could do wild magic?" I tried not to look like a witless child, but sweet Lord! I didn't have my full growth yet. A woman didn't reach her potential until she was linked to the moon, and even then, it could be another year before I had complete control.

"You have the strength," Death replied, its voice implacable.

I let my gaze drop to the flames between us and tossed another log on the fire. My mind was a blank, as fogged as an autumn river dell past sunset. After a while, I realized that Death had said the magic existed . . . and that I had the strength to learn it.

But Death had not said it would teach me.

All right. There was a rhythm to this game. I lifted my gaze back to the small, erect figure. "And what is the price of wild magic?" I asked. One thing I already knew—there was always a price, if something was worth having. I am proud to say that my voice did *not* tremble.

"The Keeper of Souls."

I straightened and stared at the face of my great-grandmother. "You want me to bring you . . . to kill the Keeper?"

"No. The Keeper must kill himself. But you will be the instrument of his death." I must have looked pretty puzzled, because Death actually kept speaking. "The Keeper upsets the balance. He has avoided the great circle for many generations. The Keeper must finish his journey . . . and his power must die with him."

"I can help bring this about?" I said carefully.

"Yes."

"And if I help . . . bring this about, you will teach me wild magic? To protect myself?" I must have sounded skeptical, because Death spoke right on top of my words.

"More. I will protect you from the Keeper."

"How?" Yeah, it was not very polite, but we were talking about my *life*.

"I will bind you to serve the master healer, the Last Healer."

That was interesting . . . I could hear the emphasis even when Death spoke of itself.

I can be obscure, too. "And?"

"Once you are bound to my protection, the Keeper can no longer bind you to the Hudson clan."

The relief was so intense I felt black creep in before my eyes. There *was* a way to protect myself. "What if he breaks the binding?" I gasped out. "He sounds more powerful than I ever dreamed of being."

Gran's lips thinned in a faint smile. "He may try. He will not like what he finds. If he breaks the bond, the binding will flow from you to him. The price of my protection is sacrificing immortality of the body."

Sacrificing immortality of the body . . . not the soul. . . . "Then we both get something," I murmured. "I get wild magic, you get a shot at the Keeper."

"There is one thing you must swear," Death added. "You will never attempt to duplicate the transferal spell of the Keeper."

Huh. "You mean how he steals power, or steals bodies?"

"Bodies," Death said simply. "Linking for a common cause is no evil—though his forcing that link may be."

I had a question I wanted to ask, but I didn't want Death to get the wrong idea. I swear, curiosity was my besetting sin. "Is there . . . is there a reason you shouldn't stretch out your life that way? Other than the fact that the Keeper does it by stealing bodies?"

Death studied me for a moment, and then said: "The soul is immortal. Consciousness is not. Physical immortality extracts a price; you would lose your humanity."

Ah.

I sat quietly, thinking about what Death had told me. What point was there in life if I was no longer human? How could I care about humans if I ceased to be one of them? Unless someday I could serve the powers on another plane of existence. And I did not need mortal flesh to guide those behind me on the path. . . .

"What have I forgotten to ask?" I said abruptly.

"You will learn wild magic. Your soul will be safe, it will not be bound to the Hudsons. You will be able to contact your mentor. What else matters to you?"

I suddenly wanted to know if some Hudson girl was off eyeing Shaw with intent to kidnap, but I didn't think that was what Death meant. As for this . . . there might be a hidden catch, but what choice did I have? Between the Miami and the Hudsons, somebody would find me.

With Death by my side, I had a chance.

Yes, I know how that sounds. But in a sense we are all Death's pupils, we practitioners—students of the great healer.

I had been offered private lessons with the master.

I was going to take them.

ELEVEN

IT'S BEEN SAID THAT ALL DEATH'S lessons are final ones, and in a way that is true. When Marta had warned me about wild magic, she'd told me that there was no way to protect yourself from failure. That was the biggest danger of casting without a circle—that you'd take one step farther than your strength. And there was no way to back up once you'd begun.

Marta's words were in the front of my mind as I went back to Hannah's little house. I'd earned that warm sponge bath, and come morning I'd get some exercise splitting logs. By then, I might even know another way to ward myself. Because there were many ways for Death to teach me magic.

One way was through my dreams.

Hannah was asleep by the time I crept back into the cabin. She'd obviously expected me to return, because she'd left several blankets out, folded on the rocker—and she'd moved to the far side of her bed.

I appreciated the offer, but I needed to go on as I'd begun. To flit in and out of Hannah's life like a ghost, maybe—if I could do it in a way that wouldn't endanger her. Still, I couldn't get accustomed to regular meals and a warm bed. It wasn't my fate to go on in comfort.

Right now I needed to fall asleep . . . I had an appointment with Death.

⁂

It should not have surprised me that Death came into my dreams as it came into my circle. I was wandering through a hardwood forest in the first blush of spring, and as I rounded a bend there was Grandsir, his buckskin jacket tossed over his wool breeches and shirt. He was twinkling at me, his flat-bowled pipe clenched in his teeth as he nodded my way.

"First things first," he said in his deep voice.

"The binding?" I asked.

Death shook my grandfather's head. "You have heard that it is dangerous to lie to the fay? It is even more dangerous to lie to me. Your very words became part of the binding I have woven. Should anything attempt to tamper with that bond, it will encompass that which tampers . . . one way or another."

I thought I understood that. Anybody who tried to steal my soul, or maybe even my magic, would be in for a big surprise. Would I find myself sharing the binding with another besides the Keeper?

Not important right now. The first thing I needed to know was warding. I hoped Death had that next in mind. "Warding, then?"

"Warding," Death agreed in my grandfather's voice. "Let us find a pond." Turning, Death wandered off down the deer trail in Grandsir's slouching walk. I stood bemused for a moment, watching the sunlight flicker green and gold across the back of his deerskin jacket. Then I hurried to catch up.

The dream pond was not far from where we'd met. It was not very large, perhaps three bodies long and two bodies wide. But it bustled with all the energy of early spring. I heard the soft buzz of insects, and the occasional croak of a sleepy toad-frog. Damselflies skimmed the surface of the water, which was dark and studded with vivid green growth.

Death slowed down by the water, walking carefully around fallen logs and clumps of weeds hiding duck nests. Then it—he—pulled his pipe from his mouth and gestured toward the water under a weeping black willow.

"What do you see?"

Oh, boy. I'd known I couldn't escape secretive teachers forever. "I see the reflection of a black willow tree. I see damselflies diving over the water, and frog eggs floating underneath, clinging to the weeds." A tiny splash greeted my words. "I see fish after bugs, and bugs after bugs—" I stopped, looking at the bubbles forming on the surface of the water. Was that an insect floating in a bubble of air?

"You will do the same," Death told me.

The same. . . . "The bubble?" I finally said.

"Yes."

"How?"

"Close your eyes and imagine yourself surrounded by one of those shiny bubbles," Death suggested. Obediently I shut my eyes and pictured walls like glittering water. "Enclose yourself completely—over the top of your head and the soles of your feet, too." I slid the bubble under my feet and folded it over my head. "Can you still hear the insects?"

I nodded, and then said "Yes" for good measure.

"Open your eyes and look through your bubble at me."

When I opened my eyes, I was looking through a rainbow. Death's tall form wavered on the other side of the shimmery wall. "How does it work?" I whispered.

"Eyes will see what they can, but minds won't find you through that," Death said with satisfaction in his voice. "You can form that shield out of any available water, in the air or on the ground. Even when the air is bone-dry, if there's snow around, or a stream still trickling by, you can form a bubble."

"This ward doesn't protect from anything solid, does it?" I asked, peering out through my watery shelter.

"Ritual probes and telepathic communication," Death said tersely. "It won't stop animals or an arrow."

"Will the bubble stop a magical search if I pretend I can't see it?"

Death smiled faintly. "Think of a tree shaking mist onto your head. Think of fog wrapped around you. Think of a hot summer day, when the air is so thick you're as like to choke as to breathe. The water is there—if you let part of your mind keep that shield strong, it will hold even when it is invisible."

I experimented a bit, letting the shield fade from view. I imagined the air of early winter, when moisture still poured down from the north. The wave of weather was enough to saturate my clothes, but I pushed it back. A dream cold I did *not* need. "Is it still there?"

Death nodded. "You practice that for a while. It will keep you safe from their magic. There are ways to ward against bears and cougars, too. We will get to that anon."

So I spent the longest time letting my shield creep up around me, slowly, like real fog. After a while it felt like a second skin. The sun went under a cloud, and I learned that I had to think invisible, or the air would ripple 'round me like heat rising from a freshly plowed field. Occasionally Death made a brief comment—"You're starting to show in my mind;" "That's better—let the droplets get smaller. Think of misty mornings." And, after a time: "Fine, fine. You've got it now. That's enough for tonight."

I'd had my eyes closed again, and flicked them open. "That's it?"

Death smiled faintly. "Do you feel the hunger?"

As he said the words, I realized that I *was* hungry, despite devouring the last leg of the quail that had been too big for Hannah to finish. Had I burned up that bird leg so soon?

"That is the daily cost of wild magic. The power must come from somewhere," Death said placidly. "It comes from your own bones, and the drain is worse than what rituals take from you. Power comes from the sleeping life all around. You draw only a tiny bit when you work, but as it burns it consumes. You must set traps tomorrow, well-hidden. You will need lots of meat for these lessons."

I felt a sinking feeling in my stomach, and tried to fight it. Surely with protection from ritual magic searches, I could trap some of my own food. But trapping took time. Perhaps I'd better see if Hannah's husband had known how to use a bow and arrows. If I had to hunt deer, such a weapon would be handy.

I was up long before dawn, making porridge and working on a leg of my second quail. Then I crept outside and split a bunch of logs for her, so she wouldn't have to take her chances with the ax. I had a feeling someone in the nearby community kept an eye on Hannah, but I owed her something for that filling meal.

When I went back inside to make sure all was well, I found a shoulder sling with a flat clay water jug placed in the center of the work table. The blanket I'd used the previous night was folded and stuffed inside the dark-stained pack. I could smell the brown bread—a chunk of it was wrapped in a handkerchief and sitting by the big flask.

"Joseph said he wanted you to have his sling and jug, from his hunting days." Hannah's voice was placid as she sat and rocked in her chair. "He's not offering you the bow right now because he's afraid of you pausing that long. And butchering a deer would lure wolves and panthers to you."

Well, there was certainly truth in that. Small animals could be taken back to huts or rocky ledges.

"It's been nice having a few more ghosts around the place," Hannah went on. "Drift on by any time you'd like, though you may have to come and go in darkness."

Yes—I'd taken as much of a chance as I could. It was time to move along. I'd stay in the area a few days, try to trap some animals and maybe smoke the meat, if the wind would carry the smell west. Couldn't risk a curious Hudson nose.

Or maybe I was just stuck there until Marta found me. No sense worrying about it now—there was time yet for decisions.

A little time. . . .

I moved back outside into a soft, gray world of falling snow.

Good. No tracks.

❧ 🜍 ❧

It was time to build myself a debris hut, and I moved fast to do it. I found another area of rock teeth and then constructed the hut close to the southeast face of the boulders. What with the steady sift of powder, the heap of leaves and pine branches was slowly buried under several inches of snow.

After the hut was built, I went around and carefully set some snares on rabbit runs. I was low on sinew—whoever found my traps had taken the line—so I really needed to catch another animal, if only for more sinew! Finding evening primrose or another strong fiber plant wasn't going to happen, not in the month of Ice. I'd end up peeling the inner bark of some tree.

As I worked, I was aware of odd thoughts flickering into my mind. I could see slivers of cedar wood and glossy holly leaves, as well as tiny green mistletoe branches. Clumped together, I saw them burning in a bonfire of leaves and wood. I was standing where the smoke could cover me, and coughing up a storm.

But the next flicker of sight was of a deer walking right past where I stood, as if I wasn't even there.

I paused, my hands stilling. Was this another lesson? Was Death trying to tell me that the smoke of those plants could make me invisible—no, unnoticeable? Interesting . . . and those were things I could put my hands on, after I was done with the snares. I hadn't planned on a fire that night, but for that kind of protection, I'd build a fire! Were words necessary, or did the smoke do everything?

The silence of the forest was a palpable thing, like the quicksilver caress of silk. I moved along the trails like a ghost, rigging my half-dozen traps, protected by my mental bubble. Later, I'd check the snares for prey—animals often came out in a light snow. In the meantime, I had the rest of my quail to eat, and Hannah's brown bread. Compared to several days ago, it was a feast.

❧ 🕮 ❧

I'd returned to my circle of hunched rock men; building a fire by my hut seemed too chancy to me. I'd found the elements of my daydream without too much trouble—in fact, there was a lot of cedar in the small fire burning before me.

Was my circle still intact, or did I need to make another one? I was gonna need that meat just to keep my blood healthy. As I thought about whether I could do Marta's spell for illuminating ritual lines, I noticed through the flames a darkening of shadows.

To my surprise, it was my older brother Dolph sitting across from me. What was he doing here uncalled?

"Why have you come without the ritual?" I asked carefully. You see, I'd heard that Death arrived uncalled only when it was planning on collecting a soul.

"I was called, and I am now bound," Death with Dolph's face said. "As long as a part of the binding touches you, I shall easily return."

I nodded at this, as if it made some sort of sense to me. "The plants I thought of this afternoon . . . is the smoke the important part?"

"Smoke and willpower," was Death's reply.

"And after I do this . . . people and animals just won't notice me?"

"That is correct."

"But I'm not invisible," I persisted, feeling my way through things.

Dolph cocked his head to one side and studied me. "There is no way to make the body incorporeal. However, there is a ritual that bends light around a form, hiding it from naked sight. And there are ways to hide scent."

"Can the ritual be sensed?" I asked.

"Yes. That is why you must learn to use odors to create certain spells. Though they seem odd, they are undetectable. Right now that is the most important thing. I will also teach you several difficult incantations which will focus your will . . . you may need the results."

It felt very odd to have Death looking at me out of Dolph's eyes but speaking in the dry voice of Gran. *Difficult things*? That bubble trick hadn't been simple.

"What next?" I asked him.

Dolph let his gaze drop to the flames for a moment, and then his pale eyes flicked back in my direction. "There are two basic spells you must learn. There is the hex for destruction, for deterioration of natural things, and there is control of the many winds."

An incantation for destruction . . . maybe more than one. Wind could be gentle and nurturing, but it could also peel the shingles off a house and knock you off your feet. I wasn't sure what good these spells would do me, but I needed to ward and to hide—Death was teaching me how to do that. Death was holding up its side of the bargain; I needed to hold up mine.

"All right," I said quietly. "Where do we start?"

"Mushrooms," Death replied.

I couldn't help it—I started laughing. "Isn't this the wrong season for mushrooms?" I finally got out.

"Not in the dreamtime," Death responded.

There was no answer to this, of course, so I nodded my agreement and started to extinguish my small blaze. Time to find out if my leaf hut was warm.

It was more than warm—what with my huge, shaggy pile and the blanket Hannah had loaned me, I was almost hot. But come the middle of the night, I'd be cooling off, so I used everything. I knew the snow piling up on the roof would protect me even more.

If Death was correct, I no longer had to hide beneath the mind of a bird—the bubble alone would protect me. I knew I could ground myself in my sleep—I could hang onto a bird's thoughts in my sleep. Surely I could learn how to hide all of me in a bubble while I slept.

That night's lesson started with mushrooms—only mushrooms. I found myself on a deer trail in the middle of a rainy summer day. Before me was a fairy ring. It had several kinds of mushrooms growing in the circle, a few I recognized as edible—and a few I knew for sure were dangerous. There was also a 'shroom I didn't recognize.

"Remember," Death whispered in my ear, and the new type of mushroom seemed to stir in the strong, rainy wind. "Eat of these, and you will see the auras of all living things without entering the trance state. Eat enough of the mushrooms, and the very forces that bind together the universe will become a woven pattern of light before you."

"Can you learn to do this without the mushrooms?" I thought to ask.

"Yes. But it takes time. You must learn to relax, no matter what the outside distractions. For some people, that is almost impossible."

Huh. True enough. But mushrooms didn't always agree with me—my head felt stuffy after eating them. Maybe I'd try to learn how to see without help.

"If this can be learned without mushrooms, why don't practitioners do it?" I thought to ask.

"Some do know how," was Dolph's quiet answer. "Some don't. Marta knows about seeing auras. She doesn't know that you can see the bonds that hold all God's miracle together."

Something occurred to me, then. "Is it a sin to break God's bonds?"

Death appeared next to me in the body of my older brother. "You won't break God's connection to each part of the universe. You'll only break what's holding the tiny pieces together . . . like when you burn a log, you're breaking the log's connections to being a tree. But the ashes are still the building blocks of a tree, and have their place in God's plan."

Okay. That I could do . . . like sawing down a tree without using a saw, so to speak. I stared down at the mushrooms again. Lord and Lady, I hated trying new mushrooms. When you made a mistake on mushrooms, there was no turning back—you ate enough, you were dead. With a couple of mushrooms, you ate *any* and you were dead.

The question was, did I trust Death? It's said Death doesn't lie . . . but you have to know what questions to ask. Surely he wanted me alive, to be the instrument of catching the Keeper.

"Is there a limit to how many of this kind of mushroom I can eat?" I decided to ask.

"It will not poison you, but too many would send you into a stupor," said Dolph's voice. "The danger is in being discovered by your enemies while in that state."

I'll say. I didn't offer this observation aloud.

I wanted this knowledge—I admitted it to myself. Even if I wasn't planning on breaking bonds all over the place, I wanted to see the light of life. Perhaps if I knew what I was looking for, I could find it another way. . . .

I knelt down in the wet grass and picked the freshest of the mushrooms. After wiping them carefully on the glistening green blades at my knee, I bit into one. It had what I think of as typical mushroom taste—not a lot—but it was still firm, so it wasn't unpleasant. How many to get the effect?

"Wait," said Dolph's voice.

Perhaps only one . . . perhaps I'd leave my gaze on the ring so that I wouldn't confuse myself.

After a while, I realized there was a soft cloud of golden light around the still-growing mushrooms, and a carpet of pale green haze above the grass. Slowly I lifted my eyes. I'd thought I needed a lot of this to see the bonds of life—

"Plants are alive, and so have auras," Death whispered. "Even in winter, you can tell a dead tree from a live one."

The woods beyond were rimmed in light. I saw soft browns and blues, reds and yellows, and more kinds of green than I could count. I stood, and we walked down the deer path into the next clearing. A turkey startled and took wing, skimming to the opposite end of the meadow. His aura was pulsing red and yellow, his behavior nervous.

The shapes of light helped me pick out several does hiding on the next deer path just inside the forest. Their auras had green and blue in them, as well as a dash of yellow.

"Do the colors mean the same in animals as humans?" I said aloud.

"Black should be avoided, and brown does not signal illness, but otherwise the meanings are similar."

'Course, practitioners all had different theories on which color meant what. . . . I looked down at the other two mushrooms I carried in my left hand. *Maybe I'd better sit down.* So I did, right there at the edge of the meadow. Then I chomped another mushroom.

It took both of the 'shrooms to understand what Death had been talking about. An interlocking haze of golden threads finally appeared around me, almost everywhere I could see. My own body remained solid, and so did the trees, the grass, the turkey— Was it the air we breathed that I was looking at?

"You will see the bonds of the lightest things first," Death told me, and I wondered if he was dipping into my mind. "Eat enough of those mushrooms, and even the bonds holding together a rock will become visible."

Rocks had bonds? I was impressed, but I was too dizzy to say so aloud.

"We will start with something simple. Come with me." He extended a hand to help me up, and I discovered that in this time and place, Death was solid and warm. With his guidance, I was able to walk back up the dirt path without tripping over any roots.

Suddenly the fairy ring was before us, the cloud of golden light now almost invisible from the cross-hatched lines of light etched over it.

"The simplest way to do this is to touch what you wish to change," Death said quietly. "It can be done with a look, but that requires tremendous power. If you are ever linked with other practitioners, you will have the energy to ignite or crumble objects with a single glance." He pointed to the mushrooms. "We will use one of these."

I knelt again and set gentle fingers on one of the round, plump mushrooms. "Now what?"

"There is energy in you, power you carry with you always," Death told me. "Let some of that power flow from your hand into the mushroom."

I felt a touch inside of me, and knew Death was trying to show me where my power lived within. That tingly place close to my heart . . . I let the tingling spread through my body, washing through each part of me, and felt some of it drip from my fingertips.

The mushroom seemed to swell, then darken a bit and become shiny. The cap started to peel back, exposing black veins of spores. Slowly the 'shroom began to shrivel up. Finally the cap split along the lines of the veins, sections of mushroom pushing out and falling to the ground.

I took my hand away from the crumpled ruin of a toadstool. My thoughts and my gaze had been locked to the plant, but I still was not positive what I'd done.

"You hurried the aging," Death said simply. "Days passed in moments, because of the energy you poured into this growing thing. If you had focused on one tiny point, you could have sent power rushing into the plant—it would have exploded into a powder of spores."

A tang of hunger echoed in my mouth, but I ignored it. I was missing something here. . . . "Can anyone do this?"

"Only the strongest of the Gifted," was the reply.

The horror of what I had done swept over me, and I felt cold to the marrow. "Could you do this to an animal—to a person?"

"With enough power," Death said, and his voice was very even, a control Dolph had never had in life. "Mostly you will do this to dead things—if you needed a rope to rot and fall away, or a stockade wall to collapse. The heat of your power can burn up many things. This is a simple way to channel that strength."

Death never honey-coated anything. "The logs would dry and splinter . . . could you lure termites to wood, to destroy it from within?" My mind whirled with endless possibilities.

"Luring would not be necessary—the decay caused by your touch would draw them."

I stared at my hand, but I did not say aloud what I was thinking.

I was truly Death's apprentice.

❧·𝕯·❧

The last thing Death told me to do that night was pick up a pebble and do to it what I'd done to the mushroom. I had to remember to focus on a point. Holding out my hand flat, I placed the stone in my palm and then extended my arm. I wasn't looking forward to flying chips of rock.

Warmth crept along my skin, heating up the pebble. The stone had been damp from the rain; a section cracked off from the water heating— "Expanding," Death said. I'd kept my gaze on the yellowish surface, waiting . . . waiting. . . .

Suddenly the tiny rock exploded in a shower of sand. Exhaustion swept through me; I wasn't sure I could keep holding my head up.

"Remember the cost of wild magic," Death reminded me. "That is why we do this in your dreams. You would need much food to replenish your strength."

I considered that. "Then the weakness isn't real? I mean, I won't feel tired and ravenous tomorrow?"

"Your hunger will increase slightly, but not as if you had done this in the real world." Once again Death offered me a hand, pulling me to my feet. "Enough for this night. You learn quickly. Catch your hares and use your bubble and your scents. You have much more to learn, and you will need your strength."

❧ 𝕯 ❧

Wild magic was simple . . . and more difficult than I could explain. Marta could whisper a spell and squeeze water from the air; I could convince myself that *I* was water, and draw an underground stream to the surface, or create a pond where only a puddle existed.

As with water, so with fire. Pull the escaping heat from dark earth or the reflection of sunlight on water, and a flame could dance on your hand.

A bonfire could coil at your feet.

With enough power, I could lay hands on an animal, any animal, slide into its mind . . . and become that animal, forcing myself into the form.

I did not have the kind of power to imitate a shape-shifter—not yet. But Death told me that once I was moon-touched, I would.

"You can even learn to sing to the winds. Eventually they'll answer you . . . and may even come at your call."

In the course of days spent trapping and trying to walk without leaving a trail, and nights dreaming magic lessons, I finally noticed that my poltergeist had disappeared. Had I lost it when Erik brought us over so great a distance? Or had I frightened it away by my new lessons?

I didn't know. Time to figure that out later. Now there was only the next rabbit—the next turn of wild magic. Several nights I got lucky and caught enough hares to leave Hannah a few. But mostly I struggled to keep up with my own needs.

My pants were much looser than they'd been, and I could tell my face felt thinner. Wild magic would protect me, but it demanded its due.

There came a night free of snow or even clouds, the air bitterly cold, the moon hanging old in the sky, and I realized I had been missing a long time. The month of Ice had passed—it was now the month of Wind. First Marta had to find me, then she had to travel to get me. . . .

No telling how long I would be in my latest leaf hut. I'd made it as thick as a squirrel's nest, and just as warm and waterproof. The only problem was that it smelled like I did—burnt cedar, holly, and mistletoe. All I could hope was that it was a weird enough combination that anyone passing nearby would think fire had swept through during the last rainstorm, or that trappers had burnt a mixed bag of deadwood.

That night Gran came to me, and I found myself sitting on the front porch of a house I didn't recognize, in a place I did not know. I could smell salt in the cold, heavy air, and the view was of a cliff. Below there was deep blue water as far as the eye could see. Somewhere beyond I could smell the smoke of burning leaves. It was very peaceful, and I felt relaxed, as if my cares had been taken away.

"This was the house your great-grandfather brought me to as a bride," Gran told me, her raspy voice soft. "We lived here until he died, and then I went west with your grandparents. You have kin still living in this place." I waited for her to tell me where we were, but that wasn't the story she'd come to tell me.

"It's time for you to learn how to summon the whirling wind," Gran said suddenly. "This is a great power, one of the most dangerous we possess. We do not use it on a whim, or to frighten the foolish. We use it for protection—for ourselves, and for those we love. Only a madman tangles with a practitioner who has mastered the whirling winds."

The old woman stood slowly, rearranging her full skirt over the thick pad of petticoats beneath. "Come, child. Walk with me." Carefully she stepped down the two porch steps and across the scythed lawn. Gran—Death—was heading for the cliff. I rose to follow.

Above the golden haze of mist and tangy smoke, I could see a front moving our way. It was one of those big thunderstorms that sometimes appear at the end of summer. Did they also appear on this coast, or was the weather here something that Death controlled?

"It is easiest the first time to let nature help you build the twisting wind," Gran said as she walked. "Our line has been given the strength to draw twisters from any cloudy sky. However, it is simplest when the feel of the air changes suddenly from cool to warm, or hot to cold."

Gran stopped abruptly at the end of the mown grass. "We will work over the water—it will be safer that way."

That startled me out of my dreamy detachment. Could my dreams affect things in the real world? I grew hungry from my actions here. "You said 'our line.' Do you mean the line of Schell practitioners?"

"Yes," Gran answered, turning toward me. "Our line was among the strongest ever to manifest. With ritual, we controlled the winds."

Momma's line, not Papa's. So Marta couldn't do this—at least not in *any* kind of weather—or simply didn't know how to do this. And the others did it with ritual, with a circle and protection. . . . I swallowed with a suddenly dry throat. "How do you go about this?" I said aloud.

"When cold and hot air collide, the cold usually slips beneath the warm and forces it up. Like in a house with a loft—it's always warmer upstairs?" I nodded my understanding. "To call the twisting wind, you must convince a finger of cold air to reach ahead of the line of clouds, and press down upon the warm air, trapping it close to the ground." Her hand reached out and down, as if playing charades.

"If the winds high above are strong, the warm and cold air will begin to swirl together. Within that whirling circle of air, smaller, tighter whirlpools will form." Gran demonstrated again, one arm making a large circle while the other made a tiny whirl within the big area. "Twisters fall from the clouds to the earth . . . waterspouts rise from the sea to the sky."

"Do we control them the same way?" I thought to ask.

"They are wind and water—we call them, we send them away," Gran said succinctly. "The secret is to spin the air close to the source. If you would raise whirling water, stir the winds close to the surface of the sea. If you would raise twisting air, stir the winds high above."

She tilted her head and gave me a narrow look. "This takes more energy than anything you have tried. It will drain you, but once you have done it, you will remember forever. When you become kin to the moon, it will be much easier."

Drain me. Not encouraging. I wondered if that meant even in the real world . . . I wondered if it meant my shields would weaken.

"I will need this spell?" I said aloud.

"You may," Gran replied, and I remembered that she was Death. If she chose, she would tell me only what I asked.

So. "Is this the eastern sea, between America and the Isles?"

"It is." Very calm.

I wished I could be as calm facing what I was about to do. I'd thought about singing down the winds many times since Death spoke of it to me, and the thought still made me shiver. You see, you must be able to hold fast to a note, and carry a tune in your head, or the spell can't work.

Who was I trying to fool? I could sing, sure, but I'd never thought my voice was anything to brag about. I might get lucky, when I finished my growing, and have a voice like Aunt Sunhild's, but then again, I might croak through hymns like Aunt Dagmar.

It didn't matter. Death had told me how it worked, and expected me to try. I needed cold, heat, and moisture, and I felt the dying time of year around me. The lean, chill fury of the east was rolling toward us. I needed warmth and mist—I needed the steamy hot breeze of a southern summer.

And so I fumbled for a low note, a warm, sultry tone that echoed the dark wind from the south. When the pitch was true, I threw it from myself, letting the dry, biting north wind to my left steal the song away and carry it beyond. The bitter eastern wind burned a path through the approaching front, pushing several masses ahead of the cloud bank. I coaxed the tendrils of cold, heavy air, wilting under its weight, as I waited to see if the south wind would answer me.

One thing I knew about the winds—they loved to do what they were born to do. Unless they were so tied up it was impossible to shake loose, winds would answer a practitioner's call. No, I didn't understand why, not then—I just knew it for truth.

I felt a warm, wet tickle against my right cheek, a tiny flutter that built into a curl of breeze. In response I hauled on that finger of air from the south, nudging it down, down under that cold cap of sinewy east wind.

And the air before us began to spiral, changing the whitecaps upon the water. I kept my gaze on the great circle, squeezing the funnel tighter and tighter, feeling a strong updraft pulling at the water. How many rules of nature was I breaking? Or was I working *with* nature? I clenched my hands into fists, as if I could wrestle with the column.

Slowly water droplets began to condense in the whirling wind, a rising tube of cloud to challenge the sky. I watched without emotion as the waterspout reached the cloud bank and attached itself to the belly of the approaching storm.

It was done. I'd asked the winds to help me with the spell, and now I was finished. Some might turn the waterspout loose with no guidance at all; others would struggle to control it precisely. I was one of the latter ones—I had no reason to make everyone for miles around nervous.

This was a power of destruction. What was I going to do with it?

"You may push it out to sea, Alfreda Golden-tongue," Gran's voice said, breaking the light trance I'd been surrounded by. "There is nothing out there it can harm."

"Can I absorb some of the energy from it before I release it?" I asked tensely. Controlling this thing was a lot like restraining a dog that wanted to fight—letting go might be worse than hanging on.

I could hear the rustle of Gran's petticoats and knew she'd turned back toward me again. "Not yet," she said, and her voice was gentle. "After you are moon-touched, you will be able to reclaim what you used to launch it, and a bit more besides."

Enough, then. I nudged the waterspout with my mind, trying to shove it out to sea.

I nudged too hard. The churning funnel exploded like wet pine in a roaring fire, water and wind flying everywhere. Dizziness took hold of me, and I sank down in a heap right where I stood.

"I warned you," Gran's rusty voice said mildly.

"What should I do now?" I managed to say.

"Rest. And eat something before you sleep again, it will keep hunger from waking you."

Then I woke without warning, as if someone had grabbed my shoulder. My stomach was tumbling, but there was no sickness involved—I just felt like I was starving. Rabbit . . . I had some smoked bunny left. It's not my favorite meat, but better than messing with deer, and you can't whack a quail every day. There were acorns, too, and winter tea, now cold but still nourishing.

The food helped, a little bit. I needed something different to eat, something like cattail sprouts. There was a stream just north of here, it might run slowly enough to let cattails grow. I'd check in the morning. . . .

❧ 🐚 ❧

I didn't know I'd wake up hungry enough to gnaw my own arm. The rest of the winter tea made my stomach a touch happier, but I couldn't fool it for long. I felt weak and shivery, and knew my last lesson had taken a lot from me.

It was then I realized that my bubble had faded. Panicked, I threw it up again, making sure it completely surrounded me. *How long was it down?*

Time to move. I'd been here long enough—this was my second leaf hut, actually. I was a full mile from the last spot, and farther from the river. But from the feel of the power south of here, there were many Hudsons strong enough to sense where I might be. I needed to—

I heard crackling nearby, the snapping of ice from too much weight crossing it. Did the hut smell enough like cedar and the other ingredients to turn eyes away? Or had I finally run out of luck?

Suddenly a picture was inserted into my mind, as clearly as I'd seen cedar, holly and mistletoe. My head was filled with a great wooden horse, half the height of huge stone walls. I knew that image. It was not exactly like the drawing in my father's book of ancient history, but Death must have seen the real thing thousands of years ago. That thought made me shiver, even as I wondered if I had been betrayed.

Do you mean me to be a Trojan Horse?

My private lessons were over. Payment had come due.

TWELVE

I WAS MORE FORTUNATE THAN most folks, because I knew who and what I was—and I accepted it. I was born with the Gift, and more . . . I had the Sight. I'd been taught the past well, and how to watch the changing weather of the present. The future spoke to me, when it chose. But I couldn't speak *for* the future . . . I only passed on hints and rumors.

There were storm clouds looming in the present, and the future had been silent for a long time. While learning to trap for pelts, I had often wondered what the animals felt when they realized they had no way out.

Now I knew.

There was more crackling and scuffing, closer to my hidden entryway. I clutched my blanket around my shoulders and held my breath. Could they hear my heartbeat? It sounded like a blacksmith working, at least to me.

"We know you're around here, miss," called a reedy male voice. "The Keeper felt you last night, and we started north at midnight. Best not to play any more games. If he has to send young Erik back to that Cat Hollow place for something else of yours, he'll do it."

I gripped my arms tightly, and inhaled slowly and deeply. I knew what the fellow meant. With some object that was close to me—my comb, or a hair ribbon—they could cast a directional spell. It might not be powerful enough to break through my wild wards, but it would tell them what area to look in. I'd be back to the beginning . . . hiding from both magic and trackers.

Did they truly know I was here? Had Erik already used something small of mine as a focus? It seemed worth it to wait. If they finally discovered the leaf hut, which looked a lot like a snowbank, then I was caught. The snow was too deep down here to run. It had been a trade-off, the rocky riverbank for the draws. But at night it got colder than you could imagine up on those stones—sometimes cold enough to flake the rock face.

I'd needed the insulation of the snow. Now the drifts had defeated me. And perhaps something else. . . . There was no reason to be thinking of the Trojan horse, not here and now. I'd bet any amount of money that Death had slipped that thought into my mind. If so, it was a message. I figured it meant one of two things. Either I was to watch for a Trojan horse, or I *was* a Trojan horse.

How long would it take me to find out which one?

How deep would they dig before giving up? All the way down to the ground?

The crunch of rotten ice, the squeak of packed snow, the snap of broken branches . . . I listened, trying to guess how many of them were out there. Were they angry? I'd kept them out here in the cold near thirty days, maybe more—I'd lost count somewhere—and who knew how the Keeper punished those who failed him?

I heard two men talking, maybe fifty feet from my hut. The voices were not clear . . . snow blocked more than cold. Something about "glowing," but that was the only word I recognized for certain.

More movement, quieter this time. Had it started snowing again? That would explain the muted footsteps before the men crunched through the ice glaze. I wasn't sure how long I sat there, wondering what was going on, but there wasn't a lot I could do. If I let my thoughts float out to eavesdrop, I might touch someone else Gifted—someone strong enough to seize my mind.

Finally the footsteps paused. "Here," an older man declared. "Look around." He was entirely too close—he sounded like he was right outside my hut.

"Come on, Miss Sorensson," the whiny one said. "It's cold as a witch's tit, and I could use a hot meal. There's food and a fire at the fort. If we start now, we'll make it back before darkness falls."

You think you *could use a hot meal?* It had been three days since I'd smoked those rabbits. I needed to check my trapline . . . I wondered if they'd give me trouble over it.

Death meant for me to get caught, now—I was pretty sure of it. Could I find a way inside that compound to contact Marta? Maybe. They used ritual magic—they had to have a permanent circle. Could I use it to communicate in some way?

It depended on how much blood magic they'd performed within the area. Too much blood, and I might not even be able to cross over the line. Your body can be contaminated without your permission, but they'd have to work long hours to get my soul.

I touched my thin face and made a decision. In the silence of winter, without being able to hunt deer, I was slowly losing my strength. The day would come when I could no longer keep a constant shield. If I waited too long, I'd have no strength to protect myself within their compound. There was no future in defiance simply to prove I could defy them.

Taking a deep breath, I said aloud: "Well, now, I guess we should break down my trapline and head south."

There was complete silence for a moment. Then, the older voice asked, "Do you need help digging your way out?"

"No." What kind of foolish question was that? If I couldn't get out on my own, I'd have smothered long ago. I grabbed my skirt and petticoat and ignored Joseph's sling and the blanket. No need to inspire questions. Maybe they hadn't gone back to talk with Hannah again.

Then I kicked open a hole to daylight. The hut might be useful to someone—or something—else, so I went out the true entrance instead of through the roof.

My shoulders had snow and leaves on them, but I didn't brush at myself. Let them think I was afraid of them. If they thought I wouldn't so much as squeak, there was a small chance I could still lose them in the forest. Quickly I stuffed the skirt and slip into the front of my coat.

I emerged into the gray light of morning, the forest a shadowy presence behind a veil of falling snowflakes. There were maybe six figures in the visible area, but I could make out no faces. None of the forms looked as slender as Erik. It was maybe twenty feet from my hut to oblivion—beyond that point, you'd have no idea how to find your way back.

It was mornings like this that made you mark a trapline somehow, so you could find it again. "The trapline goes that way," I decided to say, hoping my assumption would keep their behavior courteous.

"We got plenty to eat right now, little girl. We aren't asking you to show up with supper in hand," said the whiny one, who waited the farthest down the deer path. Was he the screechy fellow I'd heard a month and more ago? Or someone else with a discontented spirit?

"I'm not looking for supper," I said firmly. "I need to break down traps. If you take more from the forest than you can use, the forest eventually turns on you. I'd like to stay on its friendly side, if you don't mind." I didn't bother to say I wasn't going to leave any half-caught animal to starve. This type of man was more likely to accept that I had superstitions about the woods.

There was some muttering, but no one grabbed my arm to drag me away. I stepped past one of the fellows, walking carefully, but he made no move toward me. Moving on an angle up a deer trail, I headed east toward my first trap.

The wood pegs I simply left, except for the best of the bunch—that one I'd stash in my hip pouch eventually. The sinew that was still good I coiled for another day. Three out of six traps held rabbits. Maybe I could have lasted a little bit longer. . . .

I threaded the last piece of sinew through the hind feet of the hares and slung them over my shoulder. "Lead on, gentlemen," I said politely.

The grizzled man with the white beard smiled faintly and moved into the lead. The whiny one indicated that I was to go next. Several of the others followed me, while one fellow each walked the ridges to either side of us.

Huh. These boys were serious—I didn't think I had any opportunity to duck out. Maybe if a blizzard started up. . . .

I knew that there was a blazed trail not much more than a mile from my hut, and I figured that was where we were going. Sure enough, I could see solid dark masses up ahead, which were probably horses or mules. Deer wouldn't have let us get this close; one fellow kept breaking through ice, and the noise was spooking everything around.

Eight horses waited on the narrow trail, which was wide enough for maybe one wagon, if you didn't let the animal pulling drift to either side. One person was also there, sitting up in the saddle on a rangy buckskin. Male, I thought—these fellows didn't seem like the type to allow women to help them work. I wondered uneasily if I was safe with them, or if I was going to lose my virginity in a hurry.

Worrying wasn't going to help, I told myself sternly. Having another woman along might not have made any difference. I'd heard tales of women who were much worse than the rowdy trappers who sometimes passed through town.

The person on the horse was wearing some kind of fur-lined hat, with a tanned skin trailing down over his back like a cloak. It probably cut the wind pretty well. As I studied it, both man and horse turned slightly, churning snow, and I recognized Erik's cool eyes. For a man folks thought would be in a panic over losing me, Erik looked awfully calm. I'd have expected him to look either relieved or pleased. He just seemed bored.

"Well, you led us a merry chase," he said drily.

I fixed a hard eye on him and asked, "I don't suppose you're ready to explain yourself?"

Erik's glance flicked over to the grizzled older man. "Boost her up on Whitey." Gathering up his reins, he pulled his horse's head around and started south. The others moved quickly to mount up, while the oldest man gestured toward the one white horse.

I hadn't really expected an answer. Not yet.

⁂

That blizzard I'd ordered didn't put in an appearance, but the thick, fine snow continued to sift upon us the entire day. Walking down a blazed path was much faster than crawling over ice and river boulders—I didn't think I'd gotten more than twenty miles north of where I'd woken up, but this pretty well confirmed it.

A short break around midday kept my bladder from busting, and gave me a taste of my first wheat in over a month. The bread had been baked fresh that day and had no grit in it. I hadn't realized how much I'd missed the soft, chewy texture. Rabbit could keep you going, but I'd been eating older animals, and the meat got tougher each season they survived.

Several hours past our camp, the road widened again. It was now four horses across, and seemed cleared of most stumps and boulders. In response I could feel the muscles in my back and neck start to tighten. We were getting closer to a settlement—what had that one fellow told those trappers? Heaven's Road? Was that the name of the Hudsons' town?

A bit farther the snow level dropped to the horses' fetlocks. I'd heard something about scraping the road free of piled snow. Now much farther?

I didn't ask. No one had said anything at all since we'd started riding—not to me, not to each other. The whiny fellow *had* given me a once-over with his eyes while we stopped to eat that bread and venison jerky, and muttered something about me being a big one. Both Erik and I had turned a cold gaze on him, and he had shut up quickly.

Were they afraid of Erik?

Or of me?

Sure enough, within a mile of the road widening, the shadowy presence of log buildings could be seen through the haze of falling snow. There was no way to tell if this was the same little village I had escaped from—it had been too dark. Whether from the cold or something else—could it be Sunday, and everyone attending a service?—we saw no movement around any of the structures.

The horses were tired, but they seemed to increase their speed as we passed the last house. They knew they were almost home. This side of the village had also been scraped recently. A wide trace spread out before us, vanishing in a veil of sifting powder.

Somewhere beyond the heavy clouds the sun was setting. The gloom beneath the trees oozed out into the path, obscuring my sight like heavy smoke. A tiny breeze was pushing at our backs, and I for one was ready to stop riding. I did think briefly about rolling off the horse and rushing into the murk, but I shrugged off the thought. They knew the area—I didn't. Right now, Death was more on their side than mine. I'd just have to go along and see what there was to see.

There was a glow off in the distance . . . torches, maybe. We were heading in that direction. Erik had lengthened his lead, the older man right at his heels. I was boxed neatly in the center; they weren't taking any chances I might slip away again.

There was a greater darkness before us, rising like a monstrous thunderhead. It was outlined in light. Was it always like this, or was it for our benefit? We had less than a quarter mile to go, whatever was before us.

I concentrated on the heavy footfalls of the stumbling horses, their tread muffled in the continuous snow. What kind of people were these Hudsons? Normal people caught up in an old man's evil? Willing accomplices to his mischief? Vicious in their own right? Whoever and whatever they were, I was somehow going to have to survive until Marta could find me. I knew I had patience and some learning . . . how much cunning did I have?

I was about to find out.

The dark shape before us suddenly separated into two distinct masses—the sky above, and a wall at least fifteen feet high. A bunch of big old trees had gone into the making of what looked like a stockade. Torches lined the top, spaced at intervals so there were no shadowed spots visible. I could see the bulk of a tower, down to the right. There was a wide swath of open ground between the woods and the wall.

Whom were the Hudsons defending against? Was this a fort left from territorial disputes with the French? Did the entire region come here when the Miami went on the warpath?

Or was this to help protect the Hudsons from their neighbors?

Odd. Those trappers passing by, and Hannah Cole, too, had seemed quite frightened by the mere mention of the Hudsons. Why did the Hudsons need physical protections? 'Course, if you were protecting from actual invasion, that might take more than a tripwire ward. . . .

We were expected; the gates slowly swung open at our approach. It was like walking into something out of legend—I'd never seen anything like this, although I'd heard about such places.

There was a walkway inside, around the top of the wall, and I could see several figures standing up there. They paid us no heed. They were watching the forest, ready to shoot at anything hostile.

Farther on in was a cluster of buildings that seemed to share common walls. I wondered if that closeness was safe. Fire was a constant threat out here, if your chimney wasn't built right. Maybe they were stone walls or something.

We headed for the big cabin in the center of the grouping. Erik had already dismounted and abandoned his horse, opening the big wooden door and disappearing into murky firelight.

I took my cue from the older fellow and waited until he got off his horse before sliding down. Lord and Lady, it was good to touch ground—I hadn't ridden that much in many months. I stretched as much as I could, what with my heavy coat still on.

"This way, child," the older man said as he reached for the heavy door. As I came up to him, he looked over at me and smiled gently. It seemed his eyes were twinkling. "You are a long drink of water, child, but you move with grace. I'm called Matthew."

"Most people call me Allie," I said simply. Now that I had ceremonial names, there wasn't much danger in bad folks knowing my baptismal name. If this fellow wanted to be nice, I'd give him room to move around.

"Welcome to Hudson-on-the-Bend," he said gravely as he ushered me though the doorway.

I went in carefully, trying to be ready for anything. Were they going to throw spells at me, or tie me to a bolt in the wall? Did they think that fence would hold me? *For a while, maybe. But just wait.*

The room was long and fairly low—I could reach up and touch the rough logs of the loft floor—and had two big fireplaces, one on either end. Most of the people inside were women, busy sewing or listening to children recite lessons. A few were still working at one fireloft, and I could smell roast chicken and some sort of venison stew.

"I've brought you a guest, Jane," Matthew announced, and one of the women adjusting the spit looked up.

An older woman at the opposite fireplace cleared her throat, setting aside her needlework and rising to her feet. "Finally," she said in a dry soprano voice.

I let my vision become slightly unfocused, so I could watch a wide range around me. Erik chose that moment to leave the building, pushing past Matthew like he was a shrub or something. No one else made a move toward us.

"Edna," Matthew said respectfully. "I thought you'd be over at your own home."

The woman who had spoken looked grimly amused. As she came over, I saw that she was wearing a fine dark wool dress, its style older but not something from her youth. It seemed from the metallic flashes in her coiled braid that she had pale, silvering hair, and she looked to be in her fifties.

"It is my duty to greet all who come among us, Matthew." There was nothing threatening in the woman's words, but I felt the hair on my neck rise. A glance at Matthew told me he was uncomfortable.

Rustling from the other fireside caught my attention, and I looked beyond Matthew to see a tall, dark-haired woman with delicate features move to his side. She touched his arm, a fleeting expression of warmth crossing her face. Then she looked over at me. "Welcome. You must be hungry. And you brought rabbits! Thank you, we will roast them tomorrow." Her voice was soft and accented—a Frenchie, it sounded like.

This Edna person seemed too important to hand a string of bunnies, but I glanced at her for permission before extending my offering to—Jane? The matriarch nodded regally, and I smiled at Jane as I handed her the string.

A young girl brought Edna a large candle in a pewter holder, and the woman held it up to get a good look at me. Her eyebrows lifted visibly. "To be expected after a month in the woods," said that dry, thin voice. "She'll need a scrubbing before we take her to the ceremonial hall. And presentable clothes. Wherever did you find those pants?"

I gave her an even look. "I always wear pants under my skirt in the winter. It's cold where I come from."

The matriarch's gaze shifted to the delicate woman next to Matthew. "Feed her a bit, Jane. Not too much at first, we don't want her sick. It's but two nights to the dark of the moon. Then see she's scrubbed down—hair, too. Hurry up about it; we mustn't leave the Keeper waiting."

With that, Edna turned back toward her rocker by the fireplace. My audience with the queen was apparently over.

I slid my gaze back in Jane's direction. She gestured with one hand, inviting me toward the fireplace. There was no reason to pretend I wasn't cold, but I followed her with some dignity. The seats by the fireplace were all filled, so I set my bag down on the side opposite the spits, and knelt by the roaring flames.

Two of the girls present practically leapt to their feet. "Please, I'm warm, take my chair," one blurted out, the other starting, "Don't sit on the floor. . . ." They looked to be ten or so—maybe older, but not growing much yet; sisters or cousins, in similar muslin dresses

"I've got pants on," I answered, settling on the flagstone hearth. "Thank you, though." I smiled at them and then let my gaze return to Jane. She had knelt down and was busy scooping stew into a dark, oval trencher. Fishing in a jar on a shelf next to the fireplace, Jane pulled out a spoon and handed me both utensil and the half round of bread. "Thank you," I decided to say immediately. If it was terrible, it would still fill my stomach.

A glance told me the girls had settled down with the walnuts they were cracking. They kept stealing a few looks my way . . . guess newcomers weren't that common after all.

There was no subtlety to this stew—it was basic venison, onions, and some salt—but it had simmered for a long time, and it tasted good. While I worked on it, Jane cut legs and thighs off one of the seasoned chickens she had spitted, and breast meat as well. These she laid on another half round of bread, which she placed to my left. "You and Matthew share that," she said with a smile. Then she leaned over to prepare another bowl of stew.

Matthew appeared at my side with two mugs in hand. "I wasn't sure if you wanted ale, so I brought cider," he announced, setting the big pewter drinking vessels next to the roasted chicken. "Is that all right?"

You know, it's not easy to hate people who are trying hard to be nice to you. I sure hoped these folks at least had souls. I glanced and saw a clear liquid; I lifted the mug to my nose, so I knew the cider had fermented. "It's fine. I don't know if I've ever had hard cider before."

Jane hesitated in the act of handing Matthew his trencher of stew. "You've never had cider?"

I blinked at her altered tone of voice. "Oh, I drink a lot of cider, but not hard cider. Momma's hard cider is pretty potent stuff, and my cousin only makes ale and spiced cider." I wasn't sure why I was running on in a bird-witted fashion, but there you have it—tired, I guess.

Jane and Matthew exchanged glances, and then their gaze settled back on me. Something in the way they looked at each other made me wonder if Matthew had taken a younger bride for himself. Jane looked to be Momma's age, while Matthew could spot her at least fifteen years. "How old are you, child?" Jane whispered to me.

The words were so soft, I could barely hear her—I doubt either of the girls shelling nuts did. "Thirteen," I said quietly.

Jane immediately turned to the gathering of children. "Will you go put kettles on to boil, back in our fireplace?" she asked the two oldest girls.

"Of course, Aunt Jane," one of them said, and they took their bowl of nuts with them when they trooped out a back door. The air rushing in their wake was cool but not icy . . . I wondered if the door led to a hallway between buildings.

Turning back to me, Jane said "They will prepare a bath for you back in our own cabin."

That was a relief, and I felt myself relax. I really didn't want to bathe around Queen Edna, or in a place where men were walking through. I glanced over at her husband, and found that Matthew was studying me.

Matthew's eyebrows had visibly lifted. "I would have guessed you were sixteen at the least."

I felt a bit embarrassed. "My father's family is pretty tall," was all I said. I ducked back over my stew.

After I'd taken a few more bites, I lifted my gaze from the trencher. Jane and Matthew were looking at each other again.

"The Keeper will ask," Jane finally said quietly, turning back to me. "Tell him the truth—but no others." She flicked her fingers at Matthew, who took a chicken leg and his stew and stepped away from the fire. "Are you moon-touched?"

Well, that was a bit personal, since we'd just met, but there was something in Jane's soft voice—something anxious—that made me decide to answer her. "Not yet."

The woman's deep green eyes grew large. "*Pauvre petite*," she murmured. "The Keeper will not be pleased with Erik. But still. . . ." Her gaze slid to one side, as if seeing who might be close by. "You are very strong, yes? To hold the Keeper at bay so long? And before the moon has taken you. . . ." She looked back to me and said softly: "My name is Jeanette, but the Keeper cannot pronounce it, and so I am called Jane."

"Jah-nette," I repeated after her, nodding slightly. "I suppose I'll never hear Alfreda from him, either."

"You are a child," she stressed, reaching to press my hand. "After he binds you, he will ignore you. For a time." Her eyes blinked rapidly, and then she looked down at our joined hands. "There is great strength in you, little one. He will want that. . . ." She pressed my hand again, and then leaned back to rise to her feet.

As she moved away, I thought I saw tears in her eyes.

※ 🌱 ※

Turned out that back door led to a regular rabbit warren of enclosed walkways, with doors that led off into small private cabins. Apparently people did have privacy and their own homes here, but they also lived a lot closer together than anything I'd ever imagined.

The girls had filled a bathtub for me, right in front of their fireplace!

There were no words to describe the joy of a hot bath after living in the same clothes for weeks. And my hair—I was afraid half my head was falling off, but Jeanette assured me that we lose hair every day. Mine had just waited for me to loosen my braid.

One of the young girls was indeed Jeanette and Matthew's oldest daughter, Virginia, and she was delighted to dig in her mother's chests to find me something clean to wear. Her cousin Prudence was fascinated by my flaxen hair, so long and so thick, and volunteered to comb it out.

"It is like honey poured from a jar of sunshine!" Prudence announced as her efforts helped my hair to dry.

"Well, yours is like a shadow, and where I come from, the fashion is dark," I told her, wincing as she pulled a wide-toothed comb through my mane.

"Is her hair dry on top, Prudence?" her aunt asked, and I made a point of thinking *Jane* to myself. She would be Jeanette in private, but I had a feeling I shouldn't use her real name in the presence of others.

"Yes, aunt," Prudence told her. "The middle is still very wet, though."

"May I braid it?" Virginia said, walking into the firelight with an arm full of dresses.

"Sure, as long as your momma thinks you can do something with this mess." I didn't want her to think I doubted her skill, but thick, fine hair took work to control.

"I braid Momma's hair," Virginia assured me, which made me feel better. Jane's hair looked black, but it was as thick and fine as mine.

Jane gestured for Virginia to take over with my hair, and started sorting through the clothing. She'd gotten a good look at me while I was scrubbing down, and now separated out the three biggest dresses. After studying them a moment, she gave me a long look.

"These will only reach your ankles, but in such snow as we have, that is all to the good."

And quietly tells people I'm a young'un, I thought, but did not say. Jane seemed worried about my age, and yet wanted it known without words. I wondered exactly what was going on, but was afraid to ask in front of the girls. It might be something that would worry them, too.

She chose the dark brown dress with a high neck, the one that made my lack of hips plain. I was no longer completely flat-chested, but there wasn't much to notice. I'd carefully relaxed my blocks the tiniest bit, to see what I could sense about Jane and the two girls. So far, I'd felt nothing hostile—not like I got from Edna right through my protections.

Suddenly something strong brushed past my defenses—something laced with urgency. It was heading this way. I quickly pulled back behind my own shield and sent an anchor of self down rock and fire to branch through the cold soil right to the water table.

If a fragment of your soul is hidden, all of you is hidden. Cory and Marta had taught me that lesson well—no one was going to shake my grounding.

A young girl burst through the door leading to the kitchen in the great room, carrying a tray with mugs and a large clay jug. "The queen has ordered spiced cider, so all must partake," she announced, setting the tray down on a closed trunk. Without hesitation she turned and walked over to me. Close up, I could see that she was not a child but rather my age of thirteen or so, a dainty fairy with wise dark eyes set in a triangular face.

"*Veritas*," she said softly, and there was music in her voice.

I was struck speechless. Not so much by the word that Death had prophesied would become one of my names, but the sound of the word. I'd heard this voice before.

This was the voice of the river.

"Sunlight and summer sky from the mountaintop," she said conversationally. "A challenge to any. So you bested the black Hudsons. I am proud to make your acquaintance. I am called Felicity in this time and place."

"I'm Allie," I decided to say.

She nodded vigorously, her cloud of dark hair shaking free of her cap. "Well named and well met," was the response. "Be very careful, bright one," she went on without a pause, her gaze holding mine. "The Keeper tires of the queen." With that, she turned and left the cabin through the same door.

I looked over at Jane.

The woman looked uncomfortable. "Felicité," she began haltingly, her French accent pronounced "has been unsettled since serving out her apprenticeship. She is Jonathan's wife."

Wife? She didn't look any older than me!

Suddenly terror gripped me by the throat. I realized what I was thinking, and shoved the thought away. If these people thought they were going to give me to some old feller, they had a surprise coming. Jane and Matthew seemed to have worked out well enough, but Felicity was either moonstruck or very good at pretending to be.

I intended to get out of this with my mind intact.

Jane had moved to pour us all mugs of cider. "Warm yourself with this, Allie, and then we must go to the ceremonial hall. You must meet the Keeper." This last was a whisper, which did not exactly encourage me.

We all obediently drank our cider, and then Jane told the girls to prepare for bed. Gesturing toward the door into the kitchen, the woman led the way.

Few people had lingered in the big room, and we could hear someone stirring in the loft over our heads. Matthew had remained, sitting by the roasting fire and sipping a mug of ale. The woman called Edna was awake and pacing around the room.

"Finally," she said when she saw us returning. "We must hurry." Edna moved swiftly to the pegs in the front wall, removing a huge woven shawl and wrapping her head and shoulders in it. "Come along." She threw open the heavy door and disappeared into the compound.

Jane hurriedly seized my coat and her own cloak, pushing the sheepskin at me. "We must not make him wait."

As I pulled on my coat I decided not to point out that he'd waited at least an hour while I'd bathed and eaten. Jane seemed worried enough. I hoped she wouldn't be blamed for my appearance or behavior. The Keeper probably wouldn't be real happy with what he saw. Matthew was also pulling on his coat—it might be nice to have him along. He still didn't feel hostile.

In the murk of the torches lining the stockade, we could see Edna far in the lead, entering the tall building near the center of the fortress. It was fairly dark inside the structure, the wooden walls stripped of bark and polished with beeswax. One stone wall lined the south side, and a fire was blazing in the huge fireloft.

There were several circles etched into the sanded floorboards, the one in the center an upside-down pentacle. I could already tell I couldn't step into that ring. Maybe one of the other rings. . . .

Planed wooden benches lined the walls of the place, and we could see a huddled shape sitting on one of them. It was gasping and shaking, and made no move to stand up. I looked hard in that direction; I'd grown much better at seeing in near darkness, but you never knew what might be hiding in shadows.

We walked past a rack of lit tapers and two tables loaded with fragrant herbs and spices. There seemed to be several people standing down near the flames, but I couldn't make out any faces. There was one chair, a big rocker, in front of the fireplace. A veil seemed draped over the blaze, and I realized there was a fire screen before it.

Edna walked right over the burnt-in pentacle, but both Jane and Matthew stepped to one side of it. I wasn't sure if I should try this or not, but the question was answered for me. It was like an invisible wall, preventing me from moving forward. I stepped to one side as Jane turned back to fetch me, and took several long strides to catch up.

The men and women standing on either side of the fireplace were all staring at me. Most of them looked impassive, but some had definite expressions on their faces. A few looked suspicious . . . a couple were startled, or afraid.

It suddenly occurred to me that maybe the Hudsons' "guests" weren't usually as cooperative as I was being. Did they see that as strength? Confidence? Insanity?

Movement behind us made me tense up, but I recognized the flaxen head of hair as he stepped forward. It was Erik.

Wasn't it?

His skin seemed paler than usual, sweat was running down his face, and he was shaking as if in a fever. Was this whom we'd walked past? He hadn't looked like this earlier. Had he caught a cold?

A slip of conversation floated to the surface of my mind, and I pulled my breath in with a hiss. Death had said the Keeper could move into someone else's flesh. How far away could he go from his real body when he did that thing?

Had I even met the real Erik? Or had it been the Keeper all along? *Dear God.*

I was pretty sure Erik was beside me now. Which meant. . . . I turned back toward the big rocker, and found myself looking into the blackest eyes I'd ever seen. They glittered like chips of smoked glass, and carried more years in them than I could easily count.

Those eyes had more years than I could imagine living.

This, then, was Harold Hudson, the Keeper of Souls.

I swallowed slowly. I was in trouble.

Thirteen

IT HAD BEEN THE SUMMER OF MY ninth year that I met an old man who claimed to have walked with the Devil. I'd been full of questions, of course. *When did it happen? What did the Devil look like? Did he speak like normal folk, or did he just look at you, and you knew what he was thinking?*

I was heading north on the Wilderness Road on my way to Boonesborough, the old man had said, pausing to scratch at a scar on his left arm. *I was a day behind a big group, and struggling to catch up. The Shawnee were hot for scalps in those days, and I wasn't interested in running into a raiding party alone.* His eyes had grown distant, then, as his memory had rolled back.

We'd re-arranged ourselves in the porch rockers, away from prying ears. *Snow was early that year, and already deep for the month of Frost. I came around a bend in the trail, and there he was, walking along with his flintlock on his shoulder. He looked like anybody else you might pass on the trail . . . 'coon cap, weathered buckskins, had mocs like an Indian. His hair was long and blond, and his face skinny and hard as flint. He had pale blue eyes that could see to the horizon and beyond.* Lost in memory, that old man had paused for a long while.

How'd you know he was the Devil? I had finally whispered.

The old fellow had looked over his shoulder to make sure we were still alone. Then he had leaned toward me and whispered, *They say your family knows about these things, so I'll tell you. He didn't leave no tracks! He didn't throw a shadder!*

Staring at old Harold Hudson's cold, dark eyes, I was sure I was looking upon a man who'd lost his shadow long ago. I could feel an icy finger trickle down my spine, I was suddenly so scared. This was as bad as the time I faced down a cougar. Was it my imagination, or did his eyes actually glow?

There are spells that can detect a falsehood, and spells that can compel truth. Of course the Keeper would use one or the other. He didn't look like a man who took things on trust. If I could phrase everything carefully, like I was nervous, to give me time to think my words through. . . .

I didn't need to pretend to be nervous.

Keeper Hudson looked older than my great-grandmother had been when she passed on. I couldn't see much in the shadows, but he was short and thin, his hair a straw patch on top of his head. Still, his eyes were bright and his hands did not shake. I didn't plan to underestimate him.

"Edna," he said suddenly, his voice as dry as dust. His gaze remained locked with mine. The woman moved out of the shadows to stand at the Keeper's left. With her back to the fire, I could not see her face.

I didn't need to . . . I could feel her dislike from where I stood.

"What is your name?" he asked, and I swallowed at his tone. Cold as an arctic wind.

Here we go. "I was baptized Alfreda Sorensson," I replied carefully.

"That is truth," Edna commented aloud, letting me know a spell had been cast. Or that she was pretending it had been cast, just to unnerve me.

"How old are you?"

Huh. Hard to say it here without the rest of his "court" hearing. "I am thirteen."

The Keeper's eyebrows rose visibly. "When were you born?"

Hadn't I just said that? "The end of the month of Sun."

The Keeper's eyes swiveled toward Edna, who simply nodded. Then his gaze fell back upon me. "You have been honored, youngling. The house of Hudson always has need of fresh blood. You have been chosen to join our family group."

"You want to adopt me?" I wasn't in the mood for vagueness.

The Keeper almost smiled. "Not exactly. All of us are bound together . . . it is the power that runs our compound and keeps our homes safe. That we can do in two nights, during the dark of the moon. Later . . . perhaps on your fourteenth birthday . . . you will marry one of my grandsons."

It was my turn to give him a long look. *Not on your life.* "That's kind of you to offer, but I don't think my father would accept his suit," I decided to say. "Especially not this soon."

Edna actually nodded. Either she knew it for truth, or knew I believed it was truth.

The Keeper smiled slightly. "All previous arrangements have been suspended. Do you know anything about herbs?"

"Yes." *Don't offer what he don't ask*, I reminded myself.

"Do you know anything about magic?"

"Yes." If I'd said "no," they would have pried. But a simple "yes" covered a world of things.

The Keeper frowned, and contemplated me. Edna glanced in his direction, and the Keeper said: "Do you know anything of midwifery?"

So . . . they knew how to speak thought to thought. I didn't think that question would occur to a man. "Yes."

The Keeper leaned forward in his rocker. "Erik tells me you know how to trap for furs."

"Yes." This was more of a whisper. I was not sure I'd ever done anything in my life as hard as giving those one-word answers. It was torture. I was so used to *explaining* things. . . . Was the Keeper trying to push me into careless speech?

"And you have proved you can take care of yourself in the wilds." He smiled, and it was not friendly. I was pretty sure he didn't care a bit for me.

Hudson the Elder glanced up at one of the shadows to his right. "I want her warded here until the ceremony. She will eat and sleep here. She will have an escort to the privy." His eyes swiveled back in my direction. "Offensive spells will not work within the circle," he said to me. "Defensive spells will not work. If you fight us, you will hurt only yourself."

Circle? They were going to put me in a circle? How big a circle? I didn't like the sound of this at all, but there wasn't much I could do about it.

Someone must have known how the Keeper would respond. Bedding was brought out, including a nightgown. Well and good, but I had no intention of changing clothes in front of a crowd. Of course, if they wanted to use magic, they could spy on me through a mirror, or even the flames of the fire.

I didn't think I was that important to them. Why hadn't they asked more questions about my training? Did they think I had no training? Surely the Keeper had talked to Erik about me before beginning his hunt.

Then again, he was an old, old, man who had dominated his family a long time. Maybe he didn't ask questions much anymore— he just gave orders. If all I represented to him was another log on the fire of his power, he might not know, nor care, what else I could do.

What with all those lessons, surely I could do something.

ॐ 𝕯 ॐ

It turned out that there was a huge circle in the ceremonial room, a circle touching the walls. This was where they bound me in, with chalk scribbling and candles and symbols that I forced myself to read. Some were familiar signs, and some were strange, and some were just downright creepy. The candles were black wax, and I tried not to think about the ingredients used to make them. I *hoped* they were just dark beeswax.

Whatever the spell, it held me as well as a linked chain or a tall fence. I could not step over the lines of the circle unless a Hudson accompanied me. Maybe it was just as well . . . something about the shadows in that room seemed *alive*.

Lying buried under my blankets, only my nose peeking out from the sheet, I took deep breaths and tried to get a handle on my fear. I'd been fine until they left me alone in this building with only those weird candles for company. Now the unease rose in me like foam in a beer mug. I pushed back at the wave of panic, trying to get it to recede, and wondered if Death would come to me in my dreams.

Offensive spells would not work . . . defensive spells would not work; ritual, in other words. A thought occurred to me, and I rolled over on my side to face the fireplace ten feet away. What would you call wild magic? Neutral? Or did it depend on how you used the power you drew from the elements?

Did that mean wild magic could serve me there?

My lids slipped down without my telling them to, but I had no memory of dreams when I woke in the early dawn light. All I remembered was a sense of unease, as if someone was looking for me and couldn't find me.

And a sense of watchfulness . . . I was not the only living thing in that room.

I found that Death's absence didn't worry me. Death wanted Hudson; Death would not abandon its best chance yet to succeed.

With the dawn came Jane, a bowl of oatmeal and a pitcher of hot water in hand. I put my borrowed dress back on and wished for my pants. The walk to the outhouse probably would be nippy.

It wasn't nippy . . . it was *cold*. At least I had my sheepskin boots.

Jane took her time bringing me back to the ceremonial hall, giving me a tiny tour of the huge compound. There were three barns that rivaled the hall in size, holding cows, oxen, mules, and horses, as well as smaller animals such as goats, geese, and chickens. The Hudsons also had a large rabbit hutch, so Jane had been especially nice about my unnecessary string of bunnies.

"Wild ones have more flavor," she told me with a shy smile. "A gift is always appreciated . . . and it made some of the others wary." This time her smile was cynical.

"This is a good thing?" I said carefully.

We walked in silence a moment, and then Jane said, "There is a hierarchy here, much like a wolf pack's. It is a delicate game, to balance strength and invisibility. You want to be seen as powerful enough to protect yourself, but not so powerful as to attract too much attention.

"Bringing gifts when you were stolen without any possessions implies a position of strength. The others try to decide where you belong in the ranks."

"Is magical potential the only measure?" I decided to ask her.

She slid me a look out of a dark eye and then turned her gaze back to the scraped courtyard. "No. But it is the most important measure. Whom you are bound to for children, or the strength of your children, is important. Any talents and training you bring with you can be important. Trapping is not done by women, but it increases your mystery—what *else* can she do?"

"Jeanette, why are you being so good to me?" I whispered, hoping I wasn't going to upset her with the question. Someone friendly there could be a big help, but I needed to see how she reacted to suspicion. I used her real name to soften the blow, in case her kindness was genuine.

For a few minutes Jane did not speak. We walked through a crisp gray morning, birdsong surrounding us. Then she said, "Because when I was brought to the Hudsons', not much older than you, terrified and desolate with fear, Tante Maria was kind to me. She taught me what I needed to know and she protected me. In her memory, I will do my best for you."

I let my gaze trip over the small cabins backed up against the stockade fence. In someone's memory? Maybe it was also a way to gain an ally.

"Are there. . . ." I tried to remember the word my papa used when he spoke of different groups arguing about electing the president. ". . . Factions here? Is the only safety in numbers?"

Jane stopped walking and turned to face me. Her eyes were thoughtful. "You are a wise child," she murmured, her voice somber. "Yes, everyone ends up in a group. The largest hasn't many powerful people, but united it can keep the crueler family members at bay. Then there are those who enjoy what Harold Hudson has built and use it to their advantage." This was said with a curl of the lip. She turned and continued down the long side of the fort, passing the large building used for weaving and spinning.

"Others hate this place and what the Keeper does to followers and strangers alike, but do not have enough power to break free." Jane shrugged as she finished speaking. "I think you are strong, to push him away for an entire moon. So, many will court your favor. When you try to decide among shifting alliances, remember this—anything we do without the direct command of the Keeper or his wife risks punishment. You must decide why someone has taken a risk."

"Where does Felicity belong in all this?" I might not get any more information, but Felicity was the river's voice. I needed to find out how she did it, because I was pretty sure the Hudsons weren't loaning her any power for the trick. I might be reduced to her methods.

Jane seemed to shiver, and she walked faster. "There are many dark things that frame Harold Hudson's life. Some of them are so frightening, they can damage your mind. Felicity has been like that since not long after her marriage to Jonathan." Jane turned her head toward me. "I do not know if she is mad or merely a bit fey— no one has ever been able to trip her tongue. But her contribution to spells was unreliable, and no punishment seemed to cow her. She does what she pleases. Since her spinning is the finest in the household, the Keeper does not yet grow angry that she has not quickened . . . though others are not so generous."

Huh. All of it interesting, but how much was useful? Depended on how long I was trapped there.

Jane had taken me the long way around to the hall, but she couldn't stall forever. As we approached the building, I asked bluntly, "Is this thing going to hurt?"

At least she didn't pretend to misunderstand. "Not really," she said softly. "He will cut your finger to get some of your blood, and press that blood to a cut on his own hand. Then you will be bound into the circle."

"Sounds more like bound to the old man, like spokes and a wheel," I said in turn.

"He is the center; we revolve around him," Jane agreed.

"Has anyone ever tried to break the axle?" I whispered.

Her eyes grew rounder, but Jane schooled her face well. "He cannot die," was her reply. There was desolation in her words.

Jane—Jeanette—believed that. Really believed it. "All things die," I reminded her gently, and took hold of her arm as if helping her over a patch of ice.

"Not him." Her voice now was bitter. "He was old when he stole me, and I have waited twenty years for him to die."

I squeezed her arm gently as we stepped into the ceremonial hall. "*All* things die," I repeated, holding her gaze a long moment. It was all the comfort I dared give her.

Perhaps it was enough. Jane reached to hug me before taking me across the double circle. As she turned away, I thought I saw something in her eyes I had yet to see in this place.

Hope.

٭ 𝔇 ٭

It was fey Felicity who brought me dinner, which had been lovingly laid out upon a wooden tray. She had even covered the plate with a china bowl to hold in the heat.

Stew, cold chicken and fresh corn bread, along with some hot cider. No rabbit, praise the heavens! The cider was from apples I did not recognize, but it was freshly pressed and lively. These people did not have much imagination, but they did not seem to stint their extended family on food.

"Thank you," I told the young woman. "This smells very good. Do you know what kind of apples are in the cider?"

"A rose by any other name would smell as sweet," she responded with a sharp nod.

"So it's said," I agreed. "But I was just wondering. We raise fruit trees in my part of the country, and my parents might enjoy another variety."

"We are all orphans here," Felicity said, turning slightly and pacing along the curve of the circle.

"I'm not." It was a firm statement. I wasn't going to let anybody know what I was up to, but I wasn't going to pretend that I liked being snatched and forced to join the Hudson clan.

"And will you fight the running of the tide?" she asked, turning around and facing me.

I settled in old Harold's rocker, which had been left inside the big circle, and set the tray in my lap. I'd heard about tides—how the moon commanded the sea to rise and fall in its own private rhythm. "If I must."

"Fools rush in where angels fear to tread," she murmured, her pixie face closed and watchful.

"I prefer to bring the angels with me," I decided to say. I broke open my corn bread square to spread some butter on it, and told her, "I've heard your voice before. It was kind of you to keep me company while I was walking the riverbank."

Felicity stood her ground, studying me a moment. "No one need be a prisoner. The soul cannot be bound."

"I'd agree," I replied, and took a bite of corn bread. After I finished chewing and swallowing, I added, "Especially someone whose voice is as free as a bird. Do you sing to the river, or can you talk to water?" Hopefully, that was vague enough to make anyone listening think I was just humoring the madwoman.

Felicity tossed her dark cloud of hair and began pacing again. "If you would be free as a bird, you must escape this cage," were her next words. "The Keeper will pen you if he can. He grows weary . . . your strength gives him new hope." She looked over at me, and her voice dropped to a whisper. "He will renew, and then seek a wife. 'Tis said he prefers a fine beard, but you might inspire him to take youth." Shaking her head, she gripped her arms and continued pacing. "The fair-haired lad is terrified."

I started working on my stew as I worked my way through her words. The "beard" part made me think she was alluding to Hudson taking a new body. I smiled into my lap at the idea of a madwoman being the only one to really hint at what was going on in Hudson-on-the-Bend. Did Hudson usually pick someone my father's age, to get past the stripling stage? But this time . . . Erik?

The cider was still hot, and I sipped carefully, aware that Felicity was watching me out of the corner of her eye. I couldn't inspire Hudson to change his plans, could I? There had been several really beautiful young women in the crowded shadows the night before. Erik might be right—I could end up with some of the Schell beauty, but I wasn't holding my breath. Why me?

A thought flickered by, and I mentally grabbed for it. The only possible answer . . . power. Maybe Hudson didn't have a lot of interest in women anymore, not like a healthy man. Or maybe he still liked a pretty woman in his bed. But I'd bet my dowry he wanted a powerful woman even more . . . and all my teachers agreed I should end up powerful.

Mighty tempting for old Hudson. Maybe I was supposed to be for Erik, but now Hudson was thinking of Erik for himself? Youth and power in one marriage . . . and the younger a body he took, the longer he could tap me.

"I'd surely like to learn how to speak to the winds," I murmured, my voice barely audible. Could it be similar to singing down a storm?

Felicity twitched, and I knew she'd heard me. Then the door opened, and someone kicked the snow off their feet and stepped inside. I could see the white-blonde hair from where I sat. Speak of the devil in training. . . .

"And all the soap in our larder will not wash your hands clean," Felicity said evenly, giving Erik a hard look.

He kept his head lowered as he removed his overcoat, and said only, "I'll take back the tray, Felicity. You need not wait."

Felicity tossed her head once more and, with a hard, thoughtful look my way, flitted out the open doorway. Only then did Erik reach to pull the big door closed.

So. I finally had my chance, my sole chance, to let him know just what I thought of the entire business. As he looked over to me I said in my coldest voice, "Well, are you Erik today, or *him*?"

No one could hope for a better response—Erik jerked as if I'd slapped him, his face draining of all color.

"How did you know?" he whispered. "How *could* you have known?"

"You underestimated me, Erik," I whispered back. It was all the hint he was getting. Suddenly I was overwhelmed by fury—I was so mad, I was prickling hot all over. I sank my teeth into a chicken leg, since I couldn't sink them into his arm.

"No, I didn't. But I don't know how long the Keeper will underestimate you," was his weary response. He folded to the floor, his legs crossed Indian style. Fingers interlaced, a few muttered words— The light level seemed to rise in the room.

"This will make it seem like we're very good whisperers," Eric told me. So they were listening, at the least.

"What can you have to say that you don't want your family to hear?" I made this offhand, as if I didn't really care, but I knew this might be my first "faction" offer.

Erik surprised me. "I'm sorry I brought you here, Allie, but you've already proved my choice was good, hiding so long. I don't

know how you know the Keeper's secret, but there's more to it."
The youth leaned forward, his expression intense. "He can take
someone's body away from them, *forever*. If he's feeling generous,
he'll let you finish whatever life is left to his last corpse. If you
anger him, he'll just crush out your mind and soul, and take you
anyway."

Living out a couple years in a body eighty-some years old?
Generous, said the cat to the mouse before she swallowed him
head first instead of tail first.

Erik didn't need to know how much Death had told me. "So, am
I to be his next choice? Does he change sex sometimes, too?"

The youth was already shaking his head. "Far as we know, he
can only steal blood kin's bodies." His face became drawn and
bitter-looking. "Sometimes I think we're all here just to give him a
choice of the best body."

"How old is he, do you think? His thoughts?" *Now why did I
ask that?* The answer wouldn't help me, and might scare me.

"He remembers the Black Plague in London," Erik muttered.

Numbness whipped through me like a wind. I lost interest in
the rest of my chicken and set down the tray. There was warmth
left in the cider, and I clutched the mug with both hands, vainly
trying to warm my soul. I wasn't exactly sure of the dates, but I did
know the last time London had plague was in the mid-seventeenth
century . . . over 150 years before.

The first time it came to England was when it was called the
Black Death, as if there was no other . . . and that was still three
hundred years earlier.

Whether 150 years or 450 years, either was unbelievable, and
so I pushed the thought away.

"Why are you glad I'm here?" I finally said.

"Because I don't want to be his next body, and a blood relative
can't break free without help." This was said simply, as if he were
asking to borrow a cup of sugar. I straightened in surprise, but
Erik rushed on. "Allie, I know I'm asking a lot, but you're strong,
stronger than anyone I've ever met. And the moon doesn't rule
you, does it?"

I stared at his pale face and thought about what he had said. He
seemed genuinely frightened. Could he use this knowledge against
me? If he paid close attention, he'd figure it out eventually. "No."

"I didn't think so." He gave me a direct look. "The Keeper wants you wedded and bedded before you're moon-touched. It will link your power to your husband's body, and to the Keeper, if you marry before you can have children."

Not the soul . . . the body. "And the link stays, no matter who is inside the body?" I asked.

"That's what one of the oldest told me, before she died." Erik looked away, his face suddenly flushed. "One of my cousins was also in the area, looking for a bride. You *don't* want him chosen for you—even the Keeper would be better. I guarantee Samuel would have also found you. You were too strong to overlook. I'm sorry, but I had no choice."

I just gave him a hard stare. Choice or not, I was gonna work on his guilt like an old granny before I relented!

"Think about pooling our strength, Allie," he whispered. "If we can come up with something that might work, there are others who will help us. We're not the only ones who want free from the Keeper." He glanced down at the tray. "You want me to take that?"

I looked down at the demolished meal. No sense in depriving myself; I'd had little enough the past few weeks. "Can you leave the chicken?"

"Long as I don't leave the spoon or knife, sure." He reached across the circle, set the plate of chicken breast and leg aside, and picked up everything else. "Do you want more bread or cider?"

"Later, maybe." I'd already dismissed him in my mind. Here was an unexpected ally, indeed. . . . The spell light dimmed as Erik left the building, but I paid it no heed. I could still throw logs on the fire; I'd cope.

A tiny shiver ran through me, and I tried to control the kernel of fear that was sprouting in my heart. I was *not* going to be the wife of the Keeper, no matter whose body he wore.

Surely Marta could find me before my fourteenth birthday. . . .

⁂

Great-grandmother Emma was sharing a porch with me, as we watched a nor'easter come in over the sea. We did not speak . . . it wasn't necessary. We both knew a storm was coming, and when to get out of the wind, so why—

"You need the necessity," a voice said in my ear, and I felt myself leap from my dream. A swirl of confusion, and I remembered I was trapped in the main circle of a ceremonial building. The fire had been banked, leaving the slow-burning black candles as the only source of illumination. Weird shadows loomed over me, twisted by the timbers holding up the peaked roof. I tried to control my sudden, ragged breathing—that darkness was *alive.*

Felicity knelt beside me, shaking my shoulder. "Come on, I could feel your need in my sleep. Here are your boots." She shoved my sheepskin muckers at me.

What was all this? I'd gone to the privy before sleeping, I didn't need to—Something closed in my mind, and I pulled on a boot. Thank goodness I'd made my coat to cover my thighs, and that Jane had brought me long wool stockings.

It was a shivery night for an outdoor conference.

We crunched our way out to the double outhouse behind the ceremonial hall. It didn't seem as cold as it'd been earlier. One thing to be grateful for in the dead of winter was that there was almost no odor from the privy. I ducked in the right cubicle, while Felicity flowed into the left side. As I'd hoped, we could hear each other easily.

"You must give the winds what they want," Felicity said without preamble.

"What do they want?" I asked softly.

"They want challenge, they want variety, they want possibilities across the entire range of choices," was her gentle reply.

"How do we give them what they want?" Here I was, talking about an element of nature as if conscious control was involved. The only mastery I'd seen so far was my own. The precision of the whirlpool came back to me quite clearly.

"Choose the Belgian for big, heavy jobs, the plantation walker for small, elegant jobs," was her answer to me. "Make not the mistake of forcing them from their places—they go where the pattern takes them, and will do what they can."

Great. Riddles upon riddles. I could freeze to death before I figured this out. "I was convinced I heard you singing, an entire day's ride from the compound. How did you throw your voice that far?"

"The winds carry all songs, all words," she said, her voice growing softer. I listened, but could not hear what had disturbed her.

"Then why isn't the air full of conversation?" I said in turn.

"It is."

I inhaled sharply, pressing my lips tightly together to keep from hissing—and then remembered the woven net of light I'd seen in my dream. If everything was tied together by bonds invisible to the eye, why not sound that was not always received by the ear? Some animals could hear sounds a mile away, it was said, and a few humans had the trait.

"How do you make something stand out? Or pick something special out of the air?" I was impressed at how calm I made that question sound.

"That is where our Gift comes to the fore. You must call the wind to you and ask it to bear your tidings." She took a trembling breath. "My power is bound, I can send no news. But I can sing. The winds like to carry song, and they carry it as far as they can— the great storms will carry it from sea to mountain, from mountain to sea." A whisper came through the wooden wall. "Perhaps my family can hear me, and know that I still live."

"And if I try to send a message before the spell casting?" I asked.

"You will need a strong wind, or to convince a breeze to pass your words along. Where are you bound?" Felicity said simply.

I'd been listening to her too long . . . she was starting to make sense. "I want to send word to the east side of the Michigan lake, north of the Saint Joseph river, north of Fort Saint Joseph, west of Fort Detroit." If any practitioner in our greater region could hear the call, they'd relay it to Marta, I was sure.

"North," was the firm reply. "North and east. It was fate that brought you here—may you free us all. It is easiest to use what Mother Nature has already put in motion, although when unbound one can control the actual winds."

Just that easily, I had it confirmed—Felicity was using wild magic to send her songs along the breezes. "So I want to catch a ride on a big wind heading north?"

"Call into the wind, ask for its help, then send it your thoughts. When it circles you before departing, you'll know it will help you as far as it can."

Then something occurred to me. "Will the ceremonial circle stop me?"

Silence. "Maybe, I think yes," came the low words. "It is a binding spell for you. But when they will pull you into the family, there will be a moment before the new binding. If you climb the mountain of power while the Keeper does his worst. . . ."

I thought about that. Not offensive, not defensive, this spell might be able to escape during another casting. But what had the weather been like outside? There didn't seem to be much wind that night, and I couldn't hear a lot from inside the lodge.

"Can you somehow tell me—" I started to say.

"Everything all right back here?"

My heart almost stopped. The low voice was several feet away, up against the hall itself, but that was too close.

"All is well, Amory, and all will be well," Felicity said abruptly. I heard the creak of the other door opening. "Come, shall you dream?"

Inhaling slowly and deeply, I pushed open my door and stepped into snow. Quickly I glanced up at the sky, hoping to get a direction on the wind. The sky was almost clear, but a bit murky, as if a fine mist had been cast over my eyes. Some of the smaller stars were very faint.

The breeze was light and capricious, now one way, now another. How long until the wind changed?

We walked back to the front of the building, the hulking dark form of Amory on our trail. He wasn't particularly hostile, but he was suspicious—the torch light from the stockade wall did not reach us, so he couldn't see our expressions.

What I wouldn't give to avoid returning to that building. . . .

As we took hold of the door, Felicity said "The month of Wind will bring the rain and melt the frozen lands again. When the stars begin to huddle, earth will soon become a puddle."

I blinked, and looked out of the corner of my eye at her cloak-shaped figure. That was old weather lore, and generally accurate.

Straining, reaching out as much as I could with my senses, I could scarcely feel it. A change in the weather. Either Felicity was very receptive to weather patterns, or the Hudsons had set up a spell to detect them. Rain was coming. At this time of year, that most likely meant a southwest wind pushing north.

If it was a powerful enough storm, the next night I was gonna write a letter home.

FOURTEEN

A SINGLE ACTION CAN change the future.

I know this—I have done it.

Morning came early in Hudson-on-the-Bend; it was still dark when Jane and Felicity brought me breakfast and a different dress. It was dark blue, and a bit nicer . . . apparently ceremonies were an excuse to party. I had hours until I needed to change into it, however.

"Red sky at morning, sailors take warning," Felicity announced as she set corked jugs of cider and water next to my banked fire. Briskly she started stirring up the coals.

White and red morning skies promised rain to come—my front was rolling our way. Now, if some of the wind would just hang around long enough to take a message. . . .

"Good morning to you, too," I said in response as I took a tray from Jane. The odor of grits and honey rose to greet me, and the small pitcher of milk had cream on top.

"You slept well, I hope?" Jane said in her soft French accent. Only her intent look made me wonder if she suspected—or knew— something about my talk with Felicity.

"As well as you can with shadows looming over you," I replied, glancing at the black candles, which had hardly shrunk at all in size.

"Yes . . . the watchers." She looked at Felicity, which gave me time for a private shudder. So something *was* in this building with me.

Thinking about invisible critters was not a good idea. "Jane, could you bring me something to do?" I said abruptly. "A book to read, or some sewing that needs doing? Is there wool to be carded?"

Jane seemed startled, and then smiled her sweet smile at me. "There is wool, yes. We could bring a sack, and the cards."

"I'd be grateful for something to do," was all I said. I would probably do better with breaking cards—I was in the mood to rip apart some raw wool. But if they needed someone to comb the bats for spinning, I could work fine cards, too.

I wasn't ready to give in to the Hudson clan, but Jane had said something about someone "punishing" Felicity. Whoever it was that decided someone wasn't working hard enough, I didn't want that person looking my way.

Especially if it was Queen Edna.

Carding wool was a nice, quiet sort of thing to do . . . a good way to calm the mind while composing a brief message to Marta. The bag was brought after I was escorted to the outhouse (by two people, this time) and I spent a large part of the day sitting in that big rocker, break-carding wool. I actually made it through the entire flour sack of pale shearing, and then started over, using the fine cards to create rolls for spinning wool thread.

I managed two walks outside during the afternoon. During the first, I noticed that the wind had definitely veered from the south and was starting to pick up. It was the second walk that gave me real hope. The cows and sheep wandering the inside of the compound were huddled together in the shelter of one of the walls, their heads lowered and turned within.

Wet and windy weather was coming. I felt like huddling somewhere myself, but I doubted the Keeper would risk waiting until after the new moon for his ritual. It had to be tonight.

That second walk saved my sanity, as gray and wet as it was. Carding alone, or with Jane or Felicity, would have been my first choice. But sometimes there's no choice. Several of the women, curious about the newcomer in their midst, had decided to come and "keep me company."

It wasn't like I could say "No, thank you, I'm plotting an escape." So I had company.

This did mean the fire was built up, making the hall comfortable and preparing for the evening ceremony. There was a great difference in ages among the group who came stomping up to my prison. Jane brought her daughter Virginia and niece Prudence, as well as two women her own age, a much older dame, and a girl perhaps two or three years older than me.

Questions from the three younger females told me something I hadn't realized my first night in Hudson-on-the-Bend: not everyone had been present during my interrogation. Being married was no guarantee of attendance, since the oldest girl, called Maggie, was already married. There had to be a secret code that determined who stood at the Keeper's right hand.

I wondered if it was better or worse to stand quite so close to living evil.

It was hard to keep so many names straight; Maggie's was the only one I could fix in my head. It wasn't hard to remember her—with long blonde hair piled up in a coil, sapphire blue eyes, and a figure to turn men's heads, Maggie was a confident young lady.

Maggie didn't seem to like other females at all, especially strong women. She hated me on sight, I think. I didn't even have to open my mouth. Maybe she was sensitive to auras or something.

Since I was the stranger sitting there with my hair down and a borrowed, ill-fitting dress, her hostility seemed odd. Surely I was the one with reason to feel out of place.

"We hear you prefer trapping meat to cooking it," Maggie said, arranging another handful of wool on her breaking cards. Her voice was both tight and distasteful, as if suggesting I'd been some Indian's squaw.

"I like to do both," I decided to say, my hands whipping my finishing cards back and forth. If I didn't rise to the bait, it wasn't an insult. Maggie was mad enough about the bats piled at my side. I'd already gotten quite a bit done by the time the group showed up at the door, so I was resting my hands and wrists from breaking.

Some folks made bats one day and rolls the next, but I liked the change, and Jane hadn't minded bringing both sets of toothed cards.

The granny of the group reached across the drawn circle to pick up a roll and smooth it in her fingers. "Nice, delicate work, my dear," she said in her throaty voice. "Just in this you will be a welcome addition to our family." The women who looked to be Jane's age exchanged glances, but neither said anything.

How odd did they find it that I wasn't questioning them? Or getting hysterical? Maybe they didn't ask because I'd been alone so long in the forest. Did they think I'd gotten it out of my system?

Maggie was giving the elderly Hudson a dark look. So, did Maggie consider carding something she excelled at? She seemed competent, but I thought they all seemed a bit slow at their work. Then again, if I had no place to go but be sucked into the Keeper's rituals, maybe I'd be slow, too.

It wasn't a competition, was it?

These folks dressed in fine wool and muslin . . . only the two youngest looked like they might be wearing homemade clothing. Bolts from English mills cost the sun and the moon. Did the Hudsons have money, or were they trading furs and whiskey for goods?

"What did you use, Virginia, to dye your dress? Lily of the valley?" I looked up as I spoke, and the expression in the girl's eyes was surprise.

"The material came this color," was her soft response. "You can use lily of the valley to dye wool?"

"The leaves and stalks," I told her. "You can use almost anything living for color. Some things just work better than others."

"That would be fun, to create a color!"

"Takes a lot of plants," I warned her. "You have to plan ahead and put out several patches of them. After a few years, you can harvest from each plot and have enough plants to dye some yarn and keep on hand for heart problems, too."

Maggie slammed down her breaking cards on the rest of her bench and rose to her feet. As she reached the doorway the door blew in, and Felicity was there, a tea tray in hand. Her scarf was fluttering wildly in a strong breeze.

It was later in the day than I'd thought. We set aside our work for a quick cup of tea, but my mind was already on the evening ceremony. Would Marta hear my call?

It was the dark of the moon, and a strong south wind was heading straight for Hudson-on-the-Bend—a storm with enough weight behind it to take it all the way to Cat Track Hollow. Wild magic could ride that gale. If I was lucky, the Keeper's circle of power would make sure that every practitioner between the Muskegon and Kalamazoo rivers received my message.

I'd worry about Maggie later.

❧·ᗪ·❧

After all the waiting and agonizing over that ritual, it turned out to be a simple thing. The Hudsons didn't bother with special robes, they just wore their best clothing . . . at least for this ceremony. Everyone who looked my age or older was there. The candles and chalked symbols from the spell that had held me were gone, so the first thing I did was ground myself to the bedrock beneath the stockade. There was no longer anything to stop me from sending down that mental finger of thought and soul.

Or nothing strong enough to stop me.

Beeswax candles littered the room, set on log ends that erupted from the walls and shelves of stone in the fireplace mantel. The flames had been built back up, but it was the golden glow of the rolled cylinders that gave light to the hall.

Hudson and I stood inside that huge circle, with all the others gathered around. Only the grannies and granddads lined the boundaries, sitting on the benches.

Even if I wanted to tell you about the ceremony, I couldn't—most of it was in Latin, or another language I did not know. There was a rhythm to it, though, and I had a pretty good idea what each section meant. I was waiting for the Keeper to draw blood from himself and me. That was the window I'd be leaping for.

The Keeper's athame was made of black horn and silver, with delicate symbols carved into the hilt. It was one of the loveliest pieces of Craft workmanship I'd ever seen, and I kept my gaze upon it.

Although he was older than most of the people ranged against the walls, Hudson conducted the ritual with the vigor of a young man. Could he keep drawing on "temporary housing" after he returned to his own body? Or was he draining the entire compound? Did they not notice because so many of them shared the burden of the Keeper?

I shook myself a bit, to bring my mind back to the moment at hand. Thinking those thoughts might get me in trouble. But I wasn't too worried—truth to tell, immortality didn't appeal to me. It was the details of the spell that sounded interesting.

A promise was a promise. I might muse on wondrous magic, but I wasn't going to cast any of that stuff.

The tone of the chant changed again, and I felt my body slowly tense. I'd memorized what I needed to say, and then shoved it deep into my old soul. What wasn't on the surface of my mind was secret. That plea would stay buried until the very last moment.

Flames reached high in the main firepit, whipping about in the powerful updraft of the huge chimney. That was my path to the outer world, drawing magic Hudson did not expect, rising into the heart of the storm. We waited only for the exact moment of the dark of the moon.

Based on the last time I saw the dying crescent, the time was coming . . . *now*.

With a flourish, Hudson sliced open the palm of his left hand. Several older men I had not been introduced to reached for my arm, but I brushed by them and extended my matching hand to the Keeper. I ignored his lifted eyebrows, the others taking a step backward—the only reality was blood, the breaking of one binding and forming of another.

When I felt the pain, my ritual prayer soared out of me. *Great southern wind, hear my cry! I have tidings for the north, for the land between the great fresh waters. Will you carry my message home?*

His blood burned.

I flinched away from the agony, then grabbed at my thread of thought. *Marta Helgisdottir Donaltsson. Allie waits for you over two hundred fifty miles south, near the mighty Wabash. Seek her in Hudson-on-the-Bend, but beware—it is the home of sorcerers.*

I felt Hudson's spell shudder through me, anchoring my flesh to the group within the stockade, and as my vision grayed I feared I might collapse. A leg hold trap could not have closed as tightly. But my words would float with the winds. All that remained was—

There was a sudden gust, actually thrumming against the sides of the building. I heard the spiraling song of a mighty tempest as it circled the ceremonial hall, and then the pulse of the storm returned to uneven blasts of wind.

If Felicity was correct, the gale had agreed to take my message north. Now I had only to stay least in sight . . . and survive the intrigue of Hudson-on-the-Bend.

Old Harold Hudson released my hand, and it was a sign of the power that had passed between us that only a pale scar remained as evidence of my injury. The Keeper's eyes were intent, but I met his gaze without concern. He had said no ritual magic, and I had cast none. There was nothing in my mind for him to find except a prayer.

I didn't think a prayer would interest him.

These people did not understand wild magic at all, or this would have occurred to them. I finally had something to use as a weapon . . . and the Keeper had just admitted it into his circle of power.

The other Hudsons might have been ready to celebrate, having brought another into their fold, but I was very tired. A cup of hot cider and a slice of applesauce cake, maybe, and I would be ready for bed. Where would they put me now?

Suddenly the circle was broken and the crowd thinning, people heading to the tables in back where food was laid out. I let my eyes flit around, looking for anyone I recognized, but I was surrounded by strangers.

The odor of spiced cider intruded, and I looked to my right. Felicity was there, a mug in each hand, and her pixie face wore a fierce smile. She'd felt the answer of the storm, then . . . maybe my message would get though. How many miles did a storm travel in a day? If it was moving fast, Marta might know within a day and a night.

"Jane and Matthew have room for many hearts," Felicity said quietly, offering me a mug. "Leave with them, and no one will question."

Nodding, I sipped at the cider, letting my soul tip-toe through the gathering. There was a side effect to the spell . . . an awareness I hadn't expected. How could they keep any privacy, if the most sensitive among them always knew what the others were feeling?

"It is protection more than anything," Felicity said softly, almost as if she had read my thoughts. "The cruel among us cannot torture the weak without hurting themselves."

"The Keeper tolerates this?" I whispered.

Felicity looked down at the hardwood floor. "The strongest will rule the compound, even as nature demands the best survive." She lifted her gaze back to my face. "As long as no one is damaged, the Keeper does not interfere."

We'll see about that. I needed some food—meat, if I could get it—and then I was going to talk to Jane about someplace to sleep.

It looked like I had a few things to do before Marta found me.

※※※

The dream was unformed, with fog and darkness obscuring every hint of place or time. Dolph stood waiting for me there, his face calm, his expression gentle.

"Have I done as you asked?" I said aloud to him.

"You have done well," was Death's response. "Hudson's spell restrains only your body. Our binding kept your power and soul free from his taint. Now you must watch for your chance. Wild magic will trickle into the Hudsons' many spells. You must prepare yourself for a struggle. The Hudsons will not easily surrender their dominance."

"We can still stop the Keeper?" I asked as Dolph faded into the fog.

There was no answer.

The future spoke to me when it chose.

For now, the only voice was silence.

※※※

Like soil beneath the drip of a hand pump, the ritual spells of Hudson-on-the-Bend began to erode. Most practitioners used their own sweat for everyday living. Spelling a trap or casting a ward to keep vermin away was a waste of energy, because it took more strength to use magic than your hands. I'd had no idea that so many of their daily actions were governed by magic . . . or that wild magic could take so many strange turns.

Our first inkling that something was wrong came before dawn, when Jane got up to bring in the morning water for heating. I could hear her stirring down below the loft I was sharing with her four children. The clanking of pans, the snap of the outer door, the creaking winch of the well in the center of the commons—The next thing I clearly remembered was Jane's voice saying, "Matthew? What is wrong with the water?"

Uh-oh. I rolled over twice and peeked over the ledge. Trust the wild magic to immediately strike at the most vulnerable point in the stockade. Would we spend the next week melting snow and boiling the result?

"Iron," Matthew finally said. "We can still drink it."

He sounded very calm for a man staring down into a bucket of reddish water. It looked almost like someone had poured blood into the well . . . lots of blood. I pulled myself away from the edge of the loft, inching back to my part of the wall. Who would have thought things would happen so soon? Could this be coincidence?

I'd never much believed in coincidence.

I was downstairs, dressed and combing out my hair with Jane's comb, when I heard a shriek from outside. A door to a connecting building slammed open, and I could hear a woman's voice screaming in fury.

One advantage to having only boots for your feet is that you are always ready to run outside. I was into the boots in a flash and tossing my coat over my shoulders as I went into the great room where dinner and supper were prepared.

Queen Edna, her face mottled red with rage, was yelling for somebody named Robert. "An entire wall of them, rising out of the pit and covering the ceiling!" she said between repeated summons for the elusive man.

Finally a fair-haired fellow with a handsome dark blond mustache came tearing into the great room. He was still tucking his shirt into his breeches, but he had on his shoes.

"Have you forgotten everything you ever learned about suppressing growth?" Edna snarled, seizing hold of the man's arm and pulling him toward the door. "I have never seen such a spectacular failure! You must clear out this privy and reinforce the spell right away."

Privy? What could you do to a privy, except—

I ducked out the open door behind Edna and hurried through the mud to the double-seater. In passing I noticed that the rain had done its work—most of the snow had melted, exposing dirt and withered grass.

An explosive pattern of brown and cream rose from the depths of the privy, forming a cliff of mushrooms. I'd never seen such an impressive display. It looked like someone had their work cut out for them. Whatever had triggered . . . ?

How old was the wood of the walls? Decay triggered by the previous night's surge of power? Would I need to ward against my own wild training in years to come?

Standing there in the mud, my nose twitched suddenly, and I realized something else. The Hudsons had controlled the odor of their refuse heaps. This spell had somehow been affected, because I could smell both the privy and an unseen mulch pile.

A whisper of wind pushed by me, carrying the familiar, overwhelming smell of pig shit. The spell muting the barnyard odors had failed. Ah, well, perhaps a few of those boys would be handed a shovel.

"Some of those mushrooms might be edible," I said aloud as I moved over to the other side of the double-seater. I wasn't crazy about using a bewitched privy, but this was the only location I knew in this part of the stockade.

Strangely enough, there were no mushrooms on the other side of the wall. That was to be the pattern of the next few days. Things happened where you didn't expect them to happen, and failed where they should have worked. A fire suddenly went out, and one of the women needed help starting it up. I simply took a warming pan, went to the next room with a fireplace, and fetched a few coals.

"I usually use a spell to start it when it goes out," she murmured, studying her fireplace with a frown. "But the wood did not burn for me."

She didn't notice me staring at her. I remembered this one now, from the carding. One of Jane's friends. I was amazed by her words—not even so much what she said as what it meant. First that they'd be so careless as to let fires go out, and then to waste magic lighting them!

"Why do you spell your fires?" I heard myself ask.

The woman's dark brown gaze shifted my way. "To keep away mischievous sprites, of course," she said. "We always have a child or two sprouting, and that attracts all kinds of spirits."

Ah—poltergeists. All right, that made a certain kind of sense.

But if everything a sprite might mess with was spelled, what would happen now that the spells no longer worked?

꽃·ⅅ·꽃

Communities are a lot like human bodies. They're born, they grow and flourish . . . they reach their peak. Then they slowly decay, and finally die. There was nothing slow about what was happening to Hudson-on-the-Bend. The place was gonna be crazy before it collapsed into dust—you could feel the wrongness growing.

The interesting thing was, the Hudsons didn't ask me about any of it, not even if I'd ever seen such a thing happen. Maggie announced to one and all that I was a jinx, but no one actually accused me of working magic. They were that sure of their bindings.

Now that I was bound to their cause, the Hudsons didn't seem to care where I went—they merely warned me to stay away from the ceremonial hall when the Council was working.

So far, no one had been injured by spells going awry. If the wild magic hurt one Hudson, would it hurt all of them? Would it hurt me? I wondered if I *could* have some control over the wild magic floating through the compound.

I experimented as I moved through the enclosed town. Prudence didn't want to slop the pigs, now that the odor had returned, so I said I'd do it. Wasn't any worse than usual. Well, maybe a bit worse . . . when you had a spell like that, you cleaned the sty less often.

Walking to the barn gave me all sorts of possible tests of my control. I leaned against the stockade while pouring the old buttermilk into the hog trough, letting a finger of my own energy trickle into the wood. There was moss on some of the logs, what with the wet weather. Soon there would be more moss and lichen than you could imagine.

I sent a blast of heat up into the ground of the ice house, and carefully built a fireproof wall between the structure and the outside.

The next time I walked by, the ice house had a solid sheet of ice draped down one outside wall. The door was open, and I could hear worried voices within discussing the slow melting of the blocks.

Well and good. But I wasn't the only one testing my limits. That night Prudence ran screaming into the great room, telling her mother that something was in the well.

"What is it, child?" Jane asked her. "What did you see?"

"It spoke to me," Prudence said sobbing as she clung to her mother. "Just like we're speaking, only it was so far away I couldn't understand." Swallowing her tears, she gasped out, "I think it wanted me to jump in."

Jane and Prudence's mother shared a long look, and then announced that no one was to go to the well alone at night. Two— or better, three—people would fetch the evening water ration.

I was kneading dough over on one of the big tables, but I glanced up to see how people were taking the news. The older folks were either disturbed or angry . . . the younger frightened or excited, depending on their nature..

Felicity whirled by, her apron full of potatoes, a strange smile pulling at her lips.

No, I wasn't the only one playing with wild magic.

❧ ⅅ ❧

My only problem with the Hudsons was the boldest among them. There was indeed a ranking of strength in this place, and my behavior so far had thrown many people off balance. They could not decide if I was powerful or merely cunning.

One thing I had forgotten to do—I had left my protective blocks up, to keep my mind from leaking into someone else's, or eavesdropping on private thoughts.

Seems the strong Hudsons regularly bullied their way into other minds. Maggie couldn't make a dent in my wards, and she didn't like it. This made her sniping worse.

The Queen may have also tried; she still hadn't found anything about me that pleased her.

"She has added nothing to our strength, Keeper," Edna insisted in a loud voice, and I could feel her gaze upon me. I was busy serving slices of ham to people, so I couldn't speak for myself—if there was anything I could say. The kitchen was a place I could be useful, and Jane had been glad for the company, not to mention some new recipes.

"She is younger than she looks, Edna," the Keeper said calmly as he started cutting up the ham on his plate.

"Not that young." This was very even. Edna was the only woman I'd seen argue with the Keeper, and even she trod lightly.

"Women do not come into their power until they bleed." Old Harold's voice held a warning note. "She has been well trained, Edna. Use her skills for our benefit."

I tried hard to concentrate on what I was doing, but it was a struggle. Was Harold right? Did women only come into power after the moon claimed them? What did that mean about me? Was I merely early . . . or was I only skirting the power that would one day be mine?

"Sit with me, Allie." It was Erik. The line had dwindled to nothing, and I was left to find a place among people where I was uncertain of my welcome. Well, Erik had his uses—right now, he could help me keep any other young men at bay.

They were sniffing around already. It varied from simple politeness, like holding open a door for me, to compliments and even embarrassing things. One of them grabbed me when I was walking through the compound and kissed me full on the lips!

"I would keep you content, woman," he told me as he let go of me. "You'd have no interest in wandering from my bed."

The arrogance of some men. It's not whom you go to bed with—it's whom you wake up next to in the morning. Momma said the rest is just gravy, and she's been right about boys so far. But I didn't like what that hinted about this place.

"Any thoughts on our last talk?" Erik said casually, drawing me back to the moment.

I spied folk clearing out one end of a table and walked down that way. "Some," I replied, and paused to let him slide down the bench first. "I'm left-handed," I reminded him as he hesitated. Then he went ahead of me.

When we were settled, I considered what I'd been thinking about Erik. I still didn't get any bad feelings from him. Deceptive feelings, maybe, but not the evil that the Keeper and the men closest to him seemed steeped in. If I had to trust a man here, Erik might be the best choice. Matthew felt all right, but he could be a good enough sorcerer to fool me . . . and if not, he had children to think about.

Erik had only his own neck to protect—and if I was his way out of here, then he'd probably protect me, too.

Sometimes you needed to make someone believe a fib wrapped deep in a truth. I looked around carelessly, as if seeking Jane and Felicity. We were sitting with several children I did not know and the granny who had carded with me that first day. I'd since figured out that she read lips well but couldn't hear worth a fig.

I bent my head to butter my corn bread. "I've already started," I murmured.

Erik's movements were so controlled, I was pretty sure he'd heard me. Glancing up, I looked his way. His expression was solemn, and something else.

Respectful.

I'd take it. Whatever helped me keep some control on this craziness was useful. I looked back to my plate. "I may need you to watch that we're not caught between wind and water," was my next comment. I hoped that old nautical phrase made sense to him—that there were places of greatest peril. In truth, I was thinking that any minute it was going to dawn on Edna that I was the current favorite to usurp her throne—and I could tell she was powerful enough to do real damage to me, if she chose. I wasn't at her level, not yet.

That silliness on the commons also worried me. What if one of these young men decided to buck for a more powerful place in the pecking order by bedding me before Old Harold gave permission?

"I've already told Samuel to keep his hands off you, or I'll tell the Keeper what I saw," Erik said curtly, and did not bother to duck his head. He was right—if we hid all our conversation, folks might get suspicious. If they thought he was trying to get back in my good graces, that would make sense—

"And what did you see, Erik?" came the Keeper's cold, caressing voice.

The shudder that ran through me must have been visible, but no one commented on it. He'd come up right behind us, and we hadn't heard a thing.

Erik had set down his knife and fork, and his hands were resting lightly on his thighs. I suddenly wondered if we were in trouble.

"Alfreda? Is there a problem?" Again, that cold voice was very gentle.

I swallowed the bread I'd been chewing. "No, sir." I could tell this man wanted an answer, so I had to make it as light as possible. "Just someone stealing a kiss. Erik was protecting me."

"And who was this fellow with such overpowering charm?" This time the voice was only cold.

I glanced over and met Erik's eye. He was in a quiet panic. His fear seemed to filter over whatever link I had with the family, and I had to fight to keep it from overwhelming me. We were in great danger—that's what Erik's fear told me. Specifically, *he* was in danger.

Deep trouble indeed.

If someone was gonna get punished over this, let it be the culprit. "Samuel was just flirting," I said softly. No way could I repeat Samuel's promise—I had a feeling the Keeper would not be amused.

"Samuel." Now the coldness had weight to it, a huge icicle threatening to drop like a spear upon you.

"It . . . it was only a kiss, Grandfather," came a whisper from the corner.

The Keeper turned his body slightly, looking over where several of the younger adults had chosen to sit with their evening ale. Samuel was thin and dark, and could have been Jane's younger brother—handsome in his way, but his manners were brash. He'd set down his drink and was in Erik's same poised position, as if to spring to his feet.

Harold Hudson's head lowered slightly, as if nodding, and then he looked at Samuel. Simply looked.

Samuel's hands went to his throat as he gasped for air. It was a wet, rasping sound, as if water had gone down his windpipe. One arm flailed out to keep his balance, but he fell from the bench to the floor before the fire.

Lord and Lady, he's going to die. Dared we interrupt? I realized that no one had told me about the Keeper "punishing" anyone . . . how severe a punishment? Did he ever change his mind?

Couldn't let that idiot die for a kiss. "Sir, it *was* only a kiss," I said weakly, rising to my feet.

"This time." As suddenly as it began, Samuel could breathe again, painfully drawing air into his lungs. The Keeper took a step into the center of the room and said mildly: "Let this be a warning to any who might think of stealing *other* things." He paused, and then added, "I will tolerate no rudeness to the young women of Hudson-on-the-Bend. None."

Old Hudson turned and nodded to me, and then continued out of the room, down one of the connecting corridors.

His departure freed all the statues, who responded in varying ways. Jane had her arms around her two youngest and was talking soothingly to them. Several of the other youths were pulling Samuel to his feet.

I could see the collar of purple fingerprints all the way across the room.

Slowly I realized that I could breathe again. As I turned to lower my shaking body to the bench, I caught sight of Maggie, who was leaning against the stone edging of the fireloft. Her eyes were still fixed on Samuel, and she was smiling.

The smile nearly froze the blood in my veins.

Marta, please come get me. These waters are too deep.

FIFTEEN

HE HAD NO SHADOW.

It was the most vivid dream I had had in months. It began with the horrendous scene at dinner, Samuel gasping his life away—this time at my feet—and then grew worse.

After darkness fell I had started seeing fetches. The double imprint of their faces was plain; in some cases the shrouds were wound up over their heads. The fetches did not fade after I saw them. What did that mean? That their deaths were so close I could reach out and touch the caskets?

All those I'd seen in winding cloths were people I hadn't known, most of them Papa's age or older. All those I knew had already left the room for their beds. I had been grateful for that. If their time had come, I didn't want to know.

I already knew too much.

Then I was again Death's apprentice, as the compound died around me. I watched as time rushed to devour the wood of the dining hall, fungus and mold destroying the dusty pulp. The roof collapsed and flames bloomed in the debris—something must have fallen into a fireplace. A blast of swirling air against my face was hot and numbing.

I backed away from the building into chaos—stampeding animals, crying children, mothers calling to gather their households. Something smoldering erupted, a flare shooting into the air. Heat ragged at my chest and throat, pushing me back from the charred doorway.

An echo of power rang in my ears, as if a great spell had been cast, and I wondered if this destruction was because of ritual, or in spite of it. All I knew was that I had to get away, now, before it was too late.

A storm was rising.

"But how will it end?" I cried aloud, and whirled at the touch of another.

It was the Keeper, and he spoke with Death's voice.

"In wind and fire."

My instincts had not failed me. My shadow loomed from the flames beyond—but the Keeper had no shadow. . . .

I woke with a shriek, stuffing my blanket into my mouth to silence myself. Lord and Lady of Light! Was that what was coming? Sitting up, I reached to pull on the pants one of Jane's friends had washed for me. I'd just keep out of Edna's way and wear the brown dress over them. Then I crept downstairs to stuff the things from my hip pouch into the pockets of my jacket. What with winding sheets and burning buildings, my nerves were at a fever pitch.

I had to be ready.

"Allie?" It was Jane, wrapped in a blanket, standing by the edge of her bed screen. She was shivering in her bare feet. "Did you have a bad dream?"

What if she spied for the Keeper?

What if she didn't?

"It's been a really bad night," I whispered. "Something feels very wrong, Jeanette. Keep your children close, and be ready to flee. I know doom when I see it coming—I've seen it before." I stayed kneeling by the banked fire, my hand on the folded pile of my coat.

She studied me for a moment. "Always we had emergency supplies packed, when I first came to Hudson's compound—that one was south of Montreal," she whispered. "I have not forgotten how to prepare. Soon?"

"Very soon," I said softly.

"What will be our end?" she murmured sadly, reaching back to a hook on the wall for her dress.

Wind and fire. But I did not say it aloud.

༂·ⅅ·༂

We had three days of warning.

The first day, a section of the stockade collapsed under the weight of two men standing on the walkway. The second day, the roof of the horse barn began to fall in, and the big animals were moved to an enclosure on the commons.

The third day the wind changed, and an icy blast from the north reminded us that winter was not yet through with us. I tingled as though I stood in the midst of a great spell, and maybe I did. I wrapped myself against the cold and didn't care if Edna spotted my long pants. I was helping to mix chinking for the barn—I needed the protection.

Smoke poured ceaselessly from the ceremonial hall. The Council was struggling to stop the erosion of Hudson-on-the-Bend, but it didn't look as if they were having any luck.

"Who could do this to us?" I heard one man yell as I slunk by on my way back for dinner. "Who could mass so many against us?"

Had none ever dared to challenge them?

After a long morning in a rising northern breeze, I was glad to come in for hot tea, roasted beef, and fresh bread. Jane was in the great hall, shaping more loaves and preparing them to go in the huge round beehive stove that backed up to the common kitchen. It seemed that most people ate dinner and supper in the great room. Mornings were spent with smaller family groups. At that time of day, the split pea soup simmering away for supper was a friendly greeting.

"A lot of bread," I murmured to her as I took a seat across from where she shaped a loaf.

"A few others feel the same unease you do," she said quietly. "They saw me preparing a packet, and asked for the same." She glanced up at me. "We simply bake every day, and have more day-old bread available at need."

I felt a bit better about that. Granted, the Keeper was whom Death was after, but not all the people there were evil. They didn't deserve to starve because their council of elders preferred trickery to honest work.

My gaze drifted to Jane's two youngest, a boy and a girl, playing a serious game with their rag dolls. "And if they have the Gift, what will the future bring them?"

Jane's hands stopped moving. She rested them on either side of the loaf, leaning her full weight on the big pine table. Her sudden stillness frightened me. Then she lifted her head, her dark eyes moist. "They have the Gift. No child shall live who does not."

I just stared at her. "What?" I whispered, feeling stupid and slow with cold.

"It is the will of the Keeper," Jane said steadily. "The Council allows no babe to live who does not carry enough magic for powerful descendants."

My left hand slid of its own accord to cover her right one. It seemed so useless to say anything. God of my fathers, were the Hudson elders still human? The Keeper certainly wasn't, if he was killing his kin.

Maybe I wasn't so sorry after all for what was building outside like a summer storm.

Maybe it was justice . . . maybe it was retribution.

Maybe, just maybe, it was the hand of God.

❧ 𝕯 ❧

Nightfall came upon us while they shored up the stockade wall, and wild magic made a mockery of all Hudson efforts. I helped move the animals back into the barn—at least they had solid walls to block the wind—and made sure I got some soup and bread. The tingling I'd felt for days was worse, as if I was constantly rubbing wool and then touching metal. Something was coming soon, and Death would expect me to be ready.

Was anyone ever ready for Death? The strangeness of the thought teased at me.

As I wiped my bread inside my bowl for the last of my soup, I heard the sound of shouting outside. What now? It sounded like a man—

A hand reached out to seize my arm. I turned to see Jane, her dark eyes large from tension. "They say it is as if a century is passing before their eyes. The north wall is no more than a honeycomb of dust and fungus," she hissed to me. "Child, do you know what is happening here?"

Not for certain. "Has no one ever challenged the Keeper for any children he's stolen?" I whispered in turn, setting my bowl down as normally as possible.

"A few. None could stand up to him." Jane sat down next to me, any pretense at casual conversation gone. "Do you think your people could have come after you?"

I shrugged slightly. Unless they'd figured it out before I yelled for help, they were still far, far away. "I don't know. But I come from a long line of practitioners. If they all got together. . . ." I left it hanging. *Let them try to ward against ritual magic. Just don't let them think of wild magic.*

Jane—Jeanette—did not seem ready to rush off with the news. "I think," she said, her voice so soft I could barely hear her, "that I will finish packing a trunk with clothing."

"Fire!" The scream came from somewhere deep inside the compound, and we were both instantly on our feet.

"Hurry," I said, grabbing her arm and pushing her toward the connecting walkway to her home. "We don't know how fast it's spreading." The idea of fire closed my throat with fear, but Jeanette and Matthew had four young children—we had to be sure they were safe.

Jane's two older children already had their outdoor clothes on, the boy ready to bolt out the door, his older sister demanding he come back to tell her what was happening. I seized the boy's collar and hauled him back inside.

"No time for gaping!" I told him. "Go fold up the bed quilts! Hurry!" I looked out the doorway, straining to see in the gloom. "There—" I pointed, and Jane hissed in reply.

"It is Edna's home! The others will extinguish the blaze." Her voice was strained, the French accent coming to the fore.

"The great room will burn, too," I told her, grabbing for the bundles of food she'd set on a corner table. "Finish packing your trunk! We may get to scavenge, and we may not. Virginia!" The girl was immediately before me. "Can you bundle up your sister and brother?"

"Yes, Allie," she said breathlessly, and her eyes were a mirror of Jane's—Jeanette's. Soon Jane would be no more—only Jeanette would remain.

While Jeanette threw into the trunk what her family would need, I gathered some cooking utensils and the flatware. There was a big willow plate, too, but there was no guarantee we could keep it whole.

I glanced out the door again, and could see that the fire had spread to the south wall of the stockade. Too close to the barn; they'd have to let the animals go.

A gust of icy wind swirled past, making me gasp, and then Felicity was there. She was dressed in gray wool and boots, but no cloak, and looked like some winter sprite freed from the ice. "The winds like you! They have returned to help you!" Spinning like a dancer, she leapt off into the darkness.

"Felicity, wait! Don't make it worse!" I yelled, but it was useless—she'd disappeared into the growing smoke and noise. "Maybe you *are* crazy," I muttered aloud, pulling my mittens back on. Or maybe just crazy for freedom. Any which way, she wasn't going to be much help w—

I felt a snap within my head, like a ward going up around a circle, and suddenly I was taffy among many hands that were pulling for all they were worth.

"Allie!" It was Jeanette, holding me on my feet, and I realized I must have staggered. "What's wrong? Have you Seen something?"

I just stared at her. She knew about Seers. Some of them were laid low by their Seeing, but this was something else. Not just the Council drawing on us all, or surely she'd have felt it, too. More like two or three people. . . . "Having a tug of war," I muttered.

"You have Seen the great building burning?" Jeanette shook my arm to get my attention.

Yes, but that was three nights ago. "Yes," I gasped out. I felt so much power pulling at me, I didn't know what to do. It wasn't just wild magic, it felt like. . . .

Marta.

If Jeanette hadn't supported me, I'd have sat down on the floor. Lord and Lady of Light, it felt like Marta! And Cory, and I didn't know who else.

"They found me," I whispered. They'd come to take me home— but they'd have to fight the Keeper first. Would Death also take a hand?

I just hoped my head survived it.

Jeanette turned toward her son. "Take the food outside, stand right by the door, watch for your father but do not leave, do you understand me? They have freed the animals, you could be trampled." Then she shook me again. "Can you stand alone?" she asked, her voice rising over the growing confusion.

There were children to get to safety. That was first. Pushing aside the turmoil in my head, I straightened and pushed back against the wall. "I'm all right," I told her. "We need to get away from the fires—and away from the great room and the ceremonial hall. Where can we go?"

Frowning, Jeanette wrapped her own huge shawl around herself and fumbled for her gloves. "The well," she said finally. "I do not wish to go farther without Matthew. What if this is a ruse to lead us from the safety of our homes?"

Not too safe right now, my friend, I thought, but did not say it. Fastening the toggles of my coat, I said "Can we carry the trunk together?"

"Maybe," was Jeanette's response. "We can drag it to the door, at least. You hold onto them," she told Virginia as her daughter stood from bundling the little ones. "Good, John tied the quilts together." She leaned out the door to hand her older boy the quilts. "Can you bring both the food and the blankets? You may drag the food, it is well wrapped." Without further comment she ran back to the trunk she'd packed.

I was pleased to see that Jeanette understood emergencies—the trunk was a smallish one. She had bound it with stout cord, and we experimented with lifting by the side lines. Effort raised it high enough so we could get our hands under the corners.

"Why don't these things come with handles?" I muttered as I started to back up. "Clear the way, Virginia!"

Slowly we somehow got everyone and everything out next to the well. Jeanette wasn't the only one to think of that site—Prudence's mother was also there, and a woman I did not know. The children milled around us in circles, alternately excited and frightened.

Then through the smoke I spotted a wavering torch, the flame whipped by a powerful wind. Hell, Hull, and Halifax!

Felicity. Only Felicity would be summoning a gale with the blasted compound catching on fire. And from her lights, she might be right—fire might destroy those circles of power in the ceremonial hall. Without the circles. . . .

For the first time it occurred to me that there might be a lot of planning going on in this chaos. Would other members of the family, powerful sorcerers themselves, challenge Hudson?

"Jeanette, I've got to find Felicity," I said quickly.

"Surely she'd think to come here?" was the woman's taut response.

"I'm not sure she's thinking very clearly right now," I said carefully, keeping an eye on the bobbing torch. "She's not all there on the best of days, and I saw her dance by earlier."

Jeanette seized my forearm. "Don't get hurt for a madwoman, Allie," she demanded. "I feel badly about her, but you should not die for her."

"I don't intend to," I said, trying to make my voice reassuring. "Don't let anybody else wander, the horses and cattle are loose!" With that, I turned and hurried across a short open area toward the dark bulk of the ice house.

The weaving torch was heading toward the ceremonial hall. *Lord, don't let her set it on fire while there are people in there!* I touched the ice house glacier, as if to orient myself, and started off toward the big hall. A huge blast of wind hit me in the face, spiraling around me as it made its way through the commons. The strength of the gusts was definitely increasing.

A horrible thought rose in my mind, and I moved faster, heedless of goats thundering through the chaos. Felicity knew how to call the winds, and how to ask their help.

I didn't think she knew how to control them.

"Felicity! Wait for me!" Maybe, if she thought I'd help her— A warm breeze slapped me in the face, and I brushed it away, humming a low note to it, encouraging it to stay close but not whip at the fires. The delicate warmth swirled away, circling me.

The winter storm that bore down upon us had pushed heavy, cold air before it, and the clouds I'd seen that day were full of snow. Cold air on top of all this heat was dangerous.

Was I ready to stop a whirling wind?

"Felicity!" The torch had disappeared into thick smoke. I saw several men and boys fighting the blaze at Edna's home, but no one had noticed that there were flames behind us, closer to the gates. The great house had finally caught fire.

A solid wall rose up before me, the huge logs charring at the base. It was the ceremonial hall, and there was no sign of Felicity. "Felicity!" I yelled again, whirling to catch some sight of her, and then a hand reached out of the smoke and caught my wrist.

"Felicity! You must stop what you're—" I got a good look at who stood next to me, and my words faltered. He had looked small and frail sitting in his huge rocker, but the Keeper was my height, and there was strength in that grip.

I threw myself backwards, trying to break his hold, but he twisted my arm inward and back, pinning it to my spine. Whatever he'd done, it hurt—I had no idea how to pull free without snapping my shoulder or elbow.

"We are under attack, child," he whispered into my ear, his voice dry, "and I am afraid I need a great deal of power. It is disappointing to lose you, but now that I know where your family can be found, perhaps a sister will do as well." Moving sideways, the Keeper dragged me toward the doorway of the hall.

"That building is on fire!" I yelled at him, trying to slow down his steps. I couldn't simply go limp, I'd break my arm. There was no point injuring myself unless I was sure it would buy me freedom.

Not the hall; I couldn't go back in that hall. Those things might still be in there, and I'd had all of them I ever wanted, thank you.

A few dry leaves ripped by my face, whirling around me, and I recognized the little breeze I'd tamed. With a gasp I let my thoughts flare upward, stabbing at the cold sky high above us, demanding the attention of the clouds.

Frigid air dropped back down the hole I'd punched through the heat, caressing my face. I don't know what that icy northern gale thought of my chattering summery breeze, but the winds grew stronger, swifter, tearing at my hood.

We'd reached the entrance of the ceremonial hall, the doors flung wide open, and I could see several bulked forms within, conducting a ritual. They still had some sort of control—the candles did not flicker in the growing storm. I had a horrible feeling what they needed me for, and dug my heels into the mud. I was not getting near that center circle. It was broken arm time.

We stumbled over the threshold, and I gasped at the forces pushing at me. There was a whirlwind of another sort inside this hall, a maelstrom of magic, and it was sucking at me like quicksand. This was what the Keeper had intended! Whatever was going on in the circle, it had nothing to do with Hudson's own core of strength and knowledge.

This structure was his temple, and I had stepped into his place of power.

I'd brought the storm with me, and it rose to my need, pulling heat from the fireplaces, stealing energy from the candles. If I tightened the spiral, the forces might kill everyone in the building. But if I didn't summon the twister, my wards would be shredded to pieces, my mind peeled like the skin from a fruit.

Inhaling the parching air, I reached through my dissolving shield and seized the tail of the growing storm.

Dead leaves spun in a furious dance, igniting as they brushed through flames. Sparks flew from the vortex, kindling benches and walls. The winds gained power as the circle closed around me.

He was too old, too strong—he had stolen too much power. I felt the last of my protections snap, and plunged downward, following my ground, taking my soul deep into the earth below us.

Numbness suddenly left my body, a sparkling awareness I had not felt in days flooding back into my flesh. I heard the Keeper gasp, felt his grip loosen, and tore myself from his hold. I spun in place, trapped by my own whirlpool of wind, and froze at the look on his face.

The black eyes stared at me in disbelief. There was horror in them, and amazement—and, at the last, a weary respect. Then the Keeper fell choking at my feet.

I had forgotten Death's binding . . . and what would happen if anyone tried to break it. There was no time for Harold Hudson, no time left for anything. I had to stop the storm forming on top of me. Raising my hands, I halted the progression of the tightening spiral. But how to send it away?

Gently, before I lost the strength to control it, I pushed upward, trying to guide the power of the young storm back up the path it had used to the ground.

I'd forgotten I was inside the ceremonial hall.

The roof erupted with the sound of thunder, the ground shaking from the force of the explosion. Burning leaves and debris soared out into the night, the whirlwind growing vast as I loosened my grip on the winds. I half turned, suddenly fearing the Council at my back, and found them using a bench to bash a hole through a blazing wall.

From the look on the face of the last one leaving, you could not have paid them enough to go past me through the open doors.

Teach you to steal children, I had time to think, and then the wind left my fingers, and I collapsed, gasping, next to the Keeper.

What was left of the Keeper. In the stark golden light I could see a twisted, ancient hank of tanned leather, too frail to survive much handling. How long had he lived in that body?

His soul had nothing else to draw on as it resisted transformation. The voice seemed to come from outside my head, not inside. Without the binding, Death could no longer simply come to me. But when something died, Death was always near—and practitioners could see it pass by. As I watched, a tall, thin man in darkish clothing nodded my way and walked through the fiery wall.

I was shaking from the collapse of the spell and had no strength to stand. Somehow I had to crawl out of that building, or a falling timber was gonna squash me flat. One hand in front of the other. . . .

Heedless of cold or sparks, I slid to the threshold and pulled my legs around, dropping my feet onto the hard dirt before the entrance. Hadn't the entry been mud before? Was it frozen or fire-hardened earth?

I felt moisture touch my face, and looked up to see a dusting of snow joining with the haze.

Someone ran up through the misty smoke, and I bit my lip to stifle a groan. If this was a Council member, I had run out of ideas. I didn't think any winds owed me any favors.

"Allie?" I blinked once at the voice, and followed the buckskin-clad legs up to see Shaw Kristinsson decked out in a dark-stained deerskin coat.

I was so glad to see him, I thought I'd cry, and that would never do. "Did you use walnut to stain that?" I said, and although my voice trembled it did not break.

His smile was like the sun coming up. To his credit, he didn't bother asking if I could walk. When he reached for my right arm, I said, "Not that one," and he immediately changed hands.

I wasn't very steady on my feet, but Shaw wrapped his arm around my waist and kept me from falling over. Truth to tell, I hung on like a baby possum. We stood together a long moment, just clinging to each other. "This way," he said simply, and drew me into the smoke and wind.

The compound was an eerie place, the glow from the fires spread out by the glint of thousands of snowflakes. We walked through a sifting blanket of snow, the shouting and fires strangely muffled by the falling veil. Suddenly the sound of swift hooves reached my ears, and I tensed, looking for something to hide behind.

Shaw simply held up his left hand, swirling the snow before us, and the horse that appeared out of the darkness veered past us as if it had seen us a mile away.

"How did you do that?" I whispered.

"Concentration," he murmured.

Oh. I did not interrupt him again.

I was completely turned around, so I was quite amazed when a cabin loomed up. Shaw pounded only once, and Jeanette threw open the door and rushed out to seize me.

She was half-sobbing and babbling in French, much too fast for me to understand, but she seemed very glad to see us. Since Shaw would not let go, the two of them helped me into the downstairs of Jeanette's own home.

"The great room burned," she said between hiccupping sobs, "but Matthew and Robert soaked the roofs and saved the attached cabins."

"I'm glad," I told her, and I was, because we were clearly in for a heavy snowfall, and folks needed protection. "Matthew is all right?"

"Yes, yes, praise the Virgin. And look, you were right! They all came together to find you, and to free us!" She hugged me again, tightly. "It is gone," she almost hissed in my ear. "The chain on my heart is gone!"

"Old Harold is pretty dead," I told her, and normally it would have been embarrassing, how happy she looked. I placed one hand on the eating table and looked around the shadowed room. The four children were all piled on the bed, nodding toward sleep. There were quite a few people I'd never seen before—and a mountain wearing a black fur coat that came to halfway between his knees and feet.

"Well, darlin', you upset someone's applecart!" Cory's voice boomed out over the soft conversation in the background, even as a tall, slender figure stepped forward.

"Marta?" That was all I could get out. Powers that be, I was glad to see her! Why was everything always fine once Marta appeared?

My cousin didn't speak. She just studied me a moment, her blue eyes thoughtful, and then reached over and hugged me tightly. Shaw finally loosened his grip on me, and I heard the scuff of a chair behind us.

"Thought I'd lost you, girl," Marta said finally, her voice husky.

"I'm hard to lose," I assured her.

"That's what you say," I heard, and I looked over to see Erik sawing away at a cold roast, laying out meat for people. He looked a little embarrassed, but he still met my gaze. "I couldn't find you in the chaos, so I went to open the gate. This had your hand all over it, but I couldn't figure out how you were doing it."

"You never said anything to anybody," I responded as Marta helped me sit down in a straight-backed chair.

Erik flushed. "You didn't seem to need help, so I spent my time sweet-talking Edna so she wouldn't give you trouble, or keeping Samuel in line." He hit his fist against his other palm as he finished speaking, and I gathered Erik had enjoyed keeping Samuel in line.

"Thank you, Allie," he said gravely. "Thank you for my life. I was sure to be his next body, and now I've got my own back."

I nodded slightly, wrapping both hands around the mug of cider Jeanette offered me. How could I blame him? Would I have done such a thing if I had been so desperate? Something occurred to me, and I said, "Has anyone seen Felicity? I think she saved my life out there. If she hadn't started calling the winds—"

"Calling the winds?" Cory said as he removed his coat and spread it over the children.

"She was trying to make the fires worse so the hall would burn. I snagged that breeze and was holding it when the Keeper grabbed me, so I had something to use as a weapon." I shook my head over my mug. "I forgot about the first binding—I didn't need to protect myself from him—but I think I scared off the Council when the twister blew the roof off."

Silence greeted my words. Then Erik said hesitantly, "I looked for Felicity, but she wouldn't stay with me, so I helped Matthew with the fire. I told her to come back here, so maybe she will—"

There was a thumping at the door, and Shaw went to open it. I noticed both Cory and Marta raising fists that gleamed, and knew that whatever they had done to Hudson-on-the-Bend, they could still call it up at will.

A snow fairy bounced into the room, carrying a bushel filled with burlap sacks. Felicity shook herself vigorously, snow flying everywhere, and set her basket on the table.

"Are you all right?" I decided to ask.

Her face was flushed, her eyes glorious with tears. "I am free," she whispered brightly. "I can become a woman!" Then she untied the innermost bag in the woven basket, her tiny hand diving inside. Her fingers hid what she pulled from the sack, but she offered it to me.

I held my palm out flat, and she pressed into it a small, brownish red apple. "The only thing done by Hudsons worth remembering," she announced.

After a look at her, I bit into the apple. It crunched in a most satisfactory way, firm-fleshed and sweet . . . but not too sweet. This was where the wonderful cider had come from. That she remembered through a holocaust. . . . "Maybe we'd better call it Felicity?" I suggested.

"Matthew and Robert created it," Felicity said proudly. "Not with magic but with the dirt under their nails."

I offered the rest of the apple to Shaw. After tasting it, he nodded and said, "It's good." Then he added drily, "But it was an awfully long way for just an apple."

We all looked at each other for a moment, and burst out laughing. If it was tinged with fright and relief, well, can you blame us? We had survived the fall of Hudson-on-the-Bend.

We had rid the world of an ancient evil.

I was relieved to learn that we did not have to pack up and flee the compound in a blizzard—which was what had descended upon us. A good dozen buildings remained, but my nine rescuers were all crammed in with Jeanette and Matthew.

Felicity seemed unconcerned about her "husband." When I asked, she said, "We were married by the Keeper, so it was a marriage of the devil. I used forest magic to keep myself from growing up. The magic bloomed, but I did not."

We all were astonished when we figured out what she had done. To freeze your body before moon-touch, on the cusp of womanhood but not over it . . . would she ever be able to explain how she had done it? I didn't know if anyone would ever need such a trick, but I sure wanted to know how she did it!

"What did you do to the compound?" I finally said to Cory after we'd all eaten some beef and corn bread.

"Not much of anything, darlin'," was his answer. He chuckled at me, so I guess my eyes got big or something. "There was already enough going on! When you destroyed that hall, we did break the circles, and used a lot of that power to restore the balance in the weather. That's why it's snowing. We kept the rest in case some of these sorcerers gave us trouble."

"Balance? Why is the weather out of balance?" I realized that I was so tired I had no idea what he was suggesting..

Cory and an elderly practitioner glanced at each other, and Shaw actually looked embarrassed. I turned to Marta, who smiled wryly and said, "When your momma got word to me where you were, I sent out the call."

"Momma?" I would have jumped to my feet if I'd had the strength.

"Indeed. Some of us caught echoes of your words, but your momma got all of it, I think—where you were, and to beware of sorcerers. Cory, Shaw, and Joseph—" She nodded at the bald old gentleman with the full white beard. "—Were already with me. The others reached us by the evening of the fifth day." She paused to pour herself some more cider.

"We had no idea what that strange message cost you, darlin'," Cory said softly. "There was no time to waste. So we cast a great spell and seized a ride on a nor'wester heading this way. The force of all that cold and moisture coming this way, well, it built into quite a storm."

"You caused the storm?" I looked at Shaw for confirmation. He flushed, which was all I expected from him, but a blush was as good as a yes.

"It was . . . beyond belief," Shaw whispered without looking up.

I pulled my braid around to the front and picked at the thong holding it together. They had ridden a storm to get here? And my momma had been the one to get my message. I thought about my words: *Will you carry my message home?*

Winds were literal things . . . they did exactly what you asked of them. And Momma had heard me. Guess she still cared about her oldest daughter after all. Silly child. I hoped I wouldn't weep.

Someday I'd learn how to ride a storm.

"How are we getting home?" I said slowly.

Bald Joseph chuckled, a purring sort of rumble. "The hard way, Alfreda. One step at a time. But these people have plenty of animals. Perhaps we can get horses for folks like me, so we get home before the snow melts."

"It would play havoc with the weather to lure up a southern gale strong enough to get us home," Marta said gently. "It could take a year to settle things back down. There would be flooding some places and drought others. So we'll walk."

I nodded my understanding. I'd been walking for a solid month; I could walk home, if need be. Shoot, if they knew the way, we might get home in a fortnight!

All right, maybe twenty days.

"What about . . . what about the rest of the Hudsons?" I whispered.

"What about them?" Marta sounded her usual matter-of-fact self. "Wizards do not punish," she reminded me.

"Some of these people. . . ." There was no easy way to speak. "Some of them are evil. They will do this again without the Keeper."

"You're not feeling responsible for them, are you?" Marta asked me.

"No, ma'am. I did what Death asked me to do, and Death kept its side of the bargain. But there are dangerous people here, and

there are also good people who were trapped by old man Hudson."
I looked over at where Matthew and Jeanette sat side by side on a
bench rescued from the dining hall. "Will the Council let you go?"
I couldn't imagine them staying, not after the Council had killed at
least one of their children. Unless Matthew was rising in the power
web?

Matthew's voice was steady as he said, "If you will let us ride
with you, once we are a se'nnight away, I do not think they will
follow us. Your people destroyed the circles. The Council has no
extra strength to hold folks against their will."

"I'd like to go back with you, if I may," Erik said abruptly. "My
uncle may take the skin off my back, but it is nothing to what
the Council might do to me for finding someone too powerful to
control." He was watching Felicity as he spoke.

Abruptly, I said, "How did you get the power to take me south?"

Erik flushed. "I had to kill one of Uncle's horses," he muttered.
"I owe him a horse."

At least he hadn't killed Mrs. Forrest. If he felt like he owed his
relatives a horse, then maybe there was hope for him.

"What do you want, Felicity?" I asked, reaching a hand out to
her. "Do you want to find your people?"

She clasped my hand loosely, her fingers tracing my woodcraft
scars. "I have seventeen years . . . I will call the moon, and maybe
she will forgive me for turning from her. My power has done ill to
this land. I must atone." She looked up at me. "Would you have
room for me? Few spin and weave as I do. It would not be forever."
She blushed as she added the last, and I realized what I had been
seeing. How many hearts had the Keeper destroyed?

Perhaps Felicity and Erik would have a second chance together.
Perhaps she was not mad, only fey . . . and why should she be
anything less, after what she had lived through?

Wizards do not judge, either.

I glanced over at Marta. She gave me a long look in turn. *They
have been tainted by blood magic, Allie. I do not know if they
could ever become simple practitioners.*

Erik may not want it, I responded. *Felicity may feel she has to
make amends for how her power was used.* I shrugged slightly. *I'd
be happy if they were just good folks.*

My teacher smiled slightly. "Your heart is too big for your flesh, Alfreda Sorensson." She gestured for me to join her over in front of the fire, so I carefully stood and walked over to sit on the hearth.

"Now," Marta said. "What is this about a bargain with Death? The short tale first; the long one can wait."

Huh. Must have looked as bad as I felt. I took a deep breath, and then I told them. After all, it's not like I could keep wild magic a secret, now was it? Toward the end, though, I'm not sure I made a lot of sense.

When I woke halfway through the night, I found I'd been wrapped in a quilt and wedged between Felicity and Shaw in a row of bodies across the floor. *How . . . ?*

I was warm, and with friends. A dream had just told me I'd belong to the moon before winter came again.

I decided not to worry about it.

৵⁑৶

It was still snowing steadily the next morning, drifts forming over the charred timbers. We helped bury bodies; not all had been able to escape the fires, and one sorcerer had been dealt with by Marta and her friends. There was food to pack, furniture to tie to a mule, and horses to select.

I didn't see Maggie among the Hudsons we laid to rest. Wherever she was, she was avoiding me.

Couldn't say I missed her.

The remains of the Council did not seem inclined to argue with us when we said Matthew and Jeanette were taking a cow and their share of the horses and mules. Cory coolly informed the elders that he was taking ten horses as payment for the theft of his cousin, and he would select the horses.

I wasn't sure if they feared the practitioners they suspected had destroyed them—or the child they had watched summon a tornado.

As long as it didn't go to my head, I thought, I deserved a bit of respect. But I stayed out of their way. Maybe they thought I did them a favor . . . maybe they wanted revenge.

I just wanted to go home.

During all this, Joseph and Matthew found they got on very well. I wondered if the Hudson family would leave us in a se'nnight, or if they would head all the way to Fort St. Joseph, and learn the trade properly from old Joseph.

I asked Marta if we could send word to Hannah's sons and take her as far as the Greenville Trace. Marta not only had no objection, she clearly looked forward to meeting a woman who talked to ghosts.

Cory, Shaw, Matthew, and Robert were busy in the apple orchard. I wondered if it was a little early to harvest apple scions, but four burlap sacks of twigs tenderly wrapped in cloth were added to our traveling supplies. I didn't know if all the cuttings would make it, but I had felt magic in the preparation.

Perhaps the Black Hudson apple would be the memorial to all their pain.

I had no doubt that the stories about the Keeper of Souls would endure.

There was one last deed that needed doing before we left with the dawn. At twilight, we paced off a ritual circle and flattened the snow. A tiny firepit was dug and lined with rocks. When it was fully dark, I went out to perform an invocation, and the others followed to edge the ring.

I had fire, water, blood, and tobacco. It seemed silly to get flowery about it. So I was direct—I held back my ritual names, in case unfriendly ears were listening, but I accepted that Death had given me a new identity. Why Golden-tongue I did not know.

I figured I'd know eventually.

"I, Alfreda Golden-tongue, call upon Azrael, greatest of healers and teachers, for I have a question that only Death may answer. Come to me, solitary angel, for we have unfinished business." The tobacco smoke coiled lazily up into the last of the falling snowflakes, and as I watched, the dark, slender man I'd seen walk through the ceremonial hall appeared seated on the other side of the fire.

He looked like he could be Shaw's older brother, his face thin and pale, the beard a black outline along his jaw, the mustache full and smooth. But his eyes . . . his eyes were darker than Shaw's at their darkest. If you looked into them long enough, you could see stars die.

I didn't look long enough to see if stars were also born.

"Have you called Harold Hudson, the Keeper of Souls, to your realm?" I asked steadily.

"I have." His voice was husky and musical, the sound both elegant and British. We were speaking English. What did he sound like if Jeanette questioned him in French? Or Marta in Norwegian? I'd have to ask.

What did the others see?

"I am free of the Hudsons' blood magic forever?"

"You have no ties to them. When the Keeper took your shields, he took your bindings. The taint was burned away." He kept his gaze upon me, ignoring those outside the circle.

All right. Not exactly what I asked, but what I wanted to know. "Have we paid our debts to each another?" I didn't know how else to ask this question, but I wanted the slate washed clean. The next time Death and I struck a bargain, I wanted to start on level ground.

Death smiled. "I have not the authority to set you free of my realm forever, Alfreda Golden-tongue, you who are Veritas. But though we may meet at times, I promise you this—I do not wish to bring you here before your days are through. Never give up, Veritas, and I will give you time."

Then I was alone within the circle.

꠹⚅꠹

We argued about what Death's last words meant all the way back to the Michigan Territory.

I figured I'd know eventually.

I always did.

END

About the Author

Katharine Eliska Kimbriel reinvents herself every decade or so. It's not on purpose, mind you—it seems her path involves overturning the apple cart, collecting new information and varieties of apple seed, and moving on. The one constant she has reached for in life is telling stories.

"I'm interested in how people respond to unusual circumstances. Choice interests me. What is the metaphor for power, for choice? In SF it tends to be technology (good, bad and balanced) while in Fantasy the metaphor is magic—who has it, who wants or does not want it, what is done with it, and who/what the person or culture is after the dust has settled. A second metaphor, both grace note and foundation, is the need for and art of healing.

"A trope in fantasy is great power after passing through death. Well, at my crisis point, I didn't die. That means that I'm a wizard now. Who knows what I may yet accomplish?"

SPIRAL PATH

UNCORRECTED PAGE PROOFS FROM THE THIRD BOOK OF NIGHT CALLS

KATHARINE ELISKA KIMBRIEL

Spiral Path

Copyright © 2014 by Katharine Eliska Kimbriel

Book View Cafe Publishing Cooperative
   PO Box 1624 , Cedar Crest, NM 87008-1624
Dragonrain Studio
   PO Box 202045, Austin, TX 78720-2045

SCENE ONE

IT IS SAID AMONG FOLK OF different gifts, those who cannot straddle the worlds, that when a wizard is born, the very church bells announce the blessed event.

Practitioners know better than that.

Gifts are not so easily recognized, and how they reveal themselves is tricky. Shifting wind might announce the birth of an Air child. We see a sudden thunderstorm for Water children, a ghost for a Medium . . . a plant blooming out of season for an Earth babe. Even attracting a Good Friend, a friendly spirit that aids the practice of magic, can show magical potential. It's more like that, and if the child's future power is great, the sign can be felt from many miles away.

Occasionally—like during the birth of my sister Elizabeth—the wall between worlds rips open and the mysteries drop into your arms.

Sometimes literally.

From the first labor pain to her last ancient breath, my sister Elizabeth was a surprise. She always looked so normal, so agreeable, so docile . . . and then her gift seized her by the throat, and you fell back before the terror of it all. Momma wasn't due until the month of Flowers, but when my kinswoman Marta and I arrived from the south, worn thin with winter travel, the fact that it was a month early mattered not at all. Marta laid her practiced hands upon my mother and announced: *It's true labor.*

 Suddenly the household was in a tizzy. Marta was my teacher in the Wise Arts, and healthy babies were her life. She set Papa on the road to fetch Aunt Dagmar from Sun-Return, the boys to tending the animals and trap lines, and me to scrubbing clothes and grinding herbs.

⚜

Papa had given lots of thought to his own home, and had anchored our log cabin with a huge chimney open on two sides. We had a great central fire that allowed cooking in the kitchen and warmth and company for the main living area. This island of light in the midst of organized labor saved us wood and made the flow of people much easier to manage.

Right after Christmas, about when I disappeared from Marta's home, Papa and the boys built another room of our house. This small room was next to the main room, and larger than the stillroom off the kitchen. There would be a chimney for our future parlor, Papa told us, but not yet. For now, Marta and I would carry hot water and bricks to Momma while she had her baby on the birthing mattress Papa made.

Aunt Dagmar arrived and took over the kitchen, and I took up the spinning wheel, so we were ready for Momma's confinement. Momma's oldest sister didn't always approve of me—I was much too outspoken for her, plus she was a tad jealous of Momma having the only wizardly child in the current generation—but while Momma was lying in, we called a truce. I complimented Aunt Dagmar on her cooking (which was very good) and she exclaimed over my thin, fine wool thread and tight weaving. Momma was pleased to have peace in her house, and Marta merely smiled and held her tongue.

This was Momma's seventh baby to go almost the full time, and the more you had, the less time you spent in labor. Usually. Elizabeth's birth was different. Fortunately we'd made it back in time—I shudder to think of Aunt Dagmar delivering Elizabeth by herself. Of course we weren't supposed to know that Momma and Papa had decided on "Elizabeth" as the name for a girl. But the universe had already whispered it to me, long ago. I had seen Elizabeth standing by my side as I looked into a dark mirror one night. She had Momma's dainty form and dark hair, and a shy smile all her own. My reflected self could have passed for Marta in her youth. Tall and golden like my father, I represented the Norwegian side of this Sorensson family, while Elizabeth looked very Irish.

As time crawled on, pressure built throughout our big log home. Elizabeth took her time arriving. It wasn't until the second day of slow, intermittent labor that things fell into a rhythm. The boys went up to the loft room or tended stock, which kept them busy. As Momma paced, Marta carded wool, and I worked at the huge spinning wheel before the fireplace in the living room. In the kitchen Aunt Dagmar was cooking and talking non-stop, but Papa sat and kept her company—and away from Momma, Marta and me. Momma hadn't spoken about where we'd been; she'd just hugged me and said she was glad to see me safe.

Momma knew why we'd come from the south . . . that a family of sorcerers had taken me for "who knew what reason." But Momma feared the dark on the other side, and had quit training in the Mysteries after she learned herb lore. We didn't tell her anything about besting the sorcerers of Hudson-on-the-Bend. I do not know if she suspected there had been a battle, or thought Marta simply took me back from those who kidnapped me. I was alive, healthy (if thin) and not throwing up, so I wasn't pregnant. I was back with kin—nothing else mattered.

We were very practical people, back then.

"I tell you, Marta, this doesn't get—" a contraction folded Momma over in the midst of her pacing around the kitchen and living room.

"Breathe, Garda," Marta said, standing and moving over to the table. "Slow and deep; try to keep your shoulders down." Marta just stood there, tall and straight as an ash tree, hands on Momma's shoulders. I saw Momma's face ease, and I wondered if Marta had used a small magic, or just the power of her presence. "Let's check how far along things are." Bending her fair head over Momma's dark one, she walked my mother back to the new parlor room and the birthing bed.

In moments Marta peered around the doorway. "Allie, come bring the linens, quickly."

I rushed to get the towels, which were warm and wrapped around a pot of coals. By the time I was across the main room and into the parlor, Marta was holding Momma's hands through another contraction. Elizabeth was coming soon? I looked to Marta and then went down to the foot of the bed.

Papa had made a long mattress, so the baby would come out on solid padding. I felt a bit shy about helping my mother with a new baby, but I'd helped others before—Lord and Lady, I'd delivered twins! So I checked—

Pressure hit me in the face, like rising steam or opening the door to an oven. It was magic, not real heat, so I just ignored it. "Marta, I can see her!" Oops—I wasn't supposed to know the sex yet. As the top of her head peeked out, I set my fingers lightly on her hair to make sure she didn't come out too fa—

Heat slammed into my fingertips, roaring up my arm as if I had run up to a solstice fire on a cold winter's night. I could see nothing but flames, the mass heaving like a cauldron of molten sugar. Shiny black and golden, the vision was much like a bright bed of coals.

Allie, catch her! The mental words rang out like a command.

Blinded by the blazing light, I fumbled to seize hold of little Elizabeth, cursing my gift and praying I wouldn't somehow fail and hurt my mother or sister.

Earth heaved beneath my feet, trying to throw me to the ground. I could no longer separate magic from Now. The stench was awful, then choking, the rain of ash burning. I held on to the baby and leaned into the plump mattress, trying to flatten us into the softness of herbs and husks, trying to keep us from sliding off the face of a mountain—

And then the top of the mountain blew off.

Clouds—no, steam—rose into the heavens, miles into the sky, carrying rock and ash and liquid stone halfway to the rim of the world. Winds churned above, carrying evidence of the deed far and wide.

Whimpering called me back, and I was stunned to realize that *Elizabeth* was seeing what I was seeing, was casting it out into the beyond, trying to channel something she had no possible chance of understanding. *A seer. Powers that be, my baby sister is a seer.* It wasn't me, or not all me—it was Elizabeth!

It's all right, I whispered to her mind, hugging her into the clump of blankets and cradling her bloody body close. *We're safe, it's all right, it hasn't happened yet, and we will warn people that it's coming.* Over and over I tried, with silent words and warm hands, to reassure her that there was nothing to fear.

Finally I could see again, and realized that time had not stood still, that Elizabeth was totally out of Momma's womb, indeed, the afterbirth was following along in a hurry. Looking over to Marta I saw that she was bent over Momma and gently slapping her cheek.

"Marta?"

"Clean up your sister, Allie. I need to wake your Momma. Is the placenta—ah, good. Take care of her, dear, do you have your embroidery thread with you?" Marta was watching carefully, her hand on Momma's shrunken, wrinkled belly, but there was apparently nothing to fear—no bright blood, no change in her breathing, no sudden swelling. My cousin's other hand was checking Momma's pulse, and since Marta did not look concerned, I bent to tie off the cord and, when the last of the blood had drained into the baby, tied the knot.

Elizabeth was much calmer, now, as if nothing strange had happened. She made cooing noises as I wiped her clean and bundled her into a soft diaper and a warm flannel gown with a draw at the feet. My little sister looked just like one of the baby dolls with china hands and head. She'd have the Sorensson trademark, the soft, pale curls of childhood. Elizabeth would start growing dark hair around five or six—although I wasn't going to volunteer that. Once we had her in her christening gown, her pale gold hair dry and fluffy, she'd be a beautiful baby.

Had Marta felt what had happened, or had she only noticed my distress? I decided not to say anything until we were alone. My mother wanted a daughter who could be a normal little girl—at least for a time—and I didn't want to spoil that for her.

Marta had revived my mother, and helped her freshen up with a clean sleeping gown. My cousin had even stripped off the birthing sheets and put fresh linens on the bed. No need to get them both upstairs—we'd move them and burn the straw mattress later. I brought the baby over and placed her in Momma's waiting arms. "You have another daughter, Momma," I told her.

"Elizabeth," was Momma's response, her eyes shining. "We decided on Elizabeth if it was a girl."

I hurried out to the kitchen to announce the news. This brought both Papa and Aunt Dagmar over to the new parlor to see the baby. Papa, as always, turned to Momma first, kissing her cheek, his sky blue eyes only for her. Glowing, Momma showed off the latest addition to the family.

I helped Marta bundle away the sheets to the kitchen, where we plunged them into a basin of ice cold water. I thought about shouting up to the boys, but decided to let Papa tell them. A new sister was interesting, but probably not as interesting as a new brother.

After we'd made sure there were no iron stains from blood separating on the sheets, I looked over to Marta. "You felt that?" I asked as we dumped the wrung linen into a second basin.

"Oh, yes," Marta said. "Perhaps not as strongly as you did, since you were touching her, but I felt it!"

"Why? It means she's a seer at the least, doesn't it?" I went on.

"It suggests that her primary gift will be seeing," Marta answered, stirring the sheets with a pole. "I hadn't told you about that little trick of nature, because you haven't helped deliver a baby practitioner. I apologize. Until now, you were the only one of Garda and Eldon's children to have talent—the only Schell in this generation with magic, and the first born to great power in three generations."

"Our blood has thinned—that's what some say," I muttered, squeezing out Momma's nightgown.

"I don't think so." It was quite definite. "More like concentrating itself, Allie. Why only the daughters this time, I have no idea. But I predict that your brothers also carry the potential."

We stirred for a while, checking the bloodstains and rubbing cloth together to get rid of as much as we could. Bleaching was difficult in winter, since a day of sunshine was a rare event. Soap was for after we got the stains out.

"What did it mean?" I finally said aloud.

At first my cousin was silent. I worked at keeping my mouth shut. "I would guess one of two things," Marta finally said. "What we saw was either an earthquake, or a volcano exploding. But it didn't feel like it was . . . now. It felt like an echo."

"Was it an echo from the past or future?" I stopped stirring and looked at her. "Could it happen here?"

"Could a volcano erupt here?" Marta gave me one of her twisted smiles. "There have been volcanoes on this continent in the past, and there will be such explosions in the future. We are more likely to have an earthquake, right here." She actually shivered, and I didn't think it was from the cold water. "A seer on the Silk Road once passed along the sight of an earthquake. The ground cracked open, and heaved like the swell of the ocean."

"I wonder if we would have known about this so soon, if Elizabeth hadn't arrived," I murmured into the washbasin. For a moment, the water surged and glimmered, flowing like lava. I stirred the brightness, and the glittering image was gone. It appeared that the glimmer had also taken out the last stains.

Perhaps I would check my great-grandmother's *Book of Shadows,* before I troubled Marta with this little vision.

"It depends on how far away it is in time and space," Marta said, her voice calling me back to the moment. "If we get more information about it soon, then soon it will come. If we don't get anything for a season or two, it may be years away. We watch, and we wait." She started twisting the sheet, and I moved to help her. Aunt Dagmar returned in time to hang a clothesline for us, and we draped the bed linen and nightgown near the kitchen fire.

My aunt warmed some milk for cocoa, and we three had a celebratory cup before heading for our beds. As I sat on a huge pillow before the fire in the main room, something abruptly occurred to me. I looked around and made sure Aunt Dagmar had retired to the stillroom, and then turned to Marta.

"Does that sort of thing always happen when a new practitioner is born?"

Marta gave me a weary glance from her chair, and she didn't stop her slow rocking. "Not necessarily a vision, but something, yes. The people delivering the baby know, and maybe a few miles beyond."

"Do you think Cory heard Elizabeth?" I asked, referring to Momma's cousin Corrado, a practitioner who lived ten days away, in the orchard country.

A faint smile, a slight shake of the head— "I would say not," was the reply. "It usually doesn't travel far—a protection thing, I think. Family will protect a new practitioner, but there are others who might want to kill it." At my lifted eyebrows, she added: "Competition, Allie. Or there are darker users of the Arts . . . they might want a child of power for other reasons, as you well know."

"What else can happen at a birth?" Now, surely she knew where we were going with this, but I decided to get as much information as I could.

"Usually a child reveals a hint of whichever element is their strongest. A thunderstorm might erupt when Water is dominant or strong mental powers for Air masters."

"So Elizabeth is of Air? That means . . . she can do more things with Air?"

"Probably. Most seers are of Air." Marta sipped again. "It means that she will be able to master all powers associated with Air. Even if she's not good at all of them, she'll be able to use them in a pinch." Marta glanced over at me. "Air and Fire are usually men's powers, so she will be unusual in that."

"Do you have an element?" I looked at her as I asked. I'd never asked her that before. There was always something else to ask about, things that seemed more important. But my Grandmother's book hadn't mentioned this . . . yet.

Of course, I suspected the book actually hid pages from me, until I was ready for the knowledge.

I hadn't asked about the book's changing page count, either.

Marta almost dimpled. It was startling against her tanned skin and white temples. "Six animals gave birth when I was born. Earth is surely my element, if anything is."

I thought about it, and decided it seemed appropriate. "Marta, you delivered me, didn't you?"

"I have been present for every one of your momma's confinements."

"You never told me any such thing happened when I was born. In fact, people seemed surprised when I started seeing things and hearing werewolves and all." I poured myself a tiny bit of the last of the cocoa from the copper pan sitting by the fire. "What's my element?"

My cousin paused to drain her mug. "I don't know."

I blinked at her. "Nothing strange happened when I was born?"

This time, Marta's smile was only slightly twisted, that smile that meant more than one thing. She did not look my way. "I didn't say that. I just don't know which element, if any, is your strongest talent."

"What happened when I was born?"

Marta stared into the glowing coals of the fading fire. "You rushed out of your mother's womb, and in the moment between your birth and your first cry . . . the world took a sudden breath."

I sat there a while, and then said: "I don't understand."

"Neither do I, Alfreda. It was as if all creation gasped at the sight of you. I have no idea what it means." She finally looked my way. "Your momma labored long with you, and you were born with the dawn. That night, the northern lights were dancing among the stars, and we don't see them often, down here. I'd never seen them in summertime. Sheer curtains of vivid pink, sky blue, the deep blue of a butterfly wing, veils of pale green and white...someday, we'll find out if you can see the memories of another practitioner. I'll show you, then. It was worth seeing."

Marta leaned over and grabbed a folded towel, seizing the handle of the pan and pouring herself the last of the cocoa. "How is your spinning coming?"

I blinked at the turn in the conversation. "Even with all the excitement, I finished nine more full skeins today." Marta smiled her pleasure. "I think I can finish in maybe three days."

"Good," Marta said. "Let's get some sleep while we can. Morning will come early, with a new little one in the house." She rose slowly and took the cocoa pan back into the kitchen.

I banked the fire for the night, and made sure that the finished wool skeins were far from the fireplace, and that the great wool wheel was lashed tight so it would not spin on its own. The dead would rise at the sound, I promise you; it was like the rush of a mighty wind. Then I headed for the back stair to join Marta in my old room.

There was no time to waste with the spinning. Momma had not felt well, the last month, plus without me, the household output had slowed. For all Momma's squawking about how much time my study of the Mysteries took from my chores when I still lived home in Sun-Return, the truth was that I had gotten a great deal of work done. The household was not currently producing nearly what it should—evidence that I was needed and was missed. All the wool should have been spun by now, and the flax wheel humming. But wool remained to be spun, the flax untouched.

I was trying to make up for it now. We'd been here three days, and I had already spun nearly forty skeins of wool, all high-quality twist. I'd had to re-learn my mother's wheel, and being left-handed had not hurt me. Once I'd learned control of the speed of the wheel with my right hand, my left hand did everything else.

Truth to tell, I still hated plain sewing. But quilts and fancy work I could do. Fortunately for me, there was a greater demand for complicated weaving and embroidery. And a big demand for wool thread as thin as a British mill could spin.

What Momma needed was a daughter with my talent for dyes and fancy work, and no hint of the Gift that clung to our family tree. Momma hated the fact that I had power—so much power I was tingling with it by my eleventh birthday. I knew she hoped this child would be free of power.

Not likely. But there would be breathing room for Momma, who needed some years spent with a daughter who wouldn't be charging off into the woods every other minute. I didn't think Elizabeth would be the same kind of practitioner as I was shaping up to be.

Whether that was a good or bad thing remained to be seen.

❧ 𝕯 ❧

THANKS FOR READING

We hope you enjoyed this scene from *Spiral Path*, forthcoming from Book View Cafe/Dragonrain Studio.

CPSIA information can be obtained at www.ICGtesting.com
Printed in the USA
LVOW06s1716090414

381019LV00002B/591/P

[8]